T. R. Wilson started writing seriously in his early twenties. In 1986 he was awarded a rarely-achieved Distinction on the MA course in Creative Writing run by Angela Carter and Malcolm Bradbury at the University of East Anglia. Born and bred in Peterborough, he has used his intimate knowledge of the region to create the stunning background to his historical sagas.

By the same author

Master of Morholm
The Ravished Earth

T. R. WILSON

The Straw Tower

This edition published 1993 by
Diamond Books
77-85 Fulham Palace Road
Hammersmith, London W6 8JB

First published in Great Britain by
HarperCollins*Publishers* 1990

Set in Times
Printed and bound in Great Britain by
BPCC Paperbacks Ltd
Member of BPCC Ltd

For Tony and Pam

Love is not love
Which alters when it alteration finds

SHAKESPEARE Sonnet CXVI

THE HARDWICKS OF MORHOLM

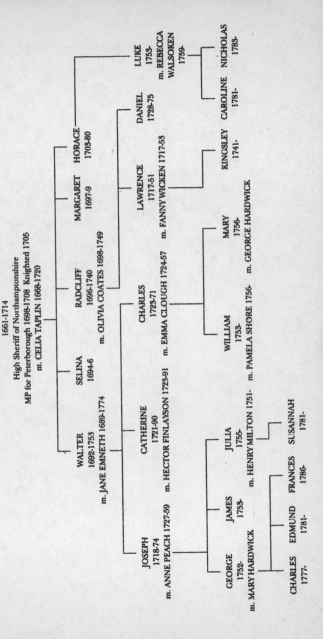

SIR ROBERT HARDWICK OF MORHOLM
1661-1714
High Sheriff of Northamptonshire
MP for Peterborough 1698-1708 Knighted 1705
m. CELIA TAPLIN 1668-1720

WALTER
1692-1753
m. JANE EMNETH 1689-1774

SELINA
1694-6

RADCLIFF
1696-1740
m. OLIVIA COATES 1698-1749

MARGARET
1697-9

HORACE
1703-80

LUKE
1753-
m. REBECCA
WALSOKEN
1759-

CATHERINE
1721-90
m. HECTOR FINLAYSON 1729-91

CHARLES
1723-71
m. EMMA CLOUGH 1724-57

LAWRENCE
1717-51
m. FANNY WICKEN 1717-53

DANIEL
1728-75

CAROLINE
1781-

NICHOLAS
1788-

JOSEPH
1718-74
m. ANNE PEACH 1727-59

WILLIAM
1753-
m. PAMELA SHORE 1756-

MARY
1756-
m. GEORGE HARDWICK

KINGSLEY
1741-

GEORGE
1752-
m. MARY HARDWICK

JAMES
1753-

JULIA
1755-
m. HENRY MILTON 1751-

CHARLES
1777-

EDMUND
1781-

FRANCES
1786-

SUSANNAH
1781-

PROLOGUE

December 1794

1

On her last night in London, Caroline saw the French prisoners-of-war.

She was waiting for a ferry-boat with her mother and father at the landing-stage below Tower Stairs. They had been to visit the Tower, and now the December dusk had come quickly, coldly down with mist on the Thames and a peppering of stars. Lanterns were already shining on board the many ships crowded downstream in the Pool, where the busy surface of the river might have been a part of the great city itself. Caroline was thirteen, and had had enough sightseeing for the day. She stood by the striped pole on the landing-stage stamping her chilled feet and thought of the supper that awaited them at their lodgings in Suffolk Street. And then the boat passed beneath them on the black water, with oil-lamps swinging at bow and stern, and her father pointed and said: 'French, I think.'

The boat was a transport barge. Huddled in the centre were about twenty men with their wrists manacled. Some were bandaged, some in dark uniform, some in rags. The lamps fore and aft illuminated the red coats of soldiers, some with muskets at the ready, and the black glazed hats of the oarsmen.

'Captured at sea, by the look of them,' her father said.

'Where are they being taken?' her mother asked.

'Well, I hear there are prison-hulks at Deptford. Probably there.'

Caroline stared down at the barge. The tide was rising,

and the boat was lifted close enough for her to make out the faces of the Frenchmen. So these were the Jacobins, the terrible revolutionaries and king-killers, with whom England had been at war for nearly two years. They did not look like monkeys, as the prints had led her to expect. They were men: chained, shabby, dejected, yet not, by their air, defeated.

It happened quickly. One of the prisoners stood up in the barge. He lifted his manacled hands towards the soldier behind him: perhaps in complaint at the tightness of the chains, perhaps simply cramped. The soldier raised his musket butt and struck the man down.

'Did you see it?' Caroline cried out. 'Father, he struck him!'

The prisoner's companions were helping him up, and the officer in the bow was shouting something at the soldier: orders, reprimands, she could not hear.

'It's wartime, Caro,' her father said. 'There'll be brutality on both sides before this war's over.'

A collier brig, black to the mast-heads, was tacking across the river, and in a moment the transport was lost to sight behind it.

'They'll not be really ill-treated,' her father said, patting her arm. 'Or no worse than our men in France. Ah! At last.' A ferry-boat was sculling towards their landing-stage, the ferryman doffing his red cap.

The ferryman handed Caroline and her mother into the boat and her father followed, telling him 'Hungerford Stairs', and then they were moving out on to the rising river, with the shape of London Bridge up ahead. Caroline looked back to try and see the transport barge again; but it was lost amongst the moving bulks of the shipping.

In a few moments she was hungry for supper again, and aware of being cold and tired. But she did not forget that sight, the baleful faces under the swinging lamplight, the red coats and the musket crashing down. Her father had spoken to reassure her, thinking she was upset; but that did not entirely describe her feelings at what she had witnessed. She had seen a little explosion of hate in the winter darkness; a glimpse of an adult world of mysteries and passions, like a prospect of a landscape into which she would soon travel.

2

Caroline's week in London, which culminated in that dramatic incident, had not been all enjoyment. Almost all, but not quite.

Caroline's brother, still at school, was deemed too young to make the trip, and so she was specially proud of going about with her parents as Miss Hardwick; as a young woman, or near enough, for the first time. They had gone to the theatres, to the Pantheon, to Hyde Park to ride in the Ring, and to Westminster with her uncle George; they had seen St Paul's, and of course the Tower. She was proud, too, of her parents – seeing them afresh in this new setting. Her mother, Rebecca, a combination of youthful spirits and mature beauty; her father, Luke, a tall well-built man who radiated energy, a merchant and shipowner, owing nothing to anyone, at ease with lord or fisherman. They were fenland people, the Hardwicks, and there was that element of the rich earth and open sky about them which seemed to be thrown into relief in the overheated drawing-rooms of the capital.

Fenlanders prided themselves on independence of mind, and Caroline was not disposed to be impressed by anything merely because one was expected to be. Still, she admired the city, laughed at its affectations, and suffered its stinks; and the only shadow on her enjoyment of the week was Richard Lindsay.

Which was unfair – as Richard was the pretext for the trip. But she couldn't help it. If she was unfair to Richard, she told herself, it was only because he seemed to court it.

Two months ago Walter Lindsay, her father's shipmaster, a valued employee of his King's Lynn mercantile house, had died. He left a son, Richard: orphaned at just fifteen, with no relatives but an elderly poor aunt and no means of support. Caroline's father and her uncle George, who was a Member of Parliament and a man of influence, had put their heads together and come up with a way to provide for the boy: a commission in the Navy. Richard had grown up with ships and hankered to go to sea; and since the outbreak of war with Revolutionary France the Navy had been hurriedly expanding. Uncle George had a friend who was newly promoted to captain of the sloop *Aristeia*, refitting at Portsmouth, and would take the boy as a midshipman on the Hardwicks' recommendation.

So, Caroline's parents had decided to take the boy down to London themselves, to get him fitted out with his uniform and all he needed, and see him off to Portsmouth. The occasion could be combined with a pleasure-stay in London, and Caroline's introduction to the capital.

Throughout that day-long coach journey down from the Fens Richard had said scarcely a word. He had stared blankly out of the coach window, his dark hair tangled over his frowning brow, a raw-boned and graceless youth. He was still grieving for his father, Caroline's mother had said.

But that could not make Caroline feel comfortable with him. Always he had been the same: prickly, dark, incomprehensible. On odd occasions they had played together as children, but without pleasure. There was something about her that he resented and made him truculent: his peculiarly piercing eyes always seemed to harden when they were on her.

Richard was with them in London three days before his departure for Portsmouth. Caroline told herself he was only the son of one of her father's employees whom they were helping out, and he would soon be gone; but still she chafed at his presence.

On the first day they had taken him to a naval tailor's in Cheapside and ordered his uniform: blue tail-coat lined with white silk, white nankeen waistcoat and breeches, tricorne hat, together with working jacket and trousers, boat cloak, and the accessories he would need – books on navigation, a sextant, a dirk, and a midshipman's chest to contain it all. Caroline's father had laid out money with a free hand: he had also arranged for the captain's agent to pay Richard an allowance for pocket-money over and above his two pounds a month pay.

Her uncle George Hardwick, with his son Charles, were also in London: George attending Parliament, with Charles, who was her favourite cousin, acting as his secretary; and the night before Richard was due to leave they all went to Covent Garden Theatre. It was by way of a treat for the boy. At the end of the evening the principals came to the footlights and led the company in a patriotic song, with a background of pasteboard ships rocking on muslin waves and the tragedienne Mrs Jordan dressed as Britannia.

> *Then hi ho, me hearties, and be of good cheer;*
> *Our island of Freedom shall never know fear:*
> *At sight of our Navy, the foeman shall blench*
> *Old England's oak walls, the Scourge of the French.*

Soon the audience were singing too, from the pit to the boxes, and a party of soldiers in the gallery were on their feet and waving their swords. Caroline, her cousin Charles, and Richard were seated together at the front of their box, and Richard was not joining in the singing. Charles, who had always been good friends with Richard, clapped him on the shoulder. 'Come on, Richard,' he said, 'you must learn to hate the French, you know, if you're to be a sailor!'

And Caroline said – and it was rude, but she could not help it – 'Why, there's no need for that: I think Richard hates everyone.'

Richard turned round and the violence of his expression startled her. He had gone white and his eyes burnt. 'You're a spoilt little miss,' he said with venom. 'You'll not treat me like that. I'm grateful to your father and your uncle – but I'm damned if I owe *you* anything.'

Caroline could not pretend she was sorry when he left the next morning. She went, of course, to see him off, with her parents and uncle George and cousin Charles, at the Bull and Gate in Holborn, where the first lieutenant of the *Aristeia* was to meet him and travel with him down to Portsmouth.

Richard was dressed in his midshipman's uniform: it made him look older, almost a man. But he was not – he was tall but thin, strong but gangling, his jaw still rounded with the last softness of childhood. An enigmatic figure, between youth and manhood.

The trunk with MR MIDSHIPMAN R. LINDSAY painted on its lid was loaded on to the coach, and the Hardwicks said their goodbyes. Caroline's mother kissed him warmly and her father shook his hand. 'Your father never let me down, Richard,' he said, 'and I don't imagine you will. Take care of yourself, and if there's anything you need don't hesitate to write to me.'

'Or me,' her uncle George said. 'Give my regards to

14

Captain Sharpe. And I expect to be giving my regards to Captain Lindsay pretty soon.'

Charles Hardwick, who never troubled to hide his feelings, hugged Richard and told him to write whenever he could: and then Caroline gave Richard her hand, and he shook it briefly without meeting her eyes.

The coach lurched away at last, thundering on the cobbles.

'He'll be a good seaman, I think,' her father said, waving his hat. 'It should be the making of him, if the war continues. Promotion's always quicker in wartime.'

'As long as he doesn't get in the way of a cannonball first,' her uncle George said grimly.

'Ah, well,' her father said, 'if it doesn't suit, perhaps we can find something else for the boy. He's a keenly enough lad, but he's got a temper. His father could be a bit of a Tartar, God rest him.'

There was a recruiting poster on the inn wall close to Caroline – *Let us, who are Englishmen, protect and defend our good* KING *and* COUNTRY *against the Attempts of all Republicans and Levellers, and against the Designs of our* NATURAL ENEMIES – and she experienced a shudder on seeing it, a kind of tremor of the spirit. She drew closer to her parents, to her uncle and cousin. Young as she was, she faced life with confidence, looking outward, but for a moment the world had suddenly reared up huge and threatening, reaching out with long fingers to touch them all.

3

So the week in London came to an end, with that last strange excitement of the French prisoners glimpsed on the dark river. The next morning Caroline and her parents

15

set out for home early, in company with uncle George and cousin Charles, for the Parliamentary session was almost over and George was anxious to get back to the fens while the weather held.

The Hardwicks had the Peterborough Fly coach to themselves, and there was much to talk about. The older ones were soon reminiscing about coach travel in the old days, when you were liable to be shaken half to death or even overturned.

'Old Mr Van Druyten, d'you remember him?' uncle George was saying. 'He always made out his will before he set out for London.'

'The turnpikes have made all the difference,' Caroline's father said. 'I remember there were places in Lincolnshire where the roads seemed to disappear altogether.'

'More often than not you had to get out and walk parts of the way to save the horses,' her mother said. 'And fleas! Always there were fleas in the cushions.'

'If there were cushions,' George said. 'Sometimes it was just straw.'

Caroline and Charles exchanged a knowing glance. 'And highwaymen, father?' Charles said. 'Highwaymen in masks being gallant to the ladies. You must have had a brush or two with them.'

'You may laugh, boy,' George said. 'I've seen a highwayman hung in chains at Alconbury more than once.'

But the Hardwicks were laughing at themselves, too, for as the children well knew they were far from the solid burghers chewing over the past that they pretended. Looking at her father and her uncle seated opposite each other, Caroline could see why folk said there was a wild streak in the Hardwicks. Her father's looks, with his shaggy black hair and brows and broad shoulders, still bore testimony to the fact that Luke Hardwick had been born illegitimate and lived rough as a boy. Though he was

16

now one of Peterborough's most prominent citizens with mercantile interests all over the fenland, there were deep graven lines in his face that denied an easy or a passive life. Her mother, too, Rebecca, had been unconventional, marrying Luke in defiance of a father who planned great things for her and never forgave her till his death. And her uncle George, though inheritor of the Hardwick land and family seat at Morholm on the edge of the fens, and an MP for Stamford, had had a rebellious reputation when young – and even now the staider gentry of the fenland referred to him as a mad radical.

The disquiet of his lean and distinguished face as yet found no echo in that of his seventeen-year-old son Charles. Charles, who was more of a dearly loved brother than a cousin to Caroline, was all openness, his mobile attractive face drinking in experience.

'Ah, you may think we spring from the Dark Ages, Charles,' his father said, 'but in one respect things haven't changed. When you were born we were at war with France – and now here we are again.'

'It was the same when I was small,' Rebecca said. 'It can't last long this time, surely?'

'I think conditions are a little different this time,' George said. 'We are fighting not just France, but a whole political and philosophical system. And our troops in Holland are back behind the Waal. In the House last week there were claims that our men there are so ill-supplied they die for lack of bandages or a warm coat.'

'But if you dare say any such thing you're called a traitor!' Charles burst out. 'And this in a war we should never have joined in the first place.'

Luke raised an eyebrow. 'Have you fathered a Jacobin, George?'

Charles coloured a little, but went on: 'I've been called that more than once by father's colleagues this past month.'

17

'There was my son quoting Paine's *Rights of Man* to Tories over their port,' said George wryly.

'I thought that book was forbidden!' said Caroline. The headmistress at her day school spoke of Thomas Paine as the brother of the devil.

'It wasn't when I bought it,' Charles said. 'I would not be allowed to sell it now. The book seems mostly self-evident good sense to me, as I said to some of the men I met at Westminster.'

'Good sense?' said Luke. 'Universal education, pensions for everyone at fifty?'

'New ideas,' said Charles. 'But that's no reason in itself to reject them. What alarms me is the way we are going backwards now out of fear of the French example. We claim we are the defenders of freedom, whilst our freedoms are taken away daily. The Corresponding Societies broken up, the presses bridled, imprisonment without trial . . . The merest suggestion of reform is seen as the – the leading edge of revolution and anarchy!'

Caroline looked at her cousin in surprise. He had always been a prey to enthusiasms, ready to join in argument for the pleasure of it: but she had not heard him talk like this before.

'Well, Charles, I'd be happy with peace in Europe at almost any price, believe me,' her father said. 'All I know is while we're at war my ships are in danger. Let 'em settle their differences and let trade thrive again.'

There was so much talk of the war these days that usually Caroline was bored by it: but now she thought of the French prisoners last night, suddenly haunted afresh by the image of those chained men, and told Charles the story.

'It must be so strange for them,' she concluded. 'Stranded in another country. Kept alive, but with no

18

comforts, no familiar things. No knowing what the future will be.'

'We none of us know that,' her uncle George said.

'Where will Richard's ship go?' said Rebecca. It was the first mention of him, and Caroline caught an inflexion of sympathy and concern in her mother's voice that pricked her with guilt as she remembered the sudden flash of antagonism between them in the theatre.

'Any number of places,' George said. 'The West Indies seems likely. Pitt's concentrating much of our strength there.'

'He'll probably be a man before we see him again,' Rebecca said.

The coachman was blowing his horn as they came into Barnet, their first stop, and when the Hardwicks rejoined the coach after the horses had been changed the conversation turned to other things.

Caroline settled back and began to think of home and count the miles, waiting for the time when her own landscape should open up before the coach, the land flat as a stage beneath an extravagant painted ceiling of sky. Yes, this was her country, the treacherous fields of black earth, the straight dykes and the willows, the crying water-birds balancing on eddies of wind, the solitary villages and the limestone towns with their great ship-like churches moored on the horizon. The visit to London had renewed her sense of kinship with this land; the visit to London had whetted her awareness of many things, not least her own changing self. The direct emotions of childhood seemed to be giving way to odd cross-currents, to movements of feeling disturbing and pleasant and mysterious as the tokens of the seasons.

Book One

CHAPTER 1

September 1799

1

'Who's that in the study with father?' Caroline asked, coming down late to breakfast.

'A Captain Woodruff,' her mother said, looking up from her letter. 'Something to do with Norman Cross, I think. There's coffee, and rolls still hot, or shall I ring?'

'No, no, that will be enough for me,' Caroline said. She stifled a yawn as she sat down. There was enough of her early-rising father in her to make her feel guilty at being late, though not enough to make her get up early. 'Woodruff . . . of course, he's the superintendent at Norman Cross. Are there more prisoners coming on the river?' She shook her head at the spaniel, Leo, who was gazing hopefully up at the table.

'I suppose so. Though the river's so high it's almost over the wharf today.'

Caroline turned to look from the bow-window across the garden and paddock to where the Nene flowed between osier willows. Her father had a small wharf there, and owned the navigation rights for this part of the river. In the sky clouds were closing together and there were specks of rain: a too familiar sight, for 1799 had been a miserably cold and wet summer. 'Perhaps the landing in Holland succeeded, and we've taken a lot of prisoners,' she said.

When Caroline had first seen the French prisoners-of-war that cold night in London five years ago she had little guessed that such a thing would become a familiar sight from the windows of her own home in Peterborough. It was two years ago, in 1797, that the great camp to contain the increasing numbers of prisoners-of-war had been built at Norman Cross, five miles south of the city. Since then she had grown used to seeing from a distance the river-barges that brought fresh batches of captured French and Dutchmen from King's Lynn, to disembark at her father's wharf and then be marched under guard across country to the camp. At first curious and occasionally hostile crowds had gathered to watch from the town bridge, but now-adays the arrivals went largely unnoticed. Caroline, how-ever, had never quite lost interest in the manacled processions of men, the glimpses of their faces, hopeless or hopeful, apathetic or curious: the set of their shoulders, slumped or defiant, as they trudged out of sight down the Yaxley road to their imprisonment.

'It looks like a bad harvest this year,' her mother said, finishing her coffee. 'Just when the country can least afford it. Your uncle George was saying near half of Morholm land is under water. You haven't forgotten we're to go to Morholm tomorrow?'

'I had,' Caroline said, pulling the bell and stretching luxuriously. Since she had finished schooling earlier that year leisure had been the pattern of her life – indeed it was expected of her – but it was still strange each morning to realize she had the day to herself. 'Is there some special reason for this party?'

'Well, I suspect there is, but George and Mary wouldn't say anything about it. Anyway, George has to go back to Westminster next week. Parliament's been called early.'

The maid came in to clear the breakfast table, and Caroline went to the window to look for a rent in the clouds. Across the river she saw the brilliant spires of the cathedral lifted above the huddled roofs of the city; to the east Borough Fen stretched away flat as an inland sea. Bad harvests, and war; they could seem a long way off

24

from this house, built by her father ten years ago at the edge of the city after he had sold the old squeezed townhouse in Stamford. With its large airy rooms, its new sash windows on three storeys overlooking the river, its porticoed door and its tiled stable and coach-house, the Bridge House was Luke Hardwick's testament, the physical expression of the urban and mercantile side of the family as Morholm was of the landed side. Here was comfort, security, a way of life that seemed solid and enduring as the great cathedral itself. Only the bitterness with which her father sometimes spoke of the war, the concentration with which he scanned the price-guides in the newspapers, and the anxiety with which he waited for the return of his ships to King's Lynn, hinted at the uncertainty that ran like a treacherous deep current under the times.

There were voices on the stairs, and then her father came in accompanied by a middle-aged man with the pigtail and tanned face of a sailor.

'My dears, this is Captain Woodruff, the governor at Norman Cross,' Luke said. 'The Captain and I have had some rather peculiar business to discuss. We may expect our very own French invasion soon.'

'Oh, not so bad as that, ladies,' Captain Woodruff boomed. He tucked his hands under his coat-tails and talked at them as if he were in a high wind. 'It concerns the French officers on parole in the city. Negotiations with France for exchange of prisoners have broken down again. The prisoners just keep on coming, and I've got my hands full at Norman Cross. The Government has directed that we appoint an agent in the city to be responsible for the paroled officers. A private gentleman of means, willing to look after them. There's the same system in Wisbech and Northampton, but most of the officers are concentrated here. There's something like fifty, Dutch and French, in the city at present.'

'I didn't realize it was so many,' Rebecca said. 'One sees so little of them.'

'Oh, they keep much to themselves, ma'am; and they have to stay within the city limits defined by the tollgates and be in their lodgings by nine at night. They're paid a small allowance by the government – and the distribution of that would be the responsibility of your husband. They would present themselves here twice weekly, so he can keep a check on them and make sure none of them jump their parole. They're a decent enough set of men on the whole. Most are resigned to sitting out the war here: there are worse places, after all.'

'What do you say, love?' Luke said. 'Would you mind?'

'No, of course not,' Rebecca said. 'As Captain Woodruff says, there can't be any harm in them.'

'It should be quite an experience to actually meet these "natural enemies" of ours face to face,' said Caroline.

'It will mean extra work for you, Luke,' Rebecca said when Captain Woodruff had gone.

'Little enough.' Luke paced down the room and picked up the *Stamford and Peterborough Courant*. 'With any luck all the prisoners will be going home soon.' Caroline watched her father scanning the print with his familiar mistrustful expression. It was one of the few times this big, barrel-chested man, with his shaggy leonine head and brimming confidence, looked vulnerable. 'If we can only have the Dutch ports open to us again – ' a habitual catechism: the French conquest of Holland, a frequent destination of Luke's ships, had hit trade hard. 'We *must* be in sight of a settlement this time. The Dutch fleet in our hands. The Austrians in Zurich. The Russians victorious everywhere. Bonaparte stranded in Egypt. Good God, what more do they want?'

* * *

26

The martial spirit was evident in Peterborough when Caroline walked into the town later that morning. Men in uniforms were a common sight: occasionally Regulars, but mostly the haphazard forces of home defence – members of the Militia Regiments, the Fencibles, and the local Volunteer associations. There were several of these, and a man's choice was often made according to which had the most fetching uniform. There were recruiting posters pasted to walls and in the bookshops patriotic prints depicting General Bonaparte as a swarthy unshaven bandit and Nelson as a Gulliver towing away the Lilliputian ships of the French.

Disregarding this boastfulness, the market, filling the square and overflowing down Narrow Bridge Street and the Long Causeway, went about the serious business of life. Prices were spiralling higher than anyone could remember, and there was a slightly feverish atmosphere to the buying and selling.

Here the produce of a huge fertile hinterland came, and here one could take the temperature of the country. The ancient city, dwarfed by the Gothic arches of the cathedral, had begun in recent years to grow faster. The presence of thousands of men at Norman Cross had stimulated the local economy. Barge traffic on the Nene and coach traffic on the new turnpike roads were increasing. A combination of enclosure and drainage failures had brought countrymen off the land to find work in the city. It was this spirit of expansion that had prompted Luke Hardwick to move here from Stamford twelve miles to the north, where he had begun to feel stifled by that town's antiquarian gentility. In recent years, too, the archaic local government of Peterborough had changed for the better, with the creation of the Improvement Commissioners, a body of which Luke was a member. The narrow streets had been newly paved and lighted with oil-lamps and the medieval drainage had been improved: and in the drive to respectability even the brutal medieval sport of bull-running, after a last defiant outbreak last year during the celebrations for the Battle of the Nile, had been finally suppressed.

Caroline, threading her way into Cross Street to call on a friend, knew this face of the city well. But she knew also the rookery of wooden hovels at Boongate, the peeling lodging-houses and ale-shops where landless labourers existed on the margin of starvation, and where smallpox and typhus bred and sporadically broke out from their ghetto like revolution. The other face, and the parading Volunteers, toasts and subscriptions, the smug cartoons of doughty John Bull, did not disguise from her the immediate effects of the war. Comfortable as she herself was, she could hardly live here and be unaware that the price of bread was rising entirely beyond the reach of the poor.

The farmers, she noticed, in their white waistcoats and top-boots, were looking especially fat.

Lucy Squire was ready for a walk, but she dithered on the threshold of her banker father's house in Priestgate, peering up at the rainclouds until Caroline took her arm and fairly hauled her out. *Eggshell-maidens*, her mother called girls who made a show of fragility, and none of her family had any patience with them.

'Frenchmen coming to your own house!' Lucy was scandalized when Caroline told her: her mouth was a round O in her round genial face. 'There's a French officer living in an attic behind my aunt's house in Midgate and she says he prays to a pagan god and washes his hands in blood!'

'Oh, and does he have a tail too?' said Caroline. 'Lucy, most of the French are still good Catholics, no matter what the atheist revolutionaries say.'

'That's just as bad! There are Catholics who meet in Wood Street and they make sacrifices in front of a picture of the Pope and say the Lord's Prayer backwards!'

'Anyway, it will give me a chance to try out all that French we had to learn at Mrs Tebbs'.'

'French isn't on the syllabus now, did you know? Mrs Tebbs won't have it any more. She offers Italian instead.' Lucy stopped in front of the dressmaker's window. 'Same old stuffs. In London the women are wearing transparent gowns with nothing underneath. They're scarcely more than petticoats. And sometimes they *damp* them . . .' she dropped her voice, or rather raised it, to a vehement whisper '. . . to make them *cling*.'

'It's a wonder they don't catch their deaths,' Caroline said.

They stopped at the Angel gateway as one of the new mail-coaches hurtled out, red wheels gleaming, full of self-importance.

'We're going to the Volunteers' Fund Patriotic Ball tomorrow. Are you?' Lucy said.

'Oh, no . . . I couldn't sing *Britons, Strike Home* again if my life depended on it! It makes me want to burst out in the *Marseillaise*.'

'But Frank Bellaers will be there. He's sure to be.'

'Well, what's that to me?'

'Oh, how can you say that! Everyone knows about you, and him. Why, Rachel Emmonsales says that when you left your glove behind at the Sedgmoors' last month, Frank Bellaers took it home and kept it with him all the time and even wore it tucked in his hat-brim when he went hunting.'

'Did he indeed!' Caroline laughed. 'And a proper fool he must have looked!'

'Caroline, you've no romance in your soul.'

'Oh, I think I have somewhere. But not for Frank

Bellaers, I'm afraid. I realize the fact that he led me into supper once or twice means we're practically engaged in some people's eyes. But really it all came to nothing, quite amicably.'

'I think he looks so handsome in his Volunteer uniform.'

'So, unfortunately, does Frank. I know gentlemen are supposed to compliment ladies on their dress, but I didn't know we had to reciprocate quite so much. I began to realize Frank and I could never be much more than friends when he constantly drew attention to how nice his legs looked in his new white pantaloons. There must be more to love than an elegant pair of knees.'

'Mrs Tebbs says one mustn't say pantaloons. One should say *unmentionables*.'

'Oh dear,' said Caroline, laughing again. 'Well, I promise not to *mention* them, as long as I don't have to *admire* them.'

Their walk had brought them to the edge of the town, where the turnpike road ran through the manor fields at Boroughbury. Lucy, who was an affectionate friend but faint of heart and leg, turned back for home, and Caroline walked on alone across the field-paths.

Here most of the blighted harvest was already in. Men were tying up a few undernourished stooks: in an adjoining hayfield the hay had rotted before it could be cut. Even now there was rain, hanging in the air rather than falling.

She had spoken the truth about Frank Bellaers. Frank could be amusing, and she liked to be amused; but it had only been the mildest of flirtations.

Caroline was eighteen, and had had an easy, civilized life which the informal atmosphere of her home, the disregard of convention that ran in her blood, had saved from a too suffocating gentility; and her evenness of temper had tended to make her laugh at rather than be irritated by the well-bred timidities of Lucy Squire and her kind and the frigid conventions of Mrs Tebbs' Academy. She was an accomplished musician, there were books aplenty at home and her mind had never wanted for stimulation; her mother in particular, with grim memories of her own puritanical upbringing, was a woman who did not believe in whalebone corsets either physical or mental.

Life had lightly touched Caroline with its fingertips, and it was to this touch that she was accustomed, rather than the blow or the caress. The homage of such as Frank Bellaers surprised her, for she had been gawky into late childhood and had filled out recently and suddenly. She had the black hair and blue eyes and fine complexion that seemed to predominate in this region, and the coming together of all this into a certain beauty, warm, humorous and lively, fresh from the shed skin of skittish adolescence, had produced tributes like that of Frank's which faintly embarrassed her. The Bellaers were an unexceptionable landowning family of the kind she was used to mixing with at parties, at balls and theatres: Frank an unexceptionable scion who, like many young men of his kind, rode to hounds, drilled with the Volunteers – this, as far as Caroline could gather, consisted chiefly in knocking turnip-heads off poles and marching in an enthusiastic straggle around Lord Fitzwilliam's lawns – and looked about him for a wife.

She could not take his attentions seriously. All the time she had felt herself to be playing a part, so decorous and appropriate was the whole business. She was irresistibly reminded of the novels where the lady tapped the gentleman's arm with a fan and blushingly said, 'Fie, sir' – and felt that if she had done such a thing Frank would have taken it quite as a matter of course.

The rain was coming down in earnest now, and Caroline turned back to the city, wishing she had put on overshoes.

For a moment there – just for a moment – a murmur of dissatisfaction had spoken inside her. Perhaps *she* was at fault . . . Would life offer her a succession of Franks, and she be unable to feel anything for them?

But the murmur soon died away. For one thing she did not even feel the matter to be as important as some girls did. She was a person, after all, complete in herself, and there was no need of a gallant arm supporting hers to reassure her of that.

She came back to Peterborough glowing and rainwet, with mud on her skirts, and laughing at the thought of Frank Bellaers with her glove in his hat. No, there was nothing there, and thankfully she suspected some other pair of blue eyes would soon engage his attention. She did not have to will herself into love for Frank Bellaers, or anyone else, for fear of being out of fashion.

She went home via the cathedral precincts. A narrow alley led through to the cloisters. Here two men deep in conversation stepped aside to let her pass. She was almost past them before she realized that they had been speaking French. As her mother said, the paroled prisoners in the town were usually inconspicuous, though an accustomed eye noticed the clothes, patched and worn, often the remnants of uniforms.

They had bowed and made room like any Englishmen. In a way it was absurd, Caroline thought: at sea, on the battlefields of Holland, they were shooting at Englishmen to kill them; here, captive, they lived alongside them normally. Did the paradox of their situation strike them too? Did they chafe at the invisible bars around the city? *Parole d'honneur* – they had given their word of honour. A position of trust. Perhaps, now her father was to be their agent and guardian, she might find out what was going on in their minds, the minds of these neighbourly enemies ambling the streets of an English town.

2

'Behold the new Deputy Lord Lieutenant of the county,' George Hardwick said. 'Something of an anti-climax, isn't it? I just had a fit of conceit when I learnt the news and had to have you over to celebrate.'

'What do I do, kiss your ring?' Luke laughed, shaking George's hand. 'Congratulations, George. You must have done something right all these years.'

'How do you feel, uncle?' Caroline said.

'*Old*,' said George. 'I await my first twinge of gout. I think the appointment is really a tribute to my reaching fifty.'

'Don't listen to him, Caroline,' Mary Hardwick said. 'He's not forty-seven. Hardly the elder statesman yet.'

'Tell that to my bones,' George said.

Caroline and her family had gone the eight miles to Morholm on horseback that morning, for the road was unfit for the carriage. Under a clearing sky they had left Peterborough and emerged into the startling openness of the fen country. They had passed the old gibbet at Millfield and skirted the low hamlets along Car Dyke. Women dressed only in their shifts were gleaning in the stubble fields. They had come through the village of Aysthorpe, past the gates of Bromswold, Caroline's mother's old home, now empty, and then, beyond the last houses of the village, Morholm came in sight.

The graceful Jacobean manor, built of local limestone, surrounded by a few trees tortured out of shape by the scouring east wind, stood on the very edge of Borough Fen. It bridged two worlds. The village was modestly handsome in the mould of many of the Northamptonshire upland villages: to the east beyond it, where Morholm land began, was a different country. Different earth, different light, different climate, different speech. It was perhaps not too fanciful to see an echo of this duality, of the civilized and elemental, in the Hardwicks.

Morholm had been home to the Hardwicks for generations, maintaining its independence between the great aristocratic estates of Burghley and Fitzwilliam. To Caroline it was a second home. So much of what she loved and valued was bound up in it, not least the family who came out to greet them in the drive. Her uncle George and aunt Mary, and their children, Charles, Edmund and Frances.

'Who's the Lord Lieutenant now? Is it Spencer?' Luke asked, as they were brought ale and cake in the summer parlour.

George nodded. 'His is the real authority. But I hope I won't entirely be a yes-man.'

'This is worrying, George,' Luke said ironically. 'Accepted by the *ancien régime* at last. Admitted to the club.'

'It does look as if I'm being driven further into their arms,' George said. 'My seat in Parliament dependent on Lord Burghley's favour. Now county lieutenant. Where are the ideals of yesterday?' He glanced across at Charles. 'I fear my Radical son has despaired of me.'

'Not at all!' said Charles. 'Even your cautious ideas, father, will be a leaven in the – the stodgy dough of our rulers.'

'I don't know whether that's a compliment or not,' said George.

Caroline and her parents were to stay at Morholm for two nights, and soon they went upstairs to change for dinner. Caroline had her usual bedroom on the top floor with a window-seat overlooking the gardens. She had thrown open the casement and was gazing out when Charles came up to find her.

'I do love this view,' she said.

'It hasn't been at its best this summer,' Charles said, sitting down by her. As he spoke a shaft of sun lit over the gardens, drawing out colour from the lawns and ragged flower-beds and dappling the orchard walk. 'Usually the wheatland looks like gold leaf.'

'A poor harvest?'

'Very poor. The turnips rotted in the ground. The wheat was scarcely thick enough to hide the fieldmice . . . You know father's to go back to London next week?'

Caroline nodded. 'Will you be going with him?'

'I don't know. I certainly enjoyed it last time. The political world is stuffed with cant and humbug and hypocrisy – but it's *exciting*. I feel involved . . . But I'm not, really. I act as father's secretary, but there's not much to do. Oh, father's happy to have me there – at least, I think so! As long as I don't begin spouting to his colleagues.'

'Well, you must be company for him. I'm sure he'd be happy for you to go with him again.'

'Yes . . . Oh, yes, it's not that.' A butterfly had blundered into the casement. Charles gently took it in cupped hands and urged it outside. 'I don't feel useful – that's the trouble. So many things I feel strongly about – as I'm afraid you know – and so little I can do.' He stood up abruptly and ran his fingers through his dark curling hair, frowning out at the mellow garden. 'D'you ever feel restless, Caroline? D'you ever feel your energies are just going up like smoke in the air?'

'Well, sometimes,' she said. 'But I'm afraid I'm constitutionally lazy anyway.'

Charles smiled. 'I suppose everybody is. Except perhaps your father!' He paced down the room and absently

35

picked up Caroline's cloak. 'I don't want for occupation, I mean, I needn't. There's always plenty to do about the estate, especially when father's away. And there's the Volunteers, of course' – he gave her a wry glance – 'though I've no relish for the drilling. But . . .'

'But they're not the things you really want to do.'

Charles nodded and winced. 'Do I sound ungrateful? God knows I shouldn't be; not when I've seen the conditions in the country this past year. With this harvest the price of bread will go sky-high . . . But you see' – Charles darted back and sat by her again – 'there's no pressure on me to do anything other than be the young gentleman of the estate and prepare to step into father's shoes. And – paradoxically, I suppose – that's what irks me.'

'Do you wish you'd gone to the university?'

'No. No, I don't regret that. Father says some of the greatest blockheads he knows went to university, and I'm inclined to agree. Besides, I never had the head for sticking at Latin and Greek.'

'They probably wouldn't have taken to having a red radical in their midst anyway,' said Caroline.

'Probably not.' Charles smiled again, and Caroline thought to herself what havoc that smile would play with some young woman's heart. That Charles was so clearly unaware of its effect added to its charm. He was now at twenty-two a handsome young man, tall and very slender and full of nervous energy, with a keen humorous face that was still boyish, and a tenor voice that was unusually melodious. The frankness and generosity of his nature had not diminished as he grew into manhood, but Caroline knew there was no one to whom he opened his heart so completely as herself.

'I should go to London with your father if I were you,' she said. 'There's sure to be some opportunity for you to

36

do something. You're not actually unhappy, are you, cousin?'

'Bless you, no,' he said, taking her hand. 'Poor Caroline. Having to listen to this when you've barely arrived – and I haven't even said how good it is to see you or asked you how you are. You *look* blooming. Is Frank Bellaers anything to do with this, I wonder?'

'Oh, no,' Caroline groaned, 'not here too! How is it gossip can travel so fast? Do they send it by carrier pigeon?'

'You forget we have the Emmonsales ladies here in this very village, and nothing escapes them. They pour out gossip from the Rectory whilst their reverend father pours out tracts telling the poor to starve in silence because it's God's will . . . I presume it's all nonsense, then?'

'Why do you presume that?'

'Because you're not blushing and giggling.'

'When did I ever blush and giggle?' she said, giving him a blow on the knee.

'Oh, I remember a time when you did. Not so much as other girls, though.'

A waft of cut hay and warmth and birdsong came in through the window, like an apology for the disappointing summer. Caroline lifted her face to drink it in. 'No,' she said, 'there's no romance between me and Frank Bellaers. I like him well enough . . . But the attentiveness! He hovers behind me with my shawl as if I were a fire and he's about to put me out.'

Charles laughed. 'I'll squash that rumour, then.'

'No, let 'em talk on if it amuses them. Tell me, do they weave no gossip around you?'

'Only that I keep a tricolour in my room to welcome the French when they invade.'

'And do you?'

Charles grinned. 'If it comes to a choice between

Bonaparte and Billy Pitt I'm not sure! No, I love England as much as the next man. I would say even more – for what England could become if she reformed herself. The Directory's ambitions are too naked now to fool anyone – though one has to admire Bonaparte's energy: he must be a brilliant man. But the ideals of the Revolution – they shouldn't be abandoned for ever just because they're being betrayed. All the more reason to remember them. Not trample on our own people as if *they* were the chief enemy. I'd like to ask our wooden-headed leaders how they expect to coerce the people into loyalty. No, they'll get loyalty if they earn it, not by these Combination Acts and spies and imprisonments without trial. And now that is my cue to take you down to dinner before you fall asleep.'

'I wasn't falling asleep!' Caroline said, taking his arm. 'Serious, though, if you were in Parliament you *could* tell our wooden-headed leaders these things.'

'Oh, I think there's more chance of them letting Bonaparte himself into the Commons!' Charles laughed. But Caroline saw her cousin's eyes kindle at the thought.

Both Morholm and the Hardwicks had seen their share of troubled times. Drainage failures on the land, debt and mortgage had once seen the estate reduced and the old mansion decrepit and almost empty. But for George and Mary Hardwick those times were past. There had been a bitter dispute between the Hardwicks of Morholm and Joshua Walsoken of Bromswold at the time of the enclosure in the 1780s; and the clandestine marriage of Joshua's daughter Rebecca to Luke Hardwick had deepened the rift rather than reconciling the two families. But dour old Joshua was dead now. Morholm held the prominent place in the village again, and George had consolidated the estate to the east with a successful programme of fen

drainage that had brought whole new areas under culti-
vation and given employment to a depressed district. The
hectic boom prices of wartime had enhanced their prosperity too – though George had an acute enough conscience and a genuine enough feeling for the local country
people who were at the sharp end of the record food
prices to perceive this as a mixed blessing.

George Hardwick had entered Parliament at the age of
twenty-eight as a Member for Stamford under the patronage of the then Lord Burghley. It had been both an
expedient and an experiment. Neither George nor his
patron had anticipated this situation continuing for twenty
years. But when the 9th Earl had died in 1793 his nephew
who inherited the Burghley title and the influence in the
borough of Stamford had shown no desire to replace
George. There had been friction since then – George
voting too much with the opposition for the conservative
10th Earl's comfort. But George Hardwick was now well
known as a man of independence and integrity at Westminster, and had been much favoured by Pitt until
recently, when his withdrawal of support for the Prime
Minister's repressive domestic policies had ended his
chances of a minor position in government. His appointment as Deputy Lord Lieutenant of the county, at a time
when anyone with faintly radical sympathies was mistrusted, was a tribute to the respect he had earned outside
of party loyalties.

George's hair had thinned and his brow was lined but
he had not put on flesh over the years, staying lean and
slightly ascetic in appearance. His wife Mary, plump and
pretty and sunny-natured, had borne three children.
Charles, the eldest, had been born in the unhappy years
of debt and decline at Morholm, and there might have
been a reflection of this in his slender physique, his
nervous alertness and sensitivity to mood. Edmund, who

was eighteen, was a placid self-sufficient boy who showed talent as an artist and would spend whole days in the fields with a sketchbook. Frances, the youngest at thirteen, was a boisterous child with a huge appetite and a cheerful dislike for all learning.

Morholm was a house that seemed exceptionally receptive to the emotions of its occupants. In the early, lean years of George and Mary's marriage, with rooms shut up and unused, it had been cold and murky, draught-haunted: the bleak wind off the fen invaded it and patches of darkness lingered in its low panelled corridors and bedrooms like fog. Now, filled by a young, prosperous family, their many interests, their voices, their abundance of vitality and hope, it was very different. The fact that in recent years George and Mary had put in fireplaces and windows in the new style, replaced dark fumed oak with white plaster and silk wallpapers and brought in slim Sheraton and Hepplewhite furniture added its share to this atmosphere. But that was simply part of the trend of the past few years, when the stateliness of powdered wigs, hooped skirts and lumbering unsprung carriages had given way to cropped natural hair, light practical gowns and fast post-chaises sleek as greyhounds, just as the ponderous armies of the *ancien régime* had fallen back before the dynamic onrush of the French revolutionaries. What really distinguished Morholm now was its stability, as the war for survival pressed harder and the world hovered in turmoil on the edge of a strange new century.

The dining-room held an echo of the older days, with its long, immensely heavy, warped oak table and the tall diamond-paned windows that sieved the light into pale lozenges. The two Hardwick families had not met for some time, and it was a noisy meal.

Only Caroline's younger brother Nicholas was an absentee. He was in his last term at school in Leicester.

'It was more his idea than mine to go back for another term,' Luke said at dinner. 'We had our doubts about that academy at first, but it's proved to be just the thing for him. He learns mathematics, modern languages – very little of the old classical education.'

'Good thing too,' George said. 'I came to man's estate knowing nothing but how to construe a passage from Ovid. And I couldn't do that very well.'

'You speak French, though, don't you, Uncle?' Caroline said.

'I did once. I fear I've lost it all. Why do you ask?'

'You can try it out on our tame Frenchmen,' Luke said. 'I'm to be the parole agent for the officer prisoners-of-war in Peterborough. Captain Woodruff came to see me yesterday.'

'Well, well,' George said. 'We've both been honoured with responsibility. Will you be able to make yourself understood?'

'Apparently most of the French have at least a few words of English. Caro can interpret for me if there's any difficulty, can't you, love?'

'My schoolgirl French,' Caroline said, 'is mainly about aunts and gardens and how many eggs are there in my basket. But I'll do my best.'

'So much for *égalité*,' Charles said drily. 'The men are locked up at Norman Cross, but the officers live in the town on parole.'

'I've only ever seen the prison camp from the road,' Caroline said. 'Have you ever been in it, uncle?'

'Not me,' George said. 'But my steward goes there with a cart most weeks. There's a market at the gate where we sell produce from the home farm. Some of the prisoners make trinkets to sell. John should be going to Norman Cross tomorrow. Would you like to go with him?'

'Oh, I would! You would, too, wouldn't you, Charles?'

'Don't let that Jacobin boy go – he'll set 'em all free!' Luke said to a laugh.

3

'It's like a town,' Caroline said. 'A whole town sprung from nowhere.'

The cart halted at the east gate leading into the camp while a sentry inspected their load – turnips, onions, bushels of peas from the home farm at Morholm. More carts and waggons were waiting outside the stockade fence behind them.

'Busy today,' John Newman said to the sentry. He clicked his tongue and they moved on, into the camp.

The Norman Cross Depot for prisoners-of-war was built on forty-two acres of ground, healthy ground well above the level of the adjoining fen, at the junction of the Great North Road and the coach road to Peterborough, and it was spread out like a panorama before Caroline and Charles, seated either side of John Newman, the Morholm steward.

Away to the left, adjoining the prison, flags flew over the barracks of the militia regiments stationed here as guard, and over the brick-built superintendent's house. The guard was changing in the barrack square. The prison camp proper, directly ahead of them, was surrounded by a strong stockade fence and, towering above it, in the very centre of the enclosure, was an octagonal blockhouse like a pepper-pot on stilts. Sentries were visible in the windows, and mounted cannon pointed from embrasures on each side. Smoke was rising from cook-houses.

A gate led into the prison wall flanked by a guardhouse with a verandah and more armed sentries; and next to this gate were the stalls of the market. In the grassed area between the prison and the outer fence carts and pack-horses crossed back and forth; and soldiers off duty, officers' wives and children walking with parasols and pet dogs, ostlers taking horses out for exercise, porters, workmen, clerks, victuallers, sewage waggons, market traders, all making up a noise and blur of colour that was like, as Caroline said, a good-sized town on a busy day. And inside the stockade, divided into four quadrangles surrounded by red-roofed wooden barracks, the reason for its existence, a prison of five thousand men.

The market stalls were collected in a rough semi-circle around the east gate of the stockade. A cannon was mounted over the gate pointing inwards at the prison. Besides the stalls there were several farm-carts like their own selling goods straight from the tailboard. There were stalls selling eggs, and milk, and fruit; clothes, wigs, combs; sweetmeats, herbals, knives and forks and needles and thread and soap and beer and candles. Of course, Caroline thought, they have everyday lives too; they're strange and foreign and captive, and enemies, but they must eat and shave and catch colds and go about the small business of living.

John Newman looped the nosebag over the horse's head and then let down the tailboard of the cart. He was a big, gentle, heavy man in his forties, with fair hair and eyebrows like bleached ears of wheat, as much a part of Morholm as the Hardwicks themselves. 'You two go look round,' he said. 'I reckon I'll not be long shifting this.'

Caroline pointed to the inner stockade. There were gaps in the struts through which could be glimpsed the teeming life within, and through the gaps several unshaven faces pressed themselves. Arms like white sticks, bone without flesh, hung out bags and hats in supplication. 'Good God, they look as if they're starving,' she said.

'Aye – those'll be the gamblers,' John Newman said. 'Terrible thing. Some of 'em locked up in here get addicted to gaming. Everybody gets a fair ration, y'see – bread, meat, cheese: the market's just for extras. But the gamblers, once their last pennies are gone, they'll lay bets wi' their clothes, and then their food. And there's always the cruel types who'll take it, and hoard it.' He looked at Caroline, who was feeling in the drawstring purse on her wrist. 'They'll only gamble it away, y'know.'

'I'll take that chance,' she said. She dropped some coppers into an outstretched hand. The arm whipped back like a snake. Through the gap in the stockade she now saw the quadrangle: a grassed enclosure surrounded by wooden barrack-huts, around which men were strolling, lounging, arguing; a couple were fencing with wooden foils, others washing clothes at a trough. Then the gap was filled by another wasted, imploring face.

The prisoners who had been allowed out of the gate to the market to sell their wares were easy to spot. They wore yellow coats and breeches and red waistcoats, a uniform that would make escapees highly conspicuous. Some were bargaining in a mixture of French and English with the market traders for food and utensils. They were men of all ages and conditions, from emaciated to plump, swarthy to blond, hideous to handsome. Militia guards paced among the stalls, watching everything.

'Mademoiselle,' a voice called. 'Mademoiselle, you wish to buy?'

Caroline saw an oldish bearded man, in the yellow uniform, beckoning her to his makeshift stall.

'Ah, these must be the things they make in the prison,' Charles said.

Some of the objects spread out on the trestle were crude: wooden pokers and toothpicks, clumsy dolls. But there were things too of astonishingly intricate workmanship. Charles indicated a model of a guillotine, grotesque and brilliant in polished white, with a flight of perfectly carved steps and tiny soldiers and drummers and even a decapitated victim, his pea-sized head smiling up from the basket.

'What is it made from?' Caroline said. 'Can it be ivory?' She smiled at the prisoner. *'Vous êtes français, oui? C'est d'ivoire, cela?'*

'Ah, non, non. Bones, only bones.' The prisoner grinned through his rusty beard. 'From the kitchens, you see?'

'And this too, I suppose.' It was a brush and comb set, slender and elegant. 'You made them all, monsieur?'

The prisoner laughed and shook his head violently.

'No, he don't make 'em, ma'am,' said a soldier behind her. 'Various of these fellows make 'em. There's a delegate from each block who brings 'em out for sale – somebody trustworthy, y'see. The makers' names are attached.'

'La guillotine not for ladies,' the prisoner said. 'This, this you like.' He handed her a small wood jewellery-box inlaid with straw marquetry. On each face was a different pastoral scene: trees, mountains, cottages.

'Why, they must spend hours and hours making such things,' Caroline said.

'Not much else for 'em to dew, ma'am,' the soldier said in his rich West Country: the Somerset Militia were currently stationed here. 'Concentrates the mind, I reckon. They're clever monkeys, right enough.'

There was more straw-marquetry work: a fan, a playing-card case, a fire-screen depicting the Crucifixion, all extremely fine. But Caroline's eye was held by a picture, propped up at the rear of the stall.

It was framed in dark wood, a panel beautifully inlaid with straw marquetry, the straw dyed in rich autumnal colours. The picture was of a tower, with a castellated top and windows, rising from a wooded landscape into clouds. The maker had used a golden dye to give the tower an appearance of being bathed in sunlight. It was a naïve picture – the tower might even have been an idealized version of the block-house that dominated the prison – but the glowing colours, the feeling of light and hope, made Caroline warm to it. There was a name on the label – *J. Bartin*, with the price, a guinea. Whoever Bartin was, she thought, it was a tribute to his spirit that he could have fashioned such a thing under these conditions.

'That'll soon be lost over a game of dice,' the soldier commented, as if disappointed in Caroline, as she handed over the money.

'Well, I was only going to spend it on gin anyway,' Caroline said lightly. '*Adieu, monsieur. Merci.*' She tucked the picture under her arm and moved away with Charles.

After another turn round the market they came back to find John Newman negotiating the sale of a last sack of onions with a young prisoner. John had no French and the boy no English, but they were finishing their business satisfactorily with sign language.

'I suppose one shouldn't be pacific at such a time,' Charles said to Caroline, 'but what a better sight that is than if they were letting off guns at each other.'

'Are there boys in the prison too, John?' Caroline said. 'He can't have been more than twelve.'

'Aye, a fair number of boys,' John said, taking off the horse's nosebag and lifting back the reins. 'Off captured ships, y'see. No place for younkers, really, is it?'

They climbed up beside John and the cart moved out on to the road leading to the outer stockade. A drover shooed his gaggle of geese out of the cart's path.

'Are there ever escapes, d'you know, John?' Charles said.

'The odd one, so I've heard. One got away not long ago by bribing a sentry. Wouldn't give much for their chances meself. I mean, imagine being stuck in France fifty mile from the sea, wi' all hands against you. No, I'd stay put and wait for the peace.'

'Not all hands would be against you, surely,' Caroline said. 'Folk couldn't feel malice for one prisoner-of-war trying to get back to his home, could they? In England or France.'

'What would you do then, Caro?' Charles said smiling. 'If you came across one of those yellow-clad Frenchies hiding out in the stable at home?'

'Give him an old coat and a drink and look the other way,' Caroline said.

'And be ravished in the meantime!' Charles said in the crusty accents of Parson Emmonsales.

'Oh, dear,' Caroline said laughing, 'I'm sure that would be the last thing on his mind.'

'Better stop a minute,' John Newman said in a quiet voice. 'Whoa, there.'

Another cart was passing in front of them, rumbling slowly in the direction of the north gate. Two soldiers preceded it; a chaplain followed. At first Caroline thought the cart was empty. Then she saw the shape covered with a linen sheet. There were bunches of herbs set round it.

The small procession passed, and John flicked the reins.

Charles broke the silence. 'Better than a bloody end on a battlefield, I suppose.'

'There's a field marked out in front of the north gate,'

John Newman said. 'They bury 'em there. Christian burial, y'know, but still . . .'

'Well,' Caroline said with an effort. 'I don't suppose the poor fellow knows whether he's buried in England or France.' But a shiver had passed over her. To die exiled and unmourned in prison . . .

She hugged the straw picture close to her, calling on life and optimism, for these were what nourished her. Against death and darkness she had always interposed the cheerful rationality of her nature. She had never been susceptible to what Lucy Squire, a great reader of the fashionable Gothic novels, called 'the horrors', and was glad to find herself still proof against them after her first sight of a dead person.

The carrier had called at Morholm while they were at Norman Cross, bringing the *Courant* and a letter for Charles.

Caroline was showing her purchase to the family, and describing the prison camp to them, when Charles, poring over his letter, gave a delighted whoop.

'It's from Richard,' he said. 'He's coming home! We can expect him in a month. After all these years!'

'Young Lindsay?' Luke said. 'I'd almost forgot him. Read it out, boy.'

'He writes from Torbay. "Dear Charles, I hope this finds you well. First my apologies for being such a poor correspondent of late, but the French have kept us pretty occupied. My respects are due to your parents, and to your uncle Mr Luke and family – I hope to present them personally very soon, for I have not forgot the debt of gratitude I owe to them in starting me off in this career, which I am pleased to say has now been attended with some success.

'"I last wrote to tell you of my transfer to the frigate

Anson for blockade duty with the Channel Fleet under Lord Bridport. She is a good ship and a contented one under Captain Barratt. The tedium of blockade is often complained of, especially whilst there are such exploits as Admiral Nelson's at the Nile; but in October last the monotony was relieved when we intercepted a French squadron off Tory. We gave chase in a heavy sea for a day and a night, and on the morning of the 12th our shot carried away the mizzen-mast of the *Hoche*, and she struck her colours after a spirited fight. We captured six of the other ships within two days. To my own great joy I was appointed acting lieutenant to the prize crew of the captured French frigate *Jalouse*, which we brought back to Torbay. Here my account becomes boastful; for Rear Admiral Warren, who commands our squadron, then recommended my becoming acting lieutenant on board the *Anson*, whose fourth lieutenant was wounded in the action off Ireland; and as such I rejoined the Western Squadron in January this year. I am deeply sensible of my good fortune in being advanced so early due to the good offices of Captain Barratt and of Rear Admiral Warren – indeed, could scarcely believe it! But now all is to be confirmed, for we are to take the *Anson* to Portsmouth for a thorough refit. I am promised shore leave then, and am told to expect a summons from the Admiralty to take my lieutenant's examination.

'"I wish I had leisure to tell you more but, as I have said, I hope to be amongst you very soon – within a month. I have written my old aunt in Stamford, and she is willing to give me a berth for the short time I expect to be ashore. I confess that all the sights of the Caribbean and the Atlantic have never quite overcome my feeling for the old fen country. Truly yours, Richard Lindsay."'

'I knew he'd not let us down,' Luke said, as Charles passed the letter round. 'And he's distinguished himself, by the sound of it. Promoted lieutenant at – what age would he be now, twenty?'

'The minimum age,' said George. 'If he passes his examination.'

'And he's safe and in one piece,' Rebecca said. 'That's the best news of all.'

Caroline looked at the strong angular script and thought of the pale silent boy they had seen off from London five years ago. It was an image very difficult to reconcile with the confident tone of the letter. Still, was there not a trace of that unpleasant pride that she had so disliked? No – she joined in the general good wishes, and in the toast that was drunk to Richard Lindsay later. The antipathy that had existed between them was a piece of the past, something that should be left behind in adolescence, like puppy fat and bad skin. She believed she had matured.

She placed the straw picture on the bureau when she went to bed that night, and the moonlight illuminated the tower in brilliant relief.

Morholm was always so quiet at night. At home in Peterborough there was always the subliminal noise of the town – late drunks from the ale-houses, the watch calling the hours, the clanking night-soil carts. Here the silence amplified her thoughts, making them large and eloquent.

And those thousands of men at Norman Cross, and the officers in their dingy lodgings in Peterborough – each with their solitary thoughts, each with their individual selfhood – cherished, held like a brimming cup . . . as one would hold a brimming cup on the swaying deck of a crowded ship.

She herself had never been lonely. The idea of loneliness afflicted her with pain.

For once in her life, Caroline was a long time getting to sleep.

CHAPTER 2

1

It was much to her father's credit, Caroline thought, that he behaved with such amiability towards the French officers who came to the house. The war news, as September ended, turned discouraging again. It would have been easy for a man in Luke Hardwick's position with so much to lose from the war, to deeply resent these men, these living symbols of all that threatened his ships and his fortune, who came twice weekly to the Bridge House to collect their allowance. Luke was a fundamentally generous man, but he could be a hard and demanding one: he had a scathing tongue at need – though it had never been turned on Caroline – and, in his mid-forties, a glowering physical presence that evinced a man of strong energies and passions. But with the paroled officers he maintained a straightforward courtesy, and kept his thoughts about the war to himself.

Ever since Nelson's victory at the Nile last year there had been high hopes that a turning-point had been reached after five long years of war: perhaps the hitherto triumphant forces of the Republic had reached the limit of their success. A second coalition including Britain, Russia, Austria and Turkey, painstakingly nurtured by Pitt with generous subsidies, had seemed to promise peace with victory. The Austrian and Russian armies had pressed the French back, and General Bonaparte's expedition to conquer Egypt and threaten Britain's Indian Empire had collapsed. Now was the time, it seemed, for the British Army to prove itself and perhaps deliver the *coup de grâce*. Two months ago the British and Russians had combined in a landing in Holland. The Dutch fleet had fallen whole into British hands. The French army in Holland had retreated.

And now, the rumours . . . There were quarrels between the British and Russian leaders. The allies had failed to consolidate their success in the Helder. And had Bonaparte evaded the blockade and escaped from Egypt? Caroline saw that the frustration of uncertainty, of rumour and counter-rumour, was a physical torture to her father. He scrutinized the local newspapers, the London newspapers, the Gazettes: angrily crumpled them, and then carefully unfolded them to read them again. Where formerly he had contented himself with a visit to the house at King's Lynn every fortnight, he now made the thirty-mile journey weekly.

Luke Hardwick's house owned several coasters, small brigs and sloops, trading up to Tyneside and down to London: theoretically these were at less risk, though French privateers increasingly made raids on coastal vessels within sight of English beaches. But Luke's chief concern was the safety of his overseas vessels, the schooners *Minerva, Undine* and *Blithe* and the brigs *Pride of Lynn* and *Sheldrake*. The *Minerva* was being refitted but the others were at sea. Before the war there had been a highly profitable trade from Lynn with the Dutch ports, where grain was in demand for the brewing industry, but the occupation of Holland had ended that. They were dependent on Baltic trade now. The Navy was clamouring for timber from the Prussian ports. But because of the depredations of enemy privateers, the Government last year had made it compulsory for all foreign-going merchant ships to travel in escorted convoy. Luke chafed at the loss of time this entailed: the ships had first to assemble with others, often at Yarmouth, to make up the convoy; and when the convoy did set sail it had to go at the rate of the slowest ship in its number – which was usually much slower than Luke's swift schooners could have sailed on their own. And when the ships arrived at port, there was the chance that so many docking at once would mean a glut of identical goods, and lower prices. Luke confessed that he was tempted to defy the law and let his ships sail alone and run the gauntlet of the privateers. He had not done so yet. But the temptation grew greater as the war dragged on.

Caroline quickly became accustomed to the paroled officers arriving at the Bridge House each Tuesday and Friday. They gathered in the carriage-yard behind the house, talking volubly in French and Dutch and scraps of English, before trooping into her father's study to receive their allowance of 1s 6d a day. She came to recognize a few of them: Delchambre, a master's mate who was fifteen and looked about ten and whose baby face brought out a chaffing paternalism in his fellows; Captain Van den Bos, an elderly courtly Dutchman with an iron hook for his left hand; and Captain Roubillard, who had fluent English and acted as a kind of spokesman-delegate for the other Frenchmen. He was an ugly, jovial, mountain of a man without a grain of self-consciousness in his hulking body; on being greeted by their spaniel Leo he dropped down on hands and knees and barked back at him and then rolled about on the floor with the squirming delighted dog, hooting with laughter.

The officers lived plainly, in attic rooms and basements, keeping to the society of their own kind, taking walks as far as the toll-bars would let them: a few sketched, some played musical instruments, others did odd jobs for occupation. They were as anxious for war news as anyone, and Luke always passed on his newspapers to Captain

Roubillard, who translated for the others. Caroline looked for the bloodthirsty Revolutionary zeal one heard so much about; but though there were certainly some officers who never shed a look of cold hostility, who took their allowance without thanks and regarded everything about them with baleful contempt, the majority were clearly waiting for news of peace. There was no possibility of an exchange of prisoners at present, and their only hope of returning home was an end to war, be the victors France or England.

There had been few new prisoners arriving either for Norman Cross or for parole since the great influx from the Nile campaign last year; but on September 25th, a Wednesday, Luke had been informed that a barge was to arrive from Wisbech, with fifteen men bound for Norman Cross and six officers to be paroled in Peterborough.

Luke was out, making enquiries about lodgings for the six, when the boat arrived at the wharf below the Bridge House. Caroline saw it from the window of the morning-room. A sergeant of militia and two soldiers were detached and brought the six officers up to the house.

The sergeant stood stiffly at the morning-room door and saluted Caroline and her mother and said he had orders to deliver these six Frenchmen into the keeping of Mr Luke Hardwick.

'My husband shouldn't be long,' Rebecca said. 'In the meantime bring your men in and I'll send for some ale and saffron cakes.'

'I'm obliged to you, ma'am,' said the sergeant, 'but we can't be leaving those fellows out there. 'Twouldn't be – '

'I meant bring them in too,' Rebecca said. 'We've plenty of ale to go round.'

'If you say so, ma'am,' the sergeant said, nervously fingering his moustache. 'We'll keep a close eye on 'em, ma'am . . . but they are Frenchies . . . if you're sure you'll be easy . . .'

'My dear man, I seem to be surrounded by Frenchmen these days, and I've come to no harm yet,' Rebecca said laughing. 'Bring them in.'

Nancy the maid – stiff-backed as she always was when there were Frenchies about – brought mugs of ale and trays of saffron cakes into the dining-room; and the sergeant and two soldiers, with muskets at the ready, ushered in the six officers, all carrying linen bundles. The Frenchmen looked startled at the two women standing there to greet them, and hurriedly bowed.

'*Bonjour, messieurs*,' Rebecca said, and then turned in some perplexity to the sergeant and said, 'Do any of them speak English?'

'I speak a little,' said one man, bowing again.

'Ah, good,' Rebecca said. 'Please, sit down, everyone. You're hungry and thirsty I'm sure. My husband Mr Hardwick, who is the parole agent here, is out at present, but he'll be back soon. He will pay you your allowance and allocate your lodgings – '

'Please,' the Frenchman who had first spoken said, 'er – a little more slowly?' and he smiled apologetically.

'*Mon père, l'agent de parole, retournera bientôt*,' Caroline said. She strained for memory, with a bizarre mental image of her French grammar-book fluttering away like a bird. 'And – oh, *il expliquera tout, oui*?' She waved a hand at the food on the table. 'Now, eat, drink, please?'

The Frenchmen sat down with grateful sighs, and after a moment the three militiamen, with considerably less ease of manner, did likewise.

'You've come from Wisbech, sergeant?' Caroline said conversationally.

'Yes, miss,' the sergeant said. 'We're quartered at Norman Cross, you understand, but we were sent to

Wisbech yesterday to escort these rogues – beg pardon, ma'am. They're off a captured ship that was brought into Portsmouth. I don't know where we'll find room for all these fellows at this rate.'

The officers were quiet as they ate except for a few remarks in French amongst themselves. Caroline, like most people of her age, had been brought up to believe that Frenchmen gabbled constantly with their arms whirling like windmills, as well as wearing wooden shoes: it was disconcerting to be disabused of so many prejudices in so short a time.

She noticed that they looked towards the one who had spoken English, though he was by no means the eldest – she guessed about twenty-seven. It was he who, when they had all finished eating, stood up and gestured the others to do so and said in his heavily accented English: 'Madame, mademoiselle, we thank you for the meal. You are very kind. And, pardon me, I have not, er, presented, introduced.' He gestured and smiled apologetically again. It was a very warm smile, a warm and grave smile. 'My name is Antoine Clairet. I am, was, *Capitaine du Frégate* La Coquille. Here is Brunet, Fabre, Renard, the lieutenants. Bourde, master. Tramond, the, er, *chirurgeon* . . .'

'Surgeon,' Caroline helped.

'Yes. So . . . we all thank you for the – hospitality' – the young captain's face registered a pleased relief as he found this word – 'and, er, that is all.' The others added *Merci, mesdames* in an array of baritones. The sergeant shook his head in mistrust.

'Well, I think everyone will be more comfortable if we absent ourselves,' Rebecca said – they were all still standing. 'Come along, Caro. Please, gentlemen, make yourselves at ease till Mr Hardwick comes back.'

'*Au revoir, messieurs,*' Caroline said. '*Mon père sera ici bientôt.*'

She felt she ought to have said something more, but what – 'Welcome to England'? 'I hope your stay here is pleasant'? The whole situation was so incongruous.

Her father was home within half an hour, and he took the officers into his study to sign their *paroles d'honneur*: and soon afterwards they and their guard were gone. Luke consigned them to Captain Roubillard, who knew the ropes and would help them settle in.

'I've managed to find room for them, but it wasn't easy,' Luke said, as they sat down to dinner. 'The lodging-houses are full, and some people just won't let rooms to prisoners-of-war, or if they do they'll only take Dutch and not French. They've had to make do with some pretty dingy berths. Oh, well, I don't suppose they went to war hoping to end up in feather beds. By the way, you'll not want the carriage tomorrow, will you, love?'

'No,' Rebecca said. 'You're going to Lynn again?'

Luke nodded. 'Sallis's timber yard is up for auction. Timber's where the profit is these days. We could store tons of timber there. And as long as the German ports stay open . . . It's a new venture, I know, but that's what happens in war. We can't stand still. As it is we're just treading water.'

Her father was pushing himself too hard. Caroline thought so and knew her mother thought so – not that Rebecca ever said as much to her. Caroline was close to her mother in many ways; but Rebecca had a self-possession that she did not compromise merely because she had a child of the same sex. And she and Luke had never been in the habit of dragging their children into the arena of their marriage – their occasional quarrels were brief and conclusive and fought without allies. What Caroline did know was that her parents were both strong-willed, and neither would give ground on something unless it was of the utmost importance. To be standing still, treading water, was anathema to her father. Oh, they were comfortable, very comfortable: Luke had lost money in the banking crisis of '97, but he had bounced back, and he had other investments besides the shipping line. But it never seemed enough. Sometimes it seemed to Caroline as if all the Hardwicks had this restlessness, this dissatisfaction, ingrained in their character. She wondered if she were the only exception.

So Luke went to King's Lynn, and Rebecca made no outward demur; and the tardy summer made a few more fitful attempts to vindicate itself, too late for the harvest but appreciated nonetheless, and Caroline spent as much time outside as possible. That meant walking, for unlike her mother who thought nothing of riding out even as far as Morholm of a morning, Caroline was no horsewoman.

The sun was hot enough on the Saturday to demand a parasol, and it had dried the low-lying river meadows towards Fletton, so she was able to stroll that way and watch the wide barges called fen-lighters that plied the green river, loaded with stone from the Northamptonshire quarries and leather and wool. The light from the open sky was brilliant and overwhelming, singling out in dense relief every reed and rush on the shore and finding specks of colour in the wings of gnats dancing in the warmth above the flat meadows.

When she saw the knot of people on the bank, and the supine figure around which they were grouped, Caroline's first thought was to turn away. It must be a body that had been fished out of the river, and though she had come out well, she thought, of that experience at Norman Cross, she had no particular wish to repeat the experiment. But then a small boy came jigging over to her, and said: 'It's a spy! A French spy under a tree!'

The people, a dozen or so, were gathered round a figure whom she recognized as the young French captain who had arrived that week. He was lying with his right arm above his head. His upturned face, even in sleep, registered a sensuous enjoyment of the sunshine. His left arm lay across his breast, with a folded telescope held loosely in the hand. He had taken off his coat and spread it under him, and his skin looked brown against his white waistcoat and breeches and open shirt.

Everyone was staring down at him. 'I been watching him from the hayfield all morning,' an elderly man said to Caroline in a hushed voice. 'Peerin' across the river through this 'ere telescope' – the man did a mime – '*spyin*'.'

'D'you reckon 'tis an invasion starting?' said another man, who gripped a pitchfork.

At that moment the young Frenchman opened his eyes, looked up at the ring of faces, and jumped to his feet in some confusion, dropping the telescope.

'Now then!' the man with the pitchfork said, backing away. A woman squealed.

'Really, what nonsense!' Caroline said. 'This is Captain Clairet. He's one of the prisoners-of-war on parole and he's just arrived. Please, put that pitchfork down.'

'What's he doing spyin' out wi' that telescope then?' said the first man. 'Thass what I want to know!'

Captain Clairet, still blinking and unsteady on his feet in the first startling unpleasantness of waking, looked at Caroline, first with dawning recognition and then appeal. 'Miss Hardwick . . . please – I have not the English to – *expliquer. Je regardais le paysage . . . je m'amusais seulement . . .*'

'Of course. Captain Clairet was merely looking at the countryside. He's a stranger here after all. A spy's hardly likely to go to sleep in full view, is he?'

'You never know,' said the first man, 'with Frenchies,'

but the others groaned and said they should have known Jack would get hold of the wrong end of the stick.

'*Messieurs*, I am prisoner,' Captain Clairet said, spreading his hands, 'no harm,' but already they were drifting away, with jibes at the unfortunate Jack. Spies were interesting, but prisoners-of-war were ten a penny.

Captain Clairet dusted down his shirt and breeches. 'Miss Hardwick, I thank you . . . I – my English, I was not able . . .'

'It's all right, Captain Clairet.' She smiled. 'It's lucky I came along – but I don't think they would have hurt you, you know.'

He blinked at her, and then smiled too, and at last laughed with great good humour. 'Yes,' he said, picking up his coat, 'I see now. I believe I was having, er, *un rêve*, a dream, yes? And then I wake and I see the faces looking, I ask myself, Where am I? You see?' He laughed again. 'I am in England, it is *bizarre*.'

Caroline watched him pluck a blade of grass out from the neck of his shirt. 'What was your dream, Captain Clairet?'

'Oh,' he shrugged, 'home. *La France. Naturellement*. I had looked at the fields, here. *Très plat,* flat, yes? Like *la Flandre*.'

'Flanders? Yes, I believe it is. This land is called fenland. That's Borough Fen over there.'

'Ah, *bon*. And then, I thought myself of home, and the sun was hot, and I was asleep.'

She couldn't help admiring someone who could fall asleep like that in a foreign place where he had been newly made a prisoner-of-war. It suggested a fundamental ease of mind that she had discerned also in the sensual lassitude with which the Frenchman had sprawled on the grass. There was something boyish about it – though he was a well-grown man, tall and big-boned – and there was something boyish too about the tousled chestnut hair through which he ran his hands and the smile that began with his dark brown eyes and spread so slowly and gravely.

'I hope your lodgings are satisfactory, Captain?' She watched him lick his lips and think – just in the way she did when working out a piece of French. 'Ah, yes,' he said. '*Ma chambre*. I have, your father has found for me, a room, a *mansarde* –' he struggled, pointed upwards. '*Au toit* – the word . . .'

'Ah, an attic room. A garret.'

'Yes.' He added with some amusement: 'It is in a place called Little's Yard.'

'Oh . . .' Little's Yard was a sunless courtyard of frowsy buildings off Narrow Bridge Street, a place that the Improvement Commissioners had been able to do little with. As if divining her thoughts he said: 'It is small, I have not many things. But you see, I am not in the prison. I am free, almost. I can go all about the city. When I, my ship was taken, I fear to be put in prison. So, I am happy.'

He looked happy, too. She lifted a hand to shield her eyes. It seemed momentarily as if the light was pouring from his figure, but it was the sun poised directly above his head. 'I'm glad,' she said. 'Well . . . *au revoir*, Captain Clairet.'

She turned to go, then turned back to him and said: 'Captain Clairet – your English . . . I don't mean it's bad, but would you like to improve it? Make your English better?'

'Certainly.'

'I have some lesson-books I used at school. For learning French – but I dare say they may be helpful the other way round.'

'Books, yes, that is what I need. My English, you see, I

61

learned it when I was young. My father spoke it very well. But' – he tapped his head – 'I lose it.'

She smiled. He made her smile, though not because she was laughing at him; just something about him, something light and sunny like the day. 'Well, next time you come to the Bridge House I'll give you the books.'

'Miss Hardwick, you are very kind. Please give my, respects, yes? to your mother and father. And thank you again. I – '

'Yes?'

He had the look of someone about to take a step forward but half-afraid to. 'It is only – in France we believe the Englishwomen are all – *les laideronnes, les chipies* – with beards, ugly, cold, yes? It is what everyone says. But you are – quite, very different!'

'Oh . . . thank you, Captain Clairet,' she said, and left him.

She was still laughing to herself when she got home. She hadn't got a beard! Well, it was a nice compliment, really, in intention at least. She went up to her room and looked out her old grammar-books, thinking occasionally of the young man's smile and the soft hollow at the base of his throat where he had pulled out the tickling blade of grass.

That afternoon a carriage drew up at the Bridge House: no humble chaise from a livery stable, but a black-glazed, yellow-wheeled, elegantly skeletal creature attended by a liveried postilion and footman. Out of this stepped a young man with long legs and fair hair, and a trim-figured girl with hair a shade darker.

The girl was Caroline's cousin Susannah Milton, and the young man she introduced was Stephen Downes, her fiancé as of last week.

'Oh, it's not that we've kept a secret of it, you know,'

Susannah said, when Caroline and her mother expressed their surprise. 'But it was in Norfolk that Stephen and I met, and I suppose we have been a little out of the way.'

Susannah and her fiancé declined an invitation to stay to dinner – they had another call to make – but they took tea in the parlour overlooking the river, told Caroline and her mother the whole story, and gave every sign of being a couple very much in love.

'I wanted to marry this young woman the very first time I saw her,' Stephen Downes said. 'It was at a concert in King's Lynn. I stared at her. No, I *gawped*. That is a marvellous word, and expresses it perfectly. I was ready to ask her there and then. But I thought, I suppose I'd better wait, it seems only proper.'

'Mr Downes!' Caroline said. 'And you expected her to have you there and then? Such conceit!'

'Oh, I only meant to ask her, you know,' the young man said, laughing and colouring. 'I never expected her to have me at all. Just to ask, you know.'

'My cousin's making fun, Stephen,' Susannah said. 'She doesn't mean it. In fact, Caro, I was soon very ready to accept, and then it was simply a question of confronting our parents. It all sounds exceeding romantic, doesn't it?'

'It does, and it is,' Caroline said. 'Mr Downes, you are a lucky man. I don't know you well enough yet to say whether Susannah is a lucky woman, but I hope I shall, and she certainly looks happy. Oh, many congratulations to you both.' She shook Stephen Downes' hand and kissed her cousin warmly.

In fact she had taken to Stephen Downes almost immediately. If he looked a little the dandy, with his open dress coat and high collar peeping over a starched cravat, and his light hair in a fashionably dishevelled Roman crop, there was no affectation in his manner. He had a humorous unmalicious face and bright blue eyes that turned constantly and affectionately to Susannah.

'You are a Norfolk man, Mr Downes?' Rebecca asked him.

'West Norfolk,' he said, turning energetically to her. 'Though they tell me that is not *true* Norfolk. My place is Great Baston, near Downham Market. Not quite on the fen, but close enough for the east wind to shake the old pile to its timbers.'

'Oh, Great Baston's beautiful,' Susannah said. 'We must have you all to stay there: all the Hardwicks. We went to Morholm this morning to give the family there the news. And to issue invitations. We plan to have a big party to celebrate our engagement. D'you remember Whittlesea Mere Feast? A sort of fair on the Mere? We've planned something similar. A water-party. Lots of pleasure-boats, an orchestra on the water, marquees on the shore. The only difficulty is the weather. It's fixed for the twelfth of October. We'll just have to hope the Indian summer keeps up.'

They made a handsome couple, Caroline decided; Susannah with her open features and dainty hands and feet, Stephen with his gentlemanly looks and long limbs of a sort of lazy athleticism. They ought to have good-looking children. And the children would be rich.

That was the chief surprise – not that Susannah was getting married, but that she was marrying so very well. When the couple had gone away again, Caroline said: 'We have understood right, haven't we? The Downes of Great Baston?'

'It must be,' Rebecca said. 'Not that I've ever met them. But they're well known. The perfect impeccable family. Very wealthy. I suppose it's really not too much of a mismatch. The Miltons may not be in the Downes' sphere but they're genteel. And Susannah's mother's a

Hardwick! Susannah's got nothing to be ashamed of, anyway. Clearly he loves her for herself.'

'Yes. Oh, yes, I know, but . . .'

'I know what you mean. One doesn't expect anyone so unconventional as the Miltons to produce a daughter who makes a good marriage at eighteen and settles down!'

Caroline thought of her uncle and aunt Milton. Her aunt Julia – born Julia Hardwick, sister to George at Morholm – was married to Henry Milton, who was the proprietor of the *Stamford and Peterborough Courant* and of the new circulating-library in Stamford. They had only the one child, Susannah. The Miltons were on good terms with the Morholm Hardwicks and with the family at the Bridge House, but they lived somewhat secludedly at Helpston and one saw little of them. Both Uncle Henry and Aunt Julia had published poetry when they were younger, and Aunt Julia had even had a play performed, if not very successfully, at Drury Lane ten years ago. They were still literary, and the house at Helpston was a rambling mess of books and papers in which Susannah's neat room was as conspicuous as a shining egg in a ragged old nest. They did rather eccentric things: just before the war they had gone to Italy – not to visit palaces but to look at barbaric mountain scenery, a taste that was new enough to be looked at askance by their more conservative Northamptonshire neighbours. But Susannah had turned out very differently: more interested in frocks than books, in dancing than debating, in society than solitude. And now she had allied herself with a rich, sociable young man with unimpeachable connections and, Caroline guessed, not an unconventional bone in his body.

It occurred to Caroline – and she was half-amused and half-disturbed by the thought – that of all the Hardwick clan, she herself had been the one expected to make such a marriage.

2

The weather was set fair for Susannah Milton's engagement party on Whittlesea Mere. The dawns of October ripened into apple-gold days, and in the evenings mist on the fen and the last drifting smuts from the stubble-burning in the fields drew a smoky cape around Peterborough. The light brought out the warmth of the old stones of the cathedral: honey tints like those in Caroline's straw marquetry picture of the tower.

The picture had been hung in the small parlour above the marble fireplace. It immediately drew the eyes of Captain Antoine Clairet, when he came in to collect the books Caroline had promised him.

She called him in as he came out from her father's study with his allowance and receipt. The books were stacked on the side-table. 'These two have translation exercises,' she said. '*Traduction*. And vocabulary.' She saw him looking at the straw tower. 'That was made by one of your countrymen. At Norman Cross. I went there a few weeks ago.'

'Ah, *les pauvres*,' he said. 'I have not seen the prison, Miss Hardwick. Thankfully. But, I hear it is not so bad, yes?'

She shrugged. 'It's a prison. But airy, I think, healthy.'

He was still looking at the picture. Her eyes described his profile: the bones strong, the eyes deeply set beneath arched eyebrows, small ears exposed by the dark hair swept back and tied in a queue.

'This tower, it makes me to think, remember, my home in France.'

'You live in a tower?'

'Oh, no, no.' He smiled. 'There is a château, very old,

66

ruineux, a ruin, yes? Near to my village. Trees, all round. And the tower very tall, very beautiful – the sun touches it in the morning. The birds, *les corbeaux* – ?'

'Crows.'

'Crows – they go there. It is very quiet, peaceful. It is what I think of when I think of my home.'

'Where is your home, your village, Captain Clairet?'

He smiled radiantly, as if being asked that question made him enormously happy. 'The village is called Torcy. It is near to Alençon, in Normandy. A very little village. *Très rustique*. My family are living there since many generations.'

'All sailors?'

'Oh, no, I am the first. I love the sea since a little boy.'

'You're quite young for a captain, aren't you?' Keeping your English simple made your conversation very direct, she was finding.

'Yes, perhaps. I am twenty-six. But you see, in the Revolution the officers of the Navy were many killed or went abroad. Everything changed. There are many young officers now, the army also. *D'ailleurs*, my ship was not large. I am made captain just two months before my ship is taken. Bad luck, is it not?' He looked at the picture again. 'I like this picture,' he said.

'So do I,' she said, and their separate smiles coincided like a brushing of hands. 'But the books, Captain Clairet.'

It was difficult. *Pilgrim's Progress* was ideal simple English, but if he was an atheist Revolutionary he would not want to read that – and if he was still a Catholic he would be similarly offended. Goldsmith's *History of England* seemed to be full of wars against the French. She had ended up, besides the grammar-books, with a book she had had as a little girl, *Selected Fables*. She flushed as she picked it up. It looked very childish; and on the fly-leaf her name was written several times, the writing growing less clumsy as she grew older. She saw him smile gently at this, and her flush deepened; having those childish characters, that small personal history observed, was as intimate and disconcerting as a flash of nudity.

'It's a book for children really,' she said apologetically. 'But I thought it might be helpful . . . the English . . .'

But he did not seem embarrassed. 'You are so kind,' he said. 'It will help very much to – occupy my time. That is good English?'

'That is very good English.'

'Captain Roubillard also helps me,' he said. 'He is, er, *un bonhomme*. A good friend.'

'That's good.'

The books were in his hand, and he was ready to go. And it was only when he was gone that she realized she did not want him to go.

She had always liked observing people – taken an objective pleasure in the revelation of their personalities, as one might in viewing scenery. But her awakened curiosity about Clairet was more. All the sympathetic interest she felt in these imprisoned foreigners thrust in their midst came to a focus in the person of the young soft-spoken captain. Her mind stood on tiptoe: the glimpses into his world, the village with the tower. The casual way he talked about the Revolution . . . but he was probably at sea then – she didn't suppose the whole French population was engaged in playing football with the heads of aristocrats the way the papers suggested.

She wanted to ask him more, and there would be no opportunity for that until the next muster day – but she saw him that same afternoon. She came through the cathedral precinct on her way to go shopping and saw Captain Clairet with Captain Roubillard in the great grassed close before the West Front. They were across by St Thomas's Chapel, watching two children playing at battledore and shuttlecock on the grass, and they waved their hats to her. When she returned the same way after her shopping she found that the two Frenchmen had been given the battledores and had taken off their coats and were playing an energetic game watched with laughing cheers by a crowd of children.

She had to stop and watch also. Captain Roubillard, his sleeves rolled up to reveal arms astonishingly hirsute, had neither reflexes nor grace, but he had good humour – his donkey's bray of a laugh boomed round the cloisters – and immense strength, so that when he managed to hit the shuttlecock he pounded it back at his young companion like shot from a gun. The children screamed with laughter as Captain Clairet dodged and ducked the feathered missile and at last caught it square in the midriff, dramatically falling flat on his back.

Then there was a rally. Captain Roubillard thundered purple-faced back and forth and Captain Clairet darted and slid, and they kept the shuttlecock in the air twenty, thirty, forty times. And then Captain Roubillard struck a low, cunning shot that sped just above the ground, and Clairet dived like a porpoise, just reaching the shuttlecock at full stretch and sending it over Captain Roubillard's head into a patch of weeds. The children cheered the young man to the echo, and Caroline bent to help him up from where he had landed flat on his face at her feet.

'Are you all right, Captain Clairet?' she said, still glowing with laughter, holding his arm.

'Ah, Miss Hardwick, thank you. Always you help me.' He grinned. '*Je l'ai déjoué, n'est-ce pas?* I win!'

'Cheat,' Captain Roubillard cried. 'An unfair stroke, Miss Hardwick, was it not? Children, was it not?'

Clairet sucked his knuckles where he had grazed them in falling. There was a faint scent of perspiration about him, and there were fragments of grass adhering to his cheek. It seemed perfectly natural for Caroline to reach up and pluck them off. 'You're always covered in grass when I see you, Captain,' she said.

'*Encore une fois*, Clairet!' Roubillard cried. 'Another game, and I'll beat you!'

'No, no, *mon vieux*, I can do no more,' Clairet said, and he passed his battledore to one of the children, and they watched as Captain Roubillard, puffing and blowing, let the little boy beat him. Caroline, standing close to Captain Clairet among the small figures, was keenly aware of their common adulthood, like a shared secret. Then the children were plucking at her skirts and saying: 'You play, miss! You play!' She had on a light muslin frock that was quite suitable, so she threw down her bonnet and played, first with Captain Roubillard and then with Captain Clairet. They played until their shadows were long on the grass, until she was too weak with laughter to lift the battledore. When the two captains finally said *au revoir* she was almost surprised – had almost forgotten they were Frenchmen. Perhaps she should not have been surprised, however, when the Butterworths called the next day.

She did not see them – or rather, she saw them coming, and ungallantly absented herself so that her mother had to entertain them alone. There were few people Caroline would actually go out of her way to avoid, but the Butterworths she could not take at any price. They had embraced a particularly saintly sort of religion. In the last few years many of the gentry had looked aghast at the Revolution in France, the upheavals and war, decided that they must have sinned, and crowded to the churches, just as politically they had hurried back to the safe reactionary ground of Pitt's conservatism. Mr Butterworth was a wealthy land agent who had had a rather racy reputation as a youth. None so pious as a reformed rake.

Mrs Butterworth had had much to do with that. She had borne him – surely miraculously, Caroline thought – a daughter, Charity, who was the most hateful little prig in fifty miles. The Butterworths were strong for the reformation of morals. They had once hustled Charity away from a concert where a flautist was playing ('playing upon the flute occasions a most improper *pursing* of the *lips*'). And it turned out, they, or someone known to them, had observed Caroline playing battledore and shuttlecock with French prisoners.

'*Gadding back and forth – skirts flying in full view – exchanging pleasantries with the Frenchmen – and in the Cathedral cloister too!*' So her mother recounted the Butterworths' shocked admonitions to Caroline.

'Why, yes, I did,' Caroline said. 'I played at shuttlecock with Captain Clairet and Captain Roubillard and some children. It was sunny and it was all good fun. Mother, surely *you* don't – '

'Oh, bless you, love, I knew it would have to be something wholly innocuous for *them* to complain about it,' Rebecca said. '*We thought you would wish to be told, Mrs Hardwick* – Pah!' She paced round the room restlessly. 'It's the way they look at *me*. As if to say, well, what can you expect from such a mother? Because I didn't go into mob-caps and mourning as soon as I turned thirty they think I'm – '

'Flighty?' Caroline said.

Rebecca looked at her daughter and her frown broke up into a laugh. 'Yes, flighty,' she said. 'Oh, little minds, Caro. Beware of little minds.'

But her mother was still inwardly gnawing – *wittling*, her father called it – that evening. Luke was inclined to laugh the whole thing off. The *Sheldrake* and *Blythe* had just come safely into his wharf at King's Lynn with full, precious cargoes of timber and hemp, and his mood was

71

genial. 'Take no notice of them, love,' he said. 'They'll soon find something else to disapprove of.'

'But it makes me want to show them what I really think of them,' Rebecca said. 'To think I just sat there and swallowed their wretched sermon . . .'

'Have them to dinner,' Luke said. 'No, no, not the Butterworths. Those officers. They're gentlemanly men. Everyone likes Captain Roubillard. And Captain Clairet seems a very sensible man: I was speaking to him the other day about deepening the wharf here. Have them to dinner, and someone from the town – the Squires or somebody – so that the news will get back to the Butterworths. Then we can all get on with our lives in peace.'

It was immediately agreed in theory, but when the day came when the French captains were to come to the Bridge House both Rebecca and Caroline were seized with doubts. Luke, however, picked them off like ripe apples. Perhaps the officers had nothing suitable to wear – their only clothes were the ones they had when they were captured. They had their uniforms, Luke said, and what could be more suitable than that? What would they like to eat – would they turn up their noses at English dishes? They were still privileged prisoners-of-war, Luke said, and if they turned up their noses at good English cooking he would personally turn them out. What about conversation – what if talk turned to the war and the Revolution and Bonaparte and things like that? *I'm* not going to bring the subject up, Luke said, and I don't suppose anyone else will be foolish enough to either. What about language – Captain Clairet's English was still shaky . . . He had enough to get by, Luke said, and anyway it will be the perfect opportunity for him to improve it. What about all the other officers, would they not feel slighted? There were half a hundred paroled officers lodged around Peterborough, Luke said, and they wouldn't fit around his dining-table unless they came in relays, and now stop fretting.

Caroline was glad of her father that day. He had a way of breasting through problems like a strong swimmer through waves. She wanted someone to whisk away the doubts and difficulties, for she wanted the evening to be a success. She wanted it to be a success as one in the eye for the Butterworths – as one in the eye for the war, if you like, a defiance of all the atmosphere of mistrust and despair and the polarization of feelings that it engendered. And she liked Captain Roubillard and Captain Clairet: though she did not so much *like* Captain Clairet – he was tantalizingly, barely known – as acknowledge the fact that he had been thrown onto her consciousness like a shadow on a screen.

The Squire family, also invited to that dinner, were clearly uneasy – especially Caroline's timid friend Lucy; but the Frenchmen were so obviously civilized, and so obviously delighted to be enjoying the natural amenities of life again in spite of war and imprisonment, that all constraint was taken away with the first course of broiled sole and shrimp sauce.

Fancy me worrying over the food, Caroline thought, when the officers, on their allowance, probably eat fat bacon and bread and little else. She thought this, seated next to Captain Clairet, watching him listen with concentration to her father talking about the harbour improvements at King's Lynn, and felt sorry for him – not in any maudlin way, but in a spirit of admiration, for the sheer resilience expressed in his attentive posture and receptive expression. She felt far more keenly his isolation, the restrictions on his spirit that his imprisonment (mitigated imprisonment though it might be) imposed, than if he had repined and cursed the English and wished himself back in *la France*.

Mr Squire, the banker, loosened with drink, went so far as to ask Captain Clairet, what did he think of this country of ours? Some breath was sharply sucked in around the table, but Captain Clairet said: 'There are many things the same as in France, but also strange things. Today I saw, at the bridge, some birds – *des oies'* – He turned to Captain Roubillard.

'Geese.'

'Geese, many geese. Hundreds of them I think. They were walking in front of a man, like sheep, yes? And they were wearing *shoes*.' He turned in bemusement to Caroline.

'Oh, they would be going to Nottingham Goose Fair,' she said. 'The farmers walk the geese through tar and sand, and it hardens on their feet to make little shoes, so they can walk long distances on the roads. They usually go after harvest so the geese can feed on the stubble in the fields.'

The young Frenchman's amused surprise at the geese wearing little shoes gave a lightness to the evening. It was a success. It was possible to forget that the captains were enemy prisoners-of-war – until they had to leave early to be in their lodgings before the parole curfew. Mr Squire even remarked after they had gone that the Captains were rather more agreeable than the *émigrés* he had met at Lady Woodhouse's a few years ago at the time of the Terror. 'Very stand-offish fellows,' he said. 'Very dandified, and always bleating about their wrongs. Understandable, of course, but one couldn't take to them. But then these fellows tonight are sea-captains. The profession of the sea has its own nobility, Frenchie or not.'

They talked of the rumours about life in France now under the Directory – a land of upstarts and loose morals, it was said, with extravagantly indecent fashions. There was a ghoulish mode for wearing the hair shorn as for the guillotine – *à la victime* – and even for completing the grim ensemble with a blood-red choker round the neck.

Caroline did the honours with tea and coffee and thought of Captain Clairet. He had addressed several remarks to her, as was natural, being seated next to her. He had told her he was working hard at his English – he did not spend all his time playing games with children! She told him about the grand party on Whittlesea Mere that she was going to, explained what a mere was, how there would be pleasure-boats and marquees and music and a feast. And, 'I wish you could be there – to see it,' she said, startled by herself, and by her tongue's dexterity in adding *to see it*: making the wish a general polite commiseration that as a prisoner in Peterborough he would be unable to see this spectacle, when in fact she had meant, *I wish you could be there*. Just that.

Lucy Squire, who had had her brothers interposed between herself and the terrible French monsters, had flashed some half-admiring, half-fearful glances across the table at Caroline, seated right next to Captain Clairet. If there was any fortitude on Caroline's part, it was not in containing fear . . . She thought back, and was almost convinced that she had never sat next to Frank Bellaers at dinner and chatted and cut up her mutton and fingered her wine-glass and all the time been aware of – been uncomfortably aware of, like a mild nausea that incommodes though one is fairly confident of being able to keep it down – a desire to touch him. A desire to reach out and touch Captain Clairet. A sort of sick pride in having him close to her – an exulting; not in the sense of showing off to anyone else, but a simple exulting of sense and spirit when his eyes turned to hers.

The attraction of the forbidden? It might be called that. But the attraction and the prohibition were separate elements, she realized; the attraction perhaps initially roused by pity and interest in his situation, but soon outrunning it.

She did not know what to do with these feelings, other than acknowledge them. To attempt to discourage them would be as dangerous, she thought, as to encourage them. She could only let the light shine on them. She could only walk round her room that night before she went to bed, barefoot in her shift but not noticing the cold, and touch things: her hairbrushes, her books, ormolu clock and jewel-box and sashes and slippers, in a strange suspicion that they were not hers at all but counterfeits that had somehow appeared in her room that night while she was looking at Captain Clairet's eyes and brows and lips and holding their shape in her mind.

CHAPTER 3

1

Charles Hardwick had been out all morning, riding to farms and big houses all around Aysthorpe. He was raising a subscription of wheat to be sold at half-price to the poor of the parish and the neighbouring parishes of Barnack, Peakirk and Northborough. The wheat crop of the home farm at Morholm formed the nucleus.

He had had fair success. He had just come from one of Morholm's tenant farms to the north, where the response had been generous despite the poor quality of the harvest. The huge prices corn was commanding meant the farmers, the larger ones at least, were still thriving. One or two had been less than forthcoming, however. They had complained that they already contributed to the upkeep of the poor through the Poor Rate, and they didn't wish to encourage idleness; and looked sceptically at Charles when he pointed out that many labourers, formerly solvent, had to rely on the parish rate to eke out wages that lagged far behind the price of food. In the end it was probably a mechanical respect for the son of the squire at Morholm that had swayed them to make a contribution. It was an ace that Charles preferred not to play: it highlighted the paradox of his position.

His last call, partly social, was to the Amorys at Leam House. With Bromswold empty, Leam was the nearest occupied big house to Morholm; and Frederick Amory, the son, was one of Charles's best friends. Leam House, a compact Palladian manor set in walled formal gardens, was two miles away across what had once been the common before the enclosure. A good new road had been laid between the neatly hedged fields, and Charles set his mare at a canter.

There was satisfaction in his errand, satisfaction in doing something practical and concreté; but there was an aftertaste of frustration that it should be necessary at all. It was a local and temporary measure, a palliative, not a cure. His father, who had gone to London to attend Parliament a fortnight ago to vote on the new militia bill, had strongly supported the idea, but then his father was part of an older paternalist tradition of landowner, deliberately conscious of responsibility to land and people. It was an aspect of his father that Charles liked and admired, but at the same time he was subtly annoyed by it, felt it would no longer do.

The weather was still fine, but the country had the subdued look of autumn. The stubble-burning was over, leaving the fields scorched blue in the fen distance. There were already elderberries in the hedges.

If Charles impatiently felt that his father's squirish concern was too cautious, his father, he was pretty sure, felt that he saw things in too romanticized a light. Charles hotly denied this, but certainly he was susceptible to the rhetoric of the *free-born Englishman*. There *was* a time, he was sure, when the average countryman had been better-fed, better-housed, and more independent – able to hold his head up. There had been a bitter argument with his father on this theme just before George had left for London. 'Oh, God, Charles, spare me the lament for Old England,' George had said, 'I hear enough cant in Westminster. It's a dangerous, sentimental fancy.'

It was that tone of condescension that could really enrage Charles's generally equable nature. He was old enough to remember the pre-war days, when good white bread and ale and bacon had seemed the labourer's birthright; when there was plentiful silver money instead of the paper money that was so common nowadays; when the very farmers had seemed different – not like, for example, the money-grabbing, pompous Mr Sumner whom he had just visited up at Maxey, with his shiny little gig and his snobbish wife. He could remember too when Pitt himself had been a reformer, before the hysteria over the French Revolution, before the muzzles had been clapped over the newspapers and the Corresponding Societies. The government were the unrealistic ones, he thought, hearing dread sedition in every decent dissenting voice.

He had worked himself into a hot sweat thinking of these things – holding a debate in his mind as was his custom – and when he arrived at Leam House he was glad to accept Louisa Amory's offer of a cool drink of small beer.

'We thought you'd gone up to London with your father,' Louisa said.

'I was going to,' Charles said, quaffing his beer and absently registering how pretty Louisa looked – her white morning-gown, with her pale skin, accentuated her large dark serious eyes. 'But my old friend Richard Lindsay is coming home on leave from the Navy, and I want to be here to see him.' I don't think you ever met him, did you, Louisa? He was an orphan, my father and my uncle Luke got him a midshipman's commission. I haven't seen him for, oh, five years. Is your father at home?'

Mr Amory was in his beloved hot-house. He was an energetic purple-faced man of close on seventy. He was, in the nicest possible way, a little crazed. He petted his exotic blooms like cats, and in the cupola on top of Leam House he kept a small, rusty, useless cannon with which he was going to blast the French when they invaded. He was generous, too, and when Charles stated his business immediately offered half of whatever was in his barns.

'Frederick's over at the smith's, complaining about how his precious hunter was shod last week,' Louisa Amory said when Charles came back from the hot-house. 'He'll be back soon. Will you have some more beer?'

Charles did, for he was one of those people who cannot refuse hospitality, and in the morning-room leading on to the stone terrace he looked over some drawings of Louisa's. She had talent and taste: she blushed at his admiration, not in the conspicuous way that hopes to be noticed, but with a genuine and painful bashfulness.

'Why, this is old Frederick!' Charles said holding up a three-quarter sketch in charcoal. 'But you've flattered him, Louisa. He looks almost human. And too slim by half.'

Louisa laughed, and after a moment said with that extreme lightness that can cost the most wrenching effort, 'Perhaps you'd like to sit for me one day, Charles.'

'Well, I'd be delighted, if you could bear to look at me that long . . . Ah, there's the original specimen.' Frederick had appeared at the French doors.

'Charles! I saw your nag outside. Oh, you're admiring Lou's scribble of me, are you? *There's* a handsome fellow for you, if you like.'

'About as handsome as modest,' Charles said. 'How are you, you conceited fellow?'

'Wretched,' Frederick said. 'Come and see my poor Jade. I reckon her hoof's permanent damaged. That smith don't know his business.'

Charles followed Frederick to the stables, where his friend seemed to spend most of his time. Frederick Amory was a horsy, hearty, overweight young man with a rider's bow legs and sorrel-coloured hair and eyelashes. His appetite was enormous and his mental horizons limited, but to the potential characteristics of an oaf he added a genial nature and a total absence of malice that made him universally liked.

'I say, Charles, what's one to wear to this water-party of your cousin's?' he said, caressing his jet-black hunter with his big freckled hands. 'I mean if there's to be music and dancing, it'll be formal; but what with sailing-boats as well – '

'Wear riding-boots like you always do,' Charles said. 'Well, I can't see anything wrong with her hoof, Frederick. You imagine it.'

Frederick grunted. 'When's your sailor friend arriving?'

'Tomorrow. I got the briefest of notes saying he would be arriving on the Stamford Fly tomorrow. Hope I recognize him. You'll meet him, of course. Cousin Susannah said I must bring him along to Whittlesea Mere.'

'Quite right. Hearts of oak. Navy's the bastion of our freedom,' said Frederick, whose political opinions were the merest reflexes.

They went outside again, and found Louisa calling to them from the carriage-sweep at the side of the house.

'It's Sukey,' she said anxiously. 'Please come . . . She's climbed up to the top of the cherry tree and can't get down – she's making such a noise . . .'

'Oh, Lou, cats can always get down,' Frederick said, stumping after her. 'You'd do best to leave the silly beast – I can't go clambering up with my gammy knee . . .'

The thin wail of a cat could be heard from the topmost branches of a cherry tree in the walled garden. Charles peered up. 'I see her,' he said. 'Shall I climb up?'

'You'd not catch me up there,' Frederick was grumbling. 'Break your neck. Leave the animal be . . .'

The first ten feet was easy, the second less so, as close-packed twigs threatened to poke his eyes out. The cat moaned with renewed despair when Charles's head appeared. Charles grabbed her by the scruff, avoided the swiping claws, and buried her in the breast of his waistcoat. He came down to a hero's welcome, from Louisa at least. 'The little beast won't thank you for it,' Frederick said. 'There – you see!' as the cat scrambled out of Charles's waistcoat and darted to its mistress.

'Oh, but *I* do,' Louisa said, all smiles and thankfulness. 'You're so very kind, Charles. Oh, did she scratch you?'

Charles put his hand in his shirt and felt the spots of blood. 'Hardly at all,' he said. He had been about to open his shirt and look, but remembered in time Louisa's exceptionally modest nature. 'Well, I ought to be off. I want to get over to Peterborough before dinner.'

'Thank you again, Charles,' Louisa said, hugging her cat. 'I'll – '

'Yes?'

'I suppose we'll see you at Whittlesea Mere,' she said quietly, her face lowered, as if she were speaking to the cat.

'Of course. We'll put this fellow in a boat and see if it sinks.'

'I'll ride as far as the pike with you,' Frederick said.

Rainclouds were getting up to the east as they struck the Heath road.

'Trouble with Lou, she's too tender-hearted,' Frederick said. 'Doesn't get out enough. Looks after pa a lot, when ma can't be bothered. Don't make the best of herself. Looking mortal plain lately.'

'Indeed she's not!' said Charles, who had an innate gallantry. 'She looks charming.'

'Still, she's eighteen now, and hardly ever mixes. Never been courted.'

'Why, you make her sound like an old maid of forty!' Charles laughed. 'I'll wager she has scores of admirers. She could take her pick.'

Frederick gave the sort of deliberate slow cough that goes as a precursor to saying something new and weighty, but in the end did not say anything.

The rain held off, and Charles was in Peterborough before noon. He wanted to let his uncle know of Richard Lindsay's imminent return.

'He'll wish to come and see you himself, of course,' Charles said.

'I'll be more than glad to see him,' Luke said. 'It's men like him who are safeguarding my ships. Ah, his old father would be proud of him.'

Luke had work to do, and left Charles in Caroline's care. She gave him tea in the room overlooking the river. Charles was struck by his cousin's appearance. Not that she looked ill – rather her usually sleepy-lidded, heavy-lashed eyes were darkly glowing like those of someone unable to sleep. She was restless about the room, constantly returning to the window, where Charles at last followed her.

There were two people down at the wharf at the bottom of the sloping garden. Charles recognized Luke's overseer. 'Repairs?' he said.

Caroline nodded, holding back the fringed curtain, the light milky on her skin. 'Father's hoping to deepen the channel. The wharf only deals in small traffic, coal-barges and so on, but you know what a perfectionist he is.'

'Who's the fellow with his coat off?'

'Oh, that's one of the paroled French prisoners. Captain Antoine Clairet. He's giving some advice. He is a sailor, you see. He knows about such things,' she added, turning to Charles as if he had challenged her.

'How do you get along with those fellows?'

'Oh, we rub along, you know. We don't really have

much to do with them.' She turned, seemingly in irritation.

'Caroline.' Charles touched her arm, and thought for a moment she was going to shake it off; but she smiled, as with an effort, and came and put her arm around him as she was accustomed to. 'Forgive my asking – is there anything wrong? You don't seem your usual self.'

'Don't I?' The look she gave him was as remote as if she were on the other side of the river. 'No, there's nothing wrong, cousin.'

'Is it the thought of Richard coming back?' he pressed. 'I mean, I know you and he never got on – if it bothers you . . .'

She looked surprised, as if she had forgotten Richard entirely, then patted his arm. 'Good Lord, no. I – How long is he to stay?'

'Oh, I don't know. Depends on when he gets his new commission. Anyway, I'll stay while he's here. Go on up to London to join father later.' That had been agreed, though not, Charles felt, entirely amicably. He thought again of their recent arguments. *You don't know what you're talking about*, had been his father's unspoken last word. But if he could only make his mark in the political world, show his father that he was in earnest . . .

He would have said something of this to Caroline, but she was looking distractedly out of the window again.

2

Caroline tried to do some embroidery, but she made the most awful cobble of it. Then she went down to the kitchen to see if she could help there. Mrs Haley had just finished her baking, and was raking out the big brick oven; the kitchen-maid was plucking a capon for dinner.

Caroline was in the way. At last, having convinced herself that she had done her best *not* to go out into the garden, she went out into the garden. Down to the river where the wharf was.

Charles had gone away. She suspected he had thought her rather offhand. She couldn't help it – not with Clairet in sight.

At the foot of the garden there were trees and a slatted seat and then a low stone wall. Beyond that was the towpath, leading to the wharf with its brick warehouse. She lingered at the end of the lawn, looked at the bright haws in the shrubbery. She remembered being warned off them as a child; they looked so colourful and tempting.

Captain Clairet had climbed on to one of the timber struts of the quay and was pointing downwards. Her father's overseer was nodding and writing something on a slate. Captain Clairet climbed nimbly up again, talking to the overseer.

Caroline bent to pluck off a fluffy head of clematis. What am I doing? she asked herself. I'm not *like* this. She had always had a sturdy amused contempt for self-tormentors. Crying for the moon . . . she had always valued her peace of mind too much. Her old self would never have done this – for she thought of herself of a few weeks ago as a separate being who could probably have given her some good advice. Her old self would have said, *Go inside, and forget about it, you're being a fool.*

The overseer lifted his hat in farewell and turned back to the warehouse.

'Captain Clairet,' Caroline called over the wall. She had to speak to him. She just had to.

'Miss Hardwick!' He came running and hopping up the towpath to the wall. The garden was banked up higher than the towpath, so she was looking down at him.

'My father said you were helping out with the wharf.'

Just to talk with him, small talk, it was enough, like a relief from pain.

'Oh, yes, it will be a simple job, I think,' he said. 'Of course, a quay made of stone would be best. The posts have rotted.'

'Aiding the commerce of the enemy,' Caroline said lightly.

'Yes . . . that is true,' he said seriously. She felt a great gulf open suddenly between them and as suddenly close when he added: 'But I cannot think of you, your father, your family as enemies. Armies, nations . . . it is different just between people. Perhaps as a captain of the Republic I should not say that. But, it is so, isn't it?'

A desperate desire for a conversation may itself paralyse speech. 'Of course,' she said, half-choking. She saw two youths from the King's School, a little way down the towpath, pushing out a small boat.

'I'm working very hard at my English, Miss Hardwick,' Clairet said. He seemed at ease, with one foot propped on the wall, lean and tanned in his shirt-sleeves. 'Each night, I have supper or play cards with Roubillard and some others, and we have, *une règle*, a rule – we speak only English. Soon it all comes back, what my father taught me.'

'Is your father still alive, Captain?' she asked, seizing this like a proffered hand.

'Yes,' he said. 'Though not my mother. He is still at Torcy, farming a little estate. That is what I hope to do, when the war is over. Enough of the sea. Back to *la terre* – the soil, yes?'

Perhaps her dry dumb gaze made him uncomfortable, for he said then, looking at his muddied hands: 'Well, I must go home and wash.'

'Come up this way, through the garden, it will be quicker,' Caroline said.

'Very well.' He stopped. 'Ah, my coat – I left it on the grass.'

He went down the towpath to the bank. He came back holding his blue officer's coat between finger and thumb. It was dripping.

'Oh – did it fall in?' Caroline said. Then she looked at his face, white, jaw rigid. The smell of urine.

'Oh, the *pigs*,' she cried, and jumped over the wall and ran down the towpath where the two youths were just sculling away. One stood up in the boat and called: 'Hey, Mon-sewer! Frenchie shite!'

The boat was soon out of sight beyond the bridge. Caroline's cheeks were burning. She turned back to Captain Clairet in deepest shame, but his expression had changed again, as if he had mastered himself. 'Well,' he said, 'that is a word I understand without translation.'

She saw at this moment what she had scarcely seen in him before – the fighting-man, the captain of a ship of war accustomed both to authority and to danger. A slightly withdrawn, glassy look came down over his eyes, normally so frank.

'Captain Clairet, I'm so very sorry – if I see those little beasts again I'll – ' She bit her lip, astonished to realize she was near tears.

'Please, it's nothing,' he said, and went to the river's edge and dipped the coat in the water and swished it back and forth. 'I can hang it to dry, and there will be no harm done. There, that is a good English expression?'

'I'm so ashamed of them,' she said. His good nature made her feel worse.

'It is their country. Such things happen, they are not often. We are still at war.'

'Oh, I'm tired of these excuses. Folk cover everything up with those same phrases. We're at war, we're at war.

87

Men nodding gravely over maps. They think of nothing else, nothing else has any meaning.'

'You forget I went to war also,' he said.

'Then the more fool you,' she burst out.

They stared at each other a moment, with very mixed feelings.

'Perhaps,' Clairet said at last. 'But still, I am an alien. Perhaps in peacetime things would not be very different. The English and the French do not love each other.'

She came very close to betraying herself at that moment. She swallowed, and said after a pause, 'No, you are not an alien.' She noticed the dripping coat again. 'Come,' she said with an effort. 'We'll go through the garden, and you can get that wet coat home.'

She went to step up on to the wall, and he put out a hand to help her. He caught sight of the dirt on his hand, and stopped. But she took the hand deliberately, and sprang up.

'What did you mean when you said such things happen?' she said, not looking at him, as they walked up the garden.

'Oh . . .' He shook his head dismissively.

'Tell me, Captain Clairet.'

'Little things. They happen to others also. There was – a dead dog. It was put outside my door.'

'Oh God.' She felt sick.

He smiled faintly. 'I hope the poor animal was not killed just for me. Little things . . . But Miss Hardwick, listen please. They are not many. Mostly I, we, find that people act very kindly – friendly, *aimable*. But, I must say it again, it is war. The world is fighting. And, I am a sailor. Much of my life was hard. Storms, battle. My ship is captured, I am taken prisoner.' He stopped, fingered a lilac leaf. 'When my ship was taken, the fight was not long, or cruel. But one of my men was killed. His head

88

broken in pieces. One moment he talks, moves, is human, the next moment – all still, *fracassé*.' His breath was coming short. 'So you see. These little things . . . they are nothing. Nothing compared to kindness – your kindness. Please, smile now. Your smile is very beautiful. I don't know if to say that in English is right . . . if it is insolent . . .' He looked at her, anxious, brows puckered.

She smiled. 'Would it be insolent in French?'

His face cleared, and he too smiled, wryly. 'Yes,' he said.

Suddenly she turned and plunged up the path, saying quickly, 'You'd better get home and dry that coat, Captain. Take the path by the stables.' She knew she must appear curt, but perhaps that was best. She went briskly up to the house, intending to go in without a backward glance. But the glance came, inevitably. He was climbing the path that led to Bridge Street. He lifted a hand in farewell and smiled at her, in a flash of – what, kindness, understanding, reassurance? All she knew was it hit her, squarely as a perfect archery shot across the distance of the garden.

Also it made her feel better. There was light where there had been shadow. Why, my dear girl, she told herself later, you are romantic at heart after all. At school the other girls were gazing in hopeless adoration at the drawing-master, and you were the one who noticed he drank gin from a medicine-bottle and had dirty fingernails . . . but all it meant was you were a little late coming to this stage.

Her feelings about Antoine Clairet could be contained, after all. Mere fantasy. She had them on a short rein. She felt she had come, painlessly, to a new self-knowledge.

The next morning she went to the draper's in Westgate to buy a ribbon neck-band to wear for the party at the Mere. Returning home up Narrow Bridge Street her thoughts were all contentedly of the party. The street was crowded: saddle horses, sedan-chairs, butter-women gossiping at the pump, boys in the cinnamon-grey uniform of Deacon's charity school, red-coated Militiamen, clerks hurrying with blue bags to the legal quarter in Priestgate, a couple of fenmen bringing poled ducks to market. It was a loved but very familiar scène, and the sight of Captain Clairet up ahead emerging from the Yards was like an arresting gold thread in the patchwork. He erupted into her placid thoughts.

He was going up towards the river, which was her direction also, so it was natural to follow him. But when he continued over the bridge, past the Bridge House, she was still following him. She could not help it. Perhaps, she reasoned, it fitted in with the girlish infatuation she had convinced herself she felt for him.

She kept him in sight over the bridge on to the London Road, an erect figure with cocked hat and white stockings. Then he turned off the road and into the trees of the orchard close on the left. Still she followed. Now her excuse was curiosity as to where he could be going.

He had taken an old brick path that led away from Fletton, through the orchard. Caroline slowed down. Unless he were going to break his parole and go beyond the city limits, she must catch him up soon.

But he seemed to have disappeared. She knew the orchard well, and could not imagine where he could be. Dappled light danced on the brick path. There were a few windfalls in the long grass. Suddenly she remembered the derelict farm buildings. Part of a stone barn and wall remained, overgrown with bramble.

She supposed he was there, for whatever reason. And now she knew she was at a threshold. If previously she had lingered in an ante-chamber, where her feelings existed as an idle supposition, a *what if*, now she might step into a place where this desperate longing was admitted as part of the real world, to be negotiated, or suppressed . . . or acted upon? Or was that another threshold, the one she must not cross, the one over which there was no returning?

There was a call of a wood-dove from somewhere as she approached the ruin of the barn. Around the crumbling stone walls was a thicket of bramble and rambler and honeysuckle and, on the other side, where there was a choked dry ditch, a stand of beeches.

She went round the wall, her skirts dragging on thorns, and stood there in a shaft of autumn sun, feeling hot and stupid. He was not there. The beech-leaves stirred faintly, colours already turning.

Then she saw him. She could not restrain an 'Oh!' of pleasure, both at seeing him, and at the cosiness of the spot he had found himself. There was thick green grass on the sloping side of the ditch beneath the mossy wall, and the trees made a screen from the wind whilst admitting a golden diffused light. The little clearing was virtually invisible from the orchard path.

Clairet had been seated on the grass, reading a book. He started to his feet, dropping the book, almost staggering backwards.

'I'm so sorry,' she said, 'I've disturbed you . . . I didn't know . . .' She had an awful feeling she was scarlet.

'Miss Hardwick – I didn't hear you . . .' He stood there looking at her.

She became suddenly urbane, out of embarrassment. 'What a charming garden you've found yourself, Captain,' she said. 'I never knew this was here. Is this a favourite spot of yours?'

He frowned round at the trees, as if he had scarcely noticed them before. 'Yes, I . . . that is, I'm afraid I am, er, a trespasser here.'

'Oh, well, the orchard belongs to Mr Squire, but I don't think he'd mind. You're not stealing away his apples, are you?'

'Apples . . . no.'

'Well, then, I'm sure it doesn't matter.' It occurred to her that he was perhaps annoyed at having this place intruded upon. 'Well, I'll leave you in peace,' she said.

'No – please.' He seemed to wake into life, and smiled. 'Miss Hardwick – will you stay a moment? Sit down. I have no house to offer you hospitality, you see. Perhaps this can be my hospitality.'

'I don't think – '

'Please. Stay a little.'

She sat miserably, joyfully, on the grassy bank. Beech-masts rustled under her shoes.

'I come here most days,' he said in a courtly tone, just as if he were entertaining her in his parlour. 'It is difficult for me to be alone, to be alone and think. My room in Little's Yard is rather noisy . . . But also I want to share this place with someone, to show how beautiful it is.' He looked up, squinting, into the trees. 'There is a little fellow who lives there – he is still afraid of me. *Un écureuil* – I don't know the word . . .'

In her tense, stupefied state Caroline could not think what he was talking about. 'A bird . . .?.'

'No, no – an *écureuil*, he's like a rat but handsome, he's red – '

92

'Oh, a *squirrel*.' She laughed. They both laughed, in a puzzled, too hearty way.

'Hospitality,' he said jumping up. 'I have offered you nothing. There are good berries here. Will you have some?' He picked a cluster of blackberries and offered them, bowing, to her.

She took them and ate them, hardly knowing what she was doing. All this had so much of the perfect quality of an idyll, and was so underscored with danger, that she was overwhelmed.

'It is strange here, neither one thing nor another,' Clairet said. She perceived that he too was talking out of nerves. 'Part of the town, part of the country, and yet neither.'

'Like limbo,' she said.

'Please?'

'Well – I think in theology it's the place between heaven and hell,' she said. 'Where the good pagans go.'

'Ah, *les limbes*.' He looked round at the clearing appreciatively. 'Yes . . . that is right. And where you and I can meet, is it not? French and English. Enemies. A special place, not in the world.'

She stirred. 'What – what book were you reading?'

He passed it to her. 'I bought it in the market.'

She saw it was *The Vicar of Wakefield*. 'Oh, this is one of my favourites. I would have lent my copy to you if – '

'Yes?'

'Forgive me. It's just the matter of religion . . .'

'Oh, I know.' He smiled. 'You think I must be an atheist? Well, many French people still believe. As for me . . . my father was an atheist long before the Revolution. He hated the priests. I suppose I have followed him, but not so far. I love to see your beautiful cathedral, for example. My father would wish to knock it down!'

'You think a lot of your father, don't you?'

93

'Oh, yes. Some people fear him.' Clairet lay back on the bank. 'He is, I think the word is the same, a *misanthrope*. He has a hot temper. When I ran away to sea he said he would never forgive me. But he is kind and gentle *au fond*. He was very strong for the Revolution, for he is a farmer and hated the Church who stole the wealth from the land. He is a man of the country, hating cities. Always he adored Rousseau. So, the Revolution was right for him.' He lowered his gaze from the sky back to Caroline, sitting with the book in her lap. 'Will you read a little to me? The page is marked. Would you mind?'

'Of course,' she said; and they exchanged a smile of such pure intimacy that she was afraid she would be unable to speak except in a croak.

'"*At a small distance from the house my predecessor had made a seat overshadowed by a hedge of hawthorn and honeysuckle. Here, when the weather was fine, and our labour soon finished, we usually sat together to enjoy an extensive landscape in the calm of the evening. Here, too, we drank tea, which was now become an occasional banquet; and, as we had it but seldom, it diffused a new joy, the preparation for it being made with no small share of bustle and ceremony . . .*"' Her eyes stole from the page to Clairet, his hands behind his head, one crossed leg idly swinging. Her throat felt swollen. '"*Sometimes, to give a variety to our amusements, the girls sung to the guitar; and while they thus formed a little concert, my wife and I would stroll down the sloping field, that was embellished with bluebells and centaury, talk of our children with rapture, and enjoy the breeze that wafted both health and harmony . . .*"'

The strong bones of his cheek and jaw worked as he chewed a blade of grass. His dark eyes were fixed on the sky. She felt with a terrible desolation that he had gone away from her.

'Don't stop,' he said. 'I love to hear your voice. English voices they say are hard, harsh. Like German speaking. I don't think so.'

'And they say English girls are cold and ugly, and Englishmen are fat and greedy, and English food is all boiled beef,' she said. 'Perhaps when you return to France you can tell them it's not entirely true.'

Clairet sat up abruptly, tossing away the blade of grass. 'You are not serious with me. You laugh at me,' he said in a changed voice.

Caroline was very still. 'Why do you say that?'

He inspected his hands. 'Why else would you consent to sit here with me? You are a lady. There is your reputation, your father – these things are the same in France. Perhaps you laugh about me with your friends. I don't know why it is you speak to me like this, show me kindness, attention. All these questions, this interest. I am glad, of course I am glad. But I think you must make a game of me.' He got to his feet, half-turned to her. 'I am a prisoner, but I am a man, not an exhibit. It is all a game. Like a pet dog. A pet Frenchman, a pet prisoner. Interesting, because I am strange, foreign. A *divertissement*.'

She sat, frozen, sick. 'I see. So you don't like to be treated pleasantly and kindly by me.'

'It is a *torture* to me,' he said with clenched violence.

There was a seething silence she was afraid to break.

'Why?' she said.

'Forgive me . . . I forget myself,' he muttered.

'Why?' she said again.

He turned to her, his face intense, perhaps hostile. 'You know some French,' he said. 'You know what it is to *tutoyer*, yes? To call someone *tu*. In English there is only the word *you*. If we were talking in French it would be only correct for us to say *vous*. Formal, respectful. But we seem to talk with *tu*. *Tu* is intimate, familiar, between friends and lovers and family. But also it can be mocking. One uses it to little children and dogs and cats and it has a little contempt.'

She drew in a painful breath that rasped her lungs. 'And that's what you think, is it?'

'When you show me this attention – this amused attention . . . I don't know, perhaps I don't know the English ways . . .' He paced across the clearing, his fists clenched, his eyes hard and lost. 'It makes me begin to hope,' he said harshly, 'hope it is real, hope for something I have no right to hope for . . . But it is better I don't say it. Because even to see you this way, to take these little kindnesses, though it hurts, it makes my life worth living . . . even if I no longer cheat myself with hope.' He flung himself down on the grass again, his face flushed and averted, as if dismissing her.

In the gale of emotion that ripped through her, she caught and held one flying realization – in all her agonies she had never considered what *he* might feel. Her mind had only reached as far as, perhaps, madly betraying herself, to his embarrassment. *This*, though terrible, impossible, was like opening a letter expecting bad news and finding oneself heir to enormous riches.

'Captain Clairet,' she said, and was surprised at how level her voice sounded, 'how do you suppose I came upon you here?'

He glanced at her, with the irritation of incomprehension, as if she had changed the subject.

'I saw you come out of the Yards, and I followed you here. And it was not to make a joke of you or spy on you or to tell my friends that I bearded a Frenchman in his den. But because I wanted to see you. It isn't easy for me to say this. If I've appeared flippant and patronizing to you it's only because that's the only way that this thing can be contained . . . this impossible thing I feel . . .'

Clairet stared at her, his lips moving slightly, then wrenched his gaze away. The silence between them seemed to stretch and swell, as if to accommodate all that they had suddenly learned.

'When I spoke just now . . .' he said. 'What I said . . .'

'We can forget it,' she said.

'*No*,' he said earnestly. 'That is – I spoke from despair. To put an end to my suffering. I expected nothing like this – no wait, please. When I was made prisoner I expected only to sit and wait for peace, be patient, quiet. Be at peace myself, if the world was not. I did not expect to be – disturbed, broken, like this. I come here to think of you, to think and think of you in despair. I spoke out so as to end all that. So you would be angry, go away from me.' He looked at her, tenderly, with forbearance. 'But that is what you are going to do anyway, isn't it?'

She ran a hand across her burning cheek, unable to look at him. 'I can't . . . it's not that . . . oh, please, understand . . .'

'Caroline,' he said – the first time. It seemed natural now. 'It's because I love you that I understand.' He looked round at the encircling trees with a sigh. 'Limbo. Yes. This is the place where we can say such things. I'm glad, now. Though I know I can never say to you the things I dream of saying – of how lovely you are, your eyes so blue, your smile and your laugh that make everything seem all right, and how just seeing you sitting there makes my heart break with happiness – '

'Antoine – please – '

'No, no. Listen. I can never say these things, all the thousand things to tell you how I feel. But before, I knew I could not, any more than I can fly. Because you would scream and hit my face and your father would have me put in the prison camp . . . but most of all because you would not want to hear them. But now I am so glad, so happy, because I know now that I *could* say them. Not in this world, not in this world of war and hate and prisons and English and French, but in another world, somewhere. To know that somewhere we could be together, though that somewhere is not made yet . . . that it's only this foolish world that prevents it. You have made me so happy. And if I have made you miserable, forgive me.'

'No,' she said, though a tear was running down her face. 'No, not you . . . Like you say, it is the world, not us . . . Oh, please believe me, if there were any way, any way at all . . .'

'Don't cry,' he said softly. He knelt beside her, not touching her. 'Please don't cry. I don't want to remember you crying.'

She got control of herself, though she could not look at him. 'I must go,' she said. 'I'm sorry. I must go.'

'So you must,' he said. He stood over her, a hand extended to help her up. She took the hand, felt its warm strength like a blow to the heart.

She was on her feet, and then her face was buried in his neck for a moment. Scent of him, rough linen of cravat, and his hands tremblingly touching her shoulders. Then she was stumbling away over the grass. 'Goodbye,' she said, choking, her skirt tearing on thorns as she blundered sightlessly into the orchard; and, when he was almost out of earshot, he answered. 'Goodbye, my love.'

She did not go home immediately. She walked to tire herself, beyond the Fletton turnpike and across the stubble fields.

She had discovered, had had revealed to her, an alarming loneliness. It was the loneliness of awareness.

All one's actions were gestures in solitude. Responsibility was eternal and absolute. Nothing could have presented that more clearly than this situation. Whatever happened now, only she could be accountable.

She was caught, trapped, between two imperatives. The imperative of the world – society, her family, her background, the world in which she had to live with all its rules and demands – and the imperative of her heart and her flesh, drawn to Antoine as to a lodestone, impatient of denial. Between these two she felt she would be crushed, her spirit pulverized.

But, *He feels for me as I feel for him* went a rapturous whisper at the edge of her conscious mind, and all the outraged shouts of reason could not drown it out.

4

An eighty-mile journey by stage-coach, despite the recent improvements to the Great North Road between London and Stamford, was still an exhausting experience. Richard Lindsay was used to discomforts, however, and did not join in the groans and complaints of his fellow passengers as the Stamford Fly lurched, thundered and shuddered its way out of Stilton, past the prisoner-of-war camp at Norman Cross and on to the last stretch to Stamford.

He had been watching the countryside, still overwhelmed by the lush green after being so long accustomed to the steely vistas of sea and sky; but now it had grown dark and the guard had lit the lamp that hung from the coach ceiling. While the other passengers talked Richard kept to his own thoughts, reserving a little solitude as he had learned to do in the crowded midshipmen's cabin.

His last shore leave had been brief and spent at Torbay: it was fully five years since he had been in the fenland, the country that he considered his home though he had no real home there. But such connections as he had were to be found in this wild flat region: the old aunt in her modest bow-fronted house in Stamford, the Hardwicks for whom his dearly loved father had worked all his life and who had taken Richard under their wing. And the memories, of his father in the cottage at King's Lynn and the ships in Lynn harbour and the windmills on the fen and the straight dykes and the bellying clouds and rushy banks alive with birds: Crowland Abbey and Peterborough Cathedral and Whittlesea Mere and the Nene and the Ouse and the duck decoys and the sluices and the forthright, independent people. The memories were his inheritance, and he was returning, though for a short space, to claim them.

The coachman blew his horn, and Richard yanked down the window to look out. The lights of Stamford, lying cradled in its valley. The spire of St Mary's Church, the great bulk of All Saints'. The air was keen and clean.

In the cobbled coachyard of the George he stretched his long legs, looked about him, felt the weight of his trunk and decided to carry it on his shoulder to his aunt's house in Scotgate, and had just hoisted it up when a voice said: 'Every inch the sailor! Welcome home at last!'

Charles Hardwick stood there, grinning.

'Good God, I never expected – Charles, it's good to see you.'

'Your letter said when you would be coming,' Charles said. 'I've been standing over there staring and wondering if it was you. You've changed so.'

'You too.' The passing of the years was borne in on both young men as they looked at each other and shook hands. Charles, who remembered Richard as a gawky, rather sullen youth, was surprised and impressed by this tall, spare man, spruce in a blue double-breasted tail-coat, with wary sailor's eyes that looked searching even when he smiled.

'You must be shaken to pieces in that coach,' Charles said. 'And you must be hungry and thirsty. The George's victuals are good as ever.'

'I supped at Stilton,' Richard said, 'but I'd be glad of a drink.'

'Rum?' Charles said with a smile.

'Not that weak landsman's stuff. Brandy for me.'

They left the trunk with an ostler and went into the taproom.

'Is that uniform what I think it is?' Charles said as a potman brought brandy.

'It is,' Richard said. 'Lieutenant Lindsay, RN, as of four days ago.'

'Congratulations! But you didn't say in your note.'

'I suppose I wanted it to be a surprise,' Richard said. 'I was all ready to come up here and wait for the summons from the Admiralty, knowing their propensity for delay, but then on Friday I was called for my examination there and then.'

'Examination – that has a doleful sound.'

'It wasn't as bad as I thought. You have to have your log-books and certificates of conduct, and when you go in you hand these over to the examining board. Three senior captains, sitting round a table very dignified. Then they give you the usual questions on trigonometry and navigation. That's the part you can prepare for. Then they tell you to imagine you're in command of a vessel on a certain station – mine was off Ushant – and they fire questions at you about what you would do. They conjure up a heavy sea and a westerly and shoals of rocks, all the time trying to trip you up. By the end I felt as if I really *was* floundering in a gale. I expected them to say, "Bravo, Mr

Lindsay, you have just driven your ship on to the rocks and lost half your crew." But somehow, I passed.'

'Lieutenant,' said Charles. 'Now you're truly on the ladder.'

'Junior lieutenant,' Richard said. 'A long climb to Captain. But no more sleeping in a crowded gunroom. No more headaches over trigonometry and navigation. Now I must wait for a new commission.'

By the light of the fire Charles could see now the more familiar lineaments of Richard; the light blue eyes, the dark hair carefully combed and tied, the strongly set jaw. His skin had a tan that was beginning to fade. 'Well, I hope it doesn't come just yet,' Charles said. 'Five years is a lot to catch up on. And there's old friends to meet. My father regretted he couldn't be here, but he's gone back early to Westminster. You must see Uncle Luke of course. In fact you can meet everybody tomorrow. My cousin Susannah's become engaged and she's holding a water-party at Whittlesea Mere. She asked me to bring you. And look, we've hired a post-chaise at Morholm to take us to the Mere. You must come with us, there'll be room enough. You will, won't you?'

Richard, dismissing a tight frown, said: 'All right. I'll be glad to.' He finished his brandy at a swallow. 'Not very accustomed to social occasions.'

Charles realized he did not just mean that he had been at sea so long. Class and background might matter less in the Navy than in some institutions, but Charles sensed that Richard was still sorely conscious of it. There was still a restive, indocile air about him. Perhaps, Charles thought, he had succeeded in this warlike profession because he was not at peace with himself. 'Pooh, naval officers are always the centre of attraction at any party now,' he said lightly. 'We civilians hardly get a look in.'

'Civilians? I thought there were none in England nowadays.'

'Oh, not quite. We're overrun with Volunteers and Fencibles charging about – even I go drilling twice monthly with the Soke Volunteers! – but the Government are scared to give arms to the common folk in case they use them to shoot Billy Pitt.' Charles stopped and looked wryly at Richard. 'Forgive me. Treason talk. Seducing His Majesty's troops from their allegiance.'

Richard smiled broadly. It made him look younger, less coiled and hard. 'You needn't apologize for me. I'm fighting the damn French but I'm not fighting them for those twice-damned donkeys in Whitehall.'

'I'm glad to hear you say that,' Charles said. 'My father and my uncle think I'm a Jacobin. Or probably a French spy. When all I want is reform at home and an end to the war.'

'That reminds me.' Richard poured more brandy; he had had three stiff glasses already but Charles suspected he had not even felt them. 'In London this morning there was a rumour – pretty well-founded I think – that Bonaparte has run the blockade and landed in France. Apparently he's the only one the people have any faith left in and they're welcoming him like a liberator.'

'Too late surely? The French are being pushed back everywhere – '

'Not now. Our army in Holland is on the retreat. I'm afraid there's a lot of life left in the Republic . . . However, till I get my commission I'm resolved to be a perfect civilian. I'll not even look at a newspaper.' He finished his drink. 'My aunt's expecting me, I'd better go. And you've got a dark ride back to Morholm . . . It's fine to see you again, Charles. We must talk more tomorrow.'

'*You* must talk,' Charles said as they went out to the

yard. 'You must have so much to tell . . . the West
Indies – '

'They look like paradise and they are the veriest hell,'
Richard said, hoisting his trunk on his shoulder. 'At
Morholm tomorrow then.'

Charles watched Richard set off towards Scotgate,
where his old aunt, his only relative, lived in a squat
cottage a few pence above poverty. An impressive but
somewhat inaccessible man. His connection with the
Hardwicks was a difficult one, complicated by obligation
and deference, of which he was sure Richard was sorely
aware. Charles hoped that he would look on him, at least,
as unequivocally friend rather than patron.

CHAPTER 4

1

The weather was perfect at Whittlesea Mere.

There was a cool boisterous wind but the sky was a generous blue, plumbing the calm shallows of the Mere with pearly colour. The Mere stretched over a thousand acres, the biggest of a chain of meres reaching to the Old Nene. Many of its shores were deep beds of tall reeds that were worth a small fortune for those who owned the rights to cutting them, and the whole place teemed with wild birds. The marquees had been set out on the western shore where the banks were firm and dry, though straw and planks had been laid down between the marquees as a precaution. Stephen Downes had met most of the cost of the occasion, and clearly he had a long purse. In the largest marquee long trestle tables were constantly replenished with food by a platoon of footmen: sides of beef and mutton, a haunch of venison, poultry, sucking pigs, pasties and mince pies, traditional roast apples and frumenty, exotic melons and pineapples, and water-ices sculpted into the shapes of churches and ships. In another tent there was drink of every description, from casks of small beer to ankers of the best smuggled brandy. A fenced ring had been constructed, and ostlers engaged from a livery stable, to look after the saddle and carriage-horses of the guests. An eight-man orchestra played from the bandstand on the bank. 'We wanted them to play on the Mere itself,' Stephen Downes told Caroline. 'Like Handel's Water Music. We could easily have popped

them in a wherry. But they complained they got seasick.'
And as well as the official entertainment, several travelling sideshows and booths had collected around the main marquees in an impromptu fair.

An observer might not have guessed this was a sparsely-populated country. The gentry who lived around the fens – seldom actually on the fens – were used to travelling for their entertainment. They had come from their townhouses in Stamford and Peterborough, from the prosperous ports of Lynn and Wisbech, from the solid limestone manors of Northamptonshire and Huntingdon, from the big bleak estates of Lincolnshire. A party of friends of Stephen Downes' had come all the way across the fens from Norwich in a cutter.

The cutter now formed part of the regatta on the Mere. A small fleet of gigs and wherries and rowing-boats had been hired and now they dotted the sparkling surface of the Mere. The white of the sails, the blue of the sky and the many colours of gowns moving amongst the striped marquees made the scene a brilliantly festive one.

Earlier in the day Richard Lindsay had called at Morholm as promised. Charles's mother, Mary Hardwick, laughingly complained at being so overshadowed as, her arm linked in Charles's, they went out to the carriage: Charles and Richard towered over her, Edmund at eighteen was still growing, and vigorous young Frances had nearly caught Mary up. 'I'm beginning to feel like a sparrow in a whole nest of cuckoos, Lieutenant Lindsay,' she said to Richard. When Caroline greeted the Morholm party at the main marquee by the Mere it took her several moments to recognize the tall man in naval uniform next to Charles: still big-boned, dark, rather saturnine, but with an air of cultivated self-control in his purposeful sailor's walk.

'Richard!' she said, in a burst of surprise.

'Lieutenant Lindsay to you, impudent girl,' Charles said.

'You're truly promoted?' Caroline said. 'Oh, many congratulations! How proud you must be! Charles read us your last letter, when it was in the offing. And I suppose we shall only just get used to calling you Lieutenant Lindsay before you become *Captain* Lindsay!'

'Just Richard will do admirably,' he said, shaking her hand. There was no opportunity for more. Caroline's father seized him.

'Let me look at you, boy,' Luke said. 'Aye, I can see your father in you now. The jaw . . . Ah, if only he could see you in that uniform!'

'Mr Hardwick. I've not forgot your generosity to me, sir. I hope I've justified your faith in me.'

'Indeed, indeed you have, boy. A pity George isn't here to see you. I know he was anxious to, but he's up at Westminster speechifying. How long are you to be ashore? – but come, and have a drink, and you can tell me everything . . .' He took Richard off to the refreshment-tent.

Caroline took this opportunity to drink another glass of wine: the occasional strictness that was in her father manifested itself in such things as young ladies drinking. She was not tipsy, but she was in a state of fine-drawn tension that required an extra glass or so to maintain its equilibrium. She had been in this febrile, supernaturally wakeful state since the momentous meeting with Antoine Clairet yesterday. To forestall thought was all. She must throw herself into enjoyment of the day. There was something hectic in her blood.

As for the to-be-happy couple who were the excuse for the feastings, they were everywhere, greeting, enquiring, and making sure everybody was comfortable, in a way that left them very little time to be wrapped up in each other. An eminently civilized attachment. Caroline was happy for them, but somehow the straightforward emotions that the occasion should conjure had tangled and become complicated inside her.

Charles soon found his friend Frederick Amory, full of food and wine, with his arm around his sister Louisa. Though so different, the two were devoted to each other. Frederick, stout in his red riding-coat and white waistcoat and beaver hat set back on his round head, looked exactly like the John Bull who was always appearing in the prints, eating plates of Frenchmen and being imperturbable.

'Would you believe this creature, Charles?' Frederick said. 'She's plaguing me to go out in a boat with her. She won't dare set her nag above a trot but she wants to risk her neck in this pesky lake!'

'He won't go with me, Charles,' Louisa said. 'And he promised pa he'd look after me.'

'He's scared, that's what it is,' Charles said. 'Scared he'll sink to the bottom!'

'Aye, so I am!' Frederick boomed, not at all put out. 'So would any sensible man be! Naught but a few planks between your arse and a watery grave!'

'Well, I've never sailed, but I can row,' Charles said. 'Will you let me be your pilot, Louisa?'

There were several wooden landing-stages with small rowing-boats tied up. Charles handed Louisa into a boat, feeling suddenly happy. He had been fretting a lot lately. This was better.

They were quiet until they had got clear of the jetty and the other boats. A lot of guests, though they might never have been in a boat before, had taken to the water: for all the drainage and road-building that had taken place in the fenland in recent years, the instinct was still somehow in their blood, from the days when fen-folk

108

sailed as naturally as they walked. At last Charles said: 'Why, Frederick doesn't know what he's missing.' It was peaceful on the Mere, with a fresh breeze blowing, and moorhens bustled past them on the green water in a companionable way. How pretty Louisa looks, Charles thought, as she smiled at him from the bow. Her gentle earnest face was framed by a cabriolet bonnet and she looked cool and unruffled in pale yellow muslin.

'Your cousin's fiancé seems an exceptionally agreeable man,' she said.

'Stephen, yes, I think so. I've only met him once or twice, but he's so easy and friendly.'

Louisa dipped her fingers in the water. 'I suppose you'll be going to London to join your father soon.'

'Soon perhaps,' Charles said. He leaned on his oars and could not help saying: 'I don't know whether he really wants me there.'

'Why ever not?'

'Oh – we tend to disagree over political matters. I'm afraid I annoy him.'

'But your father's known as a very liberal man.'

'So he is. Up to a point. But there's five-and-twenty years between us, and it makes a difference. Especially in these times. I feel I'm something of an embarrassment to him.'

'Oh, surely not.'

'Well . . .' Charles pulled on the oars again, flushing. It had been an unfair thing to say. He was conscious of talking too much about himself: Louisa, living in a household of overbearing personalities, had let him go on. 'What about you – will you be at Leam all the winter?'

'Yes,' she said simply. 'Pa's not really well enough for travelling. He's not as robust as he appears. He needs quite a lot of care.'

Charles thought without pleasure of Louisa's mother,

who was many years younger than Mr Amory and now-adays took about as much interest in the household as might a casual acquaintance staying overnight. Frederick, for all his kindly qualities, was not much help. Injustice, as always, pricked Charles with a directly personal pain. 'You should get Frederick to take you to London, or Bath, or Weymouth, just for pleasure,' he said. 'You deserve it,' and the intensity of her blush at this surprised him.

However much Richard Lindsay wished to forget about the war for a while, Luke wanted to talk about it. The news was bad – the Allies retreating again and falling out amongst themselves, General Bonaparte returning to France and rallying the Republic.

'God knows, I'm no peace-at-any-price man, Richard,' Luke said, 'but this war's grinding me down. Pitt's digging us so deep in debt to keep it going I don't see how we'll ever get out. Taxes on taxes. A tax on your carriage, but replace it with saddle-horses and they're taxed too. I never know whether my ships are going to come back or whether there'll even be any foreign ports left open to 'em. You're a fighting man, now. Tell me. D'you see any prospect of peace?'

'The French won't beat us at sea,' Richard said. 'That I can engage for. But we certainly can't beat them on the Continent alone. I wish I could give you an answer, sir. But you must remember that for my own part peace is scarcely to be desired. War is my only hope of advancement. I have no other resources.'

'True enough.' Luke peered into Richard's face, as if he suspected he still might harbour some secret knowledge about the war. 'Tell me, were there many pressed men in your last crew?'

Richard nodded. 'A majority.'

'Aye. I can scarcely keep my ships' crews now. The Press raided Boston last week and ransacked every merchant ship in harbour.'

'The system's to be deplored, but there seems no other way of keeping our forces up to strength. I'm afraid it may well be part of my duty as lieutenant to lead a press gang.'

'Ah, well, it's all an infernal mess. The paradox is I'm parole agent for these Frenchie prisoners-of-war and I can't really feel any malice towards them. Perhaps soon I'll feel differently.' Luke stared gloomily into his glass of punch. 'I'm keeping you from the fun, Richard. I tend to think everyone's as old as me. Go talk nonsense to the young ladies while you've the chance. But come and see us in Peterborough, won't you? We must talk more about this.'

A few couples had formed an impromptu dance on the grass in front of the bandstand. The music was thin and lovely in the open air and there was the smell of crushed grass bruised under the shoes of the dancers. Caroline's old beau Frank Bellaers was here today, and she was relieved to see him in obvious pursuit of another young lady. She gave him a civil nod across the refreshment marquee, feeling the wine go down and wondering how she could ever have found him even half-way attractive.

Here Richard Lindsay joined her. She found herself uneasy in the presence of his light-blue, critical, rather intractable gaze and his still surprising maturity.

'It seems strange,' she said, 'you have been half-way round the world in those five years, and come back and find me here the same as always.'

'Not entirely the same,' Richard said.

'And have you come through entirely unscathed?'

'Save for one bout of malarial fever in Jamaica,' he said. 'I was laid very low with that: there's at least a week

111

of my life of which I have no recollection. Just a gap. It's a disease that often recurs later, but so far, thank God, I have escaped.'

'Shall you be stationed there again, do you suppose?'

'I sincerely hope not.' They walked out of the marquee towards the mereside. 'Those islands are the most cruel places . . . Compared to our chill fens, of course, they look like fragments of heaven. A sky bluer than any blue you've ever seen, lush green hills and beautiful bays sparkling in the sun. But everywhere pestilence – you can feel it in the air. And hundreds of little graves where the men of our garrisons dropped like flies. Young cadets fresh out from England who died as soon as they disembarked. A foul waste of human life, and all to placate the fat slave-men and sugar-men in the City.' He stopped and glanced at Caroline, not without humour. 'I'm sorry. So much for small talk.'

'Lieutenant Lindsay – Richard – when you were involved in that action off Ireland – did you take prisoners?'

He raised his eyebrows, as if surprised at the sudden vehemence with which she had spoken. 'Certainly,' he said. 'Several hundred. They were taken to Scotland, I think, to the prison at Perth.'

'And there was no prospect of their being exchanged?'

'Hm? Oh, well, relations between England and France are so poor that exchange has virtually broken down. I can guess your reason for asking, Miss Hardwick.'

Her face must surely have gone dead white, because her heart had stopped. 'Can you?' she got out.

'You have a friend or relation imprisoned in France, am I right?'

'Oh! no, no, no.' Relief made her laugh absurdly and loudly. So lightheaded did she feel that she half-expected him to be laughing also. He was not.

'Perhaps you will share the joke with me,' he said.

'The joke, such as it is, is against myself. Don't mind me.' They had come to the edge of the Mere now, and were looking out across the water to where two young couples were rowing a boat with much squealing and laughter. He showed no inclination to leave her, but neither, she thought, did he seem pleased with her company.

'What stupid things those people are saying,' he said abruptly.

'Those people? I didn't hear. Surely they're only enjoying themselves.'

'I wish to God they would do it without screaming like a pack of hyenas.'

It was still there, that light arrogance; and it was a bait she could not help but rise to.

'You wish nothing of the kind. You wish they did *not* enjoy themselves because it piques you that you cannot do so.'

He glanced at her with bleak blue eyes. 'The spectacle of pleasure does not necessarily give pleasure. A starving man would scarcely appreciate the sight of others feasting.'

'But a well-fed man would surely find it a cheerful sight.'

'I have seen men taking pleasure in knocking the heads off chickens, but I feel no inferiority in not sharing their pleasure.'

'But you feel a *superiority* in not sharing these folk's pleasures.'

He cleared his throat. 'I am not fond of controversy for its own sake.'

'Meaning you don't like to be argued with by a woman.' Her hackles were really up now. Anger was an emotion

113

generally foreign to her, but he seemed uniquely able to call it up.

'Only a woman would argue in this inconsequential way,' he snapped. She perceived he was angry too. The air between them was like gunpowder.

'I won't trouble you with my feminine inconsequence any more, then,' she said, turning away with more casualness than she felt. She was relieved to see Stephen Downes, and to move into his lightweight, unambiguous presence.

2

Soon after midday there were toasts to Susannah and Stephen, and Susannah's father made a speech in the main marquee. The Hon. Augusta Downes, Stephen's aristocratic mother, had established herself in state in one corner of the marquee and received audiences one at a time like the Pope. Plump and healthy in green spotted silk with elbow-length gloves and a helmet-hat with a veil, she sat with one foot on a charcoal foot-warmer and sipped canary wine, looking, as Stephen whispered to Susannah, like Britannia in unbuttoned mood.

Susannah had spent most of the morning being introduced to Stephen's friends, many of whom were formidably double-barrelled and all of whom wanted to get a good look at her: but they all pronounced her a fine girl and called Stephen a lucky beggar, so that was all right. And her father, Henry Milton, had made a splendid speech, looking scholarly and distinguished, and her mother had managed to pin her abundance of wiry greying hair into a semblance of order. And she was discovering that she and Stephen made excellent hosts. What parties they would give at Great Baston! They would be the talk of the county, of all East Anglia.

Caroline forced herself to eat something after the toasts, to smother the wine she had drunk. But she felt no less restless and hectic. Her altercation with Richard Lindsay had struck sparks that still tingled. His capacity to provoke a violent reaction in her had intensified with the years, it seemed: years that had given him a commanding if no less disturbing presence to which indifference was impossible. She was not used to having her equilibrium upset like this. She joined in the dance in front of the bandstand, and danced with several young men she knew vaguely and then with her cousin Charles, who looked kindly into her face and said she was tipsy. Then Frederick Amory, who was considerably more than tipsy, came roistering up. 'Where are these wretched cockleshells, then? I'm ready for 'em. Who'll take to the waves with me? Charles?'

'Not I! You're not safe!'

'I'll come, Frederick,' Caroline said. 'I haven't been in a boat yet. We'll go together.'

'Caroline. You're an angel.' Frederick bowed low and kissed her hand, rising back to the perpendicular with some difficulty. 'I knew you'd be game. Come! Avast, lubbers, pipe me aboard and death to the French and all the rest of it.'

At the time there seemed nothing amiss with going out in a little sail-boat with Frederick Amory when neither of them knew what they were doing. 'Those fellows from Norwich have been teaching me all about this,' Frederick blustered, tugging on cords, 'and there's nothing to it . . .' Caroline took the tiller, and felt she soon had the hang of it. 'Why they make such a mystery of this business I don't know,' Frederick said. They were scudding out on to the

115

Mere quite smoothly, and Caroline found the dipping motion quite pleasant.

'Row-boat ahead,' Frederick cried. 'Fore, or is it aft? Hard a-port, or starboard. Look out, anyway!'

She yanked on the tiller, sending them lurching to one side.

'Keel haul that man!' Frederick stormed, while Caroline dissolved into helpless laughter. 'Forty lashes, and no rum for a week!' He stood with one foot on the gunwale. 'We shall make sail for the Spanish Main . . . I shall singe the King of Spain's beard – I say, Caro, the wind's getting up, isn't it?'

The breeze was more boisterous out on the Mere than she had expected. 'Perhaps we ought to take the sail down and row,' she suggested through her laughter.

'What! Mutiny – I'll have you strung from the yard-arm . . .'

She was aware of someone shouting something from a rowing-boat nearby, but she was too racked with slightly hysterical laughter to listen. 'Splice the mainbrace, and have a care for your bulwarks . . .' Frederick struck a pose, his hat aloft, one hand on his breast. Suddenly she could not see him: the sail flapped and whipped round. She was still dully thinking he had fallen on his face in the bottom of the boat when she heard the splash, and saw his sandy head disappear under the water.

She nearly went over herself, standing up to shout. She stumbled to the side of the boat. Frederick's hat was floating. There was another splash, and then she saw a head and arm, a dozen yards away. 'Frederick!' she yelled. Then she saw it was not Frederick. A dark head, white shirt. The head whipped back, mouth drawing in air, a flash of blue eyes – Richard. He trod water, then thrashed over in a dive again. When he resurfaced it was with a great gasp of effort. He had hold of Frederick by

116

the collar. Frederick's head lolled, his face moonlike. Richard struck out for the boat, trying to keep Frederick's head above the water. Caroline woke into deadly sobriety. She seized one of the oars and, crouching over the side, held it out to Richard.

Somehow between them they hauled Frederick's sodden weight into the boat. Richard clambered in and turned him on his side and untenderly thumped the water out of him. The rowing-boat from which Richard had jumped was coming alongside them: Caroline saw Charles in it.

'He's all right, isn't he?' she said, hearing her voice dry and flat. 'Say he's all right.'

'He's just swallowed a lot of water,' Richard said. 'On top of too much damned liquor.' He stripped Frederick's red coat off and heaved him on to his back again. 'We should cover him with something . . .' He looked without comment at Caroline's black silk mantle, then turned to the sail. 'Better get him to shore.'

Deftly and quickly, Richard took down the sail and then, followed by Charles, sculled the boat to the shore of the Mere where several people, including Caroline's parents, were anxiously waiting.

'Caroline . . .' Luke was white as death. 'You're safe . . . We saw . . .' Her father embraced her feverishly. Richard was pulling the boat up on to the grass bank. 'And Frederick – is he all right?' Luke added.

'Better than he deserves,' Richard muttered. In the bottom of the boat Frederick, groaning and incoherent with shivering, writhed and beat with his fist at his right knee. 'What the devil's wrong there?' Richard said, darting a fierce glance at Caroline.

'Oh – it must be his knee, he hurt it in a fall from a horse, sometimes it locks like that,' Caroline said.

Richard frowned down at Frederick a moment, then

117

abruptly pulled off the young man's boot. With a sudden poised intentness he felt the knee, his thumbs moving firmly back and forth over it, pressing down. His brows were knitted as if in an effort of memory. Caroline saw there was weed in his wet hair. 'What are you – ?'

'Sh.' The watchers fell silent. Somewhere a sandpiper called. Richard's hands tensed and gripped harder.

'My God, you'll break his leg!' Caroline said.

'Be quiet, damn you!' Richard's voice suggested he had forgotten who she was. He pressed down again.

Frederick gave a jerk and sat bolt upright. 'Oh! God – it's come back,' he gasped. 'How did you do that?' He flexed his knee, grimacing. 'I thought it was gone for good . . .' He looked with guilty, fuddled admiration at Richard. 'Thank you . . . a thousand thanks . . . Lieutenant Lindsay, isn't it?' He coughed a last drop of water. He was white, sick and chastened. 'I – can't swim, you see . . .'

'You damned fat fool. What d'you mean by taking a sail-boat out, for God's sake?' The instinctive tenderness that Caroline had seen in Richard's large strong hands a moment ago was gone: his voice was clear, quiet and dangerous. 'Risk your own stupid sot's neck if you like, but do it alone next time and we'll leave you to it – '

'Don't keep lecturing him!' Caroline burst out. 'He didn't force me to come out with him – we didn't mean any harm.'

'You're as bad as each other,' Richard said. 'You should have had more damned sense.' They stared at each other with stormy hostility.

'You'd better get out of those wet things, Richard,' put in Charles, pulling him gently away. He had just seen the look in Luke's eyes: he was not accustomed to having his daughter spoken to in that way.

* * *

118

The gentlemen who had sailed the cutter from Norwich had spare clothes on board to lend Richard, and he changed in an empty tent. It occurred to Charles as Richard undressed that out of his naval uniform his friend lacked identity: without family, without connections, he was a man who must fend entirely for himself.

'That was a remarkable thing you did with old Frederick's gammy knee,' Charles said. 'Where did you learn bone-setting?'

'Oh . . .' Richard's face softened a moment. 'When I was with the *Anson*, the first lieutenant had an arm he'd broken years before. It had never been set properly and sometimes it went fearfully stiff and useless like that fellow's knee. One cold night on the watch it went like that and he was blind with pain and I just had a try at pushing it back. I seemed to have the knack. After that he always used to send for me when it happened.'

Charles handed Richard the lieutenant's coat he had shed before diving into the water. 'You know, Frederick's not a bad fellow really,' he said.

The tight lines of Richard's face broke up in a brief smile. 'Gave him a roasting, didn't I? One gets used to a curt way of speaking at sea.'

Charles was about to say something about Caroline when a shadow fell behind him. Luke was at the entrance to the tent.

'I want a word with you, Lindsay,' Luke said, in a harsh voice.

Richard nodded towards Charles. Reluctantly and with unease, Charles left them.

'I'll say this once,' Luke said. He screwed up his eyes at the dim light in the marquee. 'I'll not make a meal of it. Just give me your apology, boy, and we'll say no more.'

Richard brushed back his damp hair. 'I wasn't aware I owed any apologies, sir.'

Luke took a step forward. The scare he had had over Caroline's safety had stirred his hot temper. 'You damn well owe me an apology, boy, for speaking to my daughter like that. And in public too!'

'I said only what I believed to be true,' Richard said coolly. 'They both took a foolish risk.'

'Now look you here, boy, I'll have you show respect to my daughter, d'you hear?'

Richard paused. 'I – hope I would show the respect to Miss Caroline that I would show any woman.'

'Not any woman! My daughter damn it. I'll have you remember who she is – and just who *you* are!'

Richard turned pale. Trembling slightly, he buttoned up his coat. 'You mean my father was your employee.'

'I'm glad you remember it. And I hope you remember too what you owe to me. I hope you remember who gave you your start in life. You needn't hide behind that fine coat. Remember where that came from!'

'You gave me my start in life, sir,' Richard said whitely. 'But this coat – this rank – came from my own exertions. I won't exchange it for a hair-shirt to satisfy you. Obligation can only go so far.'

If Luke had been in command of himself he might have reflected that here was someone with a pride and temper to match his own. 'So you think you can get on alone, do you? You, without connections? Why, you're a nobody without influence. By God, boy, you're in no position to be impudent to me!'

Richard was silent a moment. 'Others have risen before,' he said carefully. 'From just as lowly a station as mine.'

There were few men who dared to refer openly to Luke Hardwick's illegitimate origins. His face was scarlet. 'You – by God, if your father had spoken to me that way – '

120

'I'm not my father, sir,' Richard said. 'And I am not your employee.'

Luke swallowed. 'We'll see how you make your way alone, then, boy,' he said, turning to go. 'We'll see.'

3

After the Whittlesea Mere party Richard returned to Stamford, with no word to Charles of what had passed between him and Luke.

Charles had his own surmises, but kept them to himself. He was disappointed when he saw nothing of Richard the next day. Richard had clearly grown into a man who was not easy to know – and Charles found it difficult to realize that he was a couple of years Richard's senior, for he certainly didn't feel it when they were together – but he liked him and wished for his friendship. And he wanted to hear more of his experiences. At the Mere – before the boating accident – Richard had talked to Charles of his life at sea. He was economical of speech, and his narrative had a matter-of-fact quality that made even more vivid the terrible hazards and death, the miserable cold and monotony of the Channel blockade interrupted only by battering storms and gales, the foetid conditions of the orlop-deck where the men were crammed in, the surgeon's cabin with the brazier to take the chill off the knife and the red oilcloth that did not show the blood.

Two days after the Mere, Charles was leaving the Morholm gatehouse at noon after talking to the steward when he saw Richard striding across the stripped fields.

'Well! I was afraid you'd gone back to sea.' Charles shook Richard's hand, noticing the shadows under his eyes. 'Come to the house and we'll have some ale. You've walked from Stamford?'

Richard smiled. 'Got a ride on a carrier's cart. How's your friend Amory, have you seen him?'

'He's well and fine, and singing your praises!' Charles said. 'Swears the doctors have never been able to do anything with his knee, and he has an even greater respect for the men of the King's Navy since having his life saved by one.'

'Good Lord, and after I gave him such a tongue-lashing.'

'Oh, Frederick's never one to bear a grudge about anything. Louisa says he has the virtue of forgetfulness.'

'Lucky man,' Richard said. 'Louisa. That's the sister – the quiet pretty one. You seem to get along very well, Charles. Is this an attachment I see in the making?'

'Louisa? Good Lord, she's an old friend, I – I've known her for years.'

'I dare say. Perhaps I've been too long at sea to understand these things, but I would guess she has a taking for you.'

'Oh, but – you're surely mistaken,' said Charles, who was often unable to see what was under his very nose. 'Louisa . . . why, she could have her pick of men.'

'Perhaps. I like her, but she'd not be every man's ideal. And besides, it's what she thinks of you that's important.'

'Oh, no, no,' Charles said. He shook his head emphatically, and was breezily dismissive as one is with a piece of information one prefers not to assimilate. It was this discomfort which drove him to ask what he would not otherwise have ventured to ask. 'What about you, Richard? Is it true about sailors having wives in every port?'

'There's truth in it when applied to some fellows,' Richard said, narrowing his eyes and studying Morholm up ahead. 'Not me.'

He was silent then, and Charles said quietly: 'Sorry, that was hardly a polite question.'

Richard gave him a tight smile, and then patted his shoulder. 'Dear Charles, you're too good for this world. It was me who sprang that stuff about Louisa on you, remember.' He stopped and breathed in, gazing around him at the sheep in the autumn stubble-fields, the pure stark shapes of pollard willows. 'I wonder if I love this country because it's like the sea – or the sea because it's like this country. Bracing space. Same vast horizons and sky.'

Charles took Richard into the library, shooing Frances away, and they drank ale spiced with nutmeg. Richard studied the portrait of Charles's father over the mantelpiece. It had been painted by Opie a few years ago. 'A good likeness,' he said.

'I think so. Father always says it looks as if he's sitting on a nail.'

'I didn't mean to sound self-righteous a moment ago, Charles,' Richard said abruptly. 'About the wives in every port. But I just feel differently. I'll tell you.' He drank deeply. 'When I was in Jamaica recovering from the malaria I used to play at cards with some other midshipmen in the hospital. The stakes weren't high, they couldn't be. But I kept losing, and so did some of the others, and at last I spotted this fellow cheating. And then he took ship again. But then at Portsmouth this year I met up with him quite by chance. He'd grown and changed, as so had I, I suppose, but all I could think of was that he'd cheated us back in Port Royal. And I tackled him with it . . . He didn't seem to believe that I'd remembered, but I had. I didn't want his damned money. I just wanted him to come out and acknowledge the fact that he was a cheat. So you see . . . There must be only one woman for me, right or wrong, for always. That fellow couldn't believe I'd preserved that single-minded feeling about him so long – but that's how it must be, with hate or love. I can't think of any other way that would be worthwhile.'

'It's a lot to ask,' Charles said mildly.

'I know,' said Richard. He reached suddenly in his pocket. 'On the subject of gambling. That's why I couldn't see you yesterday.' He extracted a fistful of coins. 'Never knew there was so much gaming to be had in Stamford. Went up to Spalding too. Some prodigious seedy places along the river there.'

'Why?' Charles said, looking at the gold and silver.

'Your uncle. Mr Luke. When I was started off as midshipman, he gave me twenty pounds against my pay. And bought the uniform.' He spread the coins out on the table and stared at them. 'I've won enough here to pay it back.'

'I guessed you . . . clashed with him the other day.'

'I didn't come back here to quarrel with your uncle,' Richard said. The muscles in his jaw were working as he turned his heavy-lidded, unrestful eyes to Charles. 'I wanted to show him that I had made a success of it: to show that I had worked off the debt. To prove myself if you like. To prove that I was making something of myself. As he once did,' he added grimly.

'And so you have,' Charles said. But he began to perceive – knowing his uncle's sometimes overbearing manner – that being the object of patronage was anathema to Richard's complex nature. Dependence went hard with him.

'Have I?' Richard scooped the money back into his pocket. 'I'd hoped to be accepted on my own terms. Not to be continually owing something. Call it pride if you like. Well, when I give him this I won't owe a single farthing.'

'I hope,' said Charles evenly, 'that I'm not included in this quarrel.'

Richard glanced at him, then patted his arm. 'God's life, no one could quarrel with you, Charles. Least of all me.'

'You know, Richard . . . this quarrel . . . uncle Luke's a hot-tempered man. And Caroline's the apple of his eye. So perhaps it's – '

Richard stiffened. 'I know that,' he said abruptly, and Charles fell silent. He began to see too that Richard's struggle had not only been to rise above his humble birth. He suspected that the reserve, the self-control, the immaculate dress actually bespoke a man who had had to knit together the flailing threads of strong passions. Suddenly, he could picture Richard very clearly on the foredeck of a fighting ship.

'Let me drink your health in another mug of ale, Charles,' Richard said, seeming to shake off introspection. 'And then I must be off. I can get a coach in Peterborough at two to take me as far as Biggleswade. Yes, I'm going back to London. Call at the Admiralty, see if there's any news of my commission.'

'So soon? But – '

'I know. I just feel it was a mistake to come back here. Not as far as seeing you, of course. Next time we're both in London we must meet. I'll write you as soon as I can. It's just – I can't stay here. I had hoped . . . but I made a mistake. Better when I get the decks under my feet again.'

Charles was miserable. Richard had been away so long, they had just begun to be good friends, and now he was going away and there was no telling when he would see him again.

But part of friendship was insight, and Charles had enough to perceive that a fundamental element in Richard had been sorely touched.

* * *

125

Richard got to Peterborough by carrier and stowed his luggage at the Angel before walking up to the Bridge House.

Luke was in his panelled study, and when Richard was shown in he laid down his pen and looked neutrally at the young man.

'Well, boy,' he said, 'it's a little late, but if you've come to make your apology for your conduct the other day, then – '

'No, sir.' Richard took the money from his pocket and counted it carefully on to Luke's desk.

Colour rose in Luke's cheeks. 'What the devil's this?'

'Forty-eight pounds and six shillings,' Richard said. 'It represents your expenditure on me, Mr Hardwick, five years ago.' Before Luke could speak he went on: 'Don't think me ungrateful for what you did. But a man can't go on feeling grateful for ever.'

Luke leaned back and studied Richard coldly. 'Still proud, eh, boy?' he said. 'Pride's all very well. But pride in a poor lieutenant with no name, no family, who owes everything to – '

'That's why I've sought to discharge this debt, sir,' Richard said. He had the breathless stiffness of a man barely in control of himself. 'Shouldn't a man be judged on what he is, not on the accident of his birth?' He swallowed. 'Did you not rise above that? Can I not do the same?'

'Damn your impudence,' said Luke, softly and hoarsely. 'Your father showed me respect, boy – '

'There's a difference between respect and servile dependence,' Richard said. 'I've worked and striven to be worthy of my father's memory and, yes, of you, Mr Hardwick. That was why I came back here. Tell me, when will I be good enough to be accepted? Commodore? Lord Admiral?'

Luke said nothing. He got up suddenly as if he would strike the young man. But instead he gestured around him to the models of schooners and brigs mounted around the study: the ships of his merchant fleet. 'Relying on yourself, then, eh, boy? Well, well. If the war ends there'll be hundreds of junior officers discharged from the Navy. Seeking employment.' He clasped his hands behind his back and turned away from Richard. 'As you're so independent, I suppose you won't come crying to me.'

Caroline was crossing the hall as Richard left the study, his face like thunder. She knew there had been trouble between him and her father, and now as he came striding towards her, almost blindly, it seemed for one moment as if he would turn on her. But when his gaze met hers, she saw a flat, startled look in his eyes: she even seemed to see hurt there.

He bowed shortly, said her name, and saw himself out. He walked down Broad Bridge Street to the Angel to wait for his coach, and whatever awakened hopes he had brought back to the fenland he stifled and hid away.

CHAPTER 5

1

Muster day, and for the first time Caroline stayed in her room.

She could hear the voices of the French officers downstairs, but could not pick out Antoine's.

Keep away. You must keep away.

Her father was going to King's Lynn later: his ship *Sheldrake* was just in. He had been in a dark mood since the Mere party three days ago. Richard Lindsay's impact had been brief but unsettling.

Everything in her hitherto sane and measured life, it seemed, had been thrown drastically off-beam. She had changed, she knew, since that revelation in the clearing in the orchard. Her former self stood reproachful behind her on the other side of a chasm. Was there still a bridge over which to return – and did she wish to?

Perhaps she should go to King's Lynn too – though it was only for a couple of days. Perhaps she should go for a stay with her uncle Peter in London. Get away completely.

But what possible reason could she give for wanting to go away – aside from the real one that could never be confided to anyone?

Last night she had had an exhaustingly vivid dream, too directly erotic to need any interpretation. It had surprised her. She had woken with a desperate feeling of loss.

Caroline was a child of her time and had not spent eighteen years in a vacuum. She was a virgin but not innocent. For all the evangelical efforts of people like the Butterworths to reform morals and manners, it could hardly be otherwise. She had never kissed a man except formally, but she had seen people blind and disfigured with venereal disease. Pornographic prints which left nothing to the imagination were commonplace. In the country districts of the fenland young couples commonly slept together prior to marriage, to establish whether they were fertile. At school the girls had discussed in whispers what a man and a woman did in bed together, and Caroline's only comment had been that it sounded dismayingly athletic. Fashionable ladies drank chocolate in the elegant townhouses of Stamford whilst open sewers ran beneath their windows. Life was still raw, and to some extent tolerant.

But for her, the daughter of Luke Hardwick, to have these feelings about an enemy prisoner-of-war – these feelings that were no idealistic wraiths but had hot blood in their veins – it was impossibly forbidden. She knew she was playing with fire.

Oh, but she was young, wasn't she? Was it so insane and selfish, with the world senselessly fighting a war that went on and on, to want to snatch that simple, incomparable happiness of being with him?

She thought of him, and longing rose in her, turning her sick.

The officers were gone, and she went downstairs. Her mother was writing a letter at the bureau. In passing, Caroline kissed her mother's elegant auburn head, feeling a childish need for the sort of comfort her mother could no longer provide.

She saw the books placed on the table, and froze.

'Oh, Captain Clairet left those books you lent him and said to give you his grateful thanks.' Rebecca smiled at

129

her daughter. 'He certainly does seem to speak rather more fluently now.'

Caroline stared at the books. 'I'll – put them away,' she said.

Back in her room she held the books by their spines and shook them. A note, there would be a note.

She flung the books on the floor. No, there was no note. She should have known. Why should there be? She herself had said *I can't . . . it's impossible.* He was being sensible, respectful; taking her at her word.

But no – they were not all here. He had not returned the little book of fables, with her name childishly written on the flyleaf.

He had kept it. A piece of her.

The thought sustained her for a while. Oh, if only she had something of his!

Frank Bellaers keeping her glove. She had laughed about that. She had laughed about a lot of things, from her lofty height of self-sufficiency.

She would go to King's Lynn with her father. See the ships, the whalers, the bustling life of the port, forget. It would occupy her mind for a couple of days. She ran down to her father's study to ask him.

He met her at the study door. He was carrying a letter. 'Well, love,' he said before she could speak. 'That may be the last we'll see of our foreign friends and enemies.' He tapped the letter. 'From Captain Woodruff, the governor at Norman Cross. Our government has been trying to negotiate with the French again over exchange, also over who should be responsible for supplying the prisoners' clothing, and they've got thoroughly cross with each other. Apparently it may be necessary any day to cancel all parole rights and confine all the French officers in the prison camp. As a rebuke to the French. And no doubt they're preparing to do the same with our men in France.'

'But – but that's absurd, they can't do that!'

'Aye, it's ridiculous,' Luke said, seeming unsurprised at her outburst. 'Like spiteful children. Well, Woodruff says I must be prepared to round them up if and when he gets word from the Transport Office, who are responsible for the prison camps. Negotiations are still going on. I've told the men nothing. What a damn nuisance! Well, I'll not postpone going to Lynn. I'll ask old Squire to act for me if necessary.'

'That reminds me,' Caroline said, with complete command of herself now. 'I said I'd call on Lucy.'

2

Little's Yard lurked like a poor relation behind the tall townhouses of Narrow Bridge Street. An open gutter ran through the courtyard. Lines of washing, made frowsy by the smoke from ranks of chimneys, were strung between the high windows. At the blind end of the yard was an unsavoury ale-house.

Caroline had put on her plainest cloak and poke-bonnet; but still she was immediately conspicuous here. She glanced up at the garret windows. It could be any of them.

Some children were playing ring-o'-roses in the court-yard. They were shoeless and ill-fed and they looked at her with old wisdom when she approached; expecting no good of her.

'Hello,' she said.

They were still and poised.

'Somebody told me there's one of those funny men

131

living here, is that true? One of those Frenchmen. Is that right?'

A little boy gravely nodded.

Caroline looked up at the windows, and pointed to one. 'Just there. I bet he lives there.'

'No, he don't,' the boy said. He pointed proudly. 'He lives there. I've seen him.'

'My mam says if we talk to him he'll put us in the pot and eat us,' a small girl said in an unconcerned way, merely offering the information.

Caroline looked up at the window again. A small leaded dormer, slightly ajar. The door of the tall soot-blackened house stood open.

The hall smelt of damp and the faded dinners of multiple occupancy. Little pinched seamstresses and decayed dancing-teachers. A half-submerged world. The thought of Antoine here was incongruous, and sad.

She mounted the stairs, dreading to meet anyone. The realization that she was compromising herself finally by coming here was in her mind somewhere, but it seemed as irrelevant now as a childhood worry.

There were three flights to the attic storey. She was breathless. A dark passage and a latched door.

She should have tried the orchard close first. He was probably there, in the clearing, in limbo. The thought struck her with such certainty that she calmly laid her hand on the latch and opened the door, expecting an empty room.

Antoine was bending over the hearth, putting a pan on a trivet over the fire. He was in shirt-sleeves – looking informal, domestic, but not diminished. There was colour in his face from stooping, and it rose higher as he turned to see her.

'Caroline!'

'I had to come,' she said faintly.

132

'Caroline – it was dangerous – if someone sees you – '

'Oh, it doesn't *matter*.'

'Not to me.' He came forward quickly and closed the door behind her. 'But for you, if it was known . . . What is wrong?'

He did not touch her, but looked into her face with alarm.

'I had to see you – to tell you . . . You may soon be put in the prison camp at Norman Cross. All the paroled Frenchmen. The English and the French Governments are in dispute over treatment of prisoners – and they may take away the privilege of parole.' She could not look at him. 'I had to tell you.'

'So . . . in the prison.' He shook his head slowly. 'Perhaps . . . after all . . . it is for the best.'

'How can you say that?' Her whole being protested. 'How can you *say* that . . . after the other day – when you said – '

'Because it would be best for both of us – not because I want it!' he said, with some harshness. He went on more gently: 'Then I would not see you. Which is the only way. That is what we agreed. Caroline – '

'But I had to come anyway,' she said. Her eyes had gathered a swift impression of the room: an old rug on bare floorboards, a trunk, an iron bed. The scent of him, the insistent fact of his presence, was so strong here. She knew she was lost. She had crossed the threshold, though driven by pretext. She would have crossed it anyway. 'I would have come, Antoine, even if this had not happened. I would have had to, you see. In spite of what we said in limbo . . . Since then I've felt as if I were breaking in two . . . And then when I heard that you might be locked away and I would never see you again I knew that what we said, what *I* said that day was just words. Brave words, but cowardly too – yes, cowardly, because I was afraid of my own feelings. Oh, God, I want you, and it can't be denied any more than I can stop the beating of my own heart . . .'

She was exhausted by the effort of speaking, of lifting up this terrible weight of emotion. She half-fell into his arms.

Nothing can hurt me here. She pressed her face with a grateful moan into his shoulder, crushed in his quick embrace. It was all strange and yet shot through with recognition and release, a new world and a coming home. 'Oh, my love,' he said, his hand stroking the nape of her neck, 'I am so ashamed . . .'

'Why – why?' Incredulous, because nothing in the universe could ever be wrong or bad with her face pressed into his sweet-smelling neck; all was made over, it was the beginning of the millennium.

'I make you suffer so,' he said softly. He tilted her face and looked into it. 'See, there are tears,' and his lips touched her cheeks. 'No more tears, no more, Caroline, my only love.'

He stood back from her, looked at her wonderingly, then took both her hands in his and kissed them.

'You're really here.'

She nodded, gulping back something that was half a laugh and half a sob. She pulled off her bonnet. 'Yes. I'm here.'

Holding her hands he led her to an old Windsor chair near the hearth. 'Here,' he said, in a hushed, almost reverential voice, 'sit here.'

She sat, obeying him. He stood looking down at her, still with a certain wonder. 'Yes,' he said, 'that's it.'

'What is it?'

He knelt beside her, coiled and ardent. 'This is where you sit. When I think, when I dream, have dreamt . . . When I came home and opened the door sometimes I would fancy to myself *une image*, a picture, of you sitting there . . . waiting for me. Oh, but not with tears,' and he embraced her, touching her face again, 'never with tears.'

She held his face in her hands, examining his tan skin, the lights and shadows, the brown answering eyes and strong, slightly quizzical brows. 'And now – now I'm here – it's almost too late,' she said; but not with a real sadness, rather a sadness imagined and indulged, because just to hold and be held by him like this was to be utterly redeemed.

'No,' he said. 'No, it can't happen. They wouldn't take away our parole now – not now this has happened.' He kissed her with a deep possessing tenderness. 'They can't. The world can't be so cruel.'

'There's no way of knowing,' she said. 'Father and the governor at Norman Cross must just wait for the decision from the Government.' It seemed suddenly so monstrous that so much was depending on stupid diplomatic wranglings, so far away, so blind, that she clung to him with a feeling of passionate outrage: as if she had found that everyone around her had been trying to encompass her death.

'Then we must wait,' he said with great simplicity. 'This – our love – should never have happened at all. Everything has been against it from the first moment. But it was too strong.' He turned her hands over, gazed at them, kissed her palms. 'You will stay here with me, won't you? You are not about to go away again?'

'I told them I was going to see Lucy Squire,' Caroline said. 'I shall have to go back by dinner – '

'Oh, yes, I know,' he said eagerly, 'but *now* – for now you are free, yes? You can be here with me, and no one knows. I am so happy to have you here – I never dared hope it would be so.'

'Of course I'll stay,' she said, 'as long as I can.' She ran

135

her hands through his dark curling hair. A dreadful, marvellous seriousness weighed on her, as if she had caught and held some rare wounded animal that she must nurse. 'Oh, Antoine, I don't know if I can bear loving you so much.'

'I know that I can never deserve it,' he said, 'only try.'

There was a sudden startling hiss from the fire. The pan had boiled over on to the flames and nearly put them out. She laughed, with a breaking of tension across her chest. Antoine leapt up and seized the pan, burnt his fingers, nearly dropped the pan, finally found a cloth and placed it over the fire again.

'What a disgrace,' he said, sucking his fingers and laughing. '*Quelle dégringolade* . . . so, you see my domestic arrangements. The brave Captain of the Republic at home . . .'

'Oh, dear, Antoine, did you burn yourself?' She could not remember enjoying laughter so much. He pantomimed blowing on his fingers, grinned at her, lean and boyish. 'That's better,' he said, 'smiling.'

'What were you making?'

'It's just a little soup for my dinner,' he said. 'Yesterday I had a little chop of meat, so I have the bones and a few vegetables . . .'

The realization of the modest plainness of his solitary life touched her keenly. She joined him at the fire. 'Will you share it with me when it's ready?' she said, putting her arm round his waist.

'This?' He smiled. 'It is only soup . . .'

She nodded. 'I want to share it with you. To eat a meal with you.'

'Very well!' he said gaily. 'I have some bread, I even have a little wine – '

'There you are then. A feast.' She held his hands. She felt like dancing. She looked around at the room. 'And

136

this is where you live. I've wondered so often what it's like. Tried to picture it.'

'And was it so dirty?' he said with a rueful smile.

'Oh – all I could ever see was you,' she said. The room was shabby but not untidy, with a sailor's plainness. She walked slowly around it, touching things, seeing each object not for what it was but for its place in the constellation of love of which Antoine was the brilliant centre. There was a shaving-brush, razor and comb with the glazed bowl and pitcher by the bed. There was a pair of boots, and his officer's braided coat and cocked hat hanging on the door. There were a few books – her *Fables* amongst them. On the bare walls there was only an old Hogarth print. A pack of cards, a telescope, pen and ink, a clay pipe.

'This is all,' he said with a shrug. '*Château Clairet*.'

'It makes me think of a ship's cabin,' she mused aloud. 'A captain's cabin. Quite austere but comfortable.'

'My cabin on the *Coquille* was not half so big,' he said.

'And it's part French and part English. A mixture of the two.'

'Then it is just right for us.'

'And – oh, I like the view!'

He joined her at the window. It faced north across the town, towards Borough Fen. A jagged collection of roofs and gables, haphazard as if they had been washed up here by retreating water, with the tower of St John's rising stranded amongst them. In the distance the treacly brown smoke from Phipps' Brewery hung in the air, and all around them drifted the smoke from the chimneys of the town. 'You see,' he said, 'the way we are just above the smoke, as if we were resting on clouds above the city. Sometimes a bird will fly right up on to my window-sill, and he looks at me surprised, like to say "What do *you* do up here?" We have been in limbo – now, here we are up in heaven.' He pushed the latticed window further open. 'Just there, beyond the windmill, I see the green of the fields – fens, yes? And those are out of my reach. It's strange to think that if I take that road, or that road, or that one, and just keep walking till I pass the tollgates and I am in the green fields, then my parole is broken and I am a fugitive. Such a simple thing. Not like breaking down bars or shooting a guard . . . just walking.' He turned and touched her arm, as if reminding himself she was there. 'You hid from me this morning,' he said gently.

'. . . Yes.'

'It was what I expected. After what we said – in limbo. But then I thought, I must see her just once more – I will take her books and that will be an excuse, just to speak a word . . .'

She was silent, smiling, feeling life to be an impossible maze of paths whose destination one could never know in advance. One could only set out and hope.

They ate the soup, seated either side of Antoine's little desk. He had only one glass for the wine, and they shared this. The informality heightened the sense of ritual. Never, never will I forget this, thought Caroline.

'That day when I saw you asleep by the river,' she told him. 'From a distance I – thought you were a dead body. I nearly didn't come near.'

He looked at her thoughtfully. 'Did you?' Their fingers fitted companionably together around the glass. 'I – when I first came to England I nearly was.'

She waited for more.

'It seems very stupid now. I cannot quite understand. I had lost my ship, yes, but we were outnumbered . . . I had lost hardly any of my crew. I was not wounded. I was taken prisoner, so, that is a hazard of war. We come into Portsmouth, and at first we are put in a hulk. We are told we will go to Norman Cross soon – the officers probably to be paroled near the prison. So . . . why did I feel, so seriously, I wish to kill myself? For I did. I think I was afraid. Afraid of facing more things. Not just being a prisoner. Just – facing the future. I wanted to stop it all. Like hearing music and yes, you like it, and it goes on and on and you want it to stop. Does that sound foolish?'

'Not foolish. But sad. And . . . not like you.'

'Well . . . I have always thought I have a temper, er, *sanguin*. But, this strange weakness . . .' His fingers, long and tense, stroked hers absently. 'Once, off Brest, I was in charge of a small vessel – a lieutenant's command, I was not yet captain – and we were to escort some merchant ships to Le Havre. We had passed Pointe St Mathieu and gone through the Chenal du Four, my convoy was still neatly together and I was perhaps a little proud. Then there is a sail on the horizon. Sometimes the English ships make raids right into the Iroise. And my second lieutenant is looking at me, wishing to know what to do, what is my reaction . . . and I panic inside, I think, *Don't look at me – I don't know* . . . I am a blank.' Abruptly he grinned. 'The ship was a French corvette. And soon I was myself again. But this weakness . . . Anyway, at Portsmouth it was over quickly, thank heaven, and then I am feeling just glad to be alive again. And then – there was you. Something I never expected. Who knows, perhaps it is a message of fate, to show how foolish I was to look into the sea and wish to die, when something so wonderful was waiting for me.'

'I don't believe in fate,' she said after a moment.

'No?'

She shook her head. 'Don't folk have enough to contend with getting through life without inventing these imaginary adversaries behind it all? If I fail, or succeed, I'd rather put the blame or the credit to my account.'

'It is a courageous way,' he said slowly. 'But, women

are more courageous than men. We go out to battlefields and rush into the mouth of cannon. But there is no real courage, only shouting. I think of your courage, in coming here, with so much to lose.'

'It's because I love you,' she said. 'Love has its own courage. I suppose love *is* courage. A giving, a surrendering. Because I didn't want to be in love with you, Antoine. I resisted it, I was afraid.'

He looked at her soberly, attentively. 'It is easier for me. I knew there could be no hope, so in a way I was free. Oh, when you came that day when Roubillard and I played *aux raquettes* – and you threw down your hat without hesitation and played, you were so light and laughing and graceful, feet skipping. And I thought afterwards, this woman is so special, and I wondered about your life . . . I thought of the young men who must be paying court to you, and perhaps there was one you liked. And I pictured him, I had him clear in my mind, oh yes. And I was jealous of this picture – seeing him at dinner with you, dancing with you. And yet not jealous, for I wanted him to treat you well and admire you – but he could never appreciate you, I knew that.'

'And what did he look like, this phantom gentleman?'

'Oh . . . he was tall, and handsome in the English way, and he rode a fine horse and he was very attentive to you.'

She laughed and shook her head. Antoine's wry, half-serious expression was very lovable. 'Dear Antoine, there is no such beau and never has been.'

'No? Your father and mother, have they no man selected for you?'

'If they have, they haven't told me about it, and I should certainly hope to be consulted.' She was amused still, but at the same time she felt a certain awe at these

140

strange revelations of love, humbling as a glimpse of the intricate workings of the body one takes for granted.

Her eye fell on the Hogarth print on the wall and noticed it was part of *The Harlot's Progress*. Well, that was unsubtle. The Butterworths would appreciate the irony. But then all of her society would think likewise.

'What are you thinking?'

'The picture. *The Harlot's Progress*. Some would say it was appropriate.'

He looked troubled. 'I hate to think – to think that I – '

'What? Have seduced me from the path of decency?' She stood and placed her arms round his neck. 'Dear love, I've done nothing but what I wanted to do. What I *had* to do: it couldn't be denied. If there were any normal acceptable way of being with you then that would be wonderful; but since there isn't then that's all right too. I'd risk being an outcast from everyone, from all the world I know, to be with you.'

After a moment he kissed her, deeply and wordlessly.

She sat on his knee. 'There. All harlots must sit on men's knees like this. And grapes, we should have grapes or something like that. All harlots sit on men's knees and feed them sweetmeats. It's a rule.'

'Alas, no grapes! I have a little cheese . . . no good, eh?' His laughing mouth was warm against her neck. 'No, I suppose not . . . but *you* taste good enough to eat . . .'

Then they froze: a noise outside the door.

'Ah, it's all right,' he said after a moment. 'I recognize her step. It is the old woman who lives below. She wanders about, I think she is a little *toquée*.' He tapped his head. 'Sometimes she says good morning to me very friendly. Sometimes she points a finger and calls me a trike. Perhaps you can tell me what this means.'

'Oh – I'm afraid it means a man who – likes men.'

'Ah, is that all? But in France we are told all English men are like that!'

'I don't know about *all* . . .' Suddenly she felt a chill. 'Antoine – what is the time?'

He took out his watch. 'I know what you are going to say.'

They clung together. 'I can't stay any longer, oh my love, I'm sorry – they'll be sending for me at the Squires' soon . . . oh, my love, I'm so afraid . . .'

'No, no, you are not, you are too brave and strong. Caroline, if the news does come you must be brave again, and remember that I love you, I am yours always even if I am put in the prison – that simply knowing I have your love is enough to make me the happiest and proudest man in the world, even if there is no place in that world for us. Look at me, my love. We have had this wonderful hour – and if God, or fate, or whatever wills, we may have another, and perhaps another. I'll be in the orchard – in limbo – tomorrow morning. Can you come there?'

She nodded, unable to speak, clinging to him as if she were poised over an abyss from which only he could pluck her.

At the door she turned, though she willed herself not to. He smiled at her, encouraging her not to cry. 'Bless you,' he said. 'Be strong.'

Her tears flowed at last as she went down the dingy staircase. She stopped to wipe them at the landing, and the mad old woman peered out at her from her room. She was in an old petticoat with filthy stays half-undone: she looked drunk. And with her glazed fishy stare she looked like the incarnation of the forces, perhaps the fate Caroline did not believe in, that conspired against her having the one thing in her life she most desperately wanted.

Her father had gone to King's Lynn as arranged: but there were no letters for him next morning. 'No news is good news' had never been more horribly true.

But a message came to the Bridge House for Caroline's mother. It was from her friends the Mottrams at Longthorpe. Mrs Mottram's labour pains had started, and Rebecca, who as Caroline knew was a selfless and skilful nurse, had promised to be with her when the confinement came.

'I may have to stay overnight,' Rebecca said in the yard, mounting her mare with the fluid grace that was in everything she did. 'You and Nicholas came into the world with a minimum of fuss, but there's no telling with babies. Your father should be home this evening wanting a good supper – I know you can do the honours. Goodbye, love.'

So, she was alone.

She told Mrs Haley not to worry about dinner just for her -- she would have some cold meats when she was hungry.

Rain was beginning to fall from a ponderous sky. She put on her grey pelisse with the deep cape and went out.

She made for the orchard close without much hope. The rain was heavy now. At the Customs House by the bridge men were hurriedly pulling tarpaulins over a shipment of flour on the quay. The low-lying Fletton meadows were rapidly liquefying. The fallen leaves in the orchard close were resolving into slippery paste.

But he was there. Stoically crouching in the lee of the old wall, a boat-cloak over his shoulders. Beads of water decorated his hair.

'No news,' she said, pressed against him. His skin was cold and fresh; she warmed it with her lips. 'No news. Oh, my love, you're soaking. How long have you been here?'

'I don't know.' He held her close. 'You're wet too. Oh, I was afraid you wouldn't come.'

'I was afraid you wouldn't be here.' They looked at each other: all at once they were smiling. 'We should know better,' she said.

There was a quick scuttering noise in the beech trees above them, and a flash of brilliant orange. 'Look,' Antoine said. 'There he is. My little friend. What is he in English again?'

'Squirrel.'

He tried, shook his head. 'No, that is a word my lips were not made for.'

'They were made for mine,' she said.

Rain pattered down on them as they kissed.

'Even limbo is unkind to us today,' he said.

'Perhaps we'll be better off in heaven,' she said, and then added as if something urgent in her had made an impatient gesture at coyness, 'Let's go to your room, love. My mother and father are out all day. I have the day to myself. Well, no.' She stroked his face. 'My day belongs to you.'

They could not be seen walking into the city together: in a place of less than five thousand souls the risk was always there of being seen by someone she knew. Antoine went first, and she followed a few minutes later.

The sky was so thickly overcast that he had lit a candle in his room when she arrived, and he was trying to start a fire in the grate.

When the kindling at last took flame, he drew up the

144

Windsor chair to the hearth and placed her there to dry her muddy skirts.

'I have some tea,' he said, taking a box from the mantelshelf. 'It is rather like dust, but it is so expensive . . .'

Caroline recognized the low-grade Bohea tea that the poor drank. At the Bridge House they had the best hyson at sixteen shillings a pound. 'I ought to bring you some things like that,' she said, 'your allowance is so small . . .'

He looked at her with some irony. 'Ah. The charitable English lady,' he said – and she saw he was a little hurt.

'I only meant – '

'I know.' He touched her shoulder. 'Sometimes I am a little too proud. Forgive me.'

'I don't want any tea,' she said. 'Just you.'

He put the box back, and then looked down at her feet resting on the fender. 'Your boots are wet,' he said. 'You'll catch cold.'

They were short boots laced up the front, meant for walking but really not sturdy. She bent to unlace them but his hand stopped hers.

'Let me.'

So she sat back and he unlaced them and slipped them off, and then turned out the tongues and set the boots carefully on the fender. There was an admirable neatness about the way he handled things, a light dexterity. Her eyes were fixed on his hands, and there was a curious suspended silence between them.

'So . . . your mother also is away today,' Antoine said in a constrained voice, kneeling by the smoking fire, not looking at her.

'Yes.' She explained about Mrs Mottram's confinement.

'Your mother is a very kind woman,' he said, 'very warm.'

145

'Yes, she is.'

'Your father also is – I feel a high respect for him.'

'They rather like you also, I think,' Caroline said. 'Absurd, isn't it? The whole business.' She flexed her toes towards the fire. Her heart was labouring, her blood scarcely moving it seemed. 'My stockings are a little wet too.'

His hand was visibly trembling as he touched her ankle and then her calf. 'Yes,' he said. 'Caroline – '

'Please kiss me,' she said, and was promptly, fiercely taken into his arms, 'darling Antoine.' His lips seemed to scorch her neck. There was a deep bright ache in her nipples. His shirt had come loose from the waist of his breeches and she touched the hot skin of his back with shock.

'Caroline – ' His hand on the nape of her neck, he looked into her face.

'Yes, my darling?' she said. And, changing the intonation, 'Yes. Yes, Antoine.' Her vision seemed to have altered. Sensitized like her skin, it was bombarded with brilliant detail.

'Caroline . . . listen to me, please. I love you.'

'And I love you. So much – '

'What I said just now. About being proud. I hope – I try – to be honourable also.' He spoke with great effort.

'I know,' she said. 'I know, love. And you have. But don't you see, I love you and I mean it entirely . . . there's no other way for us, we have to make our own world. "Had we but world enough and time . . ." My eyes are open, Antoine.' She drew closer to him. 'My eyes are open.'

'And I am humble – humbled – that you should feel like this,' he said, persisting, his brow contracted and almost pained. 'But listen. Now – when I may be put in the prison at any time, tomorrow, the next day . . . If you

146

were to give yourself to me now, and then the order comes through and we are all put in Norman Cross and I can see you no more . . . Do you see? It is as if – I have used you. Putting your value cheap. Like, "oh, well, why not, there will be no consequence, no tomorrows." Like the breakfast for the condemned man. No responsibility. And I do not want it to be that way between us.'

'But I know you are honourable,' she said. 'And as I said, there's no place for these nice distinctions. Not for us. And suppose we were to obey those scruples – and then you were put in the prison camp tomorrow? How would you feel then? Would you not regret? Truly?'

'I – don't know.' He gazed helplessly at her. 'But you are – you are so beautiful, I am just afraid – '

'Don't be.' She caressed up and down his arms. 'You would regret it. As I would. As I would. Because you're not using me, Antoine. I am very averse to being used, believe me. It's precisely because we may have so little time that we must live it to the full. And then, if you are not put in the prison after all, so much the better.'

'You are very wonderful,' he said quietly. 'Always I find there are new things in you. And it is not that I do not want to make love to you, Caroline. I want to very much.' His hand lay lightly on her knee. 'I want to very much.'

She nodded tightly. 'And if you are put in the prison . . . you must remember that I love you. Will you?' she said as they kissed in hard, breathless kisses, and a madness made festival in her body. 'Will you, darling? And not hate yourself? Because I love you, Antoine – I do love you,' and when his hands grazed her breasts she unbuttoned the bodice of her dress and threw it back as if she were choking to death.

Gravely, he removed her chemise, and then her stockings, and she stood and stepped out of her petticoat. She

147

was intensely aware of her own naked whiteness seeming to burn like a pale flame in the room, and of the sound of the rain, on the fringe of silence, tossed in soft flurries against the window. She walked into his arms with perfect purpose as if she were walking through a doorway.

4

To get what you want can in certain circumstances be disappointing; but to find, in the getting, that you wanted it even more than you thought, engenders other feelings, no less disconcerting.

If she had been a stranger to herself at the moment of stepping naked into his embrace, she was more so now, lying propped on one elbow looking down at Antoine's face.

The fire had almost gone out, but she was not cold: the narrow bed still held the heat of their bodies. The rain had stopped, but the sky at the window was even gloomier.

They had talked, and dozed, and now in a relaxed wakefulness she looked at Antoine still lightly sleeping beside her and strove to adjust her mind's eye to the new searching light in which her life was revealed.

Her notions of the male body had been superficial – as, it turned out, had her notions of her own – and she was surprised to discover Antoine's more complete beauty. She looked down at the lean flue, hard but delicate, of the muscles on his arm thrown across the rag-work quilt, wishing to touch him but not to wake him yet.

All such conquests are mutual, and she could not deny the sense of power, seeing him there defenceless in sleep, his hair tousled, one hand curled and gripless. The most adult of acts impelled the self backwards to the naked dependence of infanthood, a surrendering of power in the trust of a reciprocal surrendering. Like becoming a prisoner-of-war.

A light woman. Ridiculous phrase, that betrayed itself. She had never felt more heavy, more drugged and sated.

Her clothes, in a heap on the floor, looked bizarre; odd cunning little scraps and contrivances to cover this body that had shown itself so spacious and elemental with its imperious demands. She had acted in the first place driven by the hard logic of love: to lay her love for him on a symbolic altar. But the satisfactions had been much more than symbolic.

Antoine had been kind to her. But his desire had been compulsive, unlocking him from a prison, and at the last he had seemed almost to fear it. Afterwards she had stroked his burning brow and soothed him back to life, like a man saved from drowning.

'I am yours, my love,' he had said. 'Remember that. I belong to you.'

And so she felt. But seeing him, calm and handsome and utterly solitary in sleep, she knew this possession to be a continual process: Love was a constant reclaiming, like reclaiming the land from the advancing sea.

She shifted in the bed, aware for the first time of pain deep in the small of her back and loins. But she had expected more. It had almost seemed as if her whole frame must fly apart, with their flesh striving together, his penetration of her, his mouth restless on her breasts. It was surprising they were both still in one piece.

She reached out to straighten his boyish hair, appalled by a tenderness too awesome for the triviality of the world. That outside there were people walking and carts trundling and horses stamping seemed scarcely believable.

He opened his eyes. They seemed to search and then reach out to her.

'Hello,' she said.

He sat up, taking her hand. 'I dreamt you were a dream,' he said, foggily, then smiled, with a profound happiness.

'Pinch yourself and make sure,' she said, sliding closer to him. 'Or shall I pinch you?'

'That was the dream,' he said, grinning.

The candle on the mantelshelf that had been wavering for some time suddenly went out, and the shadows crowded in. The autumn day was almost gone.

The dread of parting was elided in the haste of dressing and preparing; but the moment had to come, when they held each other at the door, in the unspeakable knowledge that this might be the last time.

'If the order comes tomorrow – ' he said.

'I'll come and tell you,' she said, 'somehow . . . before you . . .'

'Oh God, I can't bear it . . .'

She had no comfort to offer him. And she knew that no separation of prison walls, be they ever so thick, could surpass the agony of this severance, as she left him with a last glance at his hollow, unguarded face and at the sweet disorder of the room; and with an inward protest that cried, *Never again*?

Luke Hardwick left King's Lynn soon after noon, to be back in Peterborough by supper. The carriage-road across the Bedford Level, fair enough in summer, was liable to turn to mud in the autumn, and there was already a dome of cloud over the fens.

At the Bridge House the groom and stable-boy ran out with coach-lamps as the carriage crunched over the gravel. Caroline was there too, running to kiss her father.

'Hello, here's an odd welcome,' Luke said in surprise. 'What have you done, burnt the house down?'

150

'I think I'll box your ears next time!' Caroline said in mock outrage. 'Just pleased to see you. And I'm the mistress of the house for the moment. Mrs Mottram's labour started and mother's still with her.' Caroline was certainly pleased to see her father, but his joke had not been so far off the mark. She felt a compensating need to prove herself the dutiful daughter he must still think her, not the love-drugged stranger who a couple of hours ago had lain in a Frenchman's bed.

'I've had nothing to eat since this morning,' Luke said. 'I hope we've a good supper.'

'Surely,' Caroline said. 'A pie baked with my own hands. A thirty-mile ride and my cooking in one day – this will truly test your stomach, father.'

Luke laughed. Work and activity, as always, had restored his good humour.

'Oh, by the by,' he said as they went in. 'At Lynn I met up with the port agent, who receives the prisoner-of-war transports, and he'd just had word from the Transport Commissioners to continue with parole allocation. The government have patched matters up with the French over clothing supply and there's now no danger to parole. So we're not to lose our tame Frenchies after all. I'm glad they've seen sense. Good news, isn't it?'

'Very,' Caroline said faintly. 'Excuse me – I'll go and see about supper . . .'

In fact she ran up to her own room and, sprawled across her bed, between tears and laughter, offered up prayers of thankfulness to whatever sacred or profane power had spared her.

CHAPTER 6

1

With Richard gone, Charles resignedly tried to fit back into home life. He saw to the business of the estate with the steward, made returns on the rents to see the smaller tenants through what promised to be a hard winter, ordered repairs to fences and barns and drainage dykes. He rode with Frederick Amory, drilled with the Volunteers, attended a county meeting at the Peterborough Butter Cross and was shouted down, as usual, for calling for an end to the war.

Within a week he was bored.

Then came two letters. One was from Richard in London, saying he had his new commission: fourth lieutenant on board the *Olympia*, an eighty-gun three-decker, a renamed French prize newly fitted out to join the Western Squadron under Lord Bridport. He was leaving for Torbay immediately.

The other letter was from his father in London, saying in conciliatory tone that he was feeling the lack of company. It was like a missive from heaven.

He would go to London and stay with his father till the Christmas recess. His mother encouraged him: she had company enough with Edmund and Frances.

'You would only have chafed and fidgeted here,' she assured him. 'Take care, and enjoy yourself. And give my best love to your father. I'll need a stool to do this soon – I'm sure I must be shrinking,' she added, reaching up to kiss him.

He was so good-tempered, she thought, watching him go, that it made him difficult to read. She didn't mind him being restless, as long as whatever he was looking for really existed. To find out the goal was an illusion could be worse than not achieving it.

'If your mother could see us now,' George said, leaning back in his chair and filling his clay pipe. 'Why is it that men revert to this barbaric state when deprived of female society, even for a few days?'

The dinner-table was littered with the remains of the meal: jugs of ale, rabbit pie, and a pile of oyster-shells. Oysters were despised as a poor man's food, but both George and Charles had a liking for them, and a certain boyish complicity in their feast had restored the ease between them. Now they were drinking port. Charles leaned back lazily to stir the fire. These lodgings – half of a house in Buckingham Street – had been rented by George for his Parliamentary visits ever since he had become an MP, and they were supremely comfortable. And well-placed: you could get a boat to Westminster from the Adelphi Steps, and the coffee-houses of the Strand were close by.

'Well, at least I can report to mother that you have no London houris draping themselves around you,' said Charles.

'Good Lord, I wouldn't know where to look if they did. You know, I saw a young woman at a dinner the other day who was dressed in some transparent gauzy stuff that really, well, was hardly there. The Greek-statue idea again, I suppose, but so much for the chastity of the ancient world.'

Outside was the subdued noise of the city – the clatter of horses, the rumble of iron-shod wheels, the cries of late hawkers, the hubbub of the river, merging into a

153

susurrus like the sea, an underpinning of silence. 'A welcome change from the wind booming off the fen,' Charles said, cocking his ear to listen.

'So, who was at this county meeting?'

'Oh, it was chaired by Mr Squire and Mr Amory. A good number of farmers turned out. The resolution was about "voluntary contributions for the internal defence of the county in case of French invasion, or any riots et cetera". I got on my hind legs and objected to the notion of French invasion and riots being lumped together, as if our own people were just as much the enemy as the French.'

'And you were called a Jacobin for your pains,' said George with a smile.

'Precisely. Poor old Mr Amory looked bewildered. I think he's under the impression it's Louis XIV we're fighting.'

George laughed. 'Well, God knows who we are fighting. One hears all sorts of conflicting reports from France. It seems certain the Directory is discredited, but I don't know what will replace it.'

'General Bonaparte will have a hand in it, whatever it is,' Charles said. He glanced ruefully up at his father. 'Yes, I still have a sneaking admiration for him – if only because his name makes boobies like Parson Emmonsales foam at the mouth.' The Rev. Dr Emmonsales, Rector of Aysthorpe, was a sturdily anti-Jacobin clerical magistrate with whom both Charles and his father had clashed.

George passed his son the port. 'Come, we may as well finish it. Westminster always turns me into a toper. It must be our leader's example. They say Pitt's debts are chiefly due to his wine merchant . . . Well, boy, how long d'you intend staying?'

'Well – until you go home for Christmas – if you'll have me.'

'Excellent! These terms have been a trial lately. I know your mother would come if I asked her, but she's never really liked London.'

'No. Strange. I love it. Oh, I love the fens too, there's no place like them, but here I can – well – '

'Be a Jacobin to your heart's content?' said George.

'Something like that,' Charles said, the back of his neck tingling in spite of himself.

'I'm not mocking, Charles. Perhaps it's just when I see you get on your hobby-horse – no, that's a bad phrase – when I see you so passionate for these causes, I'm reminded of myself when younger. Perhaps,' George added diffidently, examining his glass, 'I don't like to be reminded that I've grown old and cynical.'

It was typical of Charles, who when irritated had mentally labelled his father as just that, to be pricked to his defence. 'Why, no one could accuse you of cynicism, father. You could have feathered your nest with some sinecure from Pitt long ago, if you hadn't stuck to your guns against his domestic policies. You are what I would consider the truly independent member.'

'Well,' said George, brightening, 'certainly I feel better about myself, when I consider someone like Wilberforce. Oh, I've always supported him on the abolition of the slave trade; but as for home issues . . . The slaves across the ocean he finds engaging, but the poor here on his own doorstep are not half so picturesque. And that sanctimonious odour of religion! He accounts it the devil's work to ride in a carriage on a Sunday. Strange how little religion there is in our family. I wondered if Edmund might lean to the Church, but he seems settled to painting. I suppose that's what he was doing when you left Morholm?'

'He thinks of nothing else.'

'Well, I'm no judge, but he seems to have abundant

talent. I've been thinking what to do for him. I'd be willing to set him to the Royal Academy schools, if they'll have him.'

'Now I'm here, father, is there anything I can do? Some research for a speech?'

George shook his head. 'I've not spoken yet this term. What you can do tomorrow evening is come with me to Mrs Thurrock's reception. Rich widow, likes to gather the statesmen of the land about her. Of course in netting the big fish she picks up a few small fry like me, and she's not a woman to slight. We needn't stay long.'

Charles was quite happy to stay. There were several big political fish to be seen. Mrs Thurrock took her statesmen wholesale, and there were representatives of both government and opposition at the reception. Canning, Pitt's secretary for foreign affairs, was here, and the Earl of Westmorland who was in the Cabinet, and Sheridan, the playwright turned politician, whom George knew well. Talk was lively. Charles was in his element.

It was a fine townhouse in Orchard Street, in the most fashionable part of London: every window was illuminated, making the carriage-crowded street as bright as day. Inside, amongst a great press of people, there were many dazzling women. As George had remarked, semi-nudity, together with absence of waist, seemed to be the fashion. Charles tried not to be a provincial booby and stare at the gorgeous creatures, in the finest and flimsiest muslins, with ostrich feathers and circlets of pearls in their hair and satin elbow-gloves.

'More of a turn-out than I expected,' George said. 'These autumn sittings are not popular. Country members don't like to miss the shooting season.'

Mid-way through the evening, after introductions to lots of people and several glasses of champagne, Charles went up the grand carpeted stairs in search of the cloak-rooms. The house was very large, and after using one of the new water-closets he took the wrong turn and found himself in an unlit corridor leading to bedrooms. He was about to turn back when he heard a noise behind a tall linen cupboard further down the corridor. The noise was a female voice saying 'Damn!' and it was followed by a grunt of exertion. Then what appeared to be shoes of some kind were hurled out one after another from behind the cupboard to smack against the opposite wall.

He went curiously to look, and found a young woman sitting on a chair hidden by the cupboard. She was massaging one stockinged foot.

'Well, what are you staring at?' she said, flushing, but continuing to rub her foot.

'I – I beg your pardon, I heard a noise and wondered if there was anything wrong . . .'

'Nothing,' she said, pointing, 'except those wretched shoes. They hurt like the devil.'

Charles bent to pick one up. It was made of fine gold material in flat sandal style. 'Very pretty,' he said, 'but certainly not comfortable.'

'It's supposed to be highly fashionable,' she said, attending to the other foot, 'but I refuse to cripple myself for the sake of fashion. You needn't stand there holding it like a shopman. I don't intend putting them on again.'

'What shall I do with them, then?'

She frowned, looked about her. 'There. That ghastly great Chinese vase or whatever it is. Drop them in there.'

'If you like. It seems a pity. I'm sure they were expensive.'

She laughed with brief scorn. 'I'm sure they were. What does that signify? Drop them in that vase.'

He obeyed, too bemused to do otherwise. The girl watched him and for the first time allowed him a small

157

smile. She was perhaps under twenty, but tall and slender: her gold-brown hair was dressed in the fashionable ringlets but with longer curls down the back. She had a fresh skin and arched eyebrows and a slightly tilted nose and almond eyes that were certainly beautiful if not good-tempered. 'And now I'm without a pair of shoes,' she said. 'What do you suppose I should do?'

'You are not – staying with Mrs Thurrock . . .?'

'With that grotesque, I should say not. I just sought a quiet corner where I could shed those infernal things without comment. Until *you* came blundering along.'

'My apologies again. But could you not rejoin the company just in your stockinged feet? The fashion is for classic simplicity. What could be more simple than that?'

'I hope you're not making fun of me.'

'Oh, I wouldn't dare.'

She looked as if she would snap at him, but her expression softened. 'I have an idea. But you must help me . . . Damn!'

There were voices at the end of the corridor: she pulled Charles by his waistcoat into the lee of the cupboard, putting one finger to her lips.

The voices receded as the people passed on.

'Now,' she said, 'there must be some shoes somewhere in these bedrooms. Either the gorgon's or her daughter's. While I go and look, you stand at the end of the passage and guard it.'

'Can you not merely ask Mrs Thurrock for the loan of a pair of shoes? I'm sure she – '

'Don't be a fool. Ask her for anything? Anyway, it's more fun to steal. Now, don't let anyone down here, d'you hear?'

'I'm at your command.'

Of course, he thought as he waited for her, if anyone did come this way, how would he stop them? He must

158

look pretty odd loitering here. Strangely, he didn't care at all.

But she was soon back, with an expression of triumph.

'There!' she said, hitching her skirts to show kid slippers. 'Just the thing. You know, the old hag has scores of wigs in there. I wonder if she wears different ones to arouse different lovers?'

'Does she have lovers?'

'Oh, positively. She has a *tendresse* for Parliament-men, that's why she holds these receptions. You're not a Parliament-man, are you?'

'No, I'm not anything.'

'You must be, or you wouldn't be here.' She looked him up and down critically. 'Let's see – you're the son of a North Country manufacturer who wants to turn genteel, and he's ushering you round London trying to marry you to a high-born girl.'

'Indeed I'm not!' said Charles, with some quickness; for only a saint is consistent in his ideals, and Charles's pride was touched.

'No,' she said, 'no, true, you don't have that thick-legged look that goes with trade.'

'You shouldn't trust in first impressions,' Charles said. 'After all, what do I know of you – except that you curse freely, have money enough to throw away expensive clothes, and feel no compulsion about stealing?'

She glared venomously at him: partly to forestall her reply, partly because he was thinking it, he added: 'And that you are extremely beautiful.'

Her look changed, became narrowly assessing and also, he thought, amused.

'I think I should like you if you weren't so impertinent,' she said, stepping past him, and was quickly gone.

* * *

159

The girl was nowhere to be seen in the crowds of people downstairs; and Charles almost forgot about her when his father introduced him to someone he had longed to meet. Sir Francis Burdett was a youngish Member of Parliament, hugely rich and squirish in appearance, but a prominent Radical whom Charles greatly admired. And it was gratifying to find themselves quickly on common ground. When the Radical associations, the London Corresponding Society and the United Englishmen, had been forcibly closed down last year many of their members had been imprisoned without trial. They were still there, in Cold Bath Fields prison, and Charles thought it a scandal. They talked also of the Combination Act that had just been passed strengthening legislation against any form of trade union. In the past five years, Charles said, the Government had ensured that no one could say, write or demonstrate in any way against them. Last year Gilbert Wakefield, a harmless scholar, had been sent to prison for suggesting in a pamphlet that the condition of the poor could hardly be made worse if the French did invade: he had died soon after his release.

Before they parted, Burdett invited Charles to dinner at his house in Piccadilly. Charles felt invigorated and liberated. The Government had not driven every fellow spirit underground after all.

His father had quietly absented himself. When Charles found him again and told him of his invitation he added: 'Do you mind, father?'

'You're your own man, Charles,' George said. 'Please don't think of yourself as here on any sort of condition. I don't dislike Burdett, though he's too hot-headed for me.'

'But a few hot-heads is what the country needs,' began Charles excitedly. He stopped and grinned at his father. 'Sorry.'

There was music in another room, and when they went

in to listen Charles spotted the shoe-girl, arm-in-arm with a man.

The man lifted his hand in salute to George. 'D'you know that gentleman?' Charles asked.

'Yes, slightly,' George said. 'Sir Thomas Fairburn. I'll introduce you.'

They were coming over. Charles was surprised that the young woman should be married. The surprise was not unmixed with other emotions, but perhaps it was after all to be anticipated. The man was as elegant and good-looking as his partner: starched cravat, dress coat, fashionably-dishevelled hair.

'Mr Hardwick,' he said, 'glad to see you. Some of us have made the effort, eh? How long have you been up?'

'A few weeks. Sir Thomas, may I present my son, Charles. Sir Thomas Fairburn, Miss Lydia Fairburn.'

Charles just managed to recover himself in time to take the man's proffered hand. 'How d'you do, Mr Hardwick. Haven't seen you in town before.'

'I have, father,' said the girl. 'This gentleman once showed me a little chivalry, though I swore him to secrecy.'

Sir Thomas looked from one to the other. 'When was this?'

'Oh! Only this evening. It was upstairs, but quite decent. I – suffered a little embarrassment with my dress, and this gentleman obligingly acted the part of a screen while I made the adjustment.'

Sir Thomas smiled, and looked at Charles as if to say, 'Incorrigible.' 'And you received no thanks, sir, if I know my daughter.'

'I was happy merely to be of assistance,' Charles said. The girl – Lydia – was looking at him as if daring him to tell the true story.

They went in to supper with the Fairburns: but the girl

161

– deliberately? – took George's arm and confined her talk to him. Charles was left with Sir Thomas, who was an agreeable and easy companion.

Charles's mistake was forgivable: Sir Thomas certainly looked young enough to be Lydia's husband rather than her father. He had a fine aquiline patrician face and sensitive white hands. He talked about his place up near Newmarket, where he bred racehorses; but he talked sensibly, without the airy drawl that often infuriated Charles in such men. 'One misses the shooting, coming up for this early session,' Sir Thomas said. 'But then one doesn't go into Parliament for pleasure. Are you to follow your father into political life, Mr Hardwick?'

'It may be, in the future,' Charles said diffidently.

Sir Thomas nodded. 'He's a much respected man at Westminster. Nobody's fool. I hope my daughter didn't embarrass you at all, sir.'

'Why, no, not at all.'

Sir Thomas smiled, an attractive and affectionate smile. 'Well, she's embarrassed me in public before. On one occasion at a dinner when I had displeased her she took her revenge by hailing a footman as "dear brother Tom!" and loudly claiming he was an illegitimate son whom I refused to acknowledge.' He shook his head fondly. Charles at that moment intercepted a glance of innocent sweetness from Lydia, as if she knew what was being said about her. 'I think she misses a mother's influence,' Sir Thomas went on.

'Her mother is not living?'

'Died some twelve years since.'

'I'm sorry.'

'I still miss her – for when I look at Lydia I see her mother in her.'

When they left the supper-room Charles managed to manoeuvre himself near to Lydia, though she still seemed provokingly bent on ignoring him. 'Well,' he said, 'so you know my thick-legged manufacturer of a father after all.'

She tossed her head. 'A very distinguished-looking man, I have always thought. Infinitely preferable to the young sprigs and puppies one has to meet.'

'And which am I?'

She glanced at him from lowered lashes, a smile curling her lips. 'Altogether too serious to be either.'

'Will I see you again, Miss Fairburn?'

'Oh, Lord knows,' she said, moving away from him and waving to someone across the room. With a last turn of her long beautiful neck she said: 'I've been known to ride the Ring at Hyde Park.'

It was raining when Charles and his father left the reception, and hackney-coaches were hard to come by. They walked up to Portman Square to see if one could be got there, and George answered Charles's questions about Sir Thomas Fairburn.

'Oh, I've known him slightly, from the House, for a few years,' George said. 'He owns the borough of Port-hale in Cornwall – one of these west country rotten boroughs, a few fishing cottages returning two MPs. I doubt he's ever been there. He bought the borough from the Falmouth family some years ago. He sits one seat himself and nominates the other member.'

'He must be wealthy.'

'Well, yes. The Fairburns are an old Suffolk family, but Sir Thomas was only from a minor branch and happened to get the estate near Newmarket by entail. He sold part of the land and knocked down the old house and began building a great gothic place on the site – still not finished, I hear. When he bought the Cornish borough he pledged its seats to the government: he's a strong Pittite, very conservative, gives his support to every repressive measure. In reward he got a knighthood a few years ago, and

163

he's obviously hoping to get a baronetcy. And he also got a sinecure from Pitt – Patent Inspector of Prosecutions for the Customs. A post that consists chiefly of a large salary. It enables him to go on building that great folly of a house and breeding his racehorses. He lives high, squiring that pretty daughter around: people often think they're man and wife – he looks well for forty. In short he's the epitome of place-seeking corruption and reaction. It even turns my stomach, so I can imagine how you feel.'

'Yes . . . A pity.'

'Why?'

'Oh – well,' said Charles, 'personally he's not dislikeable. I mean, it's always annoying when the enemy has a certain charm.'

The rest of Charles's stay in London was formed of two strands, both exciting. He dined at Burdett's house, and met other men of Radical sympathies. He met a printer who had been prosecuted for sedition no less than eight times, had been gaoled for printing Tom Paine's anti-religious *Age of Reason*, and had been one of the founding members of the London Corresponding Society. Charles shook this man's rough hand with profound reverence. He was introduced to Godwin, whose *Political Justice* Charles had read over and over, and whose late wife had been Mary Wollstonecraft the feminist. He came home to the Buckingham Street lodgings at night with his head spinning with arguments for the sovereignty of the people and universal suffrage.

To his father's surprise, he also took to riding in Hyde Park. His hired nag looked a poor thing amongst the sleek thoroughbreds on the backs of which young bucks sat erect as lancers; but then he was not there to show himself off.

He didn't see her: he didn't know what he expected to

say to her if he did. Then it was December, and there was news that Parliament was to adjourn in a week. He rode one last time, and there she was, cantering about the Ring on a jet-black mare, elegant in a narrow-waisted riding-habit and every inch the horsewoman.

He spurred his horse alongside her. She glanced round with the merest flicker of surprise.

'Mr Charles Hardwick,' she said.

'Miss Lydia Fairburn.'

The horses' hoofbeats rang out on the frosted ground.

'Is that poor animal yours?' she said.

'No. I suppose that rich animal is yours.'

She laughed. 'How you like to upbraid me! Well, I can assure you I shall not cast Jessamine aside as I did my shoes. Do you ride in the Park often, Mr Charles Hardwick?'

'Oftener than you, it would seem.'

'You don't mean you've been coming here looking for me? You odd creature! It's a wonder you haven't killed that poor beast.'

'I fear I will, unless we may slacken our pace a little.'

'Oh, you may go slower if you like,' she said, with a flick of her riding-crop. 'Jessamine can't bear to linger, and neither can I.'

'Shall you linger in London, now Parliament closes?'

'What's that to you?' she said, with a challenging glance. The exercise had brought a brilliancy to her fair complexion.

'What is it to me? Something. I won't say how much.'

She slackened her reins slightly. 'We leave for the country tomorrow. There, will that do?'

'Not really. Will you return to London in the new year?'

'Oh, who can look that far ahead? Father perhaps. Myself perhaps not. I may go to stay with friends.'

'Of whom I am not one.'

She shrugged. 'Why, I hardly know you.'

'True. And I would like to repair the deficiency.'

'Oh, I already have plenty of friends,' she said; then seemed to relent, and added: 'I think I should have given you one of those shoes. Then you could use it to find me. Like Cinderella.'

'Oh, no. Cinderella was much more deserving.'

She narrowed her eyes at him. He was beginning to realize that meant she was rather pleased with an answer. 'And what makes you think you are deserving to be a Prince?'

'Hope, Miss Fairburn. Hope only.'

'Well, you must *hope* to see me in London next season,' she said with a smile, and tightened the reins again. She was too fast for him, and had soon ridden away.

CHAPTER 7

1

It would have been hard for Caroline to have explained even to herself how she got through the months as winter deepened and the eighteenth century died. How she drew on more and more resources of deceit and subterfuge to continue to meet Antoine: how she discovered new aspects of her self, most of all the strength of the will when it had the fulfilment of passion as its object. Probably her mother and father noticed some change in her: she knew she felt remote from them, not indifferent but uninvolved – the Morholm family likewise. Her emotional horizons were expanding, but so, constantly, was her love for Antoine, and it took up all the room and more.

She could not have explained how the days became a steely monochrome in which the only living patches of colour were the hours spent with Antoine; how sometimes they did nothing but sit together in his room, watching the square of sky at his window and the starlings that came to the sill for the crumbs he left there; how they lost themselves down winding paths of talk, where her most inward desires and fears were laid before him, where the village of Torcy, with its ruined tower like in her straw picture and its empty church and its milkmaids in wooden pattens and its mill where Monsieur Simond lived with his twelve children, became as real to her as the stooping hamlets of the fens.

Outside – in the world beyond Antoine's room – the

British army in Holland retreated and was finally evacuated amid disillusion and acrimony with the Russian allies. People said there was no use in sending our armies to the Continent: let Europe take care of itself and the Navy take care of us. In France General Bonaparte overthrew the Directory and recreated the Constitution as a Consulate with himself as First Consul: heads nodded in England and said they always knew the Revolution would end in military government.

And in Little's Yard Caroline lay in her lover's arms and looked at his hand lying loosely across her stomach and thought: that hand is so beautiful. No other hand is precisely like that hand. I can't live without these hands, without them touching me, holding me, being part of my life.

It began to be very cold in December and Antoine's garret, stuffy in summer, took on a chill that the small fire could not dissipate. Sometimes there was ice inside the window. The frost set in hard across the flood-water of the Fletton marshes and soon there was skating there and on Borough Fen. The sun cast its winter rays across the frozen levels like gilt: race-tracks were marked out with barrels and there were bandy-matches – a kind of quoits with sticks and a lot of broken bones – and braziers and hot chestnuts on the ice. One day Antoine went there with some of the other paroled officers to try skating, and when she met him in his room later he was bruised and exhausted.

'Roubillard fell and said his leg was broken,' he said. 'I think there was nothing badly wrong but we had to carry him home. He is a fat fellow, too heavy, it was like carrying an elephant.'

He laughed, but crossly. He was looking very tired and chilled as he stretched his hands out to the fire. His face had the tight dogged look of a boy who has stayed up too long.

'Did you get a doctor to see him?' she asked.

'Doctor, no. There was nothing wrong, he was just making a fuss as usual. I fell too, it was nothing.' He rolled back his sleeve to examine his elbow, gave it up.

'Let me see.'

'It's nothing, I say.' He stared before him, then rubbed his eyes. 'I'm sorry. I don't know what's wrong with me to make me talk like this.'

'You're tired and cold,' she said, sitting on the floor beside him and leaning her cheek against his leg. He nodded, but still with a faint sulkiness.

'Sometimes the river freezes too,' she said, 'and they hold a fair on it by the bridge.'

'The marshes are all frozen past Fletton,' he said. He took his clay pipe from the mantelshelf, held it irresolutely. 'All was grey and white, *uniforme* – dykes and fields and paths all joined.' He put the pipe down. 'I could see all the way past the turnpike road, past the mill, the London road. Freedom. And I was tempted to walk. For a moment I almost did so.'

Something in his tone made her very still.

'And why didn't you?' she said.

He shook his head, made an impatient gesture.

'Why didn't you?' she persisted.

'You know why.'

'I hope I do . . .'

'Because of you, of course it is because of you.' He touched her hair. 'But – just knowing I could not go, it made me feel so strange, so tempted. I felt – a *prisoner* . . . Forgive me, Caroline. I'm fit for nothing today, a foul mood. It's just – '

'I know, I know.' She stroked his knee. Then she looked soberly up at him. 'What if I went with you?'

He smiled gently. 'You're very sweet.'

'I mean it. What if I went with you?'

He shrugged, frowning. 'Where? I am a prisoner-of-war, once I break my parole they will search for me, your father – '

'To France. What if I went with you to France?'

His hand was still moving absently on her hair while he stared blankly into the fire. 'You mean . . . Oh, but it is impossible.'

'I don't think it's impossible. But would you want it? If I were to escape with you to France?'

'Caroline . . .' His hand on her hair fell still. 'Think what you are saying.'

'I know what I'm saying. If you would take me with you, that's all that matters. You see – ' she moved a little away from him, wanting to talk clearly without the delicious distraction of his touch, and knelt to stir the fire – 'I've been thinking of this for some time. Because I feel it too – when you said you felt a prisoner: I feel that too. Meeting in this way, always lying, hiding – it cheapens everything. Just for once I would like to walk arm-in-arm with you, to listen to music with you, to sleep beside you after making love and then wake up and make love again, and watch the dawn come up together, without haste and fear. Antoine, listen.' He had risen and walked to the window. 'As I say, I've been thinking of this. Knowing I want to be with you always, *openly*. And that cannot be here, not anywhere in England. Because you're still an enemy prisoner-of-war, who happens to have a few privileges, and we could run as far as Land's End and you'd still be a hunted man. And I would be a hunted woman, come to that, for I'm not twenty-one. And there's no knowing when the war will end – it could go on for years. And so there's only one thing to do. If you jump your parole I will come with you to France.'

She had rehearsed this avowal mentally, over and over, till it had become a catechism for her, but now it was out she was overtaken by a feverish nervousness. 'Antoine?' He still had his back to her. 'What do you say?'

He seemed to give a kind of shudder, and said quietly, as if talking to himself, 'You – you would do that for me . . . But – it's not possible . . .'

'Perhaps you haven't believed me, when I've said how much I love you.' Her only fear at this moment was that he would not accept her idea – would not want her to go with him to France. There could be no worse misery than that.

'To escape . . . to be free . . . France . . .' His voice was hushed. He turned, looking suddenly exhilarated, as if he had seen a vision. 'Oh, Caroline, what kind god sent you to me?'

She jumped up and embraced him, covered him with kisses. 'Of course,' she said, 'with all my deep thinking, I don't know how we could get across to France. We can't walk gaily on to the packet-boat at Dover. "Miss Hardwick and Captain Clairet, escaped prisoner-of-war. Purpose of visit, elopement." But then there are no packet-boats now, of course, no traffic at all . . . All the French ports are closed to English ships.'

There were noises on the stairs, and they were immediately silent as usual.

When it was quiet she went on: 'You see, you must report to my father every Tuesday and Saturday, so that means a maximum of four days before you are missed. But I – well, I'd be missed straight away.'

'We are – what, fifty miles from the sea here?'

'The nearest coastal port is King's Lynn, but that deals mainly in merchant shipping to the north. Besides, there's no way of getting to France now. One might as well try to fly to the moon.' She rubbed a hand across her flushed cheeks, feeling foolish. Her ideas, having run so far, had collapsed with exhaustion.

'It *has* been done,' Antoine said slowly. He moved back to the fire, stood leaning on the mantelshelf and staring into the flames. 'There have been escapes from Norman Cross. Most men have been recaptured, but a few have got away to France. I was speaking to Lieutenant Guyot not long ago. He was in Norman Cross for a time, when his papers were misplaced. When he was there, a man got away by hiding in one of the dung-carts that go in and out of the prison. The man had been involved in smuggling before the war. He said he was going to Yarmouth, where there were people who would help him – smugglers he knew, old associates.'

'Smuggling still goes on?'

'Oh, yes. War never stops it. Smugglers are brothers.'

'And this man got away?'

'He was never recaptured.'

'Yarmouth,' she said. 'I've heard of smugglers all along that coast, but I've always thought they were just tales . . .'

Caroline was surprised at her own flat calm in talking of these things. To leave her country, her family, her friends: to sever herself from all of them, certainly for as long as the war went on, perhaps for ever; to attempt a clandestine flight, fraught with risk, with a fugitive French prisoner . . . For one fleeting second her spirit shrank from the whole idea – from Antoine and all involvement with him – and wished itself back in the trivial safety of her old life, gossiping with Lucy Squire over fashion-plates. But the second passed. The image was a sickly falsehood. Only Antoine was real.

'Did your friend say this man's name?'

'He may have done – I don't remember. But, even so – '

172

'If we knew his name I could go to the prison and ask after him. Someone at the market might know him, or know of him. A little money would go a long way.'

She touched his arm. He patted her hand briefly, but moved restlessly back to the window, his eyes averted from hers. 'Torcy,' he said, his voice growing soft and self-communing again. 'Free. Home . . . Yes. I would give up the sea. Return to farming the land. I could not continue to fight the English – it would be a mockery. And perhaps Bonaparte will make France stable again, and bring peace . . .' He turned to her. 'But there is so little I can do. You must take on so much.'

'The first thing you can do is see Lieutenant Guyot again and find out the name of the man who escaped. Then – oh, dear, Antoine – ' the tension of seriousness seemed to slip a little inside her and she half-laughed and half-sobbed – 'what will your father say when you bring me home to your village?'

After a moment he reached out to caress her, laughing a little hollowly too. 'One step at a time, my dear,' he said, and his hand trembled. 'Time enough to think of that. Let us – take one step at a time.'

The name of the prisoner who had escaped was Jean-Baptiste Massieu. That was the easy part. Now she must find a way of going to Norman Cross.

The opportunity came with the return from school, in the third week of December, of her brother Nicholas.

He was nearly seventeen now, a brisk and stocky lad with short curly hair and a pink and white complexion that made him look like an overgrown cherub. He was genial, with a quick temper like his father, and an abounding practical curiosity. As a boy, clocks and watches had never been safe from him: he always wanted to take them apart, and eventually he was allowed to because he could put them together again so unerringly. Luke had great hopes of him eventually taking control of the mercantile house. Between him and Caroline there had always been an easy affection: he had a low opinion of girls generally, but as she had never minded getting her skirts muddy, or shrunk from his wriggling collections of insects, he considered her a sort of honorary boy.

In telling him the news of the last few months she carefully placed hints about her visit to Norman Cross and how fascinating it had been. No more was needed. He was all eagerness to see for himself. So, Nicholas furnished both pretext and escort: he was a sufficiently well-grown youth to provide the protection that young ladies were universally supposed to need in riding down country roads.

'Dear life, I'd forgot what a quiet country this is,' Nicholas said as they set out on the Yaxley road. 'Last month the master took some of us on an outing to the North. To see Sheffield, and Leeds. We came to Sheffield in the evening, and the prospect from a distance is like – well, hell, I suppose – there are furnaces burning everywhere, and scores of windows lit in the great manufactories . . . But it's more exciting than hellish. There's power burgeoning there, more power than in a ship-of-the-line or an army or a court. I should love you to see it, Caro. It's a different world, the very people seem foreign.'

'I should love to see it, indeed,' said Caroline. She was sickly aware that here was another person very dear to her whom she was deceiving, and planning to go away from and perhaps never see again: unwittingly, he was conniving at it. She drove the thought away and fixed her mind on her talisman image – that of herself and Antoine looking up at the ruined tower in his village, hand-in-hand, hiding no longer.

The market inside the gate was busy as ever. For some

time Nicholas walked round with her; it was only when he began to talk with one of the militia guards – about how the camp was run and how it was drained and supplied with water – that she was able to slip away.

She found the elderly prisoner who had sold her the straw tower. To her surprise he recognized her, winking at her while a disdainful lady pawed the trinkets on his stall. When she had moved on he said: '*Mademoiselle* – Claude never forgets. You bought a picture, yes? I have more. *Voici, la madone* – *la nativité* – very beautiful, just right for the season, yes? *Noël*. Yes, I am still Christian, speak it softly! Or this – '

'Monsieur,' she said, 'I wish to ask you a question.'

The old man cocked his head on one side and stroked his beard.

'Do you – did you know of a man called Jean-Baptiste Massieu?'

The old man regarded her with a bright neutral eye, like a tame bird.

'He escaped, I believe,' she went on, 'and got away from England. At Yarmouth?'

He shrugged and looked at the sky, as if anything were possible.

'Please,' she said. 'I'm not some spy or informer. I'm – I'm trying to help someone else escape from England. A Frenchman. Your countryman. And we hear that Massieu found a way – had some contacts. Please, you must believe me.'

The old man wiped a little dust from an inlaid tea-caddy, rearranged it on the trestle. 'I believe you, perhaps, mademoiselle. But, *n'importe*. I did not know Massieu. He was in a different barrack to me.'

'But there must be someone who knew him? Who knew his plans? Please help me . . .' She drew out a sovereign from her reticule and laid it discreetly on the stall. 'I am in earnest.'

The old man put a finger on the coin, slid it towards him. Then he glanced round. There were no guards close by. He gave a short whistle to a prisoner nearby who was bargaining with a farmer over sacks of beans. 'Eh, Vierny. *Ici.*'

They talked for several minutes in a rapid dialectal French she could not follow. The other prisoner regarded her the whole time with deep suspicion. At last he nodded and moved away.

'Vierny was in the same barrack as Massieu,' the old man said, dropping his voice. 'He says Massieu was a boastful fellow and was always saying how he would run away and not be caught. He says, perhaps he can find out who are these people who helped Massieu.' He stopped and studied Caroline's face.

'Then – will you do it? Will you help?'

The old man grinned, engagingly. 'It will need money, mademoiselle. Others must be given something, if they will talk, you see?'

She found a handful of silver: she was shaking so much she almost dropped it. The old man laughed and pocketed the money. 'Never fear, mademoiselle. Claude will find it out for you. Because of your pretty face. You tell me, perhaps, who is this lucky Frenchman you help?'

'I'm afraid I can't. He's – he's on parole. I can't say more.'

'Ah, *un officier. D'accord.* Will you take then a little warning from Claude?'

She nodded.

'I have been here two years. I was in the first boat of prisoners to come here. Many prisoners have tried to get away. I have seen a man shot trying to climb the fence. *Pan!* dead. A prisoner tries to get away – prisoner, officer

176

on parole, no matter – the soldiers will seek him, and if he is caught, he goes to the hulks. Massieu was very lucky. That is all. I say this because of your pretty face. But, Claude will try to find out what you wish to know,' he concluded with a beam.

Perhaps Antoine's father is like this, she thought. It seemed unlikely, but she rather hoped so. 'Thank you, monsieur. You will be here next week?'

'*Comme toujours*.'

She was ready to go before Nicholas, who was still eagerly examining everything that could be seen of the camp. 'Well, did you buy no straw pictures this time, Caro?' he said as they mounted their horses at the gate. 'You were having a rare pi-jaw with that old Frenchie.'

'No,' she said. 'Just testing out my French.'

Throughout the following week Caroline devoted herself to helping the churchwardens organize a subscription for relief of the poor in Boongate and Fengate. It occupied her mind and was some relief to a conscience increasingly bowed by the burden of continual deception. In her meetings with Antoine they talked little about their plan: they were both waiting anxiously for Sunday and the news of Jean-Baptiste Massieu. They were unable – and even afraid – to look beyond that.

How she was to contrive to get to Norman Cross again she did not know: it had to be done, that was all. When Sunday came she agonized for an hour, then simply told her parents nothing and walked out to the stables and had her horse saddled and rode out. She should be back in less than two hours. She would just have to say she had taken a sudden fancy to go riding – unlikely, as she had never done such a thing in her life.

At the camp gate a militiaman helped her tether her horse and seemed disposed to stay with her as she entered the market. He was very young and there was a valiant attempt at a moustache on his upper lip which he stroked anxiously. Eventually she got rid of him by saying she was looking for an ornamental powder-flask for her husband, who was a dead shot with a pistol.

The old man Claude smiled when he saw her, and then to her horror laughed heartily.

'Mademoiselle, I beg you, do not look so sad! It was easier than I thought. Trust me. Now, how about this fan, fine workmanship . . .'

She thought he was teasing her, then realized a guard was passing close by. She examined the fan until he had gone.

'Ah, bad things happening this week!' Claude sighed. 'They are watching us close. The gamblers fell to fighting – always the gamblers! One was stabbed – he did not die, *grâce à Dieu*. And, we have sickness. *La fièvre typhoïde*. Very bad. But, Claude is never sick. Well, mademoiselle – you have not changed your mind?'

'No. Please, monsieur – '

'*Bien, bien*, I have the information. Vierny asked the friends of Jean-Baptiste Massieu. It was well-known. Massieu said to them, if ever they follow him and escape, go to Yarmouth, where he had friends in the trade. An inn called the White Swan. Ask for Rattler of the Haven, and mention Massieu's name.' Claude tapped his forehead. 'Always a good memory. Rattler of the Haven. *Mais c'est bizarre.*'

'Oh, monsieur, I wish there were no people watching – I would give you a kiss,' Caroline said.

Claude laughed. 'English ladies do not kiss!' he said, and looked unabashed at her purse.

'Of course, of course.' Scarcely bothering to conceal it, she gave the astonished Claude ten pounds.

178

After Christmas the frosts gave way to rain and buffeting wind. The crossing from Yarmouth would not be pleasant, Antoine warned.

They were in his room, with a paper on the desk before them, recording all the details of their plan.

There was the question of money. Antoine got the odd gift from home, when the mails got through, but it was chiefly up to Caroline. She had, after giving ten to Claude at the prison camp, about twenty-five pounds in a drawer in her room. She had also saved her dress allowances from her father, sitting up at night to alter one of her old gowns to make it look like a new one in case anybody should ask. Together they had about forty pounds.

She had enquired at the Angel about travel to Yarmouth. The Norwich Self-Defence coach could make the journey to Norwich in a day in summer, but in winter the trip was split with a night spent at Swaffham. From Norwich there were several coaches to Yarmouth, and passenger-wherries that went by the River Yare. The cost to Norwich was £1 1s 6d inside, with a charge for extra luggage.

The other expenses they had to consider were the night spent at King's Lynn; and the smugglers. She did not suppose they would carry them across for nothing. There was the matter of travel in France once they landed, but that was too vague a futurity to trouble them. Just to get safely on French soil was the main thing. From then on Antoine would carry the responsibility.

In the meantime she had been doing some smuggling herself – bringing pieces of clothing to Antoine's room. It would be impossible for him to get very far in a French captain's uniform. An old buff waistcoat and a pair of top-boots that had belonged to her brother were easily procured. A coat was a different matter. Her brother's old coats would be too small. Her father, a man without personal vanity, had only two coats in the world, so one would be missed. In the end she went to Peterborough market and bought, second-hand, a plain black riding-coat, explaining it to the curious vendor as a gift for a servant. Antoine's cocked hat, with the gold trimming removed, would pass as an English bicorne.

Antoine would report to her father with the other officers as usual on the Tuesday. On the Wednesday morning, very early, she would slip out of the house, carrying her minimum of luggage, and walk to the Angel and board the Norwich coach which left at six-thirty. Antoine, meanwhile, would walk out of the city, in his civilian outfit, to the village of Eye and join the coach there: there might be risk, however small, in their boarding the coach together. From there to Yarmouth, if any enquiries came, they had decided Antoine would be a German merchant travelling on business, and Caroline his English wife: Yarmouth had strong ties with Hamburg.

They went over the plan time and time again, searching for flaws, until they were tired and fretful with it.

'And you're sure Captain Roubillard or none of the others will notice you're gone and say something?' she said.

'Oh, they will perhaps notice, but I think they will realize I have broken my parole and hold their tongues.' Antoine stretched his arms to the ceiling, as if he would push away its lowering beams. 'Break my parole . . . Well, there is no other way.'

'Other officers have done it before,' she said. And been recaptured and put in the prison-hulks, said the unacknowledged fear.

180

She noticed the shadows under his eyes. 'You didn't sleep well again, did you?' she said. He shook his head, frowning away from her.

She was finding it difficult herself to present a normal appearance at home. What would her parents think of her? Her imagination shrank from the thought of them discovering her elopement. She returned again, obsessively, to the details of the plan, to shut out the spectacle of its great and irrevocable consequences.

3

Susannah Milton and Stephen Downes were married on Saturday 28 December 1799 at St John's Church, Peterborough.

Since their engagement party had been so extravagant there was only a small wedding-breakfast, in the upper room of the Butter Cross, for family and a few friends. Caroline did not have a tendency to cry at weddings, but she felt like crying at this one. It was probably the last time she would see all her family together.

Susannah, like a compact butterfly in satin and veil – well, with her marriage she was rather moving out of their orbit anyway, but still, never to see her again – what would she say, sensible, gentle Susannah? She would think her mad. Her Uncle and Aunt Milton, watching their daughter with proud perplexity – her aunt Julia's wayward hair already coming undone, her uncle Henry with his arm gently round hers in that carelessly affectionate way they had . . . what would they say? Perhaps they might understand a little. And the Morholm family, who were so close and so dear to her – her kind, distinguished Uncle George and practical Aunt Mary – they would be disappointed in her; and her Morholm cousins, Edmund who was going to be an artist and Frances who she suspected would grow up either very plain or very beautiful . . . would she never see them develop to adulthood?

And Charles, her favourite cousin and confidant, whom she could no longer confide in. What made it worse was that he seemed in exceptionally high spirits since his return from London with his father a couple of weeks ago, and they were spirits she could not match.

'I spent my time being a thorough Jacobin, I'm afraid,' Charles told her. 'I actually dined with Burdett. A man of excellent Radical principles, worth half of those pig-headed asses in Westminster. Can one have a pig-headed ass? Anyway, I wormed my way into several circles whose politics would make Parson Emmonsales send for the Dragoons. And I managed not to antagonize poor father too much. I may go with him again in January when Parliament reopens.'

Charles and his father were still talking amicably when they left the reception and began the ride home. Just before Christmas they had had the traditional 'Gooding Day' at Morholm, when they gave coal and food to the poor of the village, but there was still so much distress in the country that they discussed other measures. George had been corresponding with other liberal-minded MPs on the question of relief for the poor from the public funds.

'Relief from the public funds, eh? We must ask Parson Emmonsales about that,' said Charles. '"Setting a bounty on idleness and vice" would be the reply, I think.'

'Speaking of reaction,' George said, gripping his hat in the turbulent wind, 'I was talking to Stephen Downes about his place in Norfolk, and we got on to the subject of improvements, and I mentioned our friend Sir Thomas Fairburn and that gothic mausoleum he's building near Newmarket. It turns out that Stephen's a friend of the

Fairburns – families have been on good terms for years. Says Fairburn's spending a mint of money.'

'Indeed?' said Charles. While he sounded indifferent, the tantalizing image of Lydia Fairburn flashed on his mind. It was immediately followed by the memory of his cousin Susannah's insistence that he must come and stay with her and her new husband at Great Baston as soon as ever he could. 'We mean to have lots of company, winter or summer,' she had said.

If there was a way to meet Lydia again, that was certainly more promising than going to London and merely hoping. If he could get Susannah and Stephen to invite the Fairburns to Great Baston . . . Yes . . . he was full of unmistakable excitement at the thought. That his father had made his hint with this in mind – and must therefore have discerned his interest in Sir Thomas Fairburn's skittish daughter – did not occur to Charles till later, and then with mild surprise. The most candid of us consider our thoughts generally impenetrable to others – and indeed it was with surprise that Charles admitted to himself that he had been thinking about Lydia Fairburn almost constantly for the last fortnight.

4

The new century stole in without fanfares and glory. January 1800 was cold and wet, with the colourless skies and pelting rain and sleet that could make the fenland, so brilliant and generous in spring and summer, seem like the last place on earth, naked and comfortless under its vault of cloud.

There were floods around Wisbech, and the Nene swelled over the wharf and came up to the garden at the

Bridge House. The carriage-roads east were in an appalling state. Caroline and Antoine fixed the day of their flight for Wednesday the 8th, postponed it for the weather, postponed it again. The waiting frayed the nerves. In one snatched meeting, to her astonishment, they quarrelled. It was over quickly and she held him wordlessly, alarmed.

The rain and wind eased off in the third week, and it was settled. Wednesday the 22nd. They could wait no longer.

On the Tuesday Antoine reported as usual to the Bridge House to collect his allowance. As he was leaving, Caroline's mother called to him from the parlour and talked to him about the dreadful weather.

'I'm afraid this has given you no very high opinion of the English climate,' Rebecca said.

'Oh, it is not so bad, Mrs Hardwick,' he said. 'In France where I live, in Normandy, we often have very cruel winters. Now, the south of France is a very different matter . . .'

Caroline could see he was uneasy. Yet, he was still as open and courteous as ever with her mother. And a wish went through her, acute as a physical pain, that someone should burst in and announce the war was over and the English and French were friends and all the difficulties were removed, and she could announce Antoine as her intended and receive her parents' blessing.

It was this continuing feeling that prompted her that evening, when she was alone with her mother, to talk about her parents' marriage: how Rebecca's father had disapproved, how they had had to marry in secret.

Some last desperate hope was in her of reconciling her forbidden liaison with Antoine to her parents: somehow, magically, a common ground would open out between

184

them, the horrible misshapen fragments of life would suddenly fit together to a perfect pattern.

But all she could say was: 'Did you – did you not mind leaving your family to marry father?'

'Oh, I minded, of course,' Rebecca said. 'But there was no other way for us. Your grandfather was such a stern, domineering man, and it was all up to him. There was nothing but hostility between me and him by then, so it didn't matter so much. I was of age. The rest of the family soon came to terms with it. I hate to sound like a wise old matron, but time is a great healer. That's one of the few old saws that's true.'

But there were some wounds, Caroline thought, that would go too deep to heal.

She kissed her mother before going to bed. Her father was in his study; Nicholas was spending the night with friends at Market Deeping. She went into the study, and her father, at his desk, put up an absent-minded cheek to be kissed.

She felt like a murderer.

She dozed a while in an armchair in her bedroom. In the small hours she quietly began packing clothes into two carpet-bags. So many trinkets and souvenirs had to be left behind, but that was for the best. She placed the straw picture of the tower in the top of her luggage. That was to have pride of place in her and Antoine's sitting-room – a reminder of how they had been brought together, of imprisonment and exile and how they had salvaged hope and happiness from it.

185

CHAPTER 8

1

It was still dark when Caroline slipped downstairs and unbolted the front door. No one was stirring. Even the spaniel in his basket in the hall merely cocked one eye open and then settled himself again as if refraining from comment.

Outside there was mist on the river, and the shape of a barge loomed slow and stately between the bare willows. There was a wasted slip of moon. A few birds were waking.

She did not look back at the Bridge House: she couldn't trust herself. She thought with distress of the letter she had left in her bedroom. It had resolved into a series of apologies, a desperate begging for forgiveness. Nothing she could write could present her as anything but a betrayer.

In spite of the early hour, the city was by no means empty. Wednesday was market day and there were waggons rolling up Broad Bridge Street, loaded with hides and ducks and barrels of fish from the fens. She passed several people, including the watchman with his lantern and rattle who gave her a long look. A woman opened her front door to throw out the slops. An ostler led two horses back from grass. Everyone, she imagined, was ready to shout, *Look! Where is Caroline Hardwick going?*

The courtyard of the Angel was already bustling. The Norwich Self-Defence was there, and a groom was brushing out the interior. A stable-boy took her carpet-bags, and she went into the coffee-room to wait. The Dutch clock on the wall said ten past six.

She drank a cup of chocolate – she could not possibly eat – and stood at the fireplace, warming and calming herself. When the voice spoke her name she stared into the flames and refused to believe it. The voice was that of her brother Nicholas.

He came over to her, with noisy surprise, from one of the curtained eating-booths.

'Caro! What on earth are you doing here at this time?'

She smiled wanly, tried to fence him off. 'I was about to ask you the same thing. I thought you were staying with Will Sedgmoor . . .'

'Why, yes, we've been fishing all night over at the Staunch. I came in for breakfast. I've never known you rise at this hour. What are you up to?'

'Norwich Self-Defence departs in ten minutes, ladies and gentlemen,' the coachman called at the door. She started. 'I – well, I'm going to stay with friends too. At Wisbech, you remember the Robinsons . . .'

'We haven't seen them in years,' Nicholas said with sturdy scepticism. 'And you can't be travelling alone. Anyway, mother would have said . . . Caro, what's wrong?'

'Nothing, nothing. Nick, I can't tell you, I'm – I'm going somewhere, I can't tell you, please don't ask me – ' She had never imagined anything as bad as this.

'Why ever not?' Nicholas looked worried: concerned enough to drag her physically back to the Bridge House if he saw fit, she thought. 'I say, have you quarrelled with ma and pa or something like that? I mean, you can't just go soodling off like this, all alone. Caro, what is it? Are you in trouble? Tell me – '

'Nick, you must promise me – if I tell you, then you must let me go. I'm not in any trouble – I'm running

187

away, with a man who loves me very much and whom I love, and we're going away to get married . . .'

Nicholas let out a long whistle. 'An elopement! But – but I never knew you were courting with anyone!'

'It's – it's been secret, it's had to be. He's a wonderful man, but mother and father perhaps wouldn't see it that way, and besides there are reasons – '

'But why on earth are you going on the Norwich coach?' said Nicholas with a loud laugh. 'It's hardly Gretna Green! Anyway, tell me who it is. You are my sister. I don't want to think you've thrown in your lot with just anybody.'

'Hush, Nicholas, please . . .' She laid a hand on his arm. 'Nick, you do promise to keep this a secret, don't you?'

'Well, surely, if you like, but it won't stay a secret for long.'

'I know,' she said. 'I've left a letter for mother and father trying to explain. It's so difficult – '

'Why, lots of couples elope,' Nicholas said. 'What's going on, Caro? Has he got two heads or something? Are you meeting him here?'

'He's a Frenchman,' she burst out. 'An officer on parole.'

Nicholas stood back a little and let out another whistle, softer this time. 'Ye Gods,' he said. 'A Frenchie . . .' His look was not unappreciative: his sister really was exceptional for a girl. 'But if this fellow breaks his parole – '

'I know. We've got to be fast and discreet. We're – I'm going to France with him, to marry him. It's the only way, Nick, truly – '

'Aye, aye, I see that.' Nicholas shook his head. 'You certainly like to live dangerously. And this has all been going on – you've been planning this . . . A Frenchie. Damn me!' he said admiringly.

'I wouldn't do it if I weren't absolutely sure,' she said. 'And soon perhaps the war will be over, and things can be patched up.'

'How on earth are you going to get to France?'

'Yarmouth. We've found a way. Nick, the coach is waiting, and I've got to go. You're not going to try to stop me, are you? Please – '

'Stop you? Why, I've never been able to stop you doing anything you wanted to do.'

'And don't tell father where we've gone – Yarmouth I mean. I know he'd try and get me back. Please. He need never know you've seen me.'

'All right, if you say so.'

'And as soon as the war's over, you can come and see us in France, and meet him for yourself. I know you'll like him. He's going to go back to farming his land. He's a good man.'

'By God, Caro, you've got some courage,' said Nicholas. Thankfully, he seemed to be taking the news in a spirit of youthful admiration at the adventure. A couple of years older or younger, and a less robust temperament, and his reaction might have been very different. 'But are you going to be all right? I mean, have you money, and everything?'

'Yes, it's all settled. He'll take good care of me. I'll write as soon as I can. Nick, I've got to go. I'm so sorry to leave you, and mother and father, like this – but – oh, you do understand, don't you?'

Nicholas looked suddenly as if he had taken in the significance of what she was doing. He embraced her quickly and awkwardly. 'Bless you, Caro, I don't know as I do understand, but as long as you're happy – well – I just hope you'll be all right.'

The coachman called again.

She kissed her brother, gathered up her gloves and

189

reticule. 'Stay here, Nick,' she said in agitation. 'Don't come out to the coach. Please don't think badly of me. God bless.'

She ran out to the coach. The horses were restless in the traces. The coachman in his long great-coat swallowed a peg of rum and climbed up to the box. An ostler handed her in. A man in the wig and collar of a cleric and a fat woman beside him smiled a greeting. Thankfully they were strangers. Caroline busied herself with her reticule, and with great concentration managed to prevent herself from crying.

Please don't talk to me – not for a minute. The coach lurched and jolted into life. They left the innyard at a clip.

The parson spoke only to the fat woman, obviously his wife, until they had passed the turnpike and were out of the city, and by then Caroline was tolerably composed.

'A chill morning, ma'am,' the parson said cordially, rubbing his hands together as if in relish of the cold. 'Do you travel alone?'

'Er – no, my husband is to join the coach shortly – at Eye. He was detained on business there,' she said, producing a smile from somewhere. An inquisitive travelling companion was not something she had bargained for. But the cleric, after a few remarks about the weather, turned his attention to his wife again. Caroline sat back and tried to fix her mind on Antoine. She badly needed the reassuring sight of him. It was dreadful to have made Nicholas a party to her deception. The whole enterprise now seemed frighteningly random and vulnerable. Her confidence would revive once Antoine was beside her.

Mist lay damply on the bare clay fields as the coach negotiated the winding road to Eye. The flat line of the eastern horizon was brimming with pale light. In a dyke by the roadside a heron stood motionless. The parson's wife offered Caroline a comfit from a twist of paper. Caroline thanked her and refused.

The first cottages of the stone village of Eye appeared. Caroline pulled down the window and craned out. He should be waiting outside the Blue Boar in the High Street, where the coach picked up . . . She could not see him. A moment's panic, and then she realized she was expecting to see him in his uniform, as she was accustomed to. Yes, that was him, in the sober black coat she had bought, his hat worn as a bicorne. He held a portmanteau: his trunk had had to be left behind in the room in Little's Yard. He raised his hand, and the coach lurched to a halt. There was a pause while his bag was stowed in the basket, and the parson smiled at Caroline and said civilly: 'Ah, your husband, ma'am?'

Antoine climbed in with every appearance of normality, greeting Caroline casually with a 'my dear' and saying good morning to the other occupants of the coach. Only Caroline's eye remarked that his face, normally so healthily coloured, was deadly white. Whatever she was feeling he must be feeling, and more. He was a fugitive now, an escaped prisoner. From now on he must either get out of the country or be retaken and sent to the hulks. It was a prospect that neither of them had spoken of beyond the barest mention: they had recoiled instinctively, as if to talk of such a catastrophe would invite it.

These first moments would be the worst, Caroline knew. The parson and his wife were looking interested and sociable. She would have to be very strong, very calm.

'I was just remarking to your wife, sir, how cold the morning is,' the parson said beaming. 'But much colder for the poor fellows on top, I dare say,' he added, referring to the outside passengers.

'Cold, indeed,' said Antoine. 'But at least no snow.'

'Do you travel all the way to Norwich, sir?' the parson asked.

'Yes,' Antoine said stiffly.

'Ah, then we shall be companions. May I introduce myself? Ambrose Cox. Vicar at King's Cliffe. My wife.'

They introduced themselves as Mr and Mrs Franz Neuber: the names in which Caroline had reserved their seats. Neuber was a Hamburg mercantile house with which her father sometimes did business: she thought it had an unequivocally German sound. But Antoine's accent, though it was not nearly as pronounced as when she had first known him, sounded to her so obviously French . . . She trembled a little, but the Rev. Mr Cox seemed to find nothing amiss. Don't go inventing new problems, she told herself. A country parson was hardly likely to suspect anything – a foreign accent was a foreign accent.

In any case, Parson Cox liked the sound of his own voice best. Before they had crossed the river at Guyhirn he had told them about his family background, his living at King's Cliffe, his son who was in the militia, and the fever from which he had just recovered by dint of taking Dr Mercer's Assafoetida Drops.

'You are resident in Norwich, ma'am?' he asked Caroline.

'No, we – our destination is Yarmouth. Mr Neuber is a merchant,' Caroline said uneasily, and Mr Cox barely nodded before launching into an account of the sister in Norwich with whom they were going to stay while she bore her twelfth child.

'Eight of them living, God be praised,' he said. 'Though this is a sad world for a child to be born into, and who knows but it may be His beneficent will to take this twelfth back into His arms. It is a sad world, is it not?'

They agreed that it was a sad world.

'This rogue general across the water, is he man or beast?' Mr Cox said rhetorically, whilst his wife chewed comfits and nodded as if to indicate that either was all right with her. 'I am informed that on Christmas Day he sent a letter to our King proposing peace – a personal letter, as from one head of state to another. The insolence! The King would have none of it. Tell me, sir, do the good people of your German lands find the French as incomprehensible as we do?'

'Oh, indeed, sir,' Antoine said readily, and Caroline saw with relief that he had recovered his equilibrium. 'The Gallic spirit is quite foreign to us.'

'Well, our army in Holland made but little impression, alas, and Russia shows herself capricious as ever,' said Mr Cox, as if Russia were a naughty child. 'However, one still has hopes of the Austrians. My dear, I am convinced you forgot to instruct Betty to have the chimneys swept while we were away . . .'

A complex matrimonial dispute followed, and Caroline and Antoine were able for the first time to exchange a warm glance. She squeezed his hand, finding the palm damp. In spite of the fear and tension, she registered an enjoyment at travelling with him like this as his wife. Which soon she would be. It was going to be all right. She tried to communicate this with her touch.

Soon they were passing through the country of spidery orchards that marked the approach to Wisbech, and by now a mild coppery sun was well up the sky. In Wisbech the coach stopped at the Rose and Crown to change horses. Caroline and Antoine strolled a little around the town, appearing casual, talking feverishly under their breath.

'That foolish old priest,' he said. 'Does he suspect anything, do you think?'

'No, no, I'm sure of it. Everything's going well.' She

did not tell him of her encounter with Nicholas: she did not want anything to shake his fragile confidence.

'I remember this town,' he said, looking around at Wisbech with its pleasantly Dutch ambience, the stepped gables on the crescents of houses along the busy river, the warehouses and mills. 'We came this way when we are first brought to Peterborough in the prison barge. It seems a long time ago . . . a lifetime.'

'I suppose we ought to eat something before the coach is ready again,' she said. 'Are you hungry?'

He shook his head. 'We're making good time, aren't we? We're not late?'

'Yes, we're in good time. Don't worry, love.'

As they went back to the coaching inn he said: 'My God, if I can only live through this I will never fear anything again . . .' Then he made an effort at a smile and said: '*Eh bien*, now I must be Herr Neuber again. Me, a Prussian. I am much too handsome . . .'

2

Their next change was at King's Lynn, at the Duke's Head Hotel, and here Caroline's heart thundered. The town was so familiar to her. Just a few streets away were her father's wharf and warehouses and the small chequered medieval house that was their second home. Hardwick's was a name known to everyone in Lynn, and she had many acquaintances here. They risked appearing to snub the Coxes and paid for a private dinner-room.

'Antoine.' Caroline reached for his hand across the table. 'Eat something. You'll feel better – '

'I can't. I can't.' He took a deep shuddering breath, pushed away the mutton chop irritably. 'When I entered the coach I was so afraid I thought I would break down.

194

God, what am I doing . . . How long now? We are nearly half-way there, yes?'

She smiled painfully. 'Nearly.' She could not eat the food herself. She squeezed his hand, seeking the assurance of his touch, but his hand was cold and quiescent in hers.

'Begging your pardon, sir, ma'am.' The innkeeper opened the door. 'I'm sorry to ask this of ye, but we're so full up today, and here's Major Jacks of the 28th wanting a dinner, and I've scarcely room to lay a place. Would ye object, now, to sharing the room?'

The major was already in, doffing his hat and bowing. Caroline remembered the 28th Regiment of Foot was stationed at Lynn. 'I'll not disturb you, sir, ma'am, all I require is a place to set my plate,' the major boomed. He looked enormous in his red coat and epaulettes and sword and polished buskins.

'But we have paid for this room,' Antoine burst out. 'It is private, it is paid for . . .'

The sight of the soldier had thrown him into panic. 'I assure you I'll be no trouble, sir,' said the Major, and Antoine said: 'You are trouble already, this – this will not do, we have paid – ' His face was drained of colour: she was suddenly afraid he was going to bolt or rush at the major and she grabbed his arm and pulled him to his feet. 'Really, we've finished now,' she said. 'Please, take the room.'

She hustled Antoine outside to the innyard. 'That damn soldier, the uniform,' he muttered. 'I think I am discovered . . .'

'Hush, it's all right,' she said, feeling his arm taut and shaking. The worst part of his fear, for her, was that he seemed to be drawing away from her, into himself. 'There can't possibly be any search for you yet. Come, we'll sit in the coach until it's time. Come, love.'

In spite of her brave words, she knew that by now, in Peterborough, their defection must be known.

At the Bridge House, Leo the spaniel was hiding under the stairs, knowing something was wrong and not daring to go near the master.

It was Rebecca who had discovered Caroline's letter: realizing it was late even for Caroline to get up, she had gone up to her room to see if she were ill. Since then there had been chaos.

It was a joke: it had to be a joke, Luke said. He ordered all the servants up and said one of them must be in on the joke and demanded to know about it, where was she hiding, was she over at the Squires', come on damn you! and whilst his insistence grew more hysterical Rebecca sat, frozen, with a thousand recalled hints and premonitions crowding in on her.

She should have known. Like an enigmatic picture that suddenly resolves into meaning, the reviewed spectacle of her daughter's behaviour over the past few months presented its true aspect to Rebecca's mind. Caroline, who was always open, had been secretive. Caroline, who was always humorous, had been grave. Caroline, who was always full of entertaining talk, had been quiet. And last night, asking about her parents' marriage, her grandfather's disapproval . . . *I should have known*, Rebecca thought, and for the moment she could apprehend nothing but her own failure.

Luke dismissed the servants. He turned to his wife, and she suddenly thought he looked old. He said in a barely audible voice: 'It's true. It's true, isn't it?'

She nodded, sickly. 'Luke – before you do anything – '

'Well, it's true. Very well. Not for long. No.' He paced up and down, distractedly, as if looking for something. 'I'll send for Captain Roubillard and Captain Van den

196

Bos – they must know something – I'll have every one of them rounded up and they'll tell me where Clairet's taken my daughter or I'll have them all in Norman Cross, every last skulking one of them – '

'Luke, he hasn't *taken* her. She's run away with him. She's – '

'To think I've *entertained* him here,' he went on. He was not listening. 'Under my very nose. The deceit, the lies . . .' He threw a wild glance at his wife. 'They've been meeting. Somehow they must have been meeting. Did you never *suspect* anything, for God's sake? She's your *daughter*!'

'She's your daughter too!' she flared at him. 'And she's past eighteen, not eight! Am I to keep her in a nursery?'

Luke glared back at her, ran his hands through his hair. 'She – she can't have known what she was doing,' he muttered. 'That – that Clairet must have seduced her, turned her head – you know how these Frenchies are – she can't really have meant it . . .'

Rebecca privately thought Caroline, who was not naïve, probably knew quite well what she was doing. But still, she herself should have known, she should have spotted the symptoms, she prided herself on staying in sympathy with the young, on not being middle-aged and remote . . .

'We'll have her back,' Luke said decisively. 'Before dinner she'll be back. That man's a fugitive, he's jumped his parole. I'll have him taken. God, he'll rue the day he seduced my daughter – '

'Where can they have gone?' Rebecca said. 'There's nowhere for them; they can't hide . . . Oh, Caroline, what have you done . . . ?' She stroked the letter, her sorrow chiefly for the futility of her daughter's hopes.

'She says they're going to run away to France,' Luke said. 'They'll never do it.' He opened the hall door and bellowed 'John! Thorpe!' He came prowling back, twitching, volcanic. 'I'll send word to Captain Woodruff at Norman Cross. He's got two militia regiments there. I'll see the magistrates, I'll have word sent to every port on the coast, a description of Clairet. God! if I had him here, I'd thrash that bastard, I'd horsewhip him to an inch of his life. Well, he'll go to the hulks when he's caught, and I'll make damned sure those foreigners don't come near my family in future, they can collect their money from the stables, it's all they're fit for – ' He suddenly stopped, looked bewildered, and Rebecca saw there were tears in his eyes.

'Why?' he said, as they held each other. 'I thought – I thought she loved us.'

'I thought so too,' Rebecca said. 'I think she still does. No, I do. But – but there's more than one kind of love.' And she thought: poor Caroline. I'm sorry for you, falling in love so hopelessly. But I just want you back safely. I want you back.

Luke mustered Captains Roubillard and Van den Bos and a couple of the other senior officers. For all his rage, he had to admit to himself that they knew nothing about it. Captain Roubillard was as angry as himself. 'The fool,' he cried, 'the imbecile, the pig,' and he heaped Breton curse-words on his friend and raised his thick fist. 'If I saw him, I would *smash* him.'

But the imprecations of neither Luke nor Captain Roubillard could do any good. In the meantime they must wait for news from Norman Cross, where Captain Woodruff had promised to do his utmost, and despatched a platoon of militia to go upriver to Wisbech and Lynn. Mr Squire, as magistrate, put out a warrant for the arrest of Antoine Clairet as an escaped prisoner-of-war. Luke had sent his own servants on horseback to seek for news of the fugitive couple. He had mobilized every resource; but the fact remained that he had no idea where they had gone.

They sat down at last to supper at the Bridge House, though no one had much appetite, and Luke suddenly banged his fist down on the table. 'Nick!' he thundered.

'What is it?' said Nicholas, turning pale.

'The other week you went with Caro to Norman Cross, didn't you?'

'Yes, I did, she – she told me about it, and I was interested, and we went – '

'Did she speak to Frenchies there? Hm? Answer me, boy!'

'Well, yes,' said Nicholas, who had not seen his father like this for years and, a particularly fearless boy though he was, was deeply frightened of him. 'At the market stall where the prisoners' work is sold. Like the picture – the picture she took with her. But people spoke to the Frenchies there anyway, father, it's a market – '

'She often talked to the officers when they came here, anyway,' Rebecca said wearily, 'and so did I come to that. When young people start a romance they always find ways. We should know that, Luke.'

Luke glowered. 'But I wasn't a French prisoner . . . God, to think I thought that man was responsible, trustworthy . . .' He swallowed his wine and bent his bristling brows on his son again. 'But did she never say anything to you, Nick? You and she have always been pretty thick. Think, now. Did she give any hint – ?'

'*No*,' cried Nicholas. 'No, she – she didn't, and besides, I've not been back here long . . .' He excused himself, and left his father at the table, brooding and drinking.

Mr Squire and a messenger from Captain Woodruff came that evening, saying there was no news. But one of Luke's

199

servants had asked round all the coaching inns, and though there was no record of a booking in the name of Hardwick or Clairet, a boots at the Angel recalled seeing a young lady who might have answered the description of Caroline boarding the Norwich Self-Defence that morning.

3

The Self-Defence reached the market town of Swaffham in Norfolk in a cold blue dusk and put up at the King's Head for the night.

Caroline and Antoine took a room overlooking the broad market square. They were both tired and aching yet wakeful, and Antoine had been subdued since the scare over the Major in King's Lynn. She knew him as fairly abstemious, but he drank several glasses of brandy; and he continually poked and stirred the fire, complaining of the cold.

At last they went to bed, and she held tightly to him and felt herself responding as always. Fugitive and haunted as she was, it was still wonderful to lie with him like this, in a large curtained bed, not the narrow iron cot of the room in Little's Yard. But his lips were dry and hesitant on hers, and at last he threw back the covers and went to stir the embers of the fire again.

'I'm sorry, Caroline,' he said in a muffled voice, 'It is no good, I – I cannot . . .'

'It's all right,' she said.

'The thought of another journey with that foolish priest – oh, I know he cannot help it . . .'

'Imagine that poor pregnant sister of his who he's going to visit – she must dread his coming more than the labour,' she said, with an effort to laugh. It was no good. He would not respond.

Antoine went to the window and parted the curtains. His voice was hoarse as he said, 'You know, I almost wish . . .'

She watched him. 'That you could turn back?'

He sighed, came back to the bed. 'Absurd, isn't it? Having longed to escape . . . I suppose imprisonment has a kind of security. No, no. Forget I said that. There is no turning back.'

'I don't want to turn back,' she said.

He sat on the bed and ran his hands through his hair. 'You have had to lie, and hide and be afraid. All these things I have made you do . . .'

Her heart opened to him, and she kissed his lips and the sweet hollow of his neck and smiled, filled anew with love. 'Oh! you'll make it up to me,' she said gaily. 'I know you'll make it up to me, darling.'

He winced as if in pain.

At last he got back into bed, and, curled lovingly against his body, she presently slept and dreamt they were already in France, safe in the farmhouse at Torcy. But when she woke in the middle of the night, with the fire just a wink in the hearth, she felt his short breathing and saw the whites of his eyes, staring still at the heavy beams above his head.

They were a couple of miles out of Swaffham the next morning, into the gently sloping, gently wooded country of mid-Norfolk, and the Rev. Mr Cox was just embarked on an account of his views on charity-schools, when the coach rattled to a halt. After a while the guard opened the door, and said that one of the horses had cast a shoe, and they must go very gently until they could get to a smith.

At the village of Little Fransham no smith was to be found, and they had to trundle on to Wendling. There, there was another delay while the smith worked on the shoe, and they were very late getting into the town of East Dereham, where they had to change again. There were not many hours of daylight left.

When the many church towers and hilltop castle of the city of Norwich at last came in sight, the winter afternoon was fading and there was little hope of reaching Yarmouth that night. The coach put up at the ancient Maid's Head near the cathedral. They said goodbye with relief to Mr and Mrs Cox. An ostler told them, in a broad sing-song Norfolk that Caroline could just understand and Antoine not at all, that it was unlikely they would be able to hire a post-chaise at this time. 'Yew might get a wherry gooing Yarmouth from Harrison's Wharf, do you get down there queck,' he added.

So, carrying their baggage, they made the long walk down King Street to the wharves on the river near Carrow Bridge. There were several keels and wherries with black sails, some bearing precarious loads of timber. Sailors on the wharves shook their heads at Caroline's enquiries. No, they weren't stirring tonight, and besides they didn't take passengers. The *Forget-me-not* was a passenger wherry, a man with a face like sewn leather told them. 'Jepha Thain's boot,' he said. 'Thass gooing Yarmouth tomo-orrer, first light. Yew'll not git to Yarmouth afore then, ma'am, less'n you reck'n to fly.'

They trudged back to the Maid's Head. They briefly toyed with the idea of hiring saddle-horses, but the prospect of riding fifteen miles or more on a dark winter road that neither of them knew was uninviting. In the end they wearily took a room at the Maid's Head – these inns were shortening their purse – and resolved to be patient till morning.

'Well,' said Antoine with an effort, 'those boats – what is the word, wherry? – they look fast sailers. Perhaps the river is safer than the roads.'

'Of course,' Caroline said. 'There's no danger. And at least we're free of Parson Cox.'

In this way she tried to cajole his spirits up, and when they went to have supper in the Maid's Head's big stone-floored dining-room she had a genuine appetite.

The room was busy and noisy, and the flustered waiter who brought them their veal cutlets with asparagus cast anxious glances at a group of young men by the fireplace who were clearly drunk and kept proposing loud toasts. They were in motley uniforms of grey and buff with hessian boots: 'Only the local Volunteers,' Caroline whispered to Antoine.

They obviously considered themselves, however, as at least a crack Guards' regiment. They began to sing *Rule Britannia* and *Britons, Strike Home*. Then they began accosting people at the nearby tables, calling on them in a mixture of conviviality and belligerence to join them in toasts. 'A toast to the King!' they bellowed. 'You, sir, will you join us in a loyal toast to His Majesty King George?' The man did so, but somewhere across the room a wit said: 'And to his doctors, may they always be nimble with the strait-jacket,' and there was a general laugh.

The young men were not put off. Caroline had seen a frown forming on Antoine's brow and when one of the Volunteers began proposing 'Death to the French, and confusion to the enemies of old England!' she pressed her foot on his under the table. 'They're just boys,' she said.

The Volunteer who came swaying over to them was indeed a boy, no more than sixteen. He was in a stage of drink where the blissful teeters on the edge of violence. He carried a cup of punch in one hand, and did not have sense enough to make his gestures with the other. 'Sir, madam, good even to you! I know you will join us – me – I know you will join in a loyal toast, of death to the French. Eh? Death to the French!'

'Oh, I don't think death is a very nice thing to toast,' Caroline said. 'Let us toast life to the English instead.'

The young man looked at her foggily, gave a hiccoughing laugh, then frowned and waved his cup at them. 'No, no, death to the French – '

'You annoy the lady,' Antoine said in a quiet voice, putting down his fork.

The young man pouted. 'Not at all,' he said. 'All I ask is that she join me in a toast – death to the French!' and with a wild swing of his arm he spilled a little of his punch on to Caroline's dress.

Antoine was on his feet: his hand shot out and closed on the Volunteer's starched cravat. 'You stupid little boy!' he stormed, shaking him like a doll. 'You will apologize to the lady and then you will get away from here, do you hear me, yes?'

In his fury his accent was thick and the boy shouted: 'He's a Frenchie! Help me, boys, the man's a damn Frenchie!'

Caroline sprang up, pulled them apart, and fixed her eyes on Antoine, begging him, reminding him. 'Franz,' she said, 'Franz, it's all right, really,' and he subsided, slowly, into his chair. She turned to the Volunteer and said icily: 'Mr Neuber is a Hamburg merchant. Now I think you owe us both an apology.'

They did not get one, however, for at that moment the waiter reappeared with two sturdy grooms and escorted the Volunteers out.

It was about the time that Caroline and Antoine retired to their room shaken after this incident that Luke came back to the Bridge House.

All day he had had fruitless meetings with the magistrates and with the local Fencibles. The clue picked up at the Angel had led to nothing. The militia from Norman Cross had returned from King's Lynn with no news.

Luke had not slept the night before, and he had kept himself going with brandy. When he swung into the parlour that evening, with the expectant faces of Rebecca and Nicholas turned to him, the peripheral sight of Caroline's embroidery caused something to tighten and snap inside him. Luke's pride in his family was deep, fierce and embracing: to have it so casually flouted, to feel himself powerless before the whims of the daughter who had been the apple of his eye, was the bitterest gall to his hardy nature. He flung the embroidery into the fire and jammed it into the flames with his hands.

'Damn her,' he said, 'damn her, *damn her.*'

Rebecca, sick with worry, reached out to him. 'Luke – '

'I'll not have her back,' Luke said hoarsely. 'If she were to turn up at that door now I'd slam it in her face – '

'You don't know what you're saying – '

'Aye, don't I? We'll see. Those clothes she left. They'll go on the fire too. Everything . . . I suppose he promised to dress her in silks, did he, the way I've done for eighteen years?' He swept to the door. 'On the fire – everything – '

'Luke!' Rebecca pulled him back. 'She's still our *daughter.* She's young and, yes, foolish, but she's – '

'No daughter of mine!' Luke cried. 'I don't know how *you've* brought her up . . .'

'Oh, no, that won't wash,' said Rebecca furiously. 'Who was it got on good terms with Captain Clairet? Don't start saying *your* daughter wouldn't do such a thing, because she has, and burning her clothes won't make it go away – '

'Let go of me, Rebecca – '

'*Stop* it,' cried Nicholas, in an anguished voice.

They looked at him: they had forgotten him. He was sitting with his head in his hands.

Nicholas was temperamentally inclined to candour: keeping a secret did not come easily to him. He had been determined to do so through these terrible two days – but he had never imagined the effect Caroline's flight would have at home. The horrible, unaccustomed sight of his parents shouting at each other was too much for him. He desperately wanted it to stop. He was only sixteen. He sobbed out what he knew.

'And – and you never *said*?' Luke came with fearful slowness and took the boy by his shoulders. 'You knew where they'd gone and you didn't *say*?'

'Luke, don't!' cried Rebecca, as Luke leaned back and struck his son.

He had never done that before. He stood and looked, shocked, at his own hand. 'I'll have the carriage made ready,' he said mechanically.

'Luke, it's late, we can't leave tonight,' Rebecca said, putting her arms round the weeping boy.

'Then I'll go alone,' Luke said, going out.

4

The wherry *Forget-me-not* was a fine example of the black-sailed trading craft that plied the Yare between Norwich and Yarmouth. In contrast to the tall, black, single sail, the hatches and cabin sides were painted a bright vermilion, and Caroline felt a certain elation in stepping with Antoine into this strange sleek boat the next morning.

The master offered to accommodate them in the cabin,

but they preferred to stay on deck with the other passengers, mostly market-women with butter and eggs, and watch as a stiff breeze took them out of Norwich, leaving the cathedral spire behind and moving out into the flat landscape towards the sea.

Antoine had been silent and low-spirited all morning: but as the *Forget-me-not* tacked her way through the winding reaches of the Yare, past reed-shores and turning windmills, with the master calling greetings to other wherries laden with coal and timber and fish, he began to lift his face and look about him keenly.

Once she put her hand in his and he gripped it and looked round as if he had forgotten she was there and said: 'The sea, do you smell it? It's wonderful.'

The air was delightfully fresh; she couldn't smell anything in particular; but she said, 'Yes,' pleased that he was coming out of his despondency.

The wind had veered a little as they came to the broad stretch known as Breydon Water. It was a choppy crossing, and Caroline felt a little queasy, but Antoine came alive. He watched the master and his mate with admiration. 'Even here the English are good sailors,' he said, forgetting himself for a moment.

'I hope our smugglers are as good,' she said in a low voice. He did not reply.

They reached the quayside at Yarmouth in early afternoon – and now Caroline could smell the sea, but in a mixture of fish and tar and coal that made the bracing air of her own fenland seem positively soft. They went ashore at the Waterman's Arms, and found themselves confronted with the maze of narrow alleys called the Rows.

'The White Swan Inn,' Caroline said. 'Rattler of the Haven. Oh, please God, don't let Jean-Baptiste Massieu have been lying.'

Threading their way through the labyrinth of nautical

workshops and outfitters and boat-yards, amongst sailors and fishwives, they found the White Swan by the market-place, with a great stretch of baleful grey sea visible beyond the flat beach.

In the low-ceilinged taproom fishermen, wrapped in the scent of their trade, stared over their pipes at Caroline and Antoine. The landlord was a dropsical man in an old-fashioned curled wig who looked obsequious when Caroline approached him. And then astonished.

'Rattler of the Haven,' she repeated softly. 'We were told to ask for him.'

The landlord closed his eyes and shook his head and turned away.

'*Please*,' Caroline said. 'Jean-Baptiste Massieu. We had the word from him. This is – one of his countrymen.'

That got a reaction. The landlord beckoned them down some steps and opened a door. 'Step in here, if ye will,' he whispered.

It was a little wainscoted parlour. He left them in there for several minutes, then came back and closed and locked the door behind him.

'I've sent my boy for Rattler,' he said. 'Now what's this about? Don't tell me the revenuers are using ladies for agents now.'

'We've nothing to do with the revenue,' Caroline said.

'I am a Frenchman,' Antoine said. 'I have to get across to France. Jean-Baptiste Massieu, do you know the name? He escaped from the Depot at Norman Cross. He said he had – friends in the trade. He said to come here and ask for Rattler of the Haven.'

The landlord nodded. 'Aye, I know the name. And you're after getting across to France? Well, I don't know. And you, miss – begging your pardon – what's your part in this?'

'I'm going with him,' she said.

208

The landlord raised his eyebrows, then shrugged. 'As you say, miss.' He turned to Antoine. 'How long have you been on the run?'

'This is the third day,' Antoine said. 'I am an officer, I broke my parole. What do you say, my friend, is there a chance? Damn it, I *have* to get away!'

The landlord held up his hands. 'I'm saying naught. Rattler'll be here soon and you can talk to him. I've had enough trouble with the revenue as it is. You can stay in this here room and speak to Rattler, but I haven't seen you, d'you hear?'

But he brought them some wine while they waited; and at last the door opened and a big crop-haired man slipped in.

He stood with his back to the door staring at them as if memorizing their faces. He had a broad flattened nose and wore a single earring and a striped neckerchief and a short leather fisherman's coat.

'We were told by Jean-Baptiste Massieu – ' Caroline began.

'Aye, I know all that.' The man's eyes roved over them. He said in harsh guttural French to Antoine: '*Vous êtes français, vraiment?*'

'*Oui, bien sûr, Capitaine du frégate* Coquille, *pris à Brest il y a cinq mois.*'

'*Poursuivi?*'

Antoine shrugged and gently indicated Caroline.

'No one knows we're in Yarmouth,' she said. Except Nicholas . . .

'You both want to go?'

Antoine began to speak, but Caroline, with a strange inward flex of alarm, cut him off. 'Yes,' she said. 'Both of us.'

The big man turned a chair and sat astride it. 'Massieu was an old friend of mine,' he said.

'Then – you did help him escape?' Caroline said.

Rattler frowned and slid a plug of tobacco into his mouth. 'Like I said, he was an old friend. Did a lot of business.' He chewed slowly. 'We've a run set for next Thursday. Dunkirk. There'll mebbe be a place for you aboard then.'

'Next Thursday!' cried Antoine. 'But that's no good! I have to get away!'

Rattler shrugged. 'Next Thursday,' he said.

'I am a fugitive,' Antoine said, gripping the man's arm. 'Each passing day there is more risk. If I am caught I go to the hulks.'

'I know that,' Rattler grunted, shaking off his hand. 'I never axed you to go making a run for it, did I? Listen, I did Massieu a favour. Now, mebbe I'll do the same for you, out o' respect for him. I'll want money, mind you, though I suppose you guess that. But you'll have to wait. Things aren't easy for us now. Since this damned war they've put more arms on the revenue cutters, hoping to pick up French privateers on the side. There's cruisers prowling all about the Roads. We have to go extra careful. Now, you'll just have to lie up somewhere. No one knows you're in Yarmouth, you say.'

'But they'll be searching,' Caroline said. 'Not just for him but for me.'

Rattler leaned back and studied both of them, chewing. There was a fund of unspoken irony in his eyes, but he merely sighed and said: 'Well, like I say, you've made your bed . . .'

'Look.' Caroline fumbled with her purse and spilled the gold and silver on the table. 'There's thirty-five pounds here. Take it all. It's yours if you'll take us tonight.'

Rattler pursed his lips as if he were going to whistle; then he looked round for the spittoon and spat. 'I've eight crew. On a good run I reckon to make more'n a hundred pound profit. 'Twouldn't be worth my while for thirty-five.'

'Then would you do it for a hundred?' Caroline said eagerly. 'If we gave you a hundred, that would be straight profit, wouldn't it? Would you take us tonight?'

'Caroline!' said Antoine; but she turned vehemently to him. 'We'll get it,' she said. 'We'll get it.'

Rattler looked her over with something more of respect. 'If'n you can give me a hundred pound down, then mebbe I could see my way to making the trip tonight. Mind you, if – '

'Mebbe's not good enough,' Caroline said. 'I guarantee the money. If you'll guarantee to sail tonight.' She was aware of Antoine watching her: he had not known this side of her. She had not known she possessed it herself.

Rattler spat again, then put his large hand heavily down on the table. 'Do you come to Grubb's Haven around cockshut. Thass north of the Denes, off the Caister road. A quiet spot. There's a tavern with a sign of three tuns. Ask for me there. I'll be there, no misdoubt. But there's got to be a hundred pound, do you wastin' your time.'

'You'll get your money,' she said.

Rattler nodded and stood up. 'Can I axe one thing?' he said, scratching his stubbly head. 'You're an English gel. Leddy, I reckon. And you're setting for to flit to France with this gennleman? Oh, no offence, like. Just I never heard nor the like of it.'

'Grubb's Haven,' Caroline said with a smile. 'Sign of the three tuns.'

Outside the inn Antoine dropped his bag and took hold of her arms. 'Caroline,' he said. 'I know you had to say something – but we cannot get so much money – sixty-five pounds, it is absurd – '

'I have my jewellery,' she said. 'I have a pearl necklace.

A couple of rings. And a gold brooch with a fine emerald. They should – '

'You mean *sell* them? Now, here . . . ?'

Yes, why not? What good are jewels to me if we're to be stuck here and you are taken and put in the hulks? And if the jewels aren't enough I'll sell my clothes. We've come this far and I'm damned if we'll let a thing like this stop us.'

She was all energy: she could not believe that once she had been the sleepy, lackadaisical creature who could merely watch the traffic on the street for hours. Now she felt she could jump in a boat and row across the Channel single-handed if she had to.

'No . . . I can't . . .' Antoine bit his lip. 'Caroline, if you do this for me, I must – Caroline, please listen to me a moment – '

'Dear love, I'm not just doing this for you,' she said, touching his face. 'I'm doing this for *us*. Oh, Antoine, tomorrow we can be in France. *Free*. Think of it. Come . . .'

After a moment he followed her, his face set and grim.

They found a pawnshop in the Rows. She went in alone, putting on a trembling fragile look for a softening effect on the shopman. The Jewish pawnbroker stroked his beard and offered twenty pounds for the pearls and the rings. She trembled and palpitated a bit more and with the aid of a tear or two pushed him up to twenty-five. The brooch, which was beautiful and valuable, he looked at caressingly and then admitted with likeable honesty that it was worth more than his little business could give: he did not deal in such things. He suggested she try the jeweller and silversmith's in Church Square.

The jeweller offered her fifty pounds, which was less than its value. But it was all and more than she needed.

The afternoon was waning now, and they walked out to

the quayside to see the winter light fading across the sea. The long narrow harbour, with the jetty to one side, was crowded with ships – colliers and codsmacks and brigs and one Navy two-decker. The Hamburg packet that carried the mails was just coming in, flying the post-jack ensign that afforded it a precarious security from attack. There were more ships in the Roads, and a few small fishing vessels drawn up on the beach.

'I've never sailed on the sea,' she said. Salt wind stung her face. 'You'll have to look after me.'

Antoine said nothing.

After a meal at a chop-house they set out to walk to Grubb's Haven, Antoine carrying their baggage, striking a sandy path across the lonely Denes to the north of the town.

It turned bitterly cold as the sun sank, and the only light was the gleam of the sea on their right. Caroline ploughed on, still full of energy, but Antoine had fallen silent and his steps were dragging.

'Being a prisoner,' he said with a short laugh, 'makes one an idle fellow. Soft.'

'Let me carry one of the bags,' she said. 'I feel perfectly strong.'

'No,' he said. 'No . . . let me do this at least for you, Caroline.'

Soon they came to the reed-shore of the River Bure where it opened into the sea. It was a bleak spot. There were fishing-boats drawn up on the bank, and beyond the black keels she saw a light. A squat shingled cottage, with a sign swinging over the door. She gave a gasp of relief and ran up the bank, Antoine slow behind her.

The door was closed. She hammered on it, and after a moment a youth with a lantern opened up and stared at her.

'Awright, Billy,' said a voice behind him. 'Let 'em in.'

213

It was Rattler. He rose from a bench by the fire in the tiny parlour, beckoned them in. 'Close the door, Billy, and keep it shut,' he said, and led them through a passage into a malodorous room stacked with kegs and empty sacks and fishing nets. Without speaking he pulled one of the kegs into the centre of the room and upended it like a table and stood with his hands on his hips, watching them neutrally.

Caroline took the money from her bulging purse and counted out one hundred pounds on to the keg. There was silence but for Rattler's wheezy breathing. Then he pulled a pouch from his pocket and said: 'Good enough. Tonight it is.'

'Oh, thank God!' said Caroline, turning to Antoine, who was very white. 'Antoine, it's all right.'

'Now, you stop in here,' Rattler said, scooping the money into his pouch. 'I'll go direct and have the lugger unfurl sail. Tell the truth, I didn't expect ye to come, but I had my boys wait just in case. There's a smart wind and we'd best be moving straight away.' He went to the tiny window high up in the wall. 'See from this winder – over to the mouth of the river. See the mast? Thass where she'll come out. When all's ready we'll make a light three times, see? Thass when you come out to us. And be quick.'

Caroline nodded.

'Awright then.' He jangled the pouch and went to the door.

'Rattler!'

'Aye?'

'Thank you.'

He sniffed and shrugged. 'Don't thank me till we're clear o' the Roads.' Then he felt in the pouch and put three sovereigns in her hand. 'Here. There's money-changers at Dunkirk, mebbe you'll want it,' he said gruffly. 'Look for the light.' He was gone.

'Well,' said Caroline turning to Antoine, 'now we have more money than we thought. Dunkirk . . . how far is – '

'You will need that money,' Antoine said.

'Oh, well, once we're in France – '

'You must take it, not I,' Antoine said. His face was waxy in the semi-dark of the noisome little room. 'You must take it to get home to your mother and father.'

'Antoine – '

'You can't come with me, my darling,' he said. He stepped a little closer and spread his hands. 'You can't come to France, Caroline. It's no good. It was insane of us to imagine it would work. All you mean to me I can never express – all you have done for me I can never repay. But we cannot go to France together. I've been trying to think of a way to say this – '

'Antoine, don't be silly! We – we've always said it doesn't matter – I'm an English girl, you a French captain, it still doesn't mean a thing when we love each other. Let the world and the war go hang – '

'Ah, if only we could!' he said. He laid his hand on the window-ledge and looked out. 'Caroline, please don't make this more difficult for me. It wouldn't work. There is so much against it. If you go back to your family now, to your proper life, to your real life, then soon you will realize I am right, that it was all a mad dream – beautiful, yes, very beautiful to me. But impossible.'

'Of course it's not impossible!' she cried, trying to master the raving phantoms of dread rising in her. 'We've come this far! All we've had, all we've shared together, that can go on – '

'It *cannot*,' he said in a harsh breaking voice. He drew in a deep breath, and she saw his angular profile against the window, jaws working. 'Caroline,' he went on, 'I promise you that if you go home now and forget me you will be so much happier – '

'Let *me* be the judge of that! I love you – my happiness is with you – it's all wrapped up in you, everything . . .'

'Then it should not be,' he said. 'That is my fault – my most terrible fault – but it's not too late to repair some at least of that wrong. If you love me, Caroline, then go back to your home and I promise you everything will be better – '

'How can it be? It's you I want, nothing but you. To go wherever you are, to be with you, to be your wife . . . Why do you think I'm here?'

'It was a foolish dream, and we mistook it for reality,' he said dully. 'I'll never forget you, Caroline, never – please believe that – but it's better that you forget. You cannot come to France. I'm saying this the best way I can, God knows I don't want to hurt you, you of all people in the world – '

'Why can't we go?'

'Caroline, please just believe that I speak the truth and that it is for the best – '

'*Why can't we go*?' she screamed out.

He sighed with a great weariness, and shaded his eyes with his hand. 'Because, my dear,' he said, 'I already have a wife.'

She could not tell how long she had been sitting on the upturned keg staring at the sandy floorboards. Probably a couple of minutes, but in those minutes her spirit seemed to have become bowed as with an age-long burden of suffering.

Somehow her lips were framing words.

'How – how long have you been married?' she said.

His voice seemed very faint and remote, though he was still standing by the window. 'Two years, a little more.'

'Is she beautiful?'

'She – I think she is – '

216

'What's her name?' Still her lips rapped out the mechanical questions.

'Caroline, it doesn't matter what – '

'Tell me her name.'

He sighed. 'Amélie. She is from Alençon. We met there. She is at Torcy, with my father.'

'And all this *time* – all this time, while we've been planning – to go together to France . . .' Her pain scorched her. She was in the heart of the flame and even to move was agony.

'I know – I know. I should not have let it go on. I know that. It was – the prospect of freedom. Always that has been before me, tempting me, blinding me. Yes, I thought, yes, escape, escape, any way will do. And so I let it go on – our plan. Because I had to be free. And, in that respect I know I have used you.'

'*In that respect . . . !*'

'Yes! Believe me, Caroline! What we have had together – these past months – that was true, real, sincere. And then, when out of it came this plan to escape together, I – could not resist it. I was weak. A chance of freedom. I shut out all other thoughts. All the way here, on the journey, I have struggled with myself, knowing what a great wrong I am doing you, wishing to stop it there and then . . . But the lure of freedom, of France and home, was too much. I even thought, perhaps we will be caught, I will be sent away, the responsibility will be taken out of my hands . . .' He beat with his fist against the wall. 'Can you not understand what freedom means to a man, imprisoned in a foreign country with no prospect of release – a man who sees a chance of escape – how it can make him trample on feelings that were good and – and sincere. Yes, Caroline, sincere.'

'You said you loved me,' she said. She felt she could

never move again. Her body was rooted. It would melt or turn to stone.

'You must understand . . . in my imprisonment, everything seemed different. Somehow my feeling for you, and my wanting to escape and using you to do it, they became separate in my mind. What you meant to me was something very special, unique . . . But your goodness to me was too much. Yet, still I went on taking it. That is my sin. I know I have done you wrong, but believe me I did not plan to. I was weak, I let myself be carried along . . . I don't expect you to forgive me – but please, don't think that you meant nothing to me but a way to escape. You mean a great deal to me, Caroline.'

'But your wife means more.'

The silence roared between them. And she felt the approach of the knife, knowing his answer.

'Yes,' he said softly; and then there was a flash of light outside beyond the window. Another. Another.

'They are signalling,' he said. 'Caroline, please go home, and I promise you it will all be clear, soon, very soon – '

'No.' Her body lurched into life. An abyss of total darkness was before her, she was falling, he must save her, Antoine, Antoine who was everything, Antoine without whom she could not draw breath – he wouldn't let her fall, he couldn't, he couldn't . . . 'Antoine,' she cried, and she was holding on to his arms and gripping them, just keep hold of them, this body, this face, those eyes, they could not be lost to her, it would be like death. 'Antoine,' she sobbed, 'I'll go with you to France anyway. There's nothing for me here. Let me go with you to France – then I can be near you. Just to be near you, that's all I ask. You'll change your mind,' and the lights flashed again, 'you'll change your mind in France, you'll see – oh, God, don't go away from me – '

He shook her off. His face was sad and tired. 'Don't you think I've done enough to you, Caroline?' he said. He picked up his bag and opened the door. 'God have mercy on me.'

Her last sight of him was so impaired – by the dingy glass of the window and the darkness and the tears burning her eyes – and yet so clear that she felt as if she would never see anything but that image, waking or sleeping; the image of Antoine walking down the bank to the waiting boat, pausing at the gang-plank to speak to one of the figures there before jumping into the boat.

A lantern wavered in the bows, its light outlining the filling sail, and the boat began to move out as Caroline slid to the floor. Antoine was gone, and she whispered his name between her sobs while her voice grew hoarse. Antoine was gone, and receding with him was the whole sweet perspective of love, gathering up the train of past joys and future hopes and leaving in its wake nothing but an overpowering anguish which her young soul wrestled with and fought and at last surrendered to.

She lay on the grimy floor, and her cries shook her until the door was gently opened and the youth who had admitted them to the tavern said: 'Miss? Yew all right?'

She rose to her feet and wiped her face. She left the tavern, carrying her heavy bags like chains of grief. Beyond the muddy beach the sea was a moving, murmuring darkness, and no sail was visible.

5

Luke's carriage-horses had been rested many times on the long journey to Yarmouth, but still they were dead tired as they came into the town that night. They did not like the strange surroundings or the darkness or the smell of the sea, and a carriage could scarcely get round most of the narrow streets.

'Put up at an inn,' Rebecca said. 'Put up at an inn and we'll ask around in the morning. We can't search now.' She drew her pelisse round her and rocked herself. She was half-frozen, and neither she nor Luke had had any sleep since setting out last evening.

Luke looked at her with fleeting sympathy, patted her hand. He was exhausted himself. He leant out to the coachman. 'See if there's an inn with stabling, John.'

A fisherman directed them to the Wrestlers. As they rattled across the cobbles of Church Square, Luke said: 'You go straight to bed, love. I'll ask around a bit. I'll go down to the harbour . . .'

'No, Luke. Please. We can't do anything tonight. You've got to sleep. Luke, are you listening – ?'

He had yanked down the carriage window. 'John! Stop here!'

'What is it?' Rebecca said.

'Look!'

Across the empty square a girl in cloak and bonnet, carrying two carpet-bags, was walking in a painful, slow, aimless fashion, listlessly shunting one foot in front of the other, her eyes on the ground. The wind whipped her cloak back and forth. Light from an upper window fell across her.

'It is,' breathed Luke. He flung open the door. 'It's her.'

She did not at first seem to recognize them. 'Caroline,' Luke said, 'Caroline, what's happened?' and she frowned and shook her head and even tried to keep walking; until Rebecca put her arm around her and said: 'It's me, love. It's your mother and father. All's well now, love,' and then Caroline looked at her and burst into tears. 'He's gone,' she said, while her mother hugged her. 'He's gone.'

CHAPTER 9

1

Charles Hardwick, all unaware of the troubles at the Bridge House, had been in London with his father since the reopening of Parliament on 21st January 1800.

He was in the gallery on 19th February, when the suspension of Habeas Corpus was again debated by the Commons. He renewed his acquaintance with the reformer Burdett, and visited Cold Bath Fields prison himself to see the condition of the political prisoners.

Charles was delighted to find himself useful to Burdett. He collated the reformer's papers on the prisoners, drawing up details of their histories, their offences, their treatment in Cold Bath Fields; and he began writing a pamphlet of his own in which he poured withering scorn on the government's imprisoning without trial, when it had already furnished itself with enough repressive power to bring the whole weight of the state down on the mildest protest. But his feelings carried him away into cloudy invective, and he tore up each successive draft.

Charles was happy. But his happiness did not only consist in his doing work for the cause of reform at last, but in the anticipation of a letter from cousin Susannah. He had opened his heart to her – at least half-way – by saying that he knew the Fairburns, had heard that Stephen did too, and that it would be delightful if, when he took up that invitation to stay at Great Baston, the Fairburns should happen to be there also. Susannah was not obtuse; and at the end of February the letter came. She and

Stephen had the Fairburns, as well as other company, coming to stay for a week, and Charles was more than welcome.

He felt a little ashamed at the alacrity with which he abandoned the Westminster world, but his shame soon vanished on the Cambridge coach at the thought of seeing Lydia again.

There were half a dozen people already at Great Baston when he arrived, but the Fairburns were not expected for another two days. In the meantime Charles had the opportunity to admire Susannah and Stephen's great-house way of life. His cousin had clearly taken to it.

'Stephen plans great things for the grounds,' Susannah said, as she and Charles walked down the lime avenue in the frosty February morning. 'The trees that obscure the house from the east are to be cut down. It will give prominence to the specimen cedar. And beyond the lake he hopes to have a ruin. Yes, an artificial ruin,' she said, laughing at Charles's expression. 'Apparently it is quite the taste. All this is too formal. There must be a sort of wildness in the prospect.'

'Have you had any news from the Bridge House of late, Susannah?'

'No. Should I have?'

'Oh, I don't know – just that my last two letters went unanswered. Caroline's usually such a good correspondent. Oh, well, perhaps there's a letter waiting at Morholm, or in London.'

'And how do you get on there, cousin?'

'Oh, famously,' he said with enthusiasm. 'I've been meeting all sorts of people – '

'Including the Fairburns, I take it.'

Charles hesitated, looked at Susannah's gentle face,

and smiled. 'It's very good of you and Stephen to invite them here, Sue.'

'It's a pleasure. I look forward to meeting them myself. Stephen knows the Fairburns well. He says Sir Thomas is a very upright, gentlemanlike man, and that Lydia is extremely pretty and extremely headstrong, and when she rides a horse she leaves most men behind.'

'Yes,' said Charles, 'that sounds about right.'

Susannah patted her cousin's arm. 'Well, I shall say no more. Except that Stephen has a very manageable hunter in the stable called Covey that's yours to ride whenever you like.'

Charles was riding Covey about the park when the Fairburns' carriage came through the gates at midday. He saw the carriage from a distance, and galloped full tilt diagonally across the park to be at the carriage-sweep before it.

He was a few seconds behind, and Lydia was just climbing out as Covey came thundering up. She looked round in alarm at the hooves spraying the gravel, and a mad idea took hold of Charles to jump down and kiss the back of that white neck that turned so elegantly.

But instead he swung down from the saddle and put out his hand to Sir Thomas Fairburn.

'Why, Hardwick, isn't it?' said Sir Thomas in surprise, shaking his hand. 'I had no idea you would be at Baston.'

'Charles is first cousin to my wife,' said Stephen, who had just come out to the drive with Susannah on his arm. 'Whom I have yet to introduce. Sir Thomas Fairburn, Miss Lydia Fairburn – I'm proud to present my wife Susannah.' And after the introductions were over he added: 'And her cousin Charles, whom you clearly know!'

'Yes, we met Mr Hardwick in London, didn't we, Lydia?' Sir Thomas said; but Lydia was already going up the steps with Susannah. That perfect turned neck expressed utter indifference – and utter self-consciousness. Charles felt a certain satisfaction in knowing he had taken her by surprise.

Lydia proved as elusive as ever that day: Great Baston was quite large enough to avoid someone in if you chose. It was when he went upstairs to change for dinner that he came across her.

'Miss Fairburn,' he said. 'We have a habit of meeting in corridors.'

'Mr Charles Hardwick.' She gave the coolest nod. 'Excuse me, I must go and dress.'

'This is my route also.'

She walked beside him in silence. She was dressed in a Turkish robe that emphasized her willowy height, with her coils of dark hair swept up over her ears. He was admiring in contented silence when she burst out: 'Well, I may as well say I think Stephen has done very well for himself with your cousin, Mr Charles Hardwick. I like her. A very sensible woman. Stephen needs a sensible woman to keep him in order.'

'Oh, I think all men do.'

Lydia made a face as if she were inhaling some scent that might be nice or might be nasty; then she turned to him and said accusingly: 'Did you know we were coming to Baston this week?'

'Know? Why should I? I have a long-standing invitation to visit here. Susannah is my cousin, after all. Her mother was a Hardwick. I have quite as much right to be here as yourself, Miss Fairburn. Or may I call you Lydia?'

'Indeed you may not!' she said; but she looked amused. 'You are a strange creature. But I must say – ' she looked him over assessingly, her green eyes vivid and assertive as a cat's – 'your appearance is improved. Yes, considerably improved.'

'Less of the thick-legged North Country manufacturer?'

'It's not gentlemanly to take a lady's words and use them against her.'

'Even if those words are not ladylike?'

'Your notion of what is ladylike probably differs from mine.'

'Oh, I don't know,' he said. 'The sort of lady I like is one who uses unladylike words, and tells people what she thinks of them.'

'And steals shoes?'

'And most of all steals shoes.'

She smiled very slightly: she had slowed her steps until they were scarcely moving. 'How long do you stay at Baston?'

'That depends.'

'On what?'

There were flecks of amber, he saw, in those eyes. 'On how long you stay, Miss Fairburn.'

'Oh, you're impossible,' she said, turning away. 'I'll not speak another word to you – Oh! it's this passage . . .'

They faced the long gallery passage that ran the length of the main wing. 'You know,' Lydia said, 'I always have a great desire to run at full speed down this passage.'

'Let's do it, then. A race.'

She looked at him in surprise, then began to run.

She had a head start on him, but with his long legs he caught her up at the end of the passage, and both of them nearly collided with an astonished footman who emerged from the back staircase.

Breathless and laughing, they leant against the banisters, and she struck him a hard blow on the shoulder. 'It wasn't fair! You cheated!'

'Cheat, how could I cheat? You started ahead of me!'

'Well.' She wrinkled her nose. 'A gentleman would have let me win.'

'Oh, I think you already have quite enough advantages, Miss Fairburn.'

'You're a strange mixture, you know, Mr Charles Hardwick. Are you one of these Methodies, forever telling people to repent and feel guilty about everything?'

'Methody, no. But there is much in the state of the country to feel guilty about.'

'Oh, pooh, if you're one of these ranting Jacobins, you needn't try and convert me. I have wealth and position and the only change I would approve would be one that enabled me to have more of both.'

'I sincerely hope you may do: but consider those who have neither, and no possibility of acquiring them.'

'No; that is precisely what I do not wish to consider. That's what's so tiresome about you people. I have no desire to look at hovels and say, la, fie, how dreadful. Who wants to contemplate ugliness? Oh, I dare say there are a lot of things wrong and unjust and so forth, but it's no business of mine.'

'I imagine those very words were often said in France ten years ago,' he said gently.

'I'm sure they were. In France my head would have been one of the first to roll. Why, you surely don't admire that barefoot rabble?'

'Their original ideas,' he said, aware that he was growing warm. 'The ideals of freedom and reform. The sort of ideals that we in England would do well to rehabilitate, instead of turning our backs on them.'

She widened her eyes mockingly. 'Citizen Hardwick.'

'I've long been accustomed to such cheap gibes, Miss Fairburn, and they no longer have any effect.'

'Your face goes quite pink when you're angry,' she said calmly.

226

'No doubt it does,' he said, flushing more.

'My dear Mr Hardwick,' she said with a laugh, 'I really couldn't care whether you are a red revolutionary or John Bull incarnate. I find the whole subject vastly tedious. But if you are going to stand there flaring your nostrils and mentally consigning me to the guillotine then I shall leave you. In fact, I must go anyway and dress. I shall see you at dinner. Unless, that is, you put *égalité* into practice and prefer to eat in the servants' hall?'

With a husky laugh she left him, quite broken up with exasperation and attraction.

When the ladies left the table after dinner, Charles found himself talking with Sir Thomas Fairburn.

A cynical observer might have suspected him of insinuating himself with Lydia's father: in fact he genuinely found much that was agreeable in this man who was so diametrically opposed to him. Sir Thomas, with his fluent, economical speech, cool wit and restraint when it came to the port bottle, made Charles realize how unpolished were many of the gentry of his own circle. Sir Thomas had travelled a great deal before the war, even to outlandish and unfashionable places like Scandinavia. Charles listened fascinated to the older man's account of the strange climate, the vast spaces, and the northern habit of cleanliness.

'A habit,' Sir Thomas said, 'that fortunately seems to be taking root in our society. Hopefully few would now agree with Dr Johnson that they "do not love clean linen". But then the abandoning of the wig has helped in that regard. As a child I recall being quite terrified of an aunt who bore down on me crowned by an enormous powdered perruke. What will future ages think of that custom, I wonder? And all because poor Louis XIV wore one to cover his bald head.'

After dinner there were cards. Charles did not play but watched over Lydia's elegant shoulder as she laid increasingly high stakes at faro and eventually lost it all.

Getting up from the table she said to him: 'Now, are you about to upbraid me for being so careless of money?'

'Not at all,' he said: he had overcome his earlier irritation. 'A very good redistribution I call it.'

She began to move away, then stopped and said: 'I think I shall ride early tomorrow. Stephen has promised me the use of a tolerable nag.'

'I also,' Charles said. 'Perhaps we shall see each other.'

Charles rose at dawn, and the view of the park was wrapped in mist as he ate from the cold buffet laid out on the dining-room sideboard. But, Lydia was out before him.

He saw her, mounted on a fine chestnut horse, close by the great specimen cedar, quite still as if waiting for him; and he set Covey at a canter to join her, with some idea of showing off his horsemanship. But when he came within a few yards of her she suddenly set her mount off at a smart pace and galloped away from him in the direction of the lake.

It was a part of the park that Stephen had let go, in pursuit of the fashion for picturesque landscaping: between the beeches the grass was thick and hummocky, and then the ground began to dip unexpectedly. It was bad terrain for a gallop, especially in the feeble light of a winter dawn; but Lydia pounded on ahead, seemingly careless of danger, and he could only follow and trust to Covey's sure-footedness. Then Lydia turned towards the old water-meadows that fringed the lake, and to his amazement kept straight on towards the high meadow fence.

Charles actually closed his eyes for a moment when she

launched her mount at the fence. But when he opened them again she was safely over, and after cantering a little way across the meadow she pulled up and turned her horse and sat there waiting for him.

He was too far away to see her expression, but he could guess what he was expected to do. Well, Covey was a seasoned hunter, even if he was not. He dug in his heels. At the moment of the horse's leap he had a vision of himself being borne broken-necked back to the house, and of what a test that would be to Susannah's qualities as a hostess; but he landed safely, and when he came up to Lydia she was smiling.

'Well,' she said, 'Covey is certainly a different class of horse from that nag I saw you on in Hyde Park – but no, all credit to your spirit.'

'All credit to yours, Miss Fairburn,' he said, short of breath. 'But are you always so reckless on horseback?'

'Oh, not always. But I thought to see how intent you were on following me. I hate a faint-heart.'

Charles patted Covey's neck. 'I was most intent on following you,' he said. Looking at the girl, trim and slender in a black riding-habit and a broad tilted hat, her beauty as cool and sparkling as the dew on the grass and trees, he felt an impatient need for directness. 'I would have followed you a great deal further, Miss Fairburn, believe me.'

She seemed to take no account of this remark, but urged her horse gently on towards the lakeside, and said: 'Do you ride much at your place – where is it? Northamptonshire?'

'Morholm is on the fenland just north of Peterborough. Yes, riding is necessary to get from one place to another. It is a country of large distances, and we keep no carriage.'

'And there, I suppose, you are terribly rural and bucolic and isolated?'

229

'Rural, I suppose. But no more, I would think, than at your place near Newmarket.'

'Oh, Stanningford.' She laughed. 'That's father's child. We're not there very often. I prefer London. Perhaps when Stanningford's finished I may take to it – but I begin to doubt whether it ever will be. But you and your father, I imagine, are the perfect squires, hm? Discussing turnips with the tenants.'

'Miss Fairburn, if you are trying to provoke me –'

'I am succeeding, and I am sorry. Shall we get down? Perhaps I shall be less arrogant on foot.'

There were willows on the south shore of the lake, and they tied their horses here and walked on by the lakeside. Sunlight was ripening, and the mist across the park was almost gone.

'You must not think me meaning disrespect to your father or yourself or even your turnips,' she said. 'But . . .'

'But?'

'Oh . . .' She aimed a swipe at the long grass with her riding-crop. 'It's just seriousness that I can't abide. Seriousness about anything. Now, just a moment ago, you were about to become serious, and I stopped you and talked about horse-riding. And you thought, what an irritating woman this is. But you see, one gets on much better if one is not serious in life. When we met in London, and you did not mind a bit about that business with the shoes, I thought, well, *there* for once is a man not full of grave pomposity – pompous gravity – which-ever. You see?'

'I see. But seriousness need not be automatically tedious.'

She looked sceptical.

'For instance, I came out this morning with a most

230

serious intention of getting to know you better, Miss Fairburn.'

'Why? To convert me to Jacobinism?'

'Something much more serious than that.'

She made an impatient gesture. 'There you are, you see. That is precisely what I do not want you to do, Mr Charles Hardwick. Just as, if you were to lecture me on the wants of the poor, I should be very inclined to echo Marie Antoinette as regards their eating cake – though she was a very silly tiresome woman who deserved to get her head chopped off for her bad taste.' She stopped, breathed deeply, looking across the park to the long symmetrical façade of Great Baston. 'Now, for example, I might make a comment on how beautiful Great Baston is – but no doubt to you it is a symbol of tyranny and corruption.'

He was silent a moment. Then he said quietly: 'You do me a wrong, Miss Fairburn. I don't believe that in seeking to secure the liberties of the broad mass of the people one is letting in the bloodthirsty Jacobin. I don't wish to see Great Baston consigned to the flames. Nor do I wish to lecture you, though it may seem as if I have just done so. And I may as well say that I did connive at visiting Great Baston when you would be here. For reasons that at the time I did not perceive as entirely "serious"; but which I now realize are most serious. Or whatever word you would prefer.'

She turned her crop in her hands, frowning slightly. 'What a speech. Is that where your future lies, Mr Hardwick? Following your father, and mine, into that bear-pit we call the mother of parliaments?'

He shrugged hopelessly, feeling himself trapped again in her distracting net of flippancy. 'Perhaps. Where does your future lie, Miss Fairburn?' he said, with a little spasm of bitterness.

She surprised him by suddenly taking his arm and pressing him to walk on. 'I'm a worldly creature,' she said. 'In your gallant way,' she said as he was about to speak, 'you want to say no, no, Miss Fairburn, you are not as worldly as you think. But I assure you I am. I like to have the best of everything and have no use for anything second-rate. I feel no shame about that. It's the way I was brought up. When the dog sits by the table you throw him scraps of offal and best veal and he wolfs them both down with no distinction because he has never known any better. I want only veal. And champagne, and satin, and a phaeton with a pair of greys, and never to worry about anything. I mean to marry money, and spend it well, and make the old hags of Portman Square jealous and be able to snub the ones I don't like.'

'When you say,' said Charles, aware of a certain tightness in his throat, 'when you say you mean to marry money, do you mean marry *for* money, irrespective of anything else?'

'Oh, well, I'd prefer it if the man was good-looking rather than ugly, and clever rather than stupid, of course, but the fortune is the important thing. I mean, I do have money but I would like more, and marriage is the only way to get more. And as for notions of happiness in marriage – well, I think any two people who propose to set up house together and expect to be all in all to each other for the rest of their lives are absurdly unrealistic. Money is the thing that can make such an unnatural way of life bearable.' She released his arm. 'And now you think me an appallingly mercenary little cynic.'

He looked into her eyes. 'Isn't that what I'm meant to think?'

For the first time she looked uncomfortable herself. She turned back towards their horses and said: 'There, now you are driving me into the arms of earnestness again. Charles – and I have called you Charles now but you *may not* call me Lydia – it's because I like you that I don't wish to be serious with you. Or for you to be serious with me. I like you because you run down corridors with me, and argue with me and get provoked and think none the worse of me for it. And on those terms . . .'

'On those terms, Lydia,' he said, 'I shall continue to be serious with you. Whether you like it or not. And I shall continue to believe that you are not the worldly creature you pretend.'

'Even if I prove otherwise?' she said, as she prepared to remount and he bent to make a step for her foot.

He straightened, looked at her sitting with negligent grace in the saddle. 'Even then.'

He was not surprised when she rode off towards the house without him, but though he did not try to catch her up he followed her.

The week at Great Baston, enlivened with music and cards and billiards and hunting and fishing and all the occupations of country-house life, passed all too quickly for Charles. Opportunities to be alone with Lydia Fairburn there were, but they were dependent on her whim. Sometimes she deliberately sought his company; at other times seemed deliberately to avoid it. Always her brittle armour of flippancy kept him at an ironic distance, and he searched for the chink that he thought must be there.

In the meantime his acquaintance with Sir Thomas ripened and even, despite their differing ages and outlooks, approached friendship; until the last day of the Fairburns' stay, when, with dismal rain preventing outdoor pursuits, Charles joined Sir Thomas and their host in the library to look over Stephen's collections of prints and books.

There was a large portfolio of the satirical prints of

Gillray, Rowlandson and others; and in coming across one of General Bonaparte, portrayed as the usual diminutive crook-nosed brigand, Charles commented: 'I wonder how long they can go on portraying the First Consul as a pygmy, now that he is master of France and much else besides.'

'I'm surprised to hear you using that absurd upstart title Bonaparte has adopted, Mr Hardwick,' said Sir Thomas, who was idly looking along the glass-fronted bookshelves.

Charles shrugged. 'The French constitution has been reshaped as a Consulate. That is his title.'

'In that land, no doubt,' Sir Thomas said airily. 'We can scarcely acknowledge such an adventurer as a head of state.'

'We acknowledge our monarchy, and they are descended from just such an adventurer – William the Conquerer.'

'The English monarchy has been sanctified by time and precedent.'

'Well, Bonaparte is still the head of state, whether we acknowledge him or not.'

'The Bourbon dynasty is the only legitimate government of France,' Sir Thomas said.

Charles laughed. 'You surely can't believe the French monarchy will return. Even if it were desirable that they should.'

'It's a magpie collection, I'm afraid,' Stephen put in, anxiously leafing through the prints for something uncontroversial. 'Some of it was my father's, he – '

'Do you mean to say you are an advocate of republican government, Mr Hardwick?' said Sir Thomas, with frost in his voice.

And here Charles was rather guilty of the long-ingrained habit of defending whatever position he found himself in. 'Well, it has shown signal success in both America and France,' he said.

'Government by rabble?' Sir Thomas said. 'I think you are jesting with me, Mr Hardwick.'

'Maps were his particular favourite,' Stephen said, urgently rummaging. 'He obtained some fine ones of Portuguese drawing, which – '

'Certainly republican government may have its faults,' Charles said. 'But our own is scarcely so perfect that we may criticize others.'

Sir Thomas, by the bookcase, was very still and poised. His grey eyes did not leave Charles. 'My dear sir,' he said softly, 'perhaps you will enlighten me as to these glaring imperfections.'

'An unrepresentative parliament, based on an absurdly small and incoherent franchise, and riddled with corruption,' said Charles readily. He was so used to sailing on the winds of debate that he did not consider for a moment the personal application of this to Sir Thomas. 'An arbitrary concentration of power, that has been ruthlessly employed in the last decade to erode the Englishman's every liberty.'

'. . . How old are you, Mr Hardwick?' Sir Thomas's voice was barely audible.

'I'm twenty-two.'

'So I would have thought.' Sir Thomas resumed his scanning of the bookshelves. 'Your political education, however, is sub-adult. I'm surprised at your father.'

'I have attended the Westminster terms with my father on several occasions, Sir Thomas,' said Charles, ignoring the crackling antique maps that Stephen was desperately flourishing in front of him, 'and I don't consider myself an innocent. The abuses of our system of government were made plain to me from an early age.'

'Mr Downes,' said Sir Thomas, whose normally pale

ascetic complexion was suffused with pink, 'I'm pleased to see Burke's *Reflections on the Revolution in France* on your shelves. Perhaps you would lend it to Mr Hardwick to enlighten what appears to be a sadly immature mind.'

'Oh, Burke,' Charles snorted, 'I thought Tom Paine had put paid to Burke's arguments once and for all.'

'Paine?' As Sir Thomas said the word his face expressed it. 'Here, in this library filled with the accumulated wisdom of ages, you cite that atheistical mountebank's name?'

'Surely. The government may have banned his books – but his championing of the rights of man is more relevant than ever.'

Sir Thomas's face was too handsomely well-bred to form a sneer, but it came close. 'The rights of man, as you call them, are guaranteed by the British constitution,' he said.

'What constitution? We have none. Nothing that protects a man from imprisonment without trial for speaking or writing a word against the government. Nothing that allows him to protest at his starvation being made the price for continuing a fruitless crusade that benefits only the speculators and fund-holders. Nothing that prevents Pitt quartering barracks on the people to keep them in submission.'

'I have heard all this before,' Sir Thomas said in a seething voice, 'but I never thought to hear it from a man of apparent gentility and education. The government has acted in the best interest of the country, Mr Hardwick, in preventing the spread of the Jacobin contagion; it has valiantly protected the laws and the rights of property without which the country cannot stand. Indeed, it has saved England, for we had become too lax, from setting out on the path of anarchy ourselves. And if the common people feel anything but due submission and loyalty to the statesmen who lead them, then it is because of agitators like yourself, putting thoughts into their heads that would never occur to them – '

'The man who has to pay a shilling for a sixpenny loaf knows very well what is behind it, believe me,' Charles said, 'and he knows where the profit is going. And that is why we must reform the representation of Parliament and much else besides before it's too late.'

'I am a justice of the peace at Stanningford, Mr Hardwick,' Sir Thomas said, 'and let me tell you that if you had publicly said these things in my parish I could and would have had you brought before the sessions. Not from personal malice, but because I believe it is my duty to the country to put down all such levelling sentiments. I will do you the justice, however, to believe that this apparent radicalism consists chiefly in youthful *naïveté*.'

'My radicalism is most heartfelt,' said Charles heatedly, 'and so it is with many others, in spite of all that corrupt magistrates can do.'

'You insolent puppy!' said Sir Thomas, with such violence that both Charles and Stephen jumped; and Charles suddenly became aware of how angry Sir Thomas was. 'I'd have every one of your Jacobins cooling their heels in prison! They're nothing but a rabble who would bring down every institution of property and authority!'

'Gentlemen, please,' Stephen cried, 'let us leave political debates to the Commons, eh? Consider this neutral territory . . .'

'It is not a matter of political debate, Mr Downes,' said Sir Thomas going to the door. 'It is a matter of plain subversion. I really think you should warn your wife of the dangerous mischief that has found its way into her family.'

'I'm sorry for that, Stephen,' Charles said, when Sir Thomas had gone.

'Oh, never mind, cousin,' Stephen said, relieved that the shouting was over. 'You know, whenever politics came up my father always used to turn the subject to the diseases of livestock. I think I must learn to do the same.'

Though Sir Thomas might not have believed it, Charles brought no personal malice to such arguments. Once his own blood had cooled, he was ready to meet Sir Thomas on cordial terms again. But Sir Thomas did not speak to him that evening; and when he saw Lydia later in the drawing-room she said: 'Is it you who's been quarrelling with my father?'

'Yes,' he said. 'Well, arguing. It was not meant to be personal. Why, has he said something?'

'He doesn't need to. I can always tell when he's been put out of humour.'

'And now I am out of favour.'

She gave him one of her coolest, most remote looks. 'Whoever said you were *in* favour? All I know is now I shall have to put up with his black mood. Oh, you men, all thinking you and you alone can set the world to rights. I've no patience with any of you.'

And indeed, having begun the week so hopefully, he got nothing more from her. It was only as the Fairburns' carriage was being got ready the next morning, with the whole company turning out in the drive to see them off, that he managed to speak a word to her alone, and ask if he might call on her in London.

'I don't know when we shall be in London,' she said.

'Then I shall keep calling until you are.'

She narrowed her eyes at him. 'Oh, very well. But you must promise not to get into arguments with father. Why can't you just say God save the King and death to Boney like everyone else, Mr Charles Hardwick?'

It would make things a lot easier if I could, Charles thought, as the Fairburns went to their carriage, and Sir

Thomas gave him a nod that clearly indicated that their differences were far from forgotten or insignificant.

2

At the Bridge House, callers who asked after Caroline were told she was ill with a cold. She could not face anyone. The débâcle of her elopement had been kept secret. Only Mr Squire, of necessity, knew the details, but then there were the servants . . . For the moment however the storm was confined within the house, and there it must blow itself out. For several days it raged, with Luke as its centre.

The journey home from Yarmouth, with a silent and numb Caroline sitting between her mother and father, had been a time only for thankfulness that they had got her back. Afterwards the rage began.

Some of it was directed at Nicholas, whom Luke considered an accessory. The boy trembled before his father and wished himself back at school. But most of it was for Caroline.

And her passivity seemed to further infuriate him. She sat like a statue while he paced up and down and flung words at her, words that spun endlessly down the same paths of frustration, disappointment, and incomprehension.

'Are we ogres? Is that it? Have we made life so unbearable for you that you must do something like this? Let me think. No, I don't recall beating you. Or starving you, or not letting you do what you wanted.'

The words bounced lightly off Caroline's consciousness, which crouched and brooded over the image of Antoine as a young animal will cling to the dead body of its mother. She sat with her hands in her lap and stared at the shattered pieces of the future.

'It's the lying that cuts me,' Luke said. He blew out a great exasperated sigh. 'You must be a cold fish, Caroline, that's all I can say. You must be damned hard. To go on deceiving us all that time, to go on in that bare-faced way, so cool . . .' He gave a broken, dangerous laugh. 'That takes a special sort of duplicity. Something rotten about it . . . Of course, you've made me look a fool, though that's incidental. Me responsible for the paroled prisoners and my own daughter helps one escape and means to take off with him. Squire will have to take over as agent: I'm no good for it now. There's been no word, you know, so one assumes the rogue got off to France. Is that a satisfaction to you, Caroline? Well, lucky for him. If I got hold of him he wouldn't live. He'd wish he'd never been born. But, he had you well and truly twisted round his finger, didn't he? And you were just going to leave us, snap, like that. Did it never occur to you for a single second just what you were doing? A Frenchie, a prisoner-of-war? Did you not feel one moment of shame?' He took her roughly by the shoulders. 'Answer me, damn it!'

'Father, *don't*,' Nicholas appealed.

'And you,' Luke said scathingly. 'Letting her go off. Not saying a word till it was nearly too late. Don't think I've forgot your part in this. I'd expected better of you, boy. God, was I wrong to expect a – a modicum of truth and decency from my children?' He turned fiercely on Caroline again, his face flushed, a vein beating at his temple. 'Haven't you anything to say for yourself, girl? I'll not be patient for ever!'

It was then that Rebecca intervened. Caroline recognized immediately the final authoritative note in her mother's voice.

240

'Luke. This has got to stop. Caroline, go up to your room, please. You too, Nick.'

Her voice had its effect on Luke too. When their children had gone he sat heavily by the fire, stared grimly at the hearth.

'It's got to stop, Luke,' she said, standing close to him but not touching him, tall and graceful and serious. 'You know it must.'

'Am I just to let the whole thing drop?' he said. 'Pretend it never happened?'

'We can't pretend that. But Caroline's here. She's safe. She's not in France with Captain Clairet. Yes, we may as well say his name. It was him, not a monster. She's young. She's made a bad mistake. It will be forgotten in time. Not yet, perhaps, but it will be. She may have betrayed us, but she's been betrayed herself. Whatever hurt and incomprehension we're feeling she's feeling too, and more. He used her – but you only have to look at her to know how much he meant to her, however misguidedly. Oh, I know it's hard, hard to feel that she's been lying to us, carrying on a secret affair. Perhaps it's hard to feel that – that she's grown up. That's part of having children. No matter how close you may think you are as a parent, no matter how confidential, how understanding, there's always some regard in which your children are entirely alien to you. Strangers. And that's as it should be – because they're individuals too. And Luke, I can't bear to have these recriminations going on all the time. Truly, love, I can't bear it. I know she's feeling sorrow – and that's why she can't talk about it. No, I'm not making excuses for her. But we've got to have some sort of peace in this house, love. Else things will never get better.'

Frowning at the fire, Luke took his wife's hand and pressed it to his face.

* * *

So, as January gave way to February, there was an uneasy peace of recuperation. Still Caroline moved about in a sort of dream, eating little, doing nothing. Her parents watched her discreetly and tried to behave normally. Once she walked down to the garden and the wharf, and they were encouraged; but when she came back Rebecca saw she was wearing her kid slippers, and they were soaked: she hadn't even noticed.

That night Rebecca tapped softly on Caroline's door and went in. Caroline was sitting in her usual posture on the bed, with her hands on her lap. Caroline remembered indistinctly that she had sat on the upturned keg in the smugglers' tavern in just this position, while Antoine tore her soul apart: it was as if she had never been able to move from it since.

Rebecca pulled the curtains to, trimmed the candle that was smoking on the bureau. And there she noticed the straw picture of the tower, propped against the wall. Seeing it, she felt a reflected pang of the agonies of young love, and in uncomplicated sympathy she sat on the bed and took her daughter in her arms.

Caroline leant her head on her mother's shoulder, and after a long time she said, with a dry, tearless sort of groaning: 'I did love him, mother . . . I did. I didn't see anything wrong, I didn't mean . . . I just loved him so . . .'

'I know, Caro,' said Rebecca. 'Sh. I know. It's all right.'

'And I still do . . . That's why I can't − I can't do anything, I can't forget . . . I want − I want everything to be all right again . . . but . . .'

'Sh, love. It will be. Believe me, in time . . . Your father is terribly hurt and upset, but it's because he cares for you so much, and so do I. And we're just glad to have you back with us. Your father will come round, and the quicker you do too then the better it will be – '

'It can't be all right, mother – it can't – '

'I know it seems that way now, Caro, I do know how it feels, truly. But you'll see, in time – '

'It can't be all right, mother,' Caroline sobbed, and her tears came surging up and they would not stop. 'I can't hide it. It's no good.' She held her mother's hand in both her own and rocked herself. 'It can't be all right because I've missed my courses and I've been sick and – oh, mother, I'm pregnant . . . I'm going to have his baby . . .'

3

The first snow began falling across the fenland that night and continued till noon the next day. It fell gently and meekly, whitening the windless air. In the clay fields it outlined the black furrows and dropped melting in the dykes. Along the river at Peterborough it made something ghostly and fantastic of the bare willows: it formed a chill damp crust on the backs of horses and turned to slush on the cobbles.

Caroline watched the snow from her window. The house was quiet now, though it had not been for most of that day and the previous night.

The lock on her bedroom door was broken. She had locked it against her father's rage last night, but he had broken it open.

She had fully expected him to strike her, and her mother had clung to him as if she feared the same thing. He did not, however. He had put his face close to hers and yelled, '*Is it true? Is it true*?'

Well, it was, of course. She had known for sure for several days.

Normally she would not have locked the door: she would have faced her father. But now she had something else to consider. Antoine's child. After the first shock of realization something fierce and utterly single-minded had taken root in her. Antoine's child. He was not gone, entirely. She hugged herself protectively.

She had hugged herself like that through the night, while candle after candle was lit and her father stood over her and was horribly, supernaturally business-like. At first he was going to turn her out on the street; but then he seemed to stiffen, his face grew set and grim and his eyes unseeing. No. She was to be sent away. Somewhere remote, up-country, Lincolnshire, Yorkshire. Some cottager. Someone would be paid to look after her. There were baby-farms. The child would be farmed out. Money, money would do it.

While her mother, looking pale and drawn and dreadfully sad, merely sat by her, as if she had no more resources, her father was full of insane energy. He brought maps from his office. Somewhere remote. Somewhere poor, where there would be no questions asked. As for questions at home, they would say she had gone for a long stay with her Uncle Peter in London. The Morholm family would be told – no one else need know the truth. He actually got out paper and pen and ink and noted down the plans as if he were checking a cargo. His quill went scratching maniacally across the paper, hurry, whisk the horror away. If they kept moving, if they did not stop to think for a second, the monstrous shame bearing down on them could be held at bay.

Once he stopped, a light in his eyes. 'Wait. She can't be very far forward. Can it be got rid of? Is there a safe way?'

Rebecca put her head in her hands. 'Oh, *Luke* . . .'

'No. No, of course.' He nodded emphatically. 'It's not

safe. We'll send her away, and have the child provided for. Yes, that's it. Now, as for money . . .' and the quill wagged again. All the time he never addressed Caroline. She was just 'she'.

And Caroline hugged her still flat belly, no longer interested. Because she was not going to lose this child. It was Antoine's. It was everything to her. Something, after all, had been salvaged from the wreck of her life. Something to live for. It was not going to be farmed out, not going to be provided for. All she knew and all she cared about was this one light in the blackness of her humiliation and despair.

So, she was calm that day. Her father's continued, hysterical planning that kept him from breaking down, her mother's hollow ashen face, seemed remote and incomprehensible. The only thing to register from his ceaseless flow of talk was the story of her going to her Uncle Peter's in London. It presented itself to her very clearly. That was what she would do.

For the second time in a month she packed a carpet-bag, with the straw tower in the top. Her Uncle Peter was kind and understanding and she had always been a favourite of his. He would shelter and help her. She could not stay here – could not stay, after causing her parents so much pain already, as a standing shame and bane to them. But even if she could she would not. Because they were not going to let her keep her baby – Antoine's baby. She would fight for that. She would kill to keep it.

And if her Uncle Peter would not protect her, then London would. There were lying-in hospitals in London, where unmarried mothers could go to have their babies. London, a consoling anonymity.

She took some money from the drawer in her father's study; she did not feel bad about that, for it was the last thing she would ever take from him.

245

She left soon after everyone had gone to bed that night. She was not going to risk another disaster like when she had met Nicholas in the Angel. The village of Stilton, five miles south of the city – just past Norman Cross – was on the Great North Road and a centre for coaching. She would walk there, through the night. There was a moon, and the reflection of the snow made the country almost light as day.

She walked out of the quiet city: the ruts in the carriage-road were frozen into deep grooves, with here and there a crunching pool of ice. She walked through the glittering, unreal landscape, and felt as weightless and unattached as the flakes of snow that drifted on the breeze.

Book Two

CHAPTER 1

August 1800

1

'I just don't understand you,' Martha said, peering into the pot containing Caroline's dinner. 'You're still living like this and you've got family. Rich family, who'll look after you and see you get the best of everything.'

Caroline concentrated on her sewing. It was too difficult to explain.

'All right, I could see why at first. Your pa was vexed, you run away. But now you're getting so near your time – I reckon you're mad. They'd have you back. With open arms, I reckon.'

Caroline shifted her weight and held her sewing up to the light. How to explain to Martha that she had forfeited any right to expect anything from her parents? She had made such an unholy mess of her life. She could not expect anyone else to share the burden.

Besides, they would not let her keep the baby. They were going to have it taken away. Young ladies of her class and position simply did not have illegitimate babies. And her father and mother could never know how deeply she felt about this child. Kind, practical Martha certainly did not understand.

'Or what about the father? Why not turn to him?'

'I've told you, Martha, I can't.'

'Why? He ain't dead, is he?'

'. . . No.'

'Well then. You mark my words, you turning up at his door with your belly like that – it wouldn't half shake him. He'd soon do the right thing by you. Men go all to jelly when they see a woman like that.' Martha looked with bafflement at the straw picture of the tower hanging over the mantel. 'And what about when the brat's born, eh? What then?'

Caroline shrugged, and turned the piece of quilting over. 'I'll carry on doing this work. I can do it here and look after the baby.'

Martha pursed her lips sceptically.

'You could always take the baby to the Foundling Hospital. They look after 'em proper, I've heard.'

'*No.*'

Martha sighed. 'You've got your heart set on this baby, ain't you? Well, Lord knows why. I've had three and I'd gladly have given 'em away, all the pain and trouble they cause you.' She went to the window and leaned out to look at the dusty courtyard with its grey banners of washing. 'Whoo, there's no air today. What I'd give for a drop o' rain. If you're ashamed,' she went on in an unaltered voice, 'you know – to write to 'em, like – your ma and pa – I could do it for you. Ask 'em to come and collect you. I can write a fair hand. My brother learned me – he was articled to a notary. I used to make the odd shilling writing letters for the others when I was in service. Let me do it, eh?'

'You're very kind, Martha. But no. I just can't. I can't explain. Please believe me.'

'Well. If you say so. Better go and see if my boy's back yet.' She paused at the door. 'You reckon looking after a little 'un all on your own's going to be easy. I'm just warning you. If you don't it'll end up on the parish. And then it'll be took away from you.'

Caroline liked Martha, but she was glad when she had gone. She was only really at ease with solitude nowadays.

Martha was thirty and looked nearer fifty. She lived in

250

two rooms below with her sister and her surviving son, a twelve-year-old outdoor apprentice. Her husband was in the Army, but she was not sure where he was. He popped up now and then. She had been highly suspicious of Caroline when she first moved in, but gradually, perhaps motivated chiefly by inquisitiveness, she had taken her under her wing.

Martha could not understand how it was that someone like Caroline, obviously from a genteel background, should choose to leave it if she hadn't actually been turned out on the street. But there was no question of choice. The whole purpose of Caroline's life was to keep and cherish Antoine's baby. That she could not do at home – even leaving aside the paralysing shame that she felt she could not inflict on her parents.

There was no other way, for a girl of her background. London's vast indifference swallowed her and let her do what she wanted – which was to hide in a room and feel Antoine's baby growing inside her, and support herself. Which she managed to do. London was full of work for women: the only problem was keeping above starvation level.

The spring and early summer of 1800 that had elapsed since she had fled from her home had been dry, baking and monotonous. In that time she had done nothing but work, feed herself, and hide. Her mental life, such as it was, consisted in memories, in which each detail of Antoine Clairet's face and body and voice were obsessively recounted. While her fingers made the weary stitches, her mind went with the same dull repetition over every moment spent with the man whose child she bore. There was nothing so definite as longing or outrage or indignation; only a chastened brooding that never woke into a full consciousness of where she was or what she was doing. More than once Martha commented that she looked like a ghost, and indeed there was about Caroline through those long months something not fully human. She continued to live, but it was like no conception of life she had ever had. It was the way a plant or a worm lived, unreflecting and mechanical.

The war had gone on, and there had been momentous deeds. Bonaparte with heroic energy had crossed the Alps and defeated the Austrian offensive at Marengo. Whilst he confirmed the French grip on the Continent, the British strengthened their hold on the Mediterranean by at last capturing Malta. In country districts throughout England there was distress and rioting. Caroline was aware of none of these things. The only consequence of the turbulent times that touched her was the soaring price of bread.

She had never, as she had first planned, gone to her uncle Peter's. Or rather, on her arrival in London she had gone to Hanover Square and gazed across at her uncle's house and gone away again.

She could not thrust herself on him. A deep self-contempt was her chief and constant consciousness: the full recoil of her feeling, after Antoine's flight, was driven against herself and not him. She could not begin to hate him, only continue to hate herself. And in this self-abasement she could not face uncle Peter.

She stayed at the inn where the coach had put up, and tried to nerve herself. But the other emotion, or instinct, that governed her – her intense possessiveness towards her unborn child – prevented her finally from going to her uncle's. Peter Walsoken was a barrister, unmarried, generous and discreet and Caroline was a favourite of his. But he was her mother's brother. And he would never help her against the wishes of her parents – not help her as she wanted him to. She had a clear vision of uncle Peter telling her parents she was here, of her father coming to claim her, bearing down on her. *We'll have the child sent away* . . .

After that, things were simpler. She had a little money but it would not last long. She must have a room, and work to feed her – feed her for the sake of the baby.

It was then that the great gulf of experience between her past life and what she had elected to do was revealed. Vaguely and naïvely, she had thought of moderately genteel things like being a governess. A very few enquiries brought home to her the fact that governesses required impeccable character and family references, that they lived in the household, and under no circumstances were they pregnant.

Unmarried. Pregnancy. Badge and barrier. No matter if your name was ancient and your family rich and respected. A swelling belly and bare third finger were, together, great levellers.

So she had taken this room, in a dreary tenement off Gray's Inn Lane, and began seamstress-work. It was hard, ill-paid, insecure: the lowest common denominator of female labour. But she could do it at home – if the dingy room could be called that. She could hide, submerge herself, lose her identity. It was what she wanted. She sewed quilting for petticoats and stitched stays. She had no care for comfort or leisure, and she took as much work as she could get. It was Martha who helped her find it, introducing her at a large draper and haberdasher's in Cheapside. It was sweated work. It suited her. It was empty and automatic. It allowed her to be alone, as she wanted. Not to think, but to suspend thought and surrender to her body's basic needs – and those of its beloved lodger. Under the bed she kept two pounds from the money she had brought with her: that was for her lying-in. She wrote a letter to her parents, telling them she was

253

well and healthy and was sorry for the pain she had caused them, and saying this was the best way.

She rented her room weekly. The tenement was in a dark court called Jackson's Rents. In the yard was a solitary pump and an open drain. Below there were filthy cellar-dwellings with whole families crowded into single rooms: in the sweltering summer heat the air gusting up the stairwell was nauseously stale. But, the place was not as bad as the packed criminal rookeries of St Giles or Spitalfields or Black Boy Alley, where the Irish poor squatted beside pigs and asses. Caroline's room was on the first floor; it was cheaper because it was at the back, facing a blind wall. It contained a bed with linsey-woolsey blankets and bolster, a deal table, two cane chairs, an iron stove, two iron candlesticks, some floor-matting, poker, shovel and tongs, a few black pans hanging on the mantel, and a square of cracked looking-glass.

Her self-effacement meant she did not mind it. And sometimes when she drifted off to sleep, half-blind from sewing, she could fancy it was Antoine's room in Little's Yard.

A fierce sun seemed to blaze sixteen hours a day that summer, but Caroline was paler than any elegant lady who darted with parasol and gloves from Bond Street shop to carriage. The great city of eight hundred thousand people was to her an undifferentiated warren in which she had found a hole. She went nowhere except to the draper's in Cheapside to collect and return her work, and to the market to buy food – the bread, cheese, parsnips and occasional scrag of mutton or pig's ear on which she lived. She had no money for entertainments, but then she obscurely considered she had forfeited her right to such things, had left them behind when she cut her moorings; and she took no interest in the free entertainment that London offered. In the early morning, when the streets rang to the cries of hawkers, the sellers of asses' milk and the saloop-vendors, when the Guards marched in procession from their barracks to Hyde Park led by tall Negroes crashing cymbals, when the massive brewers' horses thundered their laden drays across the cobbles, she walked on her way to the draper's with her eyes lowered in perfect indifference. On the King's birthday, when the whole town was illuminated and there were fireworks and the streets were thronged with carriages taking ladies to St James in their voluminous Court dresses, Caroline came back from Covent Garden with her basket of cheap bruised vegetables and looked neither right nor left. There was no question of adjustment to London; she simply ignored it.

Martha was her only friend, and that was chiefly at Martha's instigation. But what she said that day about the baby and the parish roused Caroline a little. She knew that she had no claim on the parish for relief if it should come to that. When she went to the draper next day she asked him for testimony that she was a good worker. The parish officers might require assurances that an illegitimate baby would be supported and not become a burden on the poor-rates.

It was as she was passing Newgate on the walk home that it began to rain. There had been a heavy stillness in the air all morning and now the clouds seemed to come from nowhere. The big drops fell hissing in the dust, stirring up the stinks of the narrow City streets.

When she got home there was no way of drying her clothes. It was too warm and close to have a fire. She sat and worked in her shift, counting over the mental beads of grief for Antoine and love for his precious child, through the purple dusk, while the torrent of rain descended outside her open window.

She was caught in her continued love for Antoine like a fly in amber.

When she fell asleep the rain was still lashing down.

2

The August rain began to fall over the parched fens as Charles was returning home on horseback from Peterborough.

He had been with his brother Edmund to call at the Bridge House and ask if there was any news of Caroline. It was a regular ritual, and a depressing one. They were both silent as they struck the turnpike road north. The atmosphere of the Bridge House clung to them like a smell.

Aunt Rebecca had lost weight and looked sad and resigned. They were still placing advertisements in the local and London newspapers asking for news of Caroline's whereabouts, but Rebecca had accepted that wherever she was Caroline did not want to come back home. What worried her was the fact of her having a baby alone and friendless. It was a perilous enough business when you were supported by your family and had the best medical attendance.

Luke's reaction to the strain was different, and more alarming. He had thrown himself fanatically into work. The news of Bonaparte's courting of the Baltic countries, and a show of defiance from the Danes against the British right of search of neutral ships, had raised the spectre of the crucial Baltic ports being closed against British ships. Luke had embarked on a hasty expansion of his timber-yards in King's Lynn. He went constantly back and forth to Lynn, and took Nicholas with him. Nicholas was suffering for his part in Caroline's elopement. Luke saw it all as a concerted effort to hurt and humiliate him, and as one of the protagonists had run away in shame, the other must bear the full brunt of his grieving bitterness.

Charles and Edmund had both noticed the change in Nicholas. Physically he was as sturdy as ever, but his eyes had a cautious look. When his father spoke to him Nicholas seemed almost to flinch. They never saw him at Morholm, for he was always busy with his father, either at the timber-yards and warehouses in Lynn, or accounting at the Bridge House.

There had been a sharp hectoring tone in Luke's voice when speaking to Charles too. 'Well, what's your precious Bonaparte planning, boy?' he had demanded. 'You're always abreast of Jacobin notions. If he woos the northern powers to his side we may as well give in. What's our damned Navy doing? Cannon-shot's the best persuader. Or has the Navy all gone soft like Nelson?'

Charles had no answer. The last letter he had had from Richard Lindsay was some time ago and it was brief: he was with the Channel Fleet which had just come under Earl St Vincent, and the new admiral had imposed a strict discipline that meant long cruises and no shore leave.

'I wonder if we should speak to mother and father,' Charles said. 'About Nicholas, I mean. He's a strong lad, but he can't take that strain. Perhaps they might persuade uncle Luke to let up a little.'

'Perhaps,' Edmund said. 'But I wouldn't fancy anyone trying to moderate uncle Luke at the moment. Maybe Caroline will come home soon.'

Edmund's peaceable stoicism, which could be restful, was irritating Charles. But in his heart of hearts he had to confess to an intermittent smart of jealousy of his younger brother. Edmund had been accepted to study at the schools of the Royal Academy, and was going up to

London in the autumn: his father had agreed to support him for a year.

Not that Charles had ever wanted to be a painter – he was envious because Edmund knew precisely what he wanted and his feet were set firmly on the path to achieving it. Edmund's aspirations were a source of satisfaction to him: Charles's were the opposite.

He had had a frustrating time since his stay at Great Baston. He had gone with his father to London in the spring, and called at the Fairburns' townhouse in Curzon Street almost before he had unpacked. But on a sudden whim the Fairburns had decided to go to Bath and spend the season there; and when Parliament closed, and George was ready to go home, they were still away. So, there was no knowing in what regard he was held by either father or daughter; and the news that George did not intend going up to Westminster till the new year was a further trial to Charles's normally elastic temper.

The brothers rode in silence, and it looked as if they might reach Morholm before the rain began. But as they left Werrington and joined Morholm land, the clouds that formed a vault from horizon to horizon, from the scrub of Helpston Heath to the line of Borough Fen, broke suddenly. The rain pelted from a sky the colour of a bruise.

'We'd have welcomed this a couple of months ago,' Charles said. After a succession of wet summers, they had had a solid ten weeks of scorching heat. Across the reclaimed fen fields the wheat and barley were bleached and brittle between blackened hawthorn hedges. When they had cut the hay at Morholm it had been like matchwood, and the bean-crop had withered. They had begun the corn harvest at the home farm just last week, and the tenant farms had started yesterday.

The rain dashed down, and a steaming earthy smell

rose as if all the heat of the summer had been released. 'Oh, well,' Charles said, 'it'll do no harm as long as it doesn't last.'

It continued almost solidly for a week, and there were heavy showers into the first days of September. The interrupted harvest was resumed, but John Newman, the Morholm steward, shook his head pensively as Charles trudged with him across the Aysthorpe fields and saw the shockers struggling to tie up the shabby, blighted stooks.

The sudden downpour that followed the summer drought of 1800 was nothing spectacular, but it was enough to ruin the harvest all across the country for the second year running. In the fenland, where the progress and ripening of the sea of corn was constantly impressed on the eye, the effect was especially disheartening; the world was sky and soil, and they had turned malevolent.

While the gleaners picked their way through the stubble, and the waggons trundled through Aysthorpe with their depleted loads, rumours of discontent reached Morholm. The already inflated price of bread, instead of coming down with the harvest, had shot up further. Wheat was selling for the unheard-of price of 140 shillings a quarter. The Rev. Dr Emmonsales, Rector of Aysthorpe and magistrate, came over to Morholm to consult with George. He had heard of disturbances among the poor in Peterborough, and though he would not hesitate to use his powers to read the Riot Act, he felt reinforcements were needed. The 4th Royal Irish Dragoons were quartered at Northampton, and Parson Emmonsales pressed George as Deputy Lord Lieutenant of the county to request a detachment for the Soke. 'This is exactly the time when the grievances of the poorer sort are worked upon by agitators,' he said, 'and if they are given way to for one moment there will be no controlling their excesses.'

'You didn't promise him his dragoons, did you?' Charles asked afterwards.

'Of course not,' George said. 'I hope it won't come to anything, not in this district anyhow. We'll make sure our corn goes to Fenstanton's mill at a fair price. Certainly not to Tydd's. I believe he was speculating in grain last year, though we couldn't pin him down.'

It was two days later, on the 8th of September, that a messenger came galloping to Morholm from Burghley House. The Earl of Exeter, Lord Paramount of the Justices, had news of bread riots at Market Deeping, where there were several mills. The Earl had sworn in special constables and despatched them to the scene, but it would be a long time before the Dragoons could get there. George was to lead the local gentry in mustering the Soke Volunteers and go and help quell the disturbance.

Frederick Amory and his father were over from Leam House in a matter of minutes; and presently there were twenty or so horsemen milling about on the lawns in front of Morholm, talking excitedly and thrilled at actually being asked to do something. Parson Emmonsales was there, and Frank Bellaers in his hunting-coat and many others who were as familiar to Charles as his own name; the small gentry of the district, turning out to put down a riot of their own countrymen.

'I hope to God there's nothing in this,' George said, pulling on his riding-coat in the hall.

'There'll be another riot if those great loobies trample on my flower-beds,' said Mary. 'Who do they think they are? Now, be careful, George, please . . . Why does it have to be you?'

'It's my duty, love, I suppose,' said George, kissing his wife. 'It's probably all been exaggerated . . .'

Charles stood irresolute in the hall. Duty. He was a

Volunteer. His peers were going and he should too. How would it look if he didn't? But he had joined the Volunteers to resist foreign invasion . . .

George turned to look at his son. Charles could not read his expression. 'Are you coming, Charles?' he said quietly.

Charles shrugged, frowning. 'Oh, very well.'

They hallooed across country like so many foxhunters, and a few rakers in the fields watched them open-mouthed. People pressed themselves into the bridge bays as the horsemen clattered over the Welland bridge into the graceful little limestone town of Deeping, and some children, incongruously, ran after them cheering.

The crowd was outside Tydd's warehouse, and Charles saw that more than half of the few dozen were women: sturdy fen-women with sunburnt arms and lappet-caps. They had prevented a flour waggon from unloading, and one of the women was standing on the waggon and shouting up at a window above the warehouse. There were several farmers standing about doing nothing whom Charles took to be Lord Burghley's special constables, and one came running up to George at the head of the Volunteers.

'Thank God you've come, sir, we cann't do nothing to stop 'em,' he said. 'They're after tekkin' all that flour away, the rogues . . .'

'A fair price is all we're asking!' the woman on the waggon cried in a voice like an organ. 'We're asking for the miller to sell at a price we can afford! Two and six a stone,' and several voices echoed her: 'Two and six a stone!' though some people began to edge away at the sight of the horsemen.

'Where is Mr Tydd?' called George.

'There!' Arms pointed up to the first floor window, where a round face peered behind a curtain, and there were boos and catcalls. 'Frit to come down he is!' the woman on the waggon said. 'Because he knows we'll not be cheated any more!'

'If I ask Mr Tydd to come down and speak with you,' George said, raising his voice above the noise, 'will you give me your word to offer him no violence?'

There was a chorus of groans, a few cheers, and Mr Tydd made frantic negative gestures in the window.

'I understand your concern at the prices after this bad harvest,' George said, 'but if you take the law into your own hands it can only end one way, believe me. Now, if you will give me your word . . .' He was struggling to make himself heard. The woman shouted: 'Two and six a stone! If he don't sell it us we'll sell it usselves, fair and proper!'

'Mr Hardwick!' Parson Emmonsales urged his horse up beside George's. 'We must act immediately. These rogues will not back down. They must be dispersed, and the constables must arrest the ringleaders.' His face was hard and red. 'You know this is what you must do, sir.'

Someone had shied mud at Frederick Amory, and he did not like it. Several other Volunteers were backing their horses round to the other side of the crowd, surrounding them. And suddenly Charles's earlier reluctance took definite shape. He wanted no part in this.

He was a Volunteer against French invasion, not civil disturbances. He would not co-operate with the draconian Dr Emmonsales against country people whose grievances he could see the reason of. 'I'm sorry, father,' he said in distress, 'I'll have nothing to do with this. I'm sorry, I – I want no part in it.'

He struggled to manoeuvre his horse out of the press, desperate to get away. The shouts and jeers were growing more violent. Before he burst out of the ring of horsemen he caught a glimpse of Frederick Amory's surprised face and heard his friend's booming voice: 'Charles, where are you going?'

Charles galloped away over the bridge and did not slow down until he was past Northborough and close to Morholm land again. There he got down and led his horse to the river and stayed there till early evening.

He was in a miserable state of confusion: angry with the world and with himself. He had run away; that was the galling thing. Faced with a concretion of the conflicting loyalties he felt, torn by his beliefs, he had merely run away and hidden. Those poor devils who could not afford bread could not run away: neither, in a different way, could his father, who had clearly felt a distaste for what he was doing but carried on because he considered it his duty.

Dreading to face his father, he went home at last.

He went to the stairs to go up and change, and saw through the open library door his father, sitting at the desk with a finished letter before him, leaning his head on his hand. Charles went softly in.

'Father?'

George looked up, and Charles saw how tired he was. 'Oh, hullo, Charles. Come in.' George rubbed his eyes and then shook some silversand over his letter. 'I've just written to Lord Fitzwilliam, asking him to intercede for some of the prisoners in Peterborough Gaol – the ringleaders were arrested, you see. He may have a moderating influence on Dr Emmonsales, who of course is all for stiff sentences.'

Charles perched on the arm of a chair. 'You've had a lot to do today.'

'I don't sit so easy in a saddle as I used to. Emmonsales has twelve years on me but he canters about like a younker.'

Charles bit his lip. 'You certainly had a right to expect your son would help you.'

George shrugged slightly and looked at his letter. 'Oh, Lord knows you had your reasons, boy. I'm just glad the whole business is over.' He paused. 'You do see why I had to do it, don't you, Charles? God knows I had some sympathy with those people – Tydd's a grasping fellow and I'd like to see him caught out . . . But there's no knowing where such things can lead. It's our own fault perhaps; when the restraining hand is so tight, the reaction's all the more violent if the grip slackens. Oh, these are difficult times. There'll be starvation this winter – literally. I don't know where it will end. The temptation is ever greater to just turn away and tend my own garden. An attitude I know you find deplorable.'

'I don't think I'm in a position to deplore any attitudes just at the moment.'

George melted a little wax on his letter and sealed it. 'Do you hear anything from Burdett?'

'I've written him once, asking if there's anything else I can do. I've had no reply yet.'

'He may be at one of his country houses. You were useful to him, though, weren't you – and could be again?'

'I suppose so.' Charles thought his involvement with the reformer was a touchy point with his father, and wondered why he had brought it up.

'Edmund goes up to the Academy schools soon,' George said. 'He's young to start in London alone. While I'm paying for his lodging, I may as well pay for two. What do you feel?'

'I – don't understand . . .'

'Look, Charles, I know you're restless here. And while things like – well, what happened today – while they go on you'll chafe all the more and one day we may even fall to quarrelling. If I were to set you and Edmund up in lodgings in London you could work with Burdett, or Whitbread, or whatever. You needn't consider it a permanent arrangement. Try it. And that way – '

'That way I won't be an embarrassment to you?'

George raised an eyebrow at his son. 'I was going to put it more kindly than that.'

'Oh, I know, father, I'm sorry,' Charles said, shaking his head. 'I would love it, of course. It's just – well, perhaps I feel a little ashamed at your having to indulge me like this.'

'The indulgence won't all be on one side. I can't deny that it would be a great relief to me to see you occupying yourself doing what you wanted instead of gnawing away inside all the time. And your keep's little enough. God knows, there are plenty of young men who plague their father with tailor's bills and gambling debts . . . Perhaps,' he added, looking wryly at Charles, 'I could understand you better if you did.'

So it was settled. Mixed in with the feelings of guilt and relief at the prospect that had so unexpectedly opened up at the end of that wretched day Charles registered one unmistakable excitement. Somehow he would see Lydia Fairburn again. And this time he would not be put off.

3

At the end of September, Martha left Jackson's Rents. She had gone out to the market-gardens north of the city where harvest labour was wanted at this season. It was an annual migration, and she told Caroline she enjoyed it, in spite of sleeping in barns and cooking your food at the brick-kilns.

Martha's advice had always been available through the small alarms and difficulties of her pregnancy; and her friendship too, though Caroline had never encouraged it simply because only solitude was bearable. Now she was quite alone. But as she approached her full term, though her mind was still the same numb wound, she felt physically strong and healthy apart from some backache.

Nothing must go wrong now.

Some of the charity lying-in hospitals did not take in unmarried women, but she had heard the Royal Lying-in Hospital did, and when by her calculations she was about a week from her time she went there to ask if they would admit her. She had assurances from the parish officers, and money to lay as a deposit for burial fees in case she should not survive the birth. The hospital was quite full, the officiating surgeon said, but he had one of the trainee man-midwives examine her and told her to come back in a week.

Four days later, her first pains began.

The great downpour that had ruined the harvest had been followed by mild warm weather, and the kind of soft autumn dawns that in the fens Caroline had loved but, being a slug-a-bed, seldom seen. It was just such a pearly dawn light that she was sleepily aware of as she lay in bed in her dingy rented room, on the morning of the 2nd of October.

It was in these waking moments, before she fully remembered her situation, that she felt at least half-way human. The haunting warmth of her dreams, which were full of shadowy images of Antoine and herself somehow united and everything made right, lingered a while, until the grim truth took hold and rendered her an automaton again.

This time, however, the pleasant glow was abruptly driven out. She had been told by Martha what to expect, and she had no doubt that this was it.

After the first alarm she found the pains were negotiable insofar as she managed to get out of bed and dress. Getting her money out from under the bed was more difficult; and when she struggled to the landing and looked at the deep stairwell she felt dizzy.

By the time she had reached the courtyard the contractions were coming more frequently. An ass's milk-seller saw her at the gate and realized immediately what was happening. Caroline pressed a shilling into her hand and begged her to find a hackney-coach or a chair for her. The milk-seller was fat and none too fleet, but she was willing. 'I'll be back in two shakes,' she said optimistically. 'Now you lean on Letty here. She'll hold you up, she's sweet-nater'd.'

And so Caroline, panting and gasping for air, leaned across the uncomplaining ass's back and waited, and in a light-headed bizarre way she thought, *Just like the virgin Mary . . . carried on an ass's back*, and almost laughed at a vision of herself jogging in labour around London on an ass and all the inns turning her away, and then she wailed a bit because Martha had said these pains were nothing to what came later . . . And then the fat woman was back, and the hackney-carriage driver was unwilling to take her 'in case she whelped in his wehicle', and she pressed more money on him till he relented. And then the journey, only a few streets but the streets were crowded and it seemed hellishly long as they bumped and lurched over the cobbles and a sewage-waggon got stuck across the way and the hackney-man yelled a stream of curse-words most of which she had never heard before . . .

At last they stopped in front of the Royal Lying-in Hospital, and the hackney-man with a show of great magnanimity gave her his arm to the door. And then there was a terrible interlude in the lobby, while an ancient door-porter fetched the visiting physician, and the

267

physician, who was a grand man of the old style with a large powdered wig and a gold-headed cane, said they were full and she had better go to the workhouse infirmary; and the porter added, as if to cheer her up, that there was a lot of hospital-fever and she had better go; and Caroline tried to convey through her groans that she had money and wasn't a pauper and moreover she was going into labour. The matron settled it, taking one look at Caroline and saying they would find room.

The place was bare and austere: Caroline saw whitewash and trestles. The iron beds ranged end-to-end along the walls were not appealing, either, but they had just been introduced as much healthier than the old wooden beds that harboured pestilence. What she most disliked, however, was the high raftered ceiling, at which she stared while a midwife examined her and then went to fetch a pitcher and basin. That ceiling seemed to catch and amplify every moan and cry from the wards. A woman across the room from Caroline repeatedly murmured, 'I'm dyin' . . . Almighty God, I'm dyin' . . .', until a midwife told her to hold her clack.

The charity hospitals were also used as training-schools, and Caroline went into labour at noon under the interested eyes of several medical students and trainee midwives, one of whom was eating an apple. One tried to examine the whites of her eyes, and she tried out some of the vocabulary she had learnt from the hackney-coachman on him.

After that they were shooed away, and a capable elderly woman midwife stayed by her, and Caroline gripped her rough arms and wished she were her mother, and the physician came by and spoke in pompous polysyllables about a dilatory presentation and the possible utilization of forceps, and Caroline lurched up on the bed partly in pain and partly with some mad idea of knocking the ridiculous wig off his self-satisfied head because he could have no idea, no one could have any idea, of what this pain was like. And she made the high ceiling echo herself, and thought the woman opposite was not far wrong when she said she was dying. And if anyone had been surprised at an apparently genteel girl coming to a place like this, they would be more surprised on hearing her, for she cursed like a fishwife.

She was even on the point of cursing Antoine, when a surprisingly loud and emphatic cry put all the other echoes in the high ceiling to rout, and everything changed.

The illegitimate child of the illicit union of a well-bred English girl and a French prisoner-of-war was an apparently healthy boy.

The physician with the wig was no longer a pompous idiot but a wise and kindly figure who presently gave her a sleeping-draught under which she sank in a state of delicious gratitude. When she woke it was evening, and the house surgeon came with candles and said she could remain until tomorrow night, all being well.

She felt clear-headed on waking. Something crucial had changed in her feelings. She intended calling the boy Antoine; but still, in the midst of the pain she had had to bear amongst the strangers and the austerities of a charity hospital, a voice of sanity had spoken. The child was Antoine's, though he did not even know it existed. It was not she alone who was responsible. She was suffering whilst he enjoyed the freedom she had bought him at the cost of her reputation, her family, everything that had made up her world. True, she had a new world now – the baby in her arms – but in the quiet euphoria following the birth something of the idealistic light that bathed her mental picture of Antoine Clairet died away. The fierce unyielding love that had sustained her through this nightmare passage of her life was concentrated now in the child, leaving only a residue for its father – a residue that, if she were not so happy, might fester into the rankest bitterness.

CHAPTER 2

1

When Caroline gave the baby's name as 'Antoine', the parish registrar frowned and wrote down 'Anthony'. The name seemed more sensible, and she kept to it.

She left the Lying-In Hospital the day after the birth. The bed was needed, and after all the women at home in the fenland would have babies and be at work in the fields the next day. But she felt terribly weak and sore, and only the rumour that there was fever in the crowded hospital spurred her to move.

The cost of her lying-in, of ward fees, and of another jolting, sickening hackney-ride back to Jackson's Rents, had depleted her carefully hoarded stock of money; and for the moment all she could do was rest after the exhausting journey. Martha's old room had been taken by a woman who worked at silk-winding at Spitalfields Market. She was a crabbed creature with a gin-soaked voice and she consented, with no good grace, to buy Caroline's provisions for her over the next three days while she rested in her room; and she pocketed the change.

Little Anthony, meanwhile, took his own nourishment and slept soundly as if his surroundings, the four discoloured plaster walls that formed the unprepossessing scene of his début, were a matter of utter indifference to him. He was a mysterious, compulsive being to Caroline, for whom babies had hitherto been lace-draped bundles occasionally presented, like embroidered pin-cushions, to be briefly admired. He was demanding and tenacious, noisily asserting his claim to life. She lifted him and pointed to the straw picture of the tower, as the only link with his father she had; but it was an empty gesture. This intense little scrap of humanity had no connection with anyone but herself. Against all the odds, she had him. It was a proud, frightening thought.

But though she would willingly have stayed in her room with her baby for the rest of her life, she had a living to earn, for both of them. After a week her money was almost gone, and she felt strong enough – she *must* be strong enough – to walk down to Cheapside and get some work.

With Anthony in her arms she knocked at the back door of the draper's. The tall house seemed unusually quiet, and it was a long time before a servant came.

'Mr Stanley's giving no work,' the maid said. 'Go away with you.'

'But I always do out-work for Mr Stanley,' Caroline said. 'Isn't he at home? Please . . .'

The maid went away muttering, and presently the draper, in an old leather waistcoat and looking seedy, came to the back step.

'Ah, 'tis you, my dear,' he said vaguely. 'Got your young 'un, I see. Brave, is he?'

'Mr Stanley, your maid said – '

'Ah, I'm sorry, gel. No work today. Nor tomorrer.' He searched absently in his pockets for a pinch of snuff.

'I don't understand.' Stanley's gave employment to dozens of girls. 'Is it because I haven't come lately? I promise I'll – '

'T'ain't that, dear. I'm not giving any work. I might even have to close up. Dabbling. That's what done it.' He shook his head, seeming to find a fund of deep reflection in the word. 'Dabbling.'

272

At last she elicited from him the fact that he had lost money. The hectic prices of wartime had caused him to abandon caution and raise loans on the strength of the booming export trade to the north. The tension with Denmark and the threat to the Baltic trade had caused the funds to plummet. He had lost a lot of money speculating and could pay for no new work in the foreseeable future.

She came away from Stanley's, with a sad, kindly warning from the draper never to go dabbling.

For a minute she stood in the middle of the Cheapside pavement, with the coaches and waggons rumbling about her, people passing in and out of the many bow-windowed shops, the steeple of St Mary-le-Bow towering above, and she froze. The prospect of being without money – not just poor, not just scrimping, but being absolutely penniless – opened before her like a black pit.

A pit of snakes. For the consequence of destitution was to apply to the parish; and that meant Anthony would be taken from her.

She trudged her way all about Cheapside that day, and down Fleet Street and the Strand and all around Covent Garden, looking for work. It was dusk when she got back to Jackson's Rents, and still she had found nothing.

There was no food on her larder-shelf but a morsel of cheese and some dregs of soup. After changing and washing Anthony and hanging his clouts from the window-line she went down and managed to beg half a loaf from the woman downstairs.

She was exhausted. Her feet were blistered but she had not the energy to go down to the pump for fresh water to bathe them. And Anthony would not stop crying. He had taken his feed but now he went on crying a dry, nerve-stretching cry.

273

She walked up and down with him, shushing and crooning. She put him down to sleep and still he went on crying. She picked him up again and walked, with pain in her blistered feet. Were new-born babies supposed to cry like this? She wished Martha were here.

Her solitary candle had burnt low by the time he was quiet. She slept a drugged, aching sleep, and woke to his cries again.

He would not feed when she drowsily put him to her breast, and at last she found flint and steel and with impatient fumbling fingers lit the stub of candle.

His cry was a thin purposeless screech now. In the sickly light she looked at the red rash on his chest and felt herself sinking, sinking down while hope and courage whirled past her like so much straw and chaff.

2

The Dispensary movement had begun in 1769 with Dr Armstrong's first Dispensary for the Relief of the Infant Poor, and since then many more had opened all over London and in the provincial cities. At the Dispensaries those who could not afford physician's fees could come for free advice and treatment from resident doctors, who also made calls to poor homes: they became aware of hygiene, were discouraged from buying poisonous quack cure-alls, and were introduced to inoculation. The doctors too began to gain insight into diseases other than those of the gouty rich; and even the idea that the sufferings of the poor were not entirely attributable to laziness and vice was beginning to be accepted.

They had even made inroads on the infant mortality rate and on the old scourge of typhus. The year 1800, however, had seen a revival of the disease, especially in the seething courts and lanes of poor London where it was endemic. And for all the improvements in the gaols and the hospitals, they were still its most fertile breeding-ground.

All this the young surgeon at the Dispensary at Aldersgate Street knew well, and all of this he wished to convey to the young woman who had brought her infant to the Dispensary first thing that morning.

Not because he expected it to be any real comfort, but because she seemed to him to be of some birth and education, her voice cultured and her clothes genteel if shabby, and liable at least to respond to what he said. But she seemed to be taking it quite well anyway.

He had known, as soon as she had brought the week-old child in that morning, that it would not live. It could not even take a dose of Peruvian bark, and it had died at the Dispensary. However, the young surgeon and the resident physician, who were conscientious men, had felt their responsibilities did not end there. The place where this woman lived was probably infectious; and moreover, the resident physician suspected her apparent calm was really stupor, and tactfully concluding that she had no husband and would be unable to pay for burial, decided they had better contact the parish officers to arrange a pauper funeral.

So the young surgeon had gone with the mute girl back to her room – in a pestilential court, as he had guessed – and insisted that the flock mattress be taken out and burnt. He had advised the landlord to have the room whitewashed with hot lime as soon as possible, and when the landlord, sweating and alarmed, had mentioned turning the girl out, the young surgeon had been very firm and authoritative with him because he was a humanitarian man, and also susceptible, for though the girl was under-nourished and ashen, she was pretty.

But, the young surgeon had other duties, and they did not include helping a nineteen-year-old girl face despair alone.

Anthony was buried the next day, the 12th of October, in the crammed parish cemetery of St George the Martyr, leaving the unwelcoming world as discreetly and quietly as he had come into it. Though perhaps he had never been of the world at all, so strange and forbidden had been his origins. For all anyone else knew about him, he might have been a figment of Caroline's imagination.

The beadle at the parish graveyard seemed to expect a tip from Caroline, and looked huffy when he did not get it.

She did not even notice him. But she had not a farthing to give him anyway. She had not eaten for two days. Everything had come to a stop, everything had been buried with Anthony in the small grave.

She did not know what to do. She felt light, empty and detached, as a ghost must feel walking about the busy scenes of the corporeal world. Her brain, inert and suspended as it was, yet seemed to discern some implacable pattern that demanded the taking away first of Antoine and now his baby. What the rest of the pattern was she could not tell.

She did not know what to do. She wandered back to Jackson's Rents, and the landlord had his kitchen-maid there scrubbing out her room. Someone, perhaps the landlord, perhaps the woman downstairs, had left a little offering of a loaf and half-a-pound of tea on her larder-shelf.

Her body did not want food. It seemed peculiar to her, foreign. When she put her hand up to the latch she was surprised at the sight of it: a weird misshapen thing she could barely control.

276

She did not know what to do. She did not want to cry. She did not want to sleep. She walked, but it was her legs that did that.

The great city was roaring about her, but it seemed to make room for her to pass. People seemed to step into the gutter to let her by, in the narrow streets of the old City; and the traffic of carts and coaches seemed to make a void for her when she crossed the road. It was as if a path was carved out for her. She wondered if this was part of the plan.

The great city roared, and it was strange. It was not like this yesterday. St Paul's swam above the smoke, a garish temple, monstrous and exotic. Familiar Cheapside was a grotto, its low doorways leading into ghastly other worlds. The spirit-booths with the lights placed behind each coloured flask had turned into dens of gnomes: she caught glimpses of their leering faces trapped in the glowing bottles. And the banks and counting-houses of Cornhill and Leadenhall Street were, she saw quite plainly now, prisons. They were gaunt fortresses and she saw on the bewigged faces in the high windows the agony of their tortures. And when a sedan-chair passed her she recognized that the bearers were cannibals and the lady inside was their captive and they were going to take her home and feast on her.

She came at last to London Bridge, and wondered if it was part of the pattern that she was to cross it – but then she saw, from the great concourse of people and beasts on it, that the bridge was about to collapse. She wondered if she should shout and warn them, but her throat was dry and paralysed. But that was the heat. For it was unbelievably hot, and though she was only in a light cloak without a cape she was sweating. Still, that must be because of the fire in the sky. Surely that was not just the sun going down. There had never been such a vivid red conflagration in the sky before . . .

And the river was strangest of all, as lights began to appear on board the ships at the docks below the Tower. Some big East Indiamen were in, and there were lascar sailors congregating on Tower Steps who stared back at her. She paused here, for there was some sort of memory attached to this place. Something involving a barge, and prisoners-of-war, and one of them being struck down. But she could not tell if it was a memory of her own or someone else's, that had got by mistake into her head along with the pain. And the pain was a bright insistent companion now with the pains in her throat and back.

But she kept walking, obedient to the pattern, and the wharves and steps of the waterside flickered in and out of the shadows, now catching ribbons of light from oil-lamps and from lanterns on the decks of the moored ships and now flinging them away again, as if they were playing hide-and-seek with her. And the ground seemed to ripple and tilt like the river-water, till she could hardly tell which was which. Once a Negro with silver earrings and a jug of liquor in his hand loomed out of the darkness, and looked in her face, and appeared not to like what he saw there. Someone rang a bell on board a ship, and the noise rammed through her head like a sharp skewer. And then below St Catherine's Stairs she saw two little boys, mudlarks, rooting about for valuables in the sludge between some cockle-boats, and their faces were those of hideous imps, and she took fright and tried to run.

Her legs were like wool. But they took her down, past a row of lodging-houses and slop-shops where sailors' coats and hats hung in the windows and looked like hanged men, down to a crumbling wharf and a smell of tar and oakum and decay. And here a flash of lucidity interposed, driving for a moment the pain and sickness from her mind.

There were no lights and the water was black as oil here. It made caressing lapping sounds around the timbers of the wharf. This, then, was the end of the pattern. She stood on the edge of the wharf. To this her sick body had directed her.

And this last relief her protesting mind denied her. She had planned the escape with Antoine and not been afraid and she had come alone to London and earned her keep and not been afraid and she had borne a child alone and not been afraid. Now, in weakness and suffering, the last grains of courage had run out. She looked at the mild dark water below her and sank down against the timber props of the wharf because she did not have the courage to throw herself in. The pain in her head was maddening and she was bathed in sweat and she did not want to live but she dared not die. It seemed like the last, fiendish cruelty.

Then the pain took her in a great clinging hug and as she surrendered she thought that perhaps this was death after all.

3

The first thing she was aware of was light: sharp spears of light that transfixed her eyes. She shut them again quickly, but the light seemed to penetrate her eyelids and rekindle the pain in her head.

There was a voice. 'Ma'am. Ma'am, will you take a sip of this?'

The voice, she decided, was not in her head but outside. She risked opening her eyes again. A man's face, middle-aged, greying hair tied back. A black stock and epaulettes.

She gulped at the drink he held to her lips. Her throat opened just enough to allow it down. Brandy, searing. She coughed.

'Rest easy, ma'am. Are you able to speak?'

There were low stained beams above her head: a brass lantern hanging. The light was not coming from that but from a window behind the man. The lantern was swaying slightly. No, she was swaying slightly.

'Do you have a pain, ma'am? Shall I send for a surgeon?'

Her brain was groping, fumbling like a blind man. Was it a workhouse? How long had she been here?

She was lying on some sort of cot. She was still in her cloak; it was muddy. 'How . . . ?' Fingers of memory were unpicking the cottony confusion in her head. 'How did . . . ?' If only she could unlock her throat.

'You're quite safe, ma'am.' The man put the brandy glass in her hand, and she managed to close her recalcitrant fingers round it. 'Some of my boys found you by St Catherine's Wharf. Had you been set upon? Robbed? Can you recollect, ma'am?'

The swaying was not her, or not all of it. She was on a ship. She lurched up and cast a wild glance at the window, with some idea of being adrift at sea. 'Where . . . ?'

'This is the *Cambrian*, ma'am. The Marine Society school-ship, off Greenwich. My name is Barratt, Captain Barratt.'

She saw now a view of docks and boats at the latticed window. She was in a cabin: there was a desk and charts and shining brass.

'Some of my boys went down in a boat to fetch provisions early this morning,' the Captain was saying. 'They found you lying insensible – feared you were dead at first, and brought you over to the ship . . .'

Pain and memory were jointly encamped in her head

now. She rubbed her temples, wondering if she could get to her feet.

'Take another drink, ma'am. Were you set upon this morning, or last night perhaps? There are rough characters along the waterside. I can send a boy to Bow Street – if it is reported directly, then – '

'No.' She had found a voice, though she did not recognize it. 'Thank you, sir . . . you are very good. I was – I was taken a little ill, I believe . . . faint . . .'

'Have you a fever, ma'am?' The Captain, with his hands under his coat-tails, was studying her closely. 'You look a little unwell now. Let me send for a surgeon – the night air – '

'No, sir, thank you.' The relentless gaze, the relentless questions, were too much. The blazing pain spreading from her head to her limbs demanded her full attention. It wanted her, like an impatient lover. She must find a hole and hide and die. 'I am – quite recovered, I'll trouble you no longer . . .' She stood, and somehow managed to stay upright. The Captain watched her anxiously.

'Where are your family, your friends, ma'am? Let me send for them. They will be anxious for you . . .'

'No, indeed, I am really recovered, sir, and I ought to go. I have not far to go. You've been very kind . . .' She leant a moment against a chair, which she was relieved to find was nailed to the floor.

'Well, if you are sure, ma'am . . . But let me at least give you one of the boys to accompany you home. I really think you are unwell – Yes?'

A youth had tapped at the cabin door and put his head round. 'If you please, sir, Lieutenant Lindsay is here and desires a word.'

'Tell Mr Lindsay I shall be with him directly.' The Captain turned back to her. 'Now, ma'am, are you quite sure . . . ?'

The words *Lieutenant Lindsay* were driven into her like nails. She was immediately convinced it must be the same Lieutenant Lindsay. A final twist of the pattern, perhaps, that he should see her like this. She must get away now.

'I must go,' she said, stumbling to the door. 'Really . . .' She could not find the door handle. Captain Barratt opened the door for her. 'I am most uneasy.' The incessant concern went on. 'Have you far to travel?'

She mumbled something as she lunged up a flight of wooden steps that looked to her dizzy sight like a mountain. She reached the top with a gasp and clung to the rope rail and a tall figure in a blue coat and cocked hat swam into her vision.

The Captain was behind her holding her elbow. 'Mr Lindsay, I'm glad to see you,' he was saying. 'This young woman was found by the boys on the wharf. I am convinced she is quite unwell but she insists . . .'

She was toppling, and Lieutenant Lindsay caught her and held her up. Well, it was all over now. She was in such pain she must be dying, and if it was to be in Richard Lindsay's arms, of all people, well, it was an irony she could appreciate. She gave a half-broken laugh.

They were talking over her head. 'Where is she living . . . ? Wouldn't say . . . Surgeon . . .'

'Jackson's Rents,' she croaked out. 'Gray's Inn Lane . . .' Her room would do to curl up and die in, if she could just get there.

Lieutenant Lindsay's voice – she could feel it rather than hear it, calm and authoritative: 'The lady plainly has a fever – I'll put her in a hackney and escort her home . . .' and the Captain: 'I'd be obliged, sir – the air of these damp mornings . . . the quickest way would be to take a boat as far as Blackfriars . . .' And perhaps they were at sea, after all, for the scrubbed deck was pitching and swooping up and down . . .

282

Mercifully, Lieutenant Lindsay did not speak to her – she would have been incapable of answering – but merely propelled her, lifted her, into a jolly-boat. A young boy in a hard glazed hat rowed them down the busy river, staring at Caroline's fainting form the whole time. At Blackfriars Stairs Lieutenant Lindsay lifted her ashore and with the same silent swiftness half-carried her up the quay and down a side-street. And then he shouted down a hackney-carriage in a seaman's voice that would carry to the crow's-nest and she was bundled into it and she slumped in the corner and gave herself up to the greedy pain.

She was hazily aware of his hand touching her forehead and then peeling back the cuff of her gown. 'My God, you're burning up . . .'

'I'm quite well, thank you,' her voice was saying, somewhere about a mile away.

'Have you looked in a mirror lately?'

'Dear, dear, I must look a sight, indeed,' her voice was saying in a delirious cracked way. And then he was silent, until the carriage stopped outside Jackson's Rents and she felt her own dead weight lifted and carried into the courtyard.

'Are you sure this is the place? Miss Hardwick?'

She had her head flung backwards with her chin up, because that was the only way to stop it flying apart, but she managed to point up to the second floor.

'Your parents are here? Your family?'

'No no. Alone,' said her far-away voice, and then it disappeared altogether and she could not find it.

Caroline seemed to be unconscious when Richard laid her on the bed. He managed to take off the damp cloak and cover her with the counterpane. Their entrance had been observed by the woman downstairs and by the landlord, who occupied the house next door, and they had followed Richard up to the threshold and were staring at the prostrate girl and plying him with questions.

'I know less than you,' he said. 'She was found by the waterside and I brought her here, which she said was her home.'

'And you know the girl, sir?' said the landlord, a hoarse, stout little man, with a touch of prurience.

'She – I am a friend of her family.'

'Wasn't aware she had any, sir – oh, not that I doubt you. She's always been very secretive. I know what's took her. Same as took her child. And I went and had the room cleaned and scrubbed – '

'Her child?'

The landlord quailed a little before Richard's gaze. 'Why, yes, sir. Poor mite was buried yesterday. Didn't live above a week. She was carrying it when she come here, you see – the old story.' The man made a significant gesture to the third finger of his left hand. 'But I took her in,' he added. ''Tis not for me to judge. She worked hard seamstressing and always paid her rent. Seemed a genteel sort of creature. All on her own. The old story . . .'

'Is there a physician to be had nearby?' Richard said.

'Well, there's Dr Worth over at Aldersgate. He came when her child was took. Only a strip of a fellow – '

'Have you a servant you can send for him? If you please. At once.'

'As you say, sir.' The landlord studied Richard in a sideways manner. 'But you think to stay in here, sir? I mean, if 'tis the same fever as what took her baby, you'd best keep away. I'm a feeling man and a Christian, but I'll come no nearer than this door.'

Richard looked at Caroline. He did not like those red spots on her arms and neck or the way she held her head.

'I'll stay till the doctor gets here,' he said.

'As you like, sir,' the landlord said, and after fishing a little more and getting nothing out of Richard, he and the woman sidled away.

Richard stayed where he was, looking at Caroline in the narrow bed. After a minute he raised his head and looked around him at the squalid little room, the empty hearth, a few of her clothes, some baby's clouts on a chair. He went to the window and opened it and then came back and stood by the bed.

A great many thoughts were passing, rapid and very compact, through Richard's mind. Somehow he had managed to contain his astonishment when Caroline had come staggering up towards him from the captain's cabin on the *Cambrian*, and now he stood quite still and allowed the shock to sink in.

Once she moaned a little and her hand came out, grasping and helpless. After a moment he put his hand in it and it gripped, hard and delirious, before releasing him again.

He was still standing there when the young doctor from the Dispensary arrived.

He examined her briefly and gravely before turning to Richard.

'How long has she been like this?'

'I don't know. She was found this morning down by the river where she had fallen.'

'You know her?'

'She is an acquaintance.'

The doctor wiped his hands on a handkerchief. 'You know, then, that her baby died of the typhus but two days since? It could not be saved.'

Richard licked his dry lips. 'And this . . . ?'

The doctor nodded. 'The same.'

'What can be done? Can she be put in a hospital?'

'Unhappily I would guess that is where she took the

285

disease. The growing opinion is that typhus cases should be isolated. I think she should not be moved.' He looked warily at Richard. 'She is, I take it, without means of support?'

Richard went to the window and stared with distaste at the gloomy courtyard. 'What can you do for her?' he said after a moment.

'Well, if one is young and reasonably strong there is a fair chance. I have had some success with small doses of Peruvian bark and, when the crisis is past, fresh air treatment. I believe that to be particularly effective. She will need, of course, constant nursing.'

Richard stared down into the courtyard. A half-starved dog was nosing amongst the rubbish. A mellow sun was up, but it would never penetrate to this room. He was aware of the doctor watching him.

'If you can recommend a nurse, sir,' Richard said at last, turning, 'I will engage to pay her fees as long as is necessary. Also, of course, your own fees for attendance.'

The doctor bowed slightly. 'Thank you. I believe I can engage a reliable woman to nurse this afternoon. As for my fees, I'm attached to the General Dispensary, sir – we attend the poor without charge.'

'As you wish.' Richard stood again, with his hands behind his back, looking at the girl on the bed.

'I'll mix the patient a sleeping-draught now,' the doctor said, sniffing the pitcher of stale water on the table, 'and then go and send to the day-nurse. I'll not be long. Shall you stay here, sir?'

Richard looked at his fob-watch and frowned. The air in here was bad. It was bad in more ways than one. The lack of light was oppressive.

'. . . Sir?'

He would make sure the nurse was competent. One heard unpleasant tales of these old women who did day and night-nursing. Those baby-clothes ought to be removed . . .

'Sir?'

'Yes . . . yes, I'll stay.'

4

Richard sent a note to Captain Barratt on the *Cambrian*, saying he had been detained. The ship was the training-school of the Marine Society, a charity which took home-less and destitute boys and gave them a start in a naval career. Richard had no formal capacity there. He was on shore leave after his ship had been damaged in the autumn gales, and was staying with a merchant officer he knew in Southwark. Richard had once served under Captain Bar-ratt, and was glad enough to offer his services to the Marine Society to while away the time. He went most days to the *Cambrian* to give the boys instruction in trigonometry and navigation.

He stayed all that day at Jackson's Rents. He watched as Caroline tossed and writhed with her head thrown back and her open eyes not seeing anything, until the young physician's draught took effect and she slept, unrestfully, curled and taut.

Then the day-nurse arrived, and he went down and took a turn about the courtyard while she undressed and washed the patient and got her properly to bed.

It was the lack of air, the stinks of this place that offended him. A pest spot. He was used to cramped foulness below decks but had always been able to go up to the clean breezes above. No such thing here.

Caroline Hardwick, here. Grotesque. His only link with the Hardwicks now was the occasional letter from Charles at Morholm. That brief last visit to the fens, begun in optimism and ending in bitterness, had severed the links, and he knew nothing of what had happened since. Clearly her family could not know she was living alone in such a place.

He thought for a while about the baby-clothes, the little child that had died, and about Luke Hardwick. He saw the dim outlines of tragedy and disgrace.

He went upstairs again. Caroline was sleeping, a little more peacefully it seemed. The day-nurse was calmly doing some sewing. He saw it was mourning-weeds that she was mending, and realized she probably did laying-out as well. He felt sick.

The old woman had closed the window too, and the fire was smoking. Remembering what the doctor had said he flung the window open again. The nurse gave him an unpleasant look. She did not like him, and he did not like her. She had hard, claw-like hands and when she perfunctorily wiped Caroline's forehead he saw there was no gentleness in them.

At dusk he went and ate at a pastry-cook's and came back in the evening cool to find the night-nurse there with the young physician.

Caroline was turning her head from side to side on the pillow, a horrible clockwork motion, while her hands clasped and unclasped on the counterpane.

'Can't you give her something, for heaven's sake?' Richard said.

'I don't dare give her another dose of bark,' the doctor said. 'The fever's at its height now. I'll stay until she sleeps.'

Richard put down some coins on the mantelshelf. 'That's if you need anything,' he said. He glanced at the night-nurse before he went. He did not like the look of her either. She had rheumy, bloodshot eyes and looked as if she took gin to see her through the night watches.

It was a beautiful blue night. Bright stars mirrored the lights on the river as Richard crossed Blackfriars Bridge. The tide was full.

He would go to bed and have a good sleep and in the morning he could pick up his old life. Help out at the Marine Society, wait for his ship to be refitted and set sail again. In this last year he had hidden himself in the discipline and routine of the Navy like a suit of armour.

She was being cared for. He could send more money on, to make sure she did not want while she recovered – if she recovered. Yes, he could do that. So much was only basic human kindness.

He stopped and leant on the bridge wall and looked down at a collier slipping sleekly downstream. Someone was cooking something on board and a waft came up to him, homely and warm and cheerful.

He thought of her lying unconscious on the wharf where the boys had found her. What had taken her there? Just the wanderings of her delirium? The child buried just the day before . . . Having a child. Alone.

Richard stared down into the water. He had lived a loveless year without any particular hope or aspiration, grim, dogged, mundane. His spirit had drifted, dry and sterile. Now there was an eruption in the smooth surface of his life.

He walked slowly on, into the drab lanes of Southwark. A few revelling sailors with their arms tipsily about each other passed him, falling silent when they saw his braided coat, but he did not even notice them.

His friend had already gone to bed when he reached the small porticoed house on the Bank Side, and he let himself in. It was a fairly spartan place, but neat and shipshape, with odd little souvenirs of the owner's travels dotted about. The contrast with the shabby, featureless room where Caroline lay struck Richard with terrible poignancy as he lit a candle in his own room, with its broad window overlooking the river and the sea-chest for a desk and the plates on the whitewashed walls.

He took off his coat and waistcoat and eased his strapped shoulder. In the gale that had damaged his ship last month he had been injured, cracking a rib and badly bruising his chest; but it was quickly healing.

He thought of the nurse's careless hands. He had an instinctive, tactile sympathy with physical pain and the sight of sickness, rather than repulsing him, always made him want to do something practical.

There was brandy in a flask in his trunk but he found he did not want any. The ugliness of that room and the pathetic baby-clothes haunted him.

He lay down on the bed in his shirt and breeches and watched the circle of candlelight hovering about the rafters. He was a man who carried a burden of bitterness: there must be a time to lay it down.

He slept at last, peaceful in the knowledge of what he must do, and over breakfast with his friend told him he would be gone all day.

The day-nurse, perhaps reflecting that he was paying her fee, was a little more civil when he arrived at Jackson's Rents that morning. Her colleague had said the patient had had a poor night: 'Ravin', Captain, ravin' and rantin', but it's only to be expected.'

He thought Caroline looked worse: weaker, her skin colourless. Sometimes she stirred and looked about her, but her eyes were, he thought, unseeing. Once she pulled herself up and reached for the water beside the bed, but when he bent to give her a cup the nurse officiously pushed him aside. 'That's my duty, Captain,' she said, and spilt most of the water on Caroline's nightdress and clucked her tongue and wiped at it with the edge of her dirty pinafore.

The young physician came at midday, and mixed her another sleeping-draught and decided against a bleeding. Richard spoke with him on the dim landing outside the room.

'The fever has yet to break,' Dr Worth said. 'Its progress is highly debilitating, as you can see – especially on a constitution weakened by recent childbirth.'

'I wonder if I should write to her family,' Richard said, half to himself.

'They are not in London?'

'No. They – she is from the country.'

The physician nodded slightly. It occurred to Richard that he was probably being suspected as the father of the dead child. 'Well,' Dr Worth said, 'it is really a matter for you to decide, sir. One presumes that – given her condition out of wedlock and her living here alone, she was – dissociated from her family . . . ?'

Richard disliked the young man's prim phrases, and said nothing. The doctor put on his hat. 'I shall try to return this evening,' he said.

'Stay, sir,' Richard said. 'These nurses – are there no better to be had?'

'I wish there were. The trade is an unpleasant one, and sometimes dangerous on account of infection, and seems only to attract such women as these. I don't think you will find them actually negligent.'

Richard wondered. The old woman had furnished herself with more sewing and various items of food and drink, and seemed to look on the patient as only a minor distraction. To her evident consternation, Richard stayed all day, only going out to the landing when she had to wash the patient or move her to the stool. Once Caroline retched and was sick and the nurse was as scandalized at Richard's seeing it as if he had seen the girl naked.

He was shaken with pity and helplessness. As he watched her restlessly moving her head back and forth as if to shake the pain out of it, as he tried to make sense of her broken cries and murmurs, the fear that she might die came to him and would not leave.

At six the night-nurse came, and soon afterwards the doctor. Richard marked the expression on his face more than his words.

'She is very weak. She must be encouraged to take as much fluid as possible. Lots of milk. I think she is at the crisis. The delirium is very notable.' Richard saw his frown as he felt her pulse. A question rose to his lips but he could not ask it.

He walked back to Southwark, and after dinner his friend invited him to a game of backgammon. Richard tried to concentrate on the game, but the dice box shook in his hand, and he felt sick. He made an excuse and went out again.

It had turned cold; there was mist on the river, and the streets seemed empty and silent but for his own swift footsteps.

When the Western Squadron had been driven off station in the Channel gales last month, and Richard's ship had been half-wrecked, the master's mate had gone over the side. Richard knew he could not swim – and he had gone over to save him. He had managed to keep him up until a boat could be lowered. It was in getting back on board the heeling ship afterwards that he had been injured. He had been highly commended by his captain and his action mentioned in a dispatch to the Admiralty. But at the time there had seemed nothing else to do. In a way it had been easy. The course of action was there, and one took it.

But to the girl lying in the squalid room in Jackson's Rents, slipping away on a tide of painful death, he could offer no help.

Except be there . . . He had to be there.

He found he was walking faster and faster; when he got to the tenement he fairly ran up the dark stairs. And when he opened the door, he found Caroline moaning deliriously, half out of bed, and the night-nurse in a sound, comfortable sleep in the chair by the fire.

With his heart in his mouth he lifted Caroline gently back on to the pillows and lifted a cup of milk to her lips. She leaned her head on his arm and drank deeply.

'I warn't asleep, I warn't asleep,' the night-nurse mumbled unconvincingly when he shook her awake. 'Honest to God, Admiral . . .'

Another time he might have been amused at his rapid rise through the ranks of the Navy; but now his fear and concern heightened his fury. 'She was crying out,' he stormed. 'Crying out and you slept on! What d'you suppose you're paid for, woman!'

'Oh, that's nothink but contrariness,' the old woman said. 'I've nussed hundreds of 'em and it's contrariness as makes 'em do that. Leave 'em be and they mend all the better . . . Lord, sir, what are you doing?'

Richard had gathered up the woman's basket and her flask which smelt unequivocally of gin. 'Get out,' he said. 'Your services are no longer required. Take your incompetence elsewhere . . .'

'But who'll do the nussing?'

'I'll see to that.'

'You, sir – but it's not decent, you a gen'leman and her a lady, leastwise, I suppose she is – '

'*Get out.*'

When the night-nurse had gone, grumbling about it not being decent, Richard went and flung open the window:

the old woman had closed it and made the room stuffy. Then he lit more candles to push back the darkness, and stood looking down at Caroline and realized the woman was right. By normal standards it wasn't decent. He knew there was a woman living in the room below, and wondered if he should have her come and sit with him as chaperone. And then he remembered the baby and realized that in the world's eyes Caroline wasn't decent anyway, and the thought struck him with sadness and then a feeling chivalrous and protective.

To hell with it. He would look after her just as well as some gin-sodden hag only interested in her fee.

He made up the fire and put water to boil. He washed the cups and then with warm water bathed her face. He carefully brushed her hair and laid the pillows flat because she seemed more comfortable with her head back. Then he drew up a chair near the bed and was aware of his own health and strength and willed some of it to pass into her.

She began to rave again, after a period of quietness, about three, when the night was at its most dark and chill. She lurched up and tried to get out of bed with a feverish strength. Her eyes were open but he saw no recognition in them. She spoke through chattering teeth, and he caught the name Anthony or Antoine, and then the words *He didn't mean it, he didn't* . . . She was sick again, and he held the bowl and wiped her mouth with his handkerchief. He found the pillows were drenched with sweat, and he took off his waistcoat and laid it behind her head. After that she slumped back, hollow and flushed, and stared about the room.

Something was bothering her, over by the fireplace. It could not be the baby-clothes because he had put those away. At last he realized it must be the marquetry picture that was hanging there. He took it off the nail and brought it to her.

It seemed to quiet her for a while. She held it close to her and lay staring at the ceiling, breathing short and fast like a trapped animal. Then something in the corner of the room terrified her. She screamed and pointed and choked.

'Caroline!' He held her by the shoulders. 'It's all right. There's nothing there, there's nothing there, you're safe . . .' He held her down by main strength until she subsided again. At last her rigid grip on his arm relaxed and her eyes closed.

There was a trace of dawn at the window when it occurred to him that her head was resting in a normal position now instead of thrown back in that agonized way. Hardly daring to hope, he touched her damp forehead.

Yes, it was cooler. Very gently he wiped her face and pushed back her hair and then went to the window and drank in deep breaths. The morning light was creeping over the sooty wall opposite the window. It looked beautiful.

Moving softly, he went down to fetch fresh water from the pump and washed his own face and hands and then put the pan on to boil for tea. The framed picture had slipped off the bed, and he replaced it over the mantelshelf.

He drank tea and watched over her, and only now that the fever was broken did he begin to think about, and marvel at, what she had been through. Somehow – he did not even want to know how – she had conceived an illegitimate child. She had left her family – or had she been turned out? – and in this squalor she had, according to the landlord, entirely supported herself while pregnant. And then the child's dying of typhus . . . Whilst he had paced the decks in the monotony of Channel blockade duty she had gone through all this.

What was there for her now? The illness, perhaps, had

saved her from reflection on the death of her child. He thought with a renewed helplessness that when she woke to lucidity it would all come back.

He realized with a start that she was looking at him. Not through him, but at him.

'Richard.' She swallowed. 'Richard, is it you?'

'Yes. Rest easy. Are you thirsty?'

She nodded, and he gave her a drink of milk.

'How long . . . ?' Her voice was very quiet. 'How long have I been ill?'

'Two days. The fever's broken now. The doctor from the Dispensary will be here soon. Are you in pain?'

She shook her head. 'I was on a ship, wasn't I?'

'Yes, the *Cambrian*. Off Greenwich. You were ill and you'd fallen by the river and they took you on board the ship. I was there and I brought you back here.'

Her brow wrinkled in an effort of memory. Then she said, in a voice so low he could scarcely hear it: 'Do you know about – I – my baby . . .'

'Yes. Hush now. Try and sleep a little more.'

She subsided again; but then she stirred and said: 'Richard – my mother and father – they . . .'

'They don't know where you are?'

She nodded.

'I wondered if I should write them. What should I do?'

'No. Please. I . . . No.'

'Very well. Now try and sleep. We must get you strong and well again.'

She sank with a sigh into the pillows and closed her eyes. After a moment she said: 'Richard . . . will you stay by me?'

He sat down in the chair near the bed. 'Yes, of course.'

Charles and Edmund Hardwick moved into their lodgings in Greek Street near Soho Square at the end of September.

Edmund had a large airy room which he filled with canvases and sketches; Charles a smaller one which soon became quite as filled with papers. Burdett had casually given him the task of sorting through a voluminous correspondence on the Cold Bath Fields prisoners.

Charles set to work dutifully, but while he liked Burdett and believed in his sincerity he detected a certain irresponsibility and vanity about the aristocratic reformer. It made him uncomfortably aware of the paradox in his own position. He hated the thought that people might accuse him – as they accused Burdett – of being a mere dilettante.

At the shop of Jonas Spurling, however, Charles felt himself to be close to the real thing.

Spurling was the jobbing printer Charles had met through Burdett: a founder member of the London Corresponding Society who had suffered numerous prosecutions and a spell in prison for sedition. He had a tiny run-down shop in St Paul's Churchyard, which he had invited Charles to visit, and in a back room the small ruddy-faced man talked to him of his struggles in the radical movement, his acquittal at the treason trials six years ago, of the time a Church-and-King mob had smashed his windows and burnt his presses while the magistrates turned a blind eye.

There were great heaps of proofs and tracts here, a haphazard history of the radical movement before it was driven underground: not only *The Rights of Man* and *The Age of Reason* but Spence's *Pig's Meat* and Thelwall's

Tribune. 'Take some, my friend,' he said. 'I can give them to you as a gift, even if I can't sell them.'

He took a boat home with a sheaf of papers under his arm and Thelwall's sentences ringing in his head: 'I affirm that *every* man and *every* woman, and *every* child, ought to obtain something more, in the general distribution of labour, than food, and rags . . . and that, without working twelve or fourteen hours a day from six to sixty . . .'

His mind was still running on this that afternoon. He had been in London with Edmund a week now, and every day had gone to the Fairburns' town house in Curzon Street to see if they were there. The servants told him they were at Stanningford, their country house, and were not expected, but calling became a habit; so he was startled today when a footman answered the door and told him Miss Fairburn was at home.

In his surprise he stood there like an idiot, until he heard a familiar light voice say: 'Reed, is that Mr Charles Hardwick there? If so, tell him to go away.'

He stepped into the hall, and there was Lydia coming down the stairs to meet him.

'So, you have been pestering the servants about us, and absolutely haunting our house like Hamlet's father's ghost. But he haunted battlements, didn't he? Oh well.' She gave him her hand briefly.

'Haunting without hope,' he said. 'I was given to understand you and Sir Thomas were not expected.'

'Nor were we. And father's still at Stanningford, brow-beating the builders. I was bored to death and came back to town last evening.'

'All alone?'

'Well,' she lowered her voice and beckoned him into the morning-room, 'I have aunt Clarissa with me. Not really an aunt – some distant cousin of father's. But an aunt insofar as she is a lady of indeterminate age and

298

limited means and she is sometimes taken off the shelf to act as chaperone to me. She's utterly ineffectual and I do just what I like anyway, but it's a polite fiction we like to maintain. She's taken to her bed because she says the carriage-drive half killed her. It's my belief she drinks. My old governess drank. I used to bribe her with gin to let me out when I was supposed to be doing lessons. I wonder if that's why I turned out so ignorant. What do you think?'

'It sounds as if there was very little she could teach you, Miss Fairburn.'

She smiled. 'Sit down, sir, and tell me what you are doing in London. Are you here to torment your poor father again? Surely Parliament's not open yet.'

He told her, while his eyes took in her beauty afresh. She was dressed in a round gown with a high ruff of lace and long sleeves, and he liked the way this demureness contrasted with her roguish and most undemure expression. The frustration and ill humour of the summer came sharply into focus as he looked at her. If he had unconsciously looked to time to dim the fascination he was very wrong.

'So you are a gentleman of leisure, or all but? Well, I like that. I'm so glad to be in London again! Stanningford is like the end of the world. When I heard some of my friends were in town I refused to stay another minute. I packed some clothes and an aunt and was off. We go to Ranelagh this evening.' She looked at him sideways. 'Is Ranelagh one of the many things you consider tyrannical and unconstitutional and all the rest of it, Mr Charles Hardwick – or would you like to come too?'

'If you will have me, I would be delighted,' he said.

'Good. And you must stay to dinner. Aunt Clarissa's here to interpose decently between us, in the unlikely event that you should decide to ravish me over the soup-tureen. What ridiculous impositions we live under!'

The aunt who joined them at dinner was a feeble yes-woman with none of the Fairburn good looks. She was pale and blurred like an indifferently executed watercolour. The idea of this lady 'chaperoning' the fearless Lydia amused Charles.

'Do you hear from your cousin at Great Baston?' Lydia asked him. 'Is she carrying an heir to the Downes' acres yet?'

'Not as far as I know.'

'I'm glad to hear it. I like to go there, and I should be put off if there were some repulsive child crawling about the place.'

Charles said nothing, thinking of his cousin Caroline. It must be about now that her baby was due. One of his first acts on coming to London, at Aunt Rebecca's request, had been to take out more advertisements in the newspapers, but there had been no response.

'There. Once again I've said something to offend you,' Lydia said. 'Don't tell me you're a lover of children, Mr Hardwick. If I had my way they would all be kept in baby-farms, away from sight, until they were of an age to be reasonable.'

'Lydia was a beautiful baby,' put in aunt Clarissa. Her voice seemed to issue from somewhere amongst a nebulous clump of shawls and wraps. 'When she was born she had a full head of copper-coloured hair. It has darkened, of course. A most beautiful child.'

'I can well believe it, ma'am,' Charles said.

'Oh, aunt, what nonsense,' said Lydia. 'Like all babies, I was a nasty, spoiled, selfish little brat, always demanding attention and wanting things.'

'And when did you change?' said Charles with grave irony, meeting her eyes across the table.

'You had better look the other way, aunt,' Lydia said, 'because I am going to throw my plate at Mr Hardwick's head.' But instead she smiled at him wryly, and throughout dinner, until she went off to change, he fancied he caught a similar look directed at him, amused and speculative, and even intimate.

Aunt Clarissa was not going to Ranelagh – 'Lydia will be with known and respectable friends, Mr Hardwick, so I don't feel I shall be failing in my duty to Sir Thomas' – and he sat with the maiden lady in the drawing-room while Lydia dressed. Like the rest of the house, it was furnished in a spare classical taste that he guessed to be that of Lydia's mother. He was about to say something of this when he caught sight of a portrait above the marble fireplace.

'Ah, you remark the picture, Mr Hardwick?' Aunt Clarissa said weakly, weakly sipping her weak tea. 'By Reynolds. Lydia's late mother. Such a likeness. Poor creature.'

Charles got up to examine the portrait. The woman was young and very beautiful, like Lydia, but with an expression of gentle mildness that was not at all like Lydia.

. . . And how it was he did not know, but in looking at the picture his feelings about Lydia took a definite shape they had not had before.

He had moved towards her as unreflectingly as a moth towards the light, and with as little purpose: he had taken encouragement and discouragement in the same manner. He had simply been caught up in her own flirtatious orbit, and accepted their relationship on her own flippant terms. That he had refused to think of himself as in love with her, that he had not realized what lay at the heart of his restlessness and preoccupation, surprised him deeply, for it was now so obvious. Perhaps his unconscious resistance had been rooted in a realization that of all the women in the world she was the most unlikely and unsuitable for him to fall in love with. But now that the truth was faced, that fact seemed less of an obstacle, for the great surge of love that broke through him seemed to admit of no impediments.

Lydia's friends arrived, in two post-chaises, whilst she was still dressing. There was a Guards Captain with his fiancée who were only interested in each other. The other two Charles found he knew slightly. Spencer Murrow was a rich man of thirty-odd who had a large estate of reclaimed fen in the Isle of Ely: Charles had met him, and his mousey sister Isabel, once or twice socially at home. He was a tall, thin, etiolated man, half-strangled by a starched collar, with a long pointed nose that made him look like one of the caricatures of Pitt: he gave Charles a cold, fishy handshake. He was known for his Evangelical opinions, and Charles wondered what Lydia thought of him.

Ranelagh Gardens were just outside London at Chelsea. It was out of season, but there were 'enough people to make a show', as the Captain remarked, and the air was mild and sweet beneath the trees decorated with coloured lights. Lydia, to Charles's surprise, gave him her arm as they strolled by the illuminated canal. 'Now I know why you asked me to come,' he said. 'Three ladies and only two gentlemen. You required an arm to support you.'

'There was an element of that,' she conceded. She indicated the Murrows walking ahead of them. 'I suppose it is very ungallant of us to leave poor Spencer to squire his sister. You ought to accompany her, really, and talk to her about parliamentary reform. She's very serious.'

'And have her preach to me? No fear.'

'Well, that is really Spencer's province. He's quite a

scholar, you know. He has plans for an expurgated Bible, that can be read aloud in the family with propriety. For my part I think Sodom and Gomorrah sound delightful places. One just wishes it would be more specific. Though those Biblical places I always imagine to be sandy, and sand and lechery surely do not mix.'

'You've said as much to Mr Murrow?'

'Oh, well . . .' She laughed softly. 'It doesn't matter what I say to him. I'm afraid he's rather in love with me.'

'Is he now?' Charles tried to keep his voice light. 'And what makes you suppose that?'

'It's not a difficult thing to discern. All diseases have symptoms.'

They crossed the Chinese bridge, and passed a noisy party of youths, who looked like apprentices on a spree.

'The trouble with this place,' Lydia said, 'is that anyone who can pay half a crown can get in.'

'Perhaps you would have all the labouring people put out of sight in farms along with the babies.'

'It's they who produce most of the babies. My chief objection to them is the way they keep breeding. If they're so poor, why do they keep having children?'

'If they had more of the general amenities of life, perhaps they would not be so driven to resort to its most basic pleasures.'

'Well, I am quite ready to see virtue in them, but all I see is coarseness and grossness.'

'You should go to the gallery of the House of Commons some day, Miss Fairburn. There you will see our leaders and legislators, often drunk, spitting, cursing and baying, with huge dropsical bellies and red faces from guzzling all day long –'

'It seems I've exchanged one preacher for another,' said Lydia. 'You include my father, and yours, in that description?'

'No, I – '

'That wasn't fair, I know. But really, Charles, I'm not stupid. I know quite well what you think of my father. He is everything you detest, is he not?'

'He – made no secret of what he thought of my views . . .'

'And he's *right*. He's part of the ruling class, and so am I, and so are you come to that – and he's going to make damn sure it stays that way, thank heaven. I enjoy my life and I'll not change it to suit the rabble. Ours is the power, so that's that.'

'I don't believe you mean that,' Charles said after a moment.

'Oh, you'd be surprised.'

'Nothing you do could surprise me.'

They stopped a moment with the crowd waiting to move into the Rotunda.

'Poor Charles,' Lydia said. 'I really don't know why you continue to seek me out. You spend half your time burning up with indignation. I call you all sorts of names and mentally you do the same, and you want to send my father to the guillotine. Why *do* you do it?'

'Well,' he said slowly, 'you said just now about Mr Murrow being in love with you. That it has symptoms like all diseases. I don't know. I, for instance, was desperate to see you in London this spring, after Great Baston. I was a miserable bad-tempered fellow all summer. There were thoughts of your voice and your eyes and your laugh in my head all the time, where they had no business to be. And when I found you at Curzon Street today I felt as if the whole world had changed. You greeted me so readily, as if we had just met yesterday, and invited me to Ranelagh and I felt ready to burst with happiness. And when you mentioned about Mr Murrow I was violently jealous and ready to spit him on a sword or something

304

dramatic like that. I don't know whether these are the symptoms of the same disease. All I know is that I feel them.'

Lydia, for once, seemed to be lost for words. They passed into the Rotunda, a circular temple-like building where one showed off one's dress. Charles had spoken impulsively, unable to stop himself. He could not go back now. 'It seems I do have the disease, as you call it,' he said. 'But your behaviour to me – I don't know whether it is because you have not guessed how I feel or because – because you know too well, and wish it were not so . . .'

She glanced at him. 'It would be a strange sort of woman who did not like to be fallen in love with. Or man for that matter. But it depends if she is fallen in love with for the right reasons.'

'I don't understand.'

Lydia stopped and frowned. 'It's so hot and stale in here. Will it seem rude if we slip away from the others, do you think?'

'I'm prepared to risk it.'

'Come then.'

She marched him quickly out of the Rotunda and did not slow her pace until they reached the quiet yew-walks. She seemed lost in thought then, and under the hanging lanterns he admired the warm lights in her hair.

'It would be wrong of me to say I hadn't – suspected a certain odd, half-hating infatuation in you towards me – '

'*Hating* . . .'

'No, let me finish, Charles. Even when we first met, I thought there is a man who . . . We made good fencing partners. You don't mind that I have a mind of my own, you seem to like it, where most men profess themselves captivated at first and then wish I would keep quiet and agree with them like a dutiful young lady. Men like a girl to be a sort of submissive mermaid, doing a little embroidery and being fragile.'

'You're about as fragile as an amazon.'

'Now don't put me off with compliments, Charles,' she said, smiling in spite of herself. 'Well. I have the vanity to think that's what you like in me – '

'Not only that. Everything – '

'Silence, sir.' She walked on beside him, tall and graceful and long-legged. 'What I am trying to say is that you should not fancy yourself in love with me, Charles, because in spite of all that, I am not good for you. That world you despise, Charles – and I know I mock but I dare say you may be right to despise it – but I'm *part* of it, for good or ill. You need a girl who's not a selfish little money-getter and whose father is not the enemy of everything you believe in. We are so far apart . . . I suppose you realize how incensed against you my father was, that time at Great Baston?'

'We had a political quarrel. I can't believe it can have affected him so personally.'

She gave him a sceptical look. 'Don't your political convictions mean a great deal to you?'

'Yes . . .'

'Well, so it is with father. The other way round. I know enough to see there can't be any civilized disagreements, not in these times. To you, he and his kind are tyrants to be brought down. To him, you and your kind are the enemies of order and must be crushed. As for me . . . you know I belong in my father's camp. Everything about me proclaims it.'

'You're very loyal to your father, aren't you?' he said gently.

She held his arm more closely. 'Charles, I'll tell you. Something I've never spoken of. You saw the picture of my mother, didn't you? Father doted on her. And when

306

she died, he looked to me as her daughter. I became everything to him. As well as being beautiful, mother was a very good woman – not like father or me: good, kind, selfless. And since then, I have had to be the nonpareil, the paragon – living up to the standard of the woman he adored. I really think that father believes I am like her . . . And in a curious way, it's not easy being the object of all that love and trust and pride. There's a – sort of guilt. Knowing that you can never live up to it . . .'

Charles was moved. He saw for the first time the vulnerable Lydia beneath the flippant assurance: an insecurity, even a gap of self-esteem.

'So you see,' she went on, 'there's no question of my loyalty to father. There's no choice. And that's why I say I'm no good for you. I don't want you to be deluded too, into thinking I'm not the hard self-seeking creature I am.'

He began to see too – and it was with a renewal of tenderness that he saw it – that she could not really believe someone was in love with her. But with this intensified feeling for her came a fear.

'I'm flattered you should tell me this, Lydia,' he said quietly. 'No, serious now. Flattered and honoured . . . But is this a way of telling me – and if it is it's a kind way and I'm thankful – but is it a way of telling me that – that you can't love me?'

She did not look at him. 'Charles, that's not fair . . .'

'Probably not. But I have to know. All these things you've said – very well, I accept them. And, if your father disapproves of me – '

'Rather more than that, I fear.'

'Is it? What would he say if he knew we were together now?'

'Oh, that's no matter. That's all part of it – that he lets me do what I want. Anyway, you speak as if we were – oh, keeping some secret lovers' assignation – '

'Aren't we?'

She stopped and turned her face to him. Her expression was faintly quizzical. 'Are we?'

They were quite alone, screened by the tall hedges, and without knowing what he did, only knowing he had to do it, he bent and kissed her lips.

Her eyes widened in surprise, and she put up her hands to his shoulders, but hesitantly, and then her eyes closed and he held her tightly to him.

'Well,' she said at last, a little breathless, patting his cravat, 'what a cad you are, making a lady betray herself this way . . .'

'Lydia – '

'How I wish I'd eaten onions or something so you wouldn't like the taste of me . . .'

'You taste like wine,' he said, his lips in her hair.

'*Of* wine, no doubt,' she rattled on, 'I never told you I was a toper, did I – ?'

'Lydia?'

'Yes, Charles?'

'I love you. And I'm going to kiss you again.'

'No, you're not,' she said, and with a sort of resigned despair she seized him and kissed him, her hands running through his hair.

It was his turn to be breathless, when at last she released him and half-turned away.

'And now,' she said, 'you're going to think me the most heartless tease and flirt when I say it makes no difference.'

'I can feel a difference.'

'Oh, be serious, Charles.'

'You're always telling me *not* to be serious.'

'Well, this time you must. Charles . . . a lot of things that seem very nice and easy in the darkness are not so in the light of day. It's all so complicated. I don't want you to think – '

'Suppose I see your father?' he said ardently. 'Talk to him and – '

'*No.* That's just what I don't want you to think. Oh, Charles, slow down. I'm but twenty-one. Probably I don't know my own mind, as they say. Don't ask too much of me.'

'I'm twenty-three,' Charles said. 'I know my own mind, Lydia. My own heart.'

'And that's just what I hope you don't,' she said, looking at him soberly, her green eyes shaded and thoughtful. 'I think I must start being cruel to you again. When you're boiling with indignation I know where I am. When you look at me like that I – I can't cope with you.' She took his arm and moved him on, quickly, back towards the Rotunda. 'Come, we ought to join the others.'

'Must we?'

'Yes, we must. The world isn't just you and me, Charles. That's the whole point . . . Oh, let's go back to the way we were before, Charles, hm? I'll tease you and you can satirize me and we'll get on so much better. And promise me you won't approach my father when he comes to town. Promise, now.'

'I promise,' he said. He was ready to promise anything to Lydia at that moment. He would have signed his soul to the devil on the spot if she had asked him. And when they rejoined the rest of the party he made a point of being cordial to Spencer Murrow. Perhaps he knew that whatever he had to fear it was not rivals.

CHAPTER 3

1

The morning after Caroline's fever broke, the young physician came and pronounced her out of danger.

On the landing outside her room he shook his head. 'I confess I feared she would not recover, sir,' he told Richard. 'But, so much of our work is groping in the dark . . . Of course, she will be weak for some time and will need care. Above all I would recommend fresh air to ensure a complete recovery. Even if it is only to sit in the courtyard. A strengthening diet – milk, eggs, some lean meat. And some mild occupation when possible, for her mind needs healing as much as her body. The memory of her child will be very fresh yet.' He seemed to assume now that Richard would provide the care. Richard shook his hand and went back into the room.

She was lying flat and pale and still, only her eyes moving. Richard smiled and came and stood a little way from the bed.

'Well,' he said, 'what can I do for you now? Are you hungry?'

'I believe I am rather,' she said.

'Good. Good.' He walked to the fireplace and back again. 'Well, I shall go and buy provisions. Eggs, I think, oatmeal, perhaps a little minced chicken would not come amiss . . .'

'Richard. I still don't quite understand . . .'

He stopped and waited.

'I've been very ill haven't I?'

'Yes.'

She nodded slowly. 'I've had the same fever that took Anthony, haven't I? Anthony was my baby . . .'

'Don't speak of it.'

'No, no, it's all right. I'm just trying to set my thoughts in order. When I was ill they seemed to fly all around like birds. I remember now. Anthony was buried, and then I walked and walked, and I must have collapsed by the river, and then they took me in on the ship – and you were there.'

'Yes, that's right.'

'And – and you've looked after me since then?'

'Of course. You were very ill, you needed treatment,' he said hurriedly. 'And when I brought you here from the ship, I – found there was no one else.'

'No. No one else.' She swallowed. 'I was having a baby, you see, and – I had to come away. They don't know where I am.'

'Yes, yes, I understand.'

'It's so strange . . . When I heard you were on that ship, I felt I had to get away, I couldn't bear that you should see me – oh, because I wanted to die, Richard, it was terrible – '

'Hush. You mustn't talk like that.'

'But I still can't believe . . . You've taken care of me. I'm alive.'

He cleared his throat. 'The physician from the Dispensary was very good,' he said stiffly. 'Now, I must go down to the market – '

'I've no money, Richard,' she said. 'I was working as a seamstress, you see. There was no one else – '

'I know.' He frowned and came and stood by the bed. 'Caroline, I realize all this. And now you must listen to me. I have money, quite enough to look after you, and ample leisure till I am recommissioned. My ship is in

Portsmouth being refitted, and I'm staying with a friend across the river. So, that's what I'm going to do if you'll allow me. There's no one else, and I'm glad to do it. If you would like me to write to your parents – or your cousins at Morholm, perhaps, if you'd prefer, then I'll be glad to do that too.'

She looked up at him, perplexedly, as if something about him was changed and she was trying to work out what. 'Richard,' she said huskily, 'you say you'll do this for me – and it's so kind – but you don't know, you see, what happened . . . how I got to be here, alone. And if you did know you wouldn't do it, you'd feel like the others, you'd have to. And you ought to know, you have a right to know – '

He lifted a hand. 'No more,' he said. 'I have no right whatsoever to know. If you want to tell me, I'll listen. If not, very well. But I can only repeat it makes no difference. I'm going to be here until you get well. That's a promise.'

'You've been to so much trouble already . . .'

'Nonsense.'

'But you have. I – don't dare ask you to look after me any more.'

His face softened. 'Oh, go on, dare,' he said. 'I'll bet you I say yes.'

She smiled, relaxing again.

'Thank you, Richard,' she said. 'I'll try to get well and strong quickly. Then you won't have any more trouble.'

He patted her hand briefly, and was gone.

She lay and thought of Anthony.

The grief was there, but it was a recognizably human one, not the ghastly despairing monster that had taken her down to the river to throw herself in. It was into a sad

312

world that she had surfaced from her fever, but it was a negotiable one.

Perhaps it was wrong, but all she could feel at the moment was peace and gratitude. To be no longer ill was wonderful: to be free from pain and nightmare and the throes of death . . . That in itself was such a gift that she could even bear the loss of her child – Antoine's child.

No, not Antoine's. He seemed a long way off. The joy and grief were hers alone, not Antoine's. And so, now, was the life she had been granted.

She looked round at the familiar room. It was cleaner and neater than she remembered it. Shipshape.

It was marvellous to lie back in comfort and feel that all responsibility was being taken from her hands and she was being cared for. She had been alone and self-reliant for so long that it felt like the headiest of luxuries. And for this care to come from the unlikeliest of sources – Richard Lindsay . . . It was so strange.

There was unease, too, alongside the deep gratitude. For despite Richard's disclaimer, she knew she would feel a guilty fraud until she could tell him the whole truth about herself and her disgrace. She owed him that, at the very least. If it meant he walked out and left her to fend for herself, then that was a fair price to pay.

She looked at the straw picture on the wall. The pang it gave her was sharp but somehow indirect, like a memory of the fever.

She slept, and when she woke Richard was back and moving about the room softly. She saw flowers by the bed. At last he noticed she was awake and came over to her.

'How do you feel?' he said.

'Rested. I like the flowers.'

He smiled faintly and went back to the fire, where a pot was bubbling. 'There's a story attached to them,' he said.

'Down at Covent Garden there was a girl selling them. Pleasant-faced country girl, poor. On an impulse I asked her if she would like to do a little nursing for a fee. For when I can't be here. Well – I'd be happy to be here all the time, but obviously there are – well, I imagine you'd like a bath and so on,' he said, stirring the pot rather vigorously. 'She seemed like a gentle, cleanly sort of girl, you see. I don't know if you recall the hired nurses we got in for you . . .'

'I remember a fat old woman bending over me,' Caroline said. 'I thought she was part of my nightmares.'

Richard laughed. 'She might well have been. Could you fancy a little porridge? I learnt my cooking in the midshipmen's mess, I'm afraid.'

It was the first solid food she had had in days. She would never have believed porridge could taste like ambrosia. Afterwards she had a little minced chicken. It was a banquet of the gods. Then he made her some tea and she sat propped up in bed drinking it while he rinsed the plates and made up the fire.

'I feel so much better,' she said. 'I feel I should be up and helping you instead of watching you.'

'You'll do no such thing,' he said sternly.

'You don't mind me watching you?'

'Not at all. I wish it were more diverting. Perhaps I'll add a few dance steps as I go.'

She liked watching him. He was a tall, big-boned young man but he did not seem to take up the room and make a clatter like so many men did. Nor did he clumsily manhandle pots and utensils. Life below decks, she supposed.

'Was your ship in a fight, Richard?'

'Only with the elements. We were nearly wrecked in a gale and only just limped back into Torbay with a jury-rig.'

She noticed he bent a little stiffly to replace the shovel and tongs. 'Were you hurt?'

'Oh, I cracked a rib and wrenched my shoulder. It's still strapped.'

'Is it painful?'

'Well, I thought it was, until I saw you under the fever. Then I knew what real pain was,' he said gently.

'I remember I was in pain,' she said, 'but I can't remember what the pain was like. Perhaps it's just as well. Richard . . . the baby-clothes. Did you – ?'

'I put them away. Was that right?'

She nodded. 'They – I can give them to someone who needs them. He – he was a sweet little thing, you know.'

'I'm sure.'

'But, somehow, he seemed not to be of this world. I hope he didn't hate me – for bringing him into it.'

There was a knock at the door. 'Ah,' Richard said, 'that will be our young nurse.'

He let the girl in, gave her her instructions, and was gone, with a promise to return in the evening, before Caroline could thank him.

So her convalescence began. Outside it was autumn, but whilst the November days shortened like curling leaves, Caroline slowly began to feel the stirrings of spring.

That day the girl, who was kind and willing, filled a tin bath and helped her into it and changed the linen on the bed, and by evening Caroline, washed and groomed and well-fed, felt better able to face Richard when he called.

He brought books for her. 'From my little library. It goes everywhere with me in my trunk,' he said.

An odd collection. Sidney's *Astrophel and Stella*, the sonnets of Shakespeare, Hakluyt's *Voyages*, Sterne's *Tristram Shandy*: it gave her a new insight into his personality. Indeed, it was strange, and pleasant, to find herself contemplating another personality, after so long drearily imprisoned in her own.

He brought candles too, and a bright ragwork rug, and more flowers: she wondered where he got them from. The gloomy little room was changing under his influence. He told her about his lieutenant's cabin on the *Olympia* – not a cabin at all but a booth made with a canvas screen. 'One learns to make the best use of the space,' he said.

She saw *R. Lindsay* written in a bold hand on the flyleaf of Hakluyt's *Voyages*, and thought of Antoine keeping her book of fables with her name written in it. Poignantly touched, both by this thought and by Richard's kindness, she said: 'This book's well thumbed. Is it a favourite of yours?'

'Oh, yes.' He smiled fondly at the tattered volume. 'I think it was that book that first gave me the hankering to go to sea. I used to read it as a boy in my father's house in King's Lynn. There was an upstairs room with a window-seat, and you could see the ships coming in to port, and I used to sit there reading and looking out. Later I used to read it to father, when his eyes failed.'

After a moment she said: 'Would you read to me? Would you mind?'

'Of course.' He smiled, and she saw he was pleased; and she felt glad.

He read for an hour. His was a good voice for reading, a clear baritone, not uneducated but with a distinct fenland intonation. It carried her away, to the exotic and outlandish places where the Elizabethan explorers were led by their endless curiosity. And she too felt the touch of curiosity: an awakening of interest in the world that she had purposefully shut herself away from. It no longer seemed quite the infinitely hostile and loveless place that she had shunned through the long months of brooding pregnancy.

316

When he closed the book she said: 'Richard, I want to tell you – how it is I come to be here and – everything. It seems only fair. Do you mind?'

He hesitated. 'If it's what you want.'

'It was in Peterborough,' she began painfully. 'It began last year . . .'

'Go on,' he said softly. He had moved away as she spoke and was leaning on the window-sill looking down into the dark courtyard. Somewhere a watchman rang a bell and called the hour.

'No one knew, it was all secret, it had to be. The man . . . we had to meet secretly . . .'

'Your parents didn't approve of him, I suppose,' Richard said with sudden harshness. 'Was he poor?'

'They . . . He was a Frenchman.' She forced the words out. 'A French prisoner-of-war.'

And so, she told the whole story. Everything: the careful plans, the flight to Yarmouth, Antoine's revelation, his going without her, her discovering she was carrying his child. The story gained coherence for her as she told it. And she saw it for the first time from the outside. No one came out of it well, she saw now, except perhaps her brother Nicholas: not Antoine, certainly not herself.

'So you see why I had to tell you,' she said. Richard was very still at the window. 'You see, don't you? I can't go on – taking all your kindness, when you didn't know what I had done, just why I had come to this. It would be cheating, trading on your generosity . . . Oh, Richard, please say something . . .'

He said, still gazing out: 'I think . . . perhaps I shouldn't be disrespectful to your father, but I think his reaction was cruel. I'm sorry. I think he behaved very badly.'

'Oh, well . . . I didn't expect anything else really. I'd

317

let everyone down so badly.' She looked at his straight motionless figure. 'It's not a pretty story. But I had to tell you.'

He turned at last. The candlelight drew the contours of his strong dark face, the light blue eyes. 'No, it's not a pretty story. And now it's told, and we've got to get you well, and I think you're more likely to do that if you forget as much as you can.'

'But – now that you know – what I did was so – '

'No, no, Caroline,' he said firmly. 'What are you expecting – that I should judge you now, on top of everyone else? I find you half-dead of the typhus that has taken your child. A child you had alone, and worked to support. A child given you by a man who made promises and skipped off and left you. And I'm to put on a moral face and pronounce my judgement? No. My God, Caroline, whatever you've done – whatever you could possibly have done – you've been punished enough, and more. All I can say is if you expected me to turn and walk out then you're wrong, very wrong.'

He spoke with deep feeling. Caroline blinked away a tear. 'I – I don't know what to say. . .'

He saw the tear, coughed and picked up his book. 'Nothing needed. Shall we have a few pages more?'

He read again, and this time she only half-listened, for her mind was busy with the new idea that someone should not think badly of her. The assumption that everyone did had been part of the burden of her own self-disgust. Tentatively, as she lay there, she lifted the burden and found it lighter.

Stranger still, that this relief should come from a man who had always seemed to mistrust and even dislike her.

At last Richard closed the book and got up and trimmed the candles. 'You know,' she said, 'I think I shall be able to get up tomorrow.'

'We'll see,' he said. 'Well, our little nurse said she was willing to do the night-watch. She lives only just across at Saffron Hill. I'll go now and recruit her. Shan't be a moment.' He frowned at her. 'What's the matter?'

'Nothing, nothing,' she said hastily. Absurdly, she felt afraid of the night without him there. She felt she would somehow slip back into the fever and the despair; it was ridiculous but . . .

'She was satisfactory, wasn't she?'

'Oh, yes, she was very good . . .' And then she burst out: 'Will you stay a little longer, Richard? I'm sorry, I shouldn't ask it, and I am getting better, really, I won't ask again, I feel such a fool but – '

'Of course, of course, hush,' he said. 'Why didn't you say?'

'I promise this will be the last time,' she said, sinking down in the bed, the panic departing again.

'Never mind that,' Richard said briskly. He scattered the ashes on the fire, extinguished all but one candle and sat down with it by the door. 'Now go to sleep and stop apologizing.'

'You could leave me as soon as I've gone to sleep,' she said drowsily, 'you must be tired yourself, and your friend will be wondering . . .'

'Go to sleep, Caroline.' He sat in the old Windsor chair and opened a book.

She sank comfortably down, with a feeling she recognized like a long-lost friend, the almost forgotten feeling of security.

She got up the next day, and leaning on Richard's arm she went down to the courtyard for a while in the morning. She was not as strong as she had thought, and Richard made her rest again in the afternoon.

Despite her promise, he sat up with her again that

319

night, and the next: she didn't have to ask. The panic, and the thought of little Anthony, tended to surface on waking, and it helped to see Richard sitting stalwart in waistcoat and shirt-sleeves in the chair by the door, his coat hanging on the chair-back. In spite of the insistence of her conscience that she should get well quickly and release him from the burden of looking after her, she had to acknowledge that her convalescence seemed to rely on his presence. She identified him with recovery and sanity.

With the return of her strength he made her go outside as much as possible: he said the doctor had recommended fresh air. A little of the old shrinking came back the first time she walked out into the busy street on Richard's arm; but he held her firmly and plunged her on into the crowds and the traffic, and soon she wondered what she had been afraid of. Though her rash had gone, and her skin was regaining colour, she still felt she must look a fright; but when she said something of this to Richard he only laughed. And she thought afterwards that if her vanity was coming back she must be getting better.

One sad journey she felt she must make. She went to the parish graveyard to lay some flowers on Anthony's grave. There was no headstone, only a wooden cross, but it seemed appropriate to the modest little plot. Richard stood at some distance, with his cocked hat under his arm; when she came out of her abstraction and looked around she could not see him for a minute. 'I'm here,' he said, 'I'm here.'

After that he began to arrange outings for them: anything that would take her outside and prevent her brooding. He surprised her with them each morning. He hired a post-chaise and they went to Wimbledon Common to see the grand review of troops before the Prince of Wales. The carriages and carts of the spectators were drawn up in a huge circle around the long lines of red-coated soldiers. There was a tremendous noise when the troops made a running fire all along the line: some horses reared and bolted. Richard brought his telescope, and through it she managed to make out the figure of the Prince of Wales, every bit as fat as the caricatures represented him.

Another day they went to Astley's Theatre, and sat among a noisy crowd in a smell of sawdust and orange-peel and watched the indescribable mixture of pantomime and circus in which trained horses galloped across the boards, performed acts of heroism, feigned equally heroic death, and generally acted the human players off the stage. They went to the water-gardens at White-Conduit House. They went out on the stage-coach to Hampstead spa, and here, though it was cold and windy, the smell of the air and the fields and the sound of birds and the sight of London as a distant town like any other seemed to advance her convalescence by weeks.

And Richard was always with her, watching carefully over her, noticing when she got tired, making sure she ate well, acting as an unobtrusive support when, through overtaxing herself or dwelling on her baby, she slipped back a little. And as she began to do most things for herself and needed him less directly, her consciousness of him as a person was enhanced.

She noticed things about him, and in repetition their familiarity gave her an obscure pleasure. It was as if she had never really observed another person before, objectively, the thousand little things that made up their particular otherness. The way he pushed his hair back from his forehead when he was concentrating on something. The way he walked up stairs, brisk and straight-backed, as if he were going up to the quarter-deck. The way he stretched his arms above his head, after he had

321

been sitting up reading to her, and rubbed his eyes with his fist, making him look young and boyish. And with that came the knowledge that the tiredness he had sustained in sitting with her was quietly, selflessly given. His generosity, she began to perceive, was of the unreflecting kind: no saintliness, only a gently determined giving.

It was deep and fundamental, like so much about him. To say that she had misjudged Richard was not strictly true. He was still the same Richard she had known – or rather, and that was perhaps the crux of it, not known. In a curious reversal, their most charged emotional interaction had been when she knew very little of him: now, in the calm, uncomplicated business of her convalescence, with everything on a cool, detached level, she was actually getting to know him closely.

There had always been an antagonistic tension between them, and now for the first time she began to analyse why. It had always seemed that her mere presence had tilted his personality over to its darker side, presenting to her the prickly reserve that baffled and discomposed her. Had it in fact been a two-way process? She had always prided herself, perhaps conceitedly, on her ease with people: perhaps, faced with someone who would not be so smoothly assimilated, she had given rein to her own resentment. And Richard's status relative to the Hardwicks had not helped. There was a distance between them which, Caroline saw now, Richard was sorely aware of. The sick-room was a no man's land, where true identities were clearer.

In coming to terms with her disastrous love for Antoine Clairet, the factor of another man imposed so constantly on her consciousness – though so differently – was a determining one. Before Antoine, she had always thought of herself as a rational creature: she had always had a clear vision of the brink along which most people, it seemed, teetered without noticing it. Self-preservation, perhaps; perhaps selfishness. Whatever, Antoine had thrown it all off balance. Once her emotions were off the leash they had gone mad with their freedom. Her love had been obsessive: only now that she was emerging from a grief equally obsessive did she perceive that.

The hard edges of Richard's personality, which were all she had seen or bothered to see before, now appeared as elements in a far more complex whole. And for all her overwhelming love for Antoine, she knew she had been guilty of the same thing with him. A less blindly compulsive love, and she might have learned the truth earlier. The sea glimpsed stormily by night could appear a place of cruel dread: under the summer sun, with boats skimming across it, a place of charm and ease. It was both, and those who knew and loved it best knew that well.

She was able to reflect on these misjudgements, to feel her rationality taking shape again like a healing wound, because of the freedom given her by those strange autumn weeks. She had nothing to do but recover; she was quite alone except for Richard; her relationship with him was so unconventional yet so formal, so intimate yet so chaste.

It was borne in on her too that, while she had been voluntarily alone since coming to London, solitude had long been natural to him. It was not that he told her of his loneliness – he would not do that – it was rather something in his bearing. He was no longer defensive as he had once been, but on walking out into the street or into a garden or theatre on one of their outings, he had a way of bracing his shoulders while his penetrating, very blue eyes scanned quickly about him. It was the instinctive reaction of a man who was used to being by himself and expecting no recognition or welcome. She had had her own experience of being cut off this year, and she began to understand that Richard's life was a pattern of such isolation. She saw the guarded pride as something more than truculence. He had had a hard struggle: his independence was perhaps a precarious foothold of self-respect, rather than an aloof height from which he looked down.

And as she was eased gently back into the world, one of her intensest pleasures was in breaking down the barrier of Richard's solitude. In their walks and outings she talked, and got him to talk, and they shared their responses to what they saw: discerning the tight, lonely hold he had had to keep on himself, she tried to promote the sheer pleasure of company. They smiled together over the courtship of Uncle Toby and Widow Wadman in *Tristram Shandy*; they reminisced together about the fens, the summer droves of meadowsweet, the whistle of the teal, the islets of willow and slim poplars; they laughed together when one cold evening Richard, revealing a talent for mimicry, burst into fen dialect, complaining his fitten were fair frawn from soodling about in the rawk and it were like to mek him mardy. For her own part, she wondered how she had managed to be alone for so long; and she wondered, too, if it were the mere fact of company she was enjoying, or if it were just Richard's company.

He seemed surprised when she asked him about his life this past year, as if he didn't expect her interest; but he told her about the dour routine of blockade duty on board the *Olympia*, about his new duties as lieutenant.

'I'm only a junior,' he said, 'but still, the contrast with a midshipman's life . . . I remember the first time we were to dine in the Captain's cabin. We strolled on the deck before dinner, and the Marine band was piping away, and I was trying to look very nonchalant – and inside I was fairly blown up with vanity and fancying myself half an admiral already. No maggoty biscuit at the Captain's table. Well, at least the promotion system means that the

Captain doesn't forget what it's like to be the smallest and lowliest midshipman. I certainly hope I never forget it.'

'How do you – when you're on blockade, how do you feel about the French ships over the horizon?' She felt a strong impulse to ask this question, coupled with a peculiar reluctance to know the answer.

'Oh, well, we scarcely see them sometimes. It is a curious situation. A sort of fencing. You have to remind yourself how important it is. I've been in sea-fights and seen how men die and it's not pretty – but all the same sometimes you wish the Frenchies would come out and break the deadlock. But then, things improved when St Vincent took command of the Channel Fleet this spring. Morale was low under old Bridport. All the important things seemed to be going on in the Mediterranean. St Vincent makes us feel useful.'

This was on a frosty morning in early December, and they were walking in St James's Park. Richard said, glancing at her: 'Are you tired?'

'No, not at all. I feel as if I could walk all day. In fact, Richard, I've been thinking I ought to go and get some work.'

'Work? What for?'

'I don't know how much you've spent on me these last weeks – no, listen,' she added as he tried to put her off. 'You've fed me and paid my rent and now I'm strong I can surely pick up seamstress work again. I ought to, I'm quite able. And then after a while I can pay you back . . .'

He frowned and said nothing. She realized he was hurt; and she was deeply pained in turn.

They walked on, and she tried to think of a way of changing what she had said; but then Richard sighed and said: 'Well, I'll tell you now. I've just had a letter sent on from Portsmouth. It's some weeks old. From your cousin Charles.'

She waited.

'It's just to tell me that he's living in London. With Edmund, who's studying at the Royal Academy. And I've been wondering – what you mean to do now.'

She felt chilly. She had averted her eyes from the future.

'It's not for me to tell you what to do, or even ask you what you intend. But any day now I should be recommissioned. There are reports in the newspapers of Russia seizing British ships in her ports, and Sweden and Denmark drawing closer to her. If the North turns against us we'll need every man. So . . . I shan't be here. And I wondered – if you think of going back to your family . . .?'

Caroline stared across at the roofs of the Palace. She felt numb and helpless. Her father and mother . . . The fear, the urge to hide, came back to her.

'Or, if you wish to stay here, whether you might like to see Charles. I believe you were always close. Of course it's entirely up to you. I know I have no claim, no right to direct . . . But I would feel easier if I knew.'

'I don't know . . . I must think. . .'

'Of course.'

After that an unrestful silence fell between them, and continued until they were back at Jackson's Rents. Richard made to leave, saying something about coming back in the evening, but Caroline checked him.

'No – Richard, won't you stay, please? There's still some of that chicken – will you eat here? Perhaps you can help me – to decide.'

'Of course. But it must be your own decision.'

They talked of other things over dinner; and after dinner, from soothing habit, Richard read to her again. He read from Shakespeare's sonnets, and she sat and looked into the fire and thought of Antoine and little

Anthony, her parents and the old life she had left behind; and felt that these couple of months since her illness, strange and somehow lovely, were a unique episode that must come to a close.

Richard's voice dwelt on her ear.

> '"Let me not to the marriage of true minds
> Admit impediments. Love is not love
> Which alters when it alteration finds,
> Or bends with the remover to remove.
> O, no! it is an ever-fixed mark,
> That looks on tempests and is never shaken . . ."'

She became aware that he had stopped, and was watching her.

'Where is Charles living?' she said.

'He has lodgings in Greek Street,' Richard said. 'I'd like to see him myself.' He closed the book. 'You know, he must have been very worried about you this past year. Your parents too of course – '

'I know, I know.'

'All I mean is – it might be easier, perhaps, to begin to be reconciled with your family through Charles.'

She nodded. Charles was the least intimidating prospect. And she could not pretend to herself that she wanted to go on living like this – now there was no child to cherish . . . She must at least let them know she was all right . . .

'As long as they'll have me back,' she blurted, in a spasm of weakness.

Richard got up, touched her shoulder lightly. 'Oh, Caroline,' he said, then moved away again. 'If there's anything sure in this world, it's that. Believe me.'

She did believe him. That was the trouble. He was her reassurance.

'Shall we go and see Charles tomorrow?'

She nodded, at last.

327

'Very well. Now I must go and change. I shall call for you at seven. You had better put on your best frock: we have tickets for the theatre at Covent Garden.'

It was delightful to go to the theatre, of course, but coming after what they had said earlier, it seemed as if it was a final outing. An inexplicable sadness came over Caroline; not connected with the baby and Antoine and the past, not connected apparently with anything.

They had three-shilling seats in the pit, and Richard had exchanged his uniform for a dark wool dress coat with a high collar and a ruffled shirt. He always dressed with care, but she was struck by the change in him.

They saw a comedy called *Ways and Means*, with an entertainment called *Peeping Tom of Coventry*. The comedy was amusing, but Caroline was preoccupied. She was reminded of going to the theatre years ago, when Richard was to begin his career at sea the next day, and she had been rude to him. Of course they were children then. But the thought pricked her as painfully as if it had happened yesterday and she convinced herself that Richard was thinking of it too.

When the interval came Richard looked closely at her and seemed to notice her abstraction. 'Are you worrying about meeting Charles?' he said.

'No, no.' She examined her gloves. 'Richard – do you remember that day years ago, when you came down to London with my family, to go to sea? And we all came here, the night before?'

'Of course.'

Her cheeks burned. She felt a desperate need to say something; to somehow convey how wrong she had been in disliking him – but no, it was more complex than that, that dark tension there had been between them. She wondered if the antagonism on her part had been a perverse resentment at being unable to penetrate his inaccessible character. She had a new, sympathetic insight into this man, driven into himself by humiliating dependence, giving away nothing of himself for fear of betrayal. She wanted to break down the defences, but she had an aching fear that he wished to keep them intact.

She said: 'I've never thanked you properly for all you've done these past weeks.' Even as she said it, with hubbub all around and music playing and fruit- and pie-vendors passing, it sounded to her weak and lame and not at all what she really wanted to say. She plunged on: 'I think if it weren't for you I'd probably be dead now – '

'Oh, nonsense.'

'Or at least – dead inside. I don't know if you can guess how deep in despair I was after the baby, how it was all – all darkness . . . Anyway, I want you to know how grateful I am . . .'

'You don't have to say this to me,' Richard said. 'You're well now, and can go back to your family. That's all the recompense I need.'

Caroline subsided, unhappily. The curtains opened again and the one-act farce began.

Caroline scarcely attended. From the knotted complexities of gratitude and apology which she had tried to tease out, she found she was holding one thread.

First she remembered, almost with disbelief, how she had been besotted with Antoine. Antoine, Antoine. Besotted and obsessed. He had dominated her life: he had *taken* her life – and how nearly, literally true that was. She saw him now as a bottomless well down which she had poured herself.

Richard, on the other hand, had liberated her.

She sat still and stared at the candlelit stage and it became a bright blur: the voices of the players dwindled

329

to a muttering in her ears. Out of her tortured confusion of feeling she traced the truth.

Why had her attempt at thanks come out so feebly? In her deepened insight into Richard she had also gained an insight into herself – the confident Miss Hardwick, daughter of Luke, against whom Richard's pride had grated – and she had not liked all that she had seen. She had reflected, too, on that last time Richard had come to the fenland, when she knew he and her father had quarrelled. Knowing her father, she began to guess what had gone on then. Life had forced Richard to continually prove himself, and it was no wonder if eventually he had grown impatient with that demand. The significance of his coming home after his promotion, proudly wearing the lieutenant's coat he had striven for, had struck her for the first time. Seeking acceptance, not indulgence.

She had never liked to be troubled or discomfited: perhaps that was why she had never made the effort to imagine herself in Richard's shoes, had preferred not to contemplate his position. Now she had been through the fire herself. But was this new position of understanding fraught with danger and pain too?

She had broken down some of the barriers between them. Now she realized, with alarm, that she wanted to break them all. And she had held back because of fear of what lay on the other side. Richard had been kind to her, considerate, sympathetic . . . but she dreaded to face the fact that his feelings went no further than that. She dreaded it, because she was falling in love with him.

Precisely when, during these last weeks, she had begun to fall in love with him it was impossible to tell. It was like pinpointing the moment when the greyness of the small hours at the window became the light of dawn. You looked around, and saw the room, and knew. Now, sitting silently beside Richard in the crowded pit, she knew where her obscure apologies and explanations had been tending. She knew the foreboding she felt was not just at facing her family and returning to the world, but a dread of losing Richard. She had progressed from sickness through convalescence to health, and her feeling for him, mysterious and inevitable as the processes of her healing body, had developed too. Dependence and gratitude and interest and respect and understanding had been drawn aside like successive veils to reveal the nakedness of love.

She was wary of it: she almost wished it were not so. Love had caused her agony before.

For the rest of the evening she was preoccupied with her discovery: that, and the necessity of revealing nothing of it to Richard. They walked quickly, talking little, through the seedy alleys around Covent Garden, where there were brothels of the lowest kind and little booths that sold pornography. It was a cold, dark night, and Jackson's Rents looked unwelcoming. Richard said he would see her up to her room.

The stairs were pitch black, and Richard went first. At the landing she heard him abruptly stop with a curse and a grunt of pain.

She reached out and touched his shoulder. 'What is it?'

'Dear God,' he groaned, 'wish I hadn't done that. My chest – where I was hurt . . .'

'You'd better come in.'

He had barged straight into the newel-post. When they finally got into her room and she had lit a candle she saw him holding his shoulder and evidently holding back some salty naval expressions.

'Is it your rib?' she said. 'Don't say it's broke again – '

'No, no, don't think so,' he said through clenched teeth. 'Bruised . . . be all right in a moment. What a shite-begotten thing to do, sorry, excuse me . . .'

'Swear away,' she said, unable to hold back a smile, 'and take off your coat and sit down and let me see. Come. It will make a change for me to do the nursing.'

She threw off her bonnet and lit another candle and put some kindling on the fire while Richard, with difficulty, took off his coat and waistcoat and gingerly opened his shirt.

Beneath the shoulder-binding was an area of discoloration, the remains of an extensive bruising, and in the centre a livid mark where he had knocked it again.

'Ow,' she said, shuddering as she saw it. 'Can you touch it? I've got a little Friar's Balsam. That might help. You'd better take off your shirt. Will you let me try?'

'All right,' he said, 'as long as you don't mind.'

He took off his shirt and she knelt down beside him and with great care smoothed the balsam on to his bruised chest. It was a supple, well-shaped body: she remembered Richard was only twenty-one. If she could have possibly told Richard that she was mentally comparing it with the memory of Antoine's, it would have been to impress on him the difference – but not in terms of favourable or unfavourable. She recalled with great clarity how she had been in thrall to Antoine's body, losing herself in its planes and scents and surfaces – *losing herself*. And Richard's body affected her differently: it bore the testimony of what it had performed and suffered, it was as eloquent of him as his voice and thoughts. It suffused her with a new tenderness. Antoine had been a physically beautiful being, presented with angelic completeness. If she should see him now she would still find him beautiful; but she knew, for all the direct carnality of their relationship, that now she would see it impartially as one saw the beauty of a child. Richard's beauty had been borne in on her subtly, piecemeal, more gravely and deeply. As she smoothed the balsam on his gently rising and falling chest

332

she thought of how it had manifested itself to her of late: how she had unconsciously noticed the muscles in his back when he bent to stir the fire, the way his hands turned the pages of a book, the way his pellucid eyes narrowed to look into the distance. She had wanted Antoine physically as a child gloatingly wants a tempting toy on a shelf. She felt that if she were to make love with Richard it would be a development of desire, not a quenching and curtailing.

Her hand stopped. She was close to betraying herself, and she must not. Out of very love for Richard, she must not. It would be a poor repayment for all his kindness to suddenly embarrass him with avowals that could only poison their friendship.

She got up. 'Does that feel easier?' she said, going to the cupboard to put the jar away.

'Much better, thank you. Stupid thing to do. Try and sleep on my back tonight.'

She busied herself at the cupboard. 'I wonder what Charles will say when he sees us. It'll be a double surprise for him, won't it . . .?'

'Yes . . . I suppose it will.'

When she turned round at last Richard was pulling on his coat.

'Well,' he said, 'we'll go and startle the poor fellow tomorrow. Don't know what he's doing in London exactly.'

'Oh, setting the world to rights, I suppose,' she said. She was having great difficulty in looking at him.

'I dare say. Well, I'll call for you early, shall I? Not too far to Greek Street.' He put on his hat. 'Good night.'

'Good night, Richard.'

She listened to his brisk footsteps echoing away down the stairs and out into the street.

2

There were two facets to Charles's life in London.

One was his deepening involvement with the radical movement – what remained of it. As his friendship with the printer Jonas Spurling ripened, he was emboldened to finish his pamphlet at last and offer it to him to be printed. It was called *Habeas Corpus: The Defenders of* Tyranny *Expos'd, with some Remarks on the urgent Necessity of a Comprehensive System of* Reform. *By C. J. Hardwick, a Friend of Liberty and Country.*

'Your title's long enough, my friend,' Spurling said. 'But you put it well and it's timely. Aye, very timely.'

'Would it come under the sedition acts?'

Spurling wheezed with laughter. 'Would it? Why, the title alone. No doubt about that. But it's up to you. I'll print and willing. I'm not afraid of being hauled before the justices again. Don't want 'em to think I've gone soft. But I'll take your name off it if you like, though that's no guarantee they'll not find you out.'

'No indeed,' said Charles. 'Let it stand.' He was under no illusions about the efficacy of one little pamphlet; but to take a stand against the censorship laws was something.

One evening Spurling took him to a meeting in the cellar of a tavern in Cripplegate. They carried printed tickets saying: 'Admit one for the Season to the School of Eloquence'. This was a cover for the activities of the remnants of the Corresponding Society, since all political clubs and societies had been outlawed. There was a miscellaneous collection of men from labourers and shoe-makers to booksellers and surgeons in the smoky room, where one of their number read a lecture and then opened the meeting to discussion. It emerged from the debate

334

that the war was generally unpopular and held responsible for the rise in prices, but recent events had clouded matters. Some were for action against the Tsar, who was a despot if ever there was one; and as for the late treaty between France and Spain . . . Charles's preoccupation, the reform of Parliament and representation of the people, seemed to get rather lost. It was inspiriting, but the talk, so clearly divorced from any hope of power, turned vague and nebulous like the pipe-smoke above them.

The other facet, of course, was Lydia.

He did not know if she surrounded herself with platoons of friends, preventing them being alone, on purpose. He suspected so, as he continued to call at Curzon Street and continued to find a buffer of company there, or else the drizzly presence of aunt Clarissa. But since that night at Ranelagh her keeping him at arm's length seemed no longer a simple strategy of teasing and more a matter of self-preservation.

Over all he felt the shadow of the absent Sir Thomas. It was her father, he was sure, that was blighting the growth of their love – or perhaps being used as a pretext. He could not yet believe that Sir Thomas Fairburn's feelings about him could be so violent simply on account of his political sympathies. He felt he must see Sir Thomas, to clear the air. Great Baston was a long time ago, after all. If he could present Lydia with the fact that her father did not really disapprove of him, he felt it might break down those brittle defences she placed against his love – and, he hoped, against her own.

So, when he heard in late November that Sir Thomas was coming up to town, he was impatient to see him. He waited a few days and then sent his card asking if he might call and pay his respects on Wednesday.

The Fairburn carriage was drawn up outside the door

when he called, and he found Sir Thomas in the hall buttoning a spencer over his coat while a footman stood by with his hat and a fur muff.

'Ah, Mr Hardwick, a brisk day, I thought we might go for a drive,' Sir Thomas said with purring urbanity. 'Reed, is the carriage ready?'

Charles, surprised, allowed himself to be propelled outside again and into the crested carriage. 'Clip over to Hyde Park,' Sir Thomas said to the coachman, and then pulled up the window and settled himself opposite Charles.

'I heard you'd returned to London, and hoped to see you, sir,' Charles said. 'It's a long time since we met at Great Baston. You've – you've been out at your country place, I understand . . .' As he spoke Charles became aware that Sir Thomas was not looking at him. 'And – and Bath also, I understand,' he went on lamely.

'You understand,' Sir Thomas said, presenting his long-nosed profile and mildly watching the trees of the park.

'Yes – at least, Miss Fairburn remarked – '

'Well, I'll give you credit for honesty.' Sir Thomas crossed his booted legs with a sigh. 'If not discretion. I'm quite aware you've been calling, Mr Hardwick.'

'I thought, as Miss Fairburn's aunt was there, and she seemed to be receiving company – '

'I'm aware you've been calling,' Sir Thomas said again, as if Charles had not spoken, 'and really I'm surprised at your effrontery. I would have thought it quite plain – and if it's not, I'll make it so now – that you are not welcome in my house, after our last meeting.'

Charles swallowed. 'You mean – you surely don't refer – ?'

'The sentiments you expressed then, Mr Hardwick, effectively place you outside the circle of my acquaintance, and most especially that of my daughter.'

'I – ' Charles had not expected this. 'If you will remind me of what I said, then perhaps – '

'Don't insult my intelligence, Mr Hardwick,' Sir Thomas said shortly and quietly. That gentle softness of voice, Charles realized, had the effect of making the listener strain forward to hear: it was a subtle way of commanding deference. 'I know all about you, sir,' Sir Thomas went on. 'I know that that shocking outburst was no freak of an argumentative moment. At first I thought it the product of a misguided, perhaps unbalanced, rather than actively mischievous mind. Since then I have discovered otherwise. And I am well aware you have been seeking to pay court to my daughter. While my back was turned.'

'That's unfair. I sought this interview with you expressly so that I could lay before you my – my regard for Miss Fairburn, my feelings – '

'You needn't spout your feelings, sir,' Sir Thomas said. 'I don't wish to hear them. I can only suppose, then, that you are very foolish or very stubborn if you hoped to put any kind of case to me for your seeing my daughter. Lydia has been brought up on the best principles, Mr Hardwick. They include, of course, politeness. It is up to me, it seems, to point out to you, as you plainly need telling, that a Jacobinical saboteur like yourself has no place in the society of my daughter. It is my duty to eradicate your kind from the body politic. It is equally my duty to see that your contagion is kept away from my family.'

Charles stared at the pale, tautly handsome man opposite him. 'And Miss Fairburn,' he said. 'Has she complained of this contagion?'

'If I thought for a moment that you had been preaching your sedition to her – '

'If I did, Sir Thomas, Lydia would be quite well able to answer it, I assure you.'

337

Sir Thomas rapped with his cane on the roof, and the carriage stopped.

'Now look you here, Hardwick,' he said, his voice dropping ever lower, 'I'll not hear you bandy my daughter's name. I don't believe she's shown you anything beyond common courtesy and if she has – '

'Aye, if she has, what then?' said Charles angrily. 'Would you prevent her seeing me?'

'I would deny her that freedom, for her own good,' Sir Thomas said. 'Yes, for her own good, if it should prove she doesn't know her own mind. The thought of her trusting nature falling prey to a mischief-maker like you turns my stomach.'

'You're fond of denying freedoms, aren't you? In government, at home, it's all one to you.' Charles was breathing hard. 'You've feathered your nest well and you'll let nothing disturb it. All this high-flown cant about her trusting nature . . . What if Lydia were to say no? What would you do – throw her in prison, send for the Dragoons?'

Sir Thomas was white. He lifted one finger: it was not quite steady. 'You'll stay away from my daughter, Hardwick. You'll not enter my house and you'll have no communication with her. You disobey me, and I'll break you. I'm a powerful man, Hardwick, I have influence, and I'll not hesitate to use it. There are men lying in prison for less than I've heard you say publicly. I can break you, sir.'

'I'm aware of those men in prison,' Charles said. 'Consigned there for speaking their minds while toadies like you draw fat salaries for doing nothing.'

Sir Thomas flung open the carriage door. 'Get out.'

The carriage lurched away, leaving Charles standing in the middle of Hyde Park. He tried to get cool, but his anger would not leave him. His only satisfaction was in making the meticulous man lose his temper.

But there was no satisfaction, really. He had sought this morning to close the gap between himself and Sir Thomas, but there was no reconciling. What had Lydia said? – there could be no civilized disagreements in these times. Lydia . . .

But Charles was an essentially civilized man. He was still taken aback when he called at Curzon Street and was told the family were not at home on several occasions. It was ridiculous. And when he directed notes there was no reply. He did not know which horrible thought to believe – that Sir Thomas was physically preventing Lydia from seeing him, that she was willingly obeying him, that she simply didn't care . . .

In this way he struggled on until one morning in early December, when two people who were very dear to him turned up unexpectedly at his lodgings.

Richard had called for Caroline that morning and gone with her to Greek Street, but he could not stay long.

'I received a summons from the Admiralty this morning,' he told her as they walked. 'Presumably my new commission. I must wait upon their lordships this afternoon.'

That she had known this must come made it no easier. But she tried to disguise her feelings. 'You must be glad at the thought of occupation again,' she said.

'Well, the position's critical enough – I feel I should be doing something. If Austria breaks we'll be alone. These are dark days.'

The dark days, it seemed, had touched them all. There was bad news from Caroline's home.

Charles was more delighted to see her than anxious for explanations of where she had been and what she had been doing: perhaps he perceived that what she most needed was a reassuring welcome. She and Richard told the barest details, how Richard had come across her by chance in London and persuaded her to get in touch with her family again, and Charles asked for no more: it would come in time. But she was keen for news of home, and Charles could not hold it back from her.

'I had a letter from mother this week,' he said. 'Perhaps you'd better read it.'

He pointed to the paragraph. Caroline sank into a chair with the letter. Richard stood at a distance.

I wish I could give you a happy account of the family at the Bridge House, Mary wrote, *but they are in a sad way there since young Nicholas's accident. He was at Luke's timber-yard in Lynn, where he has spent so much of his time of late, and was working after dark in supervising the stacking of a shipment of timber. It was dark, as I say, and there was some confusion of orders with the overseer. A load of timber toppled and Nicholas was pinned beneath it. At first there were fears he might not live, but he is a strong boy and recovering slowly tho' there were several bones broke and he cannot stir. But, the effect on Luke has been terrible to behold. In truth, Charles, I believe he blames himself. He has been stockpiling timber for some time, and since the sad business with Caroline has worked the boy hard and been very severe on him. It is as if with this accident all Luke's grief has at last come out. He does not go to Lynn any more. He sits around the house and looks greatly aged. The merchant house stands still; and indeed since this trouble with the Baltic countries there is scarce anywhere for Luke's ships to go. Many trades and manufactures here have been badly hit. Rebecca I know is worried about money, and fears the employees, &c., may not have been paid, but Luke seems sunk in apathy . . .*

Caroline put the letter down.

'Is it bad?' Richard said.

She passed him the letter. 'I must go back,' she said.

340

'Oh, God, what have I been doing? Poor Nicholas . . . father . . . I must go back.'

She stayed at Charles's lodgings for the rest of the day, whilst Richard went to the Admiralty.

Charles told her what he knew of her family since she had run away, while the picture painted in Mary's letter took vivid shape in her mind.

Well, now it was settled for her. She had to go back, to help, to do what she could. The question of forgiveness and reconciliation became academic. She just had to go.

'I'll take the coach tomorrow morning,' she said. 'Could you lend me the money, Charles?'

'Certainly. If you feel it's best. They'll be overjoyed to see you, of course. As I am. All these months, Caro, with no word . . .'

'I know. It was – well, you know why I had to get away, don't you, Charles? I suppose you heard?'

'Yes. We – well, at Morholm we were told. No one else, really.'

She nodded. 'Though no doubt the rumour soon got out . . . I had to get away, Charles. I had to keep the baby – that's all I could think of. Anyway, I managed to support myself, and had the baby. It didn't live.'

'Oh, Caroline.' Charles came and stood by her chair, his hand on her shoulder. 'I'm so sorry.'

'And then, when I was down, right down at the bottom, beyond everything, Richard found me and took care of me. I was ill and he took care of me.'

'Caroline, why didn't you turn to us? We've been so worried . . .'

'I know.' She held his hand. 'I just couldn't . . . After Antoine – the French prisoner – I just wanted to hide away, bury myself . . . the shame and the pain . . . But

341

that's over now. Richard saved me. And now they need me and I've got to go back.'

'I'll come with you, of course,' Charles said after a moment. He hated the thought of leaving London now, with everything undecided, but he ought to . . . 'You can't make the journey alone.'

'Dear Charles,' she said smiling. 'I've done so much alone this past year – one coach journey won't hurt me.'

'I suppose so.' She certainly looked more mature: well, and confident, but without the old sparkle of carelessness. 'But you must stay here tonight.' There were a hundred questions he wanted to ask but refrained from asking; but he could not help saying: 'I'm – glad Richard found you. He – he's an excellent fellow . . .'

She looked up at him, and her eyes seemed to cloud over a moment. 'Yes . . . yes, he is.'

Richard came back late that afternoon. Over dinner he told them his new orders. The *Olympia* was still in the yards: Richard was to follow his captain, who was shifting his flag to the *Desirée* at Yarmouth. With the hostility of Russia and the threat of the revival of the League of Armed Neutrality against England the North Sea fleet was being strengthened.

'Richard – I'm going back to Peterborough tomorrow,' Caroline said.

He nodded and drained his glass of wine. 'I think it's best. I'll go over to Jackson's Rents and have your things sent to the Blue Boar along with mine and book two places on the coach.'

'You'll come with me?' she said, with a little inward lurch of hope. Not to lose him quite yet . . .

'Yes, of course. You can't travel alone. I've two days to report to Yarmouth. I could get a boat round from Lynn.' He got up from the table. 'I'll go now and see about our luggage. Have you the key to your room? Ah. And you're all paid up with the landlord? Good. I'll not be long. Save me some apple-tart.'

She was not to lose him quite yet. Another day with him. That was all. Already, as he became less directly, practically needed, it seemed his manner was growing brisker, more formal, withdrawing to the proper distance. Another day, and then this strange, wonderful idyll, that had begun for her in sickness and mute despair and ended in an equally mute love, would be over.

CHAPTER 4

1

Caroline left London on the 14th of December, closing a door on a part of her life. What happened could never be forgotten: there were consequences still to be faced at home. But she was healed in body and felt herself to be virtually healed in spirit, thanks to Richard; and now she had a duty to be with her family. Tragic circumstances had estranged them, and now they would bring them back together.

Charles came to the coaching inn to see them off. He thought he would be coming home for Christmas, he said, but he could not leave London just yet. He shook Richard's hand and wished him luck on his new ship. Somehow, they were all a little constrained with each other.

And this continued on the journey. There was a third person in the coach, but it was not because of this that Caroline and Richard did not talk much. A veil of politeness had fallen between them. It seemed to Caroline to grow thicker as the journey progressed. It was as if, she thought, she was becoming 'Miss Hardwick' again to Richard as they drew nearer to the scenes of their former association.

Well, their peculiar, confidential relationship had merely been part of her illness and convalescence, she told herself. It was natural that it should fade now. It was discreet and respectful of Richard to draw back like this.

She held back the curtain and watched the rainy

countryside in a confusion of feeling. She didn't *want* Richard to be like this. It was their last day and she wanted to talk and laugh as they used to. She wanted to tell him so many things. What she did not want to face was the idea that his demeanour was a way of holding her at arm's length. She had said nothing to him of how deeply she felt for him, how desperately he mattered to her . . . And she was afraid that he was carefully guarding against any such thing.

Voices of reason spoke clamorously, trying to drown the music of the heart. She was older and wiser. She knew the penalties of love. This was no adolescent longing, such as had first drawn her to Antoine. But it was a longing, and a very profound one.

Side by side with the longing, sharpening its sting, was a maturer knowledge born of her sufferings: that the dreams of romance were not self-fulfilling, that people were more complex and less knowable than the ardent heart would like to admit.

Antoine . . . She wanted to speak too about Antoine – to find out what Richard thought. To try to explain to him how she had been deceived about Antoine and how, in the process of coming to terms with that, she had come to love Richard. But she feared to do that too: not really because she felt Richard must despise her for an affair with a French prisoner, for if that were the case he would never have drawn this close to her. No, her fear was no longer of hate, but a kindly impartiality.

She remembered a time when she was so in love that she could hardly eat for happiness. She remembered the terrible pain of losing love and the way she had retreated into solitude as the only way of bearing it. She knew she must relinquish Richard and fix her mind on her family and poor Nicholas and devote herself to them. There were lots of things in the world besides her awakening love for Richard . . . It must be contained, not expressed. She would think of him, when he had gone to take up his new commission in the inhospitable North Sea. Think of him, cherish him in her thoughts, but say nothing.

They had a meal at the Sun at Biggleswade, sitting together in a plush curtained box.

Richard said: 'I forgot to ask you. When I took your luggage from your room. There was a picture, an odd sort of thing in straw marquetry. I packed it and it only occurred to me afterwards that it might have been part of the furnishings.'

'No, it is mine.' She picked at the beef on her plate. 'It was from Norman Cross, the prisoner-of-war camp. One of the things the prisoners make to sell at the gates.'

'Ah.' Richard was not eating much either. 'Well, I didn't want us to be accused of purloining the fittings.'

She tasted her wine and said with an effort: 'Richard, when you're at sea again, will you write to – will you write to us at the Bridge House?'

He raised his eyes briefly. 'Certainly, if you wish. That is . . .'

'Yes?'

'Well – you've not said what you want me to do when we reach Peterborough. I mean – as regards seeing your parents. The fact is . . . I don't know how much you're aware of, but your father and I did not . . . well, we did not part friends.'

She waited for more, but his face had gone hard and unreadable as it did sometimes, as if he were retreating to some safe inner distance. 'Did it – did it have anything to do with me?' she ventured.

After a moment he said, almost brusquely: 'It was a fundamental matter.'

'But of course, I would like you to come in with me,' she said. 'It's because of you that I'm able to go back at

346

all. All you've done for me . . . They'll want to see you and thank you too. You forget,' she added nervously, 'I've got my own making up to do with them.'

'It'll be all right,' Richard said.

'I do hope so,' she said, gazing into the colour of her wine. 'If only we could all get back on an even keel. The way it should be. I suppose you don't know when you'll next be ashore . . . but I hope when you are that you'll come back to the fenland, to your home, and – and it can be just as if that time before never happened.'

She was aware of blushing. She hadn't meant to say so much.

Richard was frowning thoughtfully down at the cloth. 'It's good of you,' he said quietly. 'But – well, we'd better see how we get on at the Bridge House.'

The rain grew heavier as they travelled North, and several times the coach got stuck in the mud. By the time they were on the last stretch after Stilton it was a dark, foul fen night. Caroline was feeling sick with nerves, and Richard had fallen silent. When at last they got down in the yard of the Angel in Peterborough he seemed to squeeze her hand reassuringly as he handed her out of the coach, but he said nothing.

He left his luggage at the Angel, and walked beside her up Bridge Street through driving rain.

All the painful associations with Antoine Clairet that she had expected to come crowding like raised ghosts, they failed to appear as she walked through the city with Richard. She was going to see her mother and father again: an anxious loving joy overtook the fear and by the end she was almost running.

There were a couple of lights in the windows of the Bridge House, but the servant was a long time answering the door, and when he did he stood there, gaping, until

Rebecca's voice called from the winter parlour: 'Who is it, Thorpe?'

Richard followed Caroline slowly, lingering in the hall to shake some of the rain from his coat. At last he went to the parlour door.

Caroline's mother was crying and laughing and hugging her daughter all at once. In a wing chair close to the fire was her father, Luke, quite motionless, staring at the two women with a puzzled frown as if he did not know what was going on.

At last, Caroline disengaged herself from her mother and turned towards Luke.

'Father,' she said. 'Please forgive me, I . . .' and then she was taken into his arms without a word.

Luke looked old. He seemed greyer at the temples and his shoulders had a defeated slump. There was a look of pained wonder in his eyes as his daughter fell on his neck and he lifted unsteady hands to put round her.

Caroline saw the change in him, and as she glanced back at Richard, standing by the door, she saw from his expression that he had noticed it too: he looked shocked – and pitying. Silently, Caroline beseeched Richard with her gaze: *See. Don't be hard on him. I know now how gentle you can be. Please.*

Luke's eyes puckered as he looked over her shoulder at Richard in the doorway. 'Is that young Lindsay there?' he said vaguely.

'Yes, father . . . Richard brought me home. He found me and he's been so kind . . .'

Richard bowed to Rebecca and to Luke. 'Mrs Hardwick . . . sir. . . I'm glad to see you again.'

Luke's lips moved as if he were struggling to summon words. 'Richard . . . thank you for bringing my daughter back. This is the most . . . I can't . . . thank you, Richard, thank you . . .'

Richard bowed again, and quietly withdrew, going to take a room at the Angel. The scene was private and he had no place there.

They stayed up most of the night at the Bridge House. There was joy, and then sadness at the story of little Anthony, the grandchild Luke and Rebecca had never known. Luke bowed his head at that, and looked old and shrunken again. It was as if all the regret of the recent past had scored itself on his normally robust frame. He tried to say something about having driven Caroline out, but she hushed him. Reconciliation was all.

They marvelled, too, that Caroline should come to them so strong and bright after what she had been through. That, she told them, was Richard. Her story was Richard's too. There must be more than one reconciliation at the Bridge House.

There was Nicholas to be seen, too. He was still confined to bed with injuries to his legs and back. He looked pale but impatient to be up, which Caroline thought was a good sign. And when she asked him to forgive her, he widened his eyes and said: 'EH?'

'Father – he's been hard on you, hasn't he, when it should have been me?'

'Oh, *that*,' Nicholas said. 'Anyway, it was my own silly fault. It's lying here that irks me. The house at Lynn's standing still, you know. There's so much to be done.'

But when she left him to sleep he said: 'Caro. I – now you're here, perhaps you could – perhaps father will come and see me . . .'

'What? Doesn't he, ever?'

'He just comes to the door and looks and goes away again. As if he can't bear to see me . . .'

Caroline nodded, understanding.

349

Before she went to sleep at last her mother came and sat on her bed and talked with her.

'Is it true that father never goes to Lynn any more?'

Rebecca nodded. 'Since Nicholas's accident . . . He tortures himself with guilt. Up until then he drove himself and Nick, blindly, never letting up – and then it all seemed to break down. He's always been a man to hide his hurt, you see.'

Caroline looked at her mother's hand lying in her own. 'All I can say is . . . I truly never dreamed all this would happen – that all this would come of it when I ran away. But it doesn't excuse anything – '

'Now, listen,' Rebecca said. 'You're safe. Nick's on the mend. And your father seems more himself already. And we've had enough of blame and sorrow and regret this past year. Now it can all be left behind. There'll be no more recriminations. Your place is here, and we're so happy to have you back, I just can't say how happy . . .' She looked fondly and anxiously at her daughter. 'And you're truly recovered?'

'Yes. I am. Recovered in all ways. I feel sad for the baby, but I know I can go on living, I feel strong. And when I passed the place Antoine Clairet used to live tonight, I was afraid I might . . . But I felt nothing. It's over. And you've Richard to thank.'

'So I shall tomorrow,' Rebecca said. 'I'm afraid it will embarrass him but I shall give that young man a very hearty kiss. He will come, won't he? He knows he's welcome, very welcome?'

'Oh! I think so,' Caroline said, and was aware of a kernel of sadness right at the heart of her joy.

Richard presented himself at the Bridge House after breakfast the next morning, and was duly kissed by Rebecca.

350

'But now you must go away again so soon!' Rebecca said. 'We've hardly begun to thank you. Is there no way . . .?'

'I really must be off today, ma'am. I must report to my new ship at Yarmouth. Besides, I've been an idle fellow long enough.'

'Richard.' Luke came forward slowly. The two men eyed each other. Caroline watched them, in the grip of an emotion fused from the love she felt for both of them. She knew they were both proud men. *Let it be all right.* She watched as Luke put out his hand and Richard, after a moment, grasped it.

'We didn't part on good terms the last time, Richard,' Luke said. 'And if we're to part again so soon, I want you to know that you go with – with a father's thanks and good wishes and – and hopes that as soon as you're ashore again you'll come here and let me thank you properly.'

'Well,' Richard said, 'it's little enough I've done, sir . . .' He seemed to brace himself. 'But thank you. I shall be glad to.'

He sat with them for a while, and then Caroline suggested he go up and see Nicholas.

'It must be some years since you saw him,' she said as they mounted the stairs. She was rattling away out of nerves. 'He'd only be a boy then. He seems to be on the mend – but I'm hoping your presence will work wonders on him as it did with me.'

Richard smiled at her. 'What nonsense.'

The minutes were draining away as Richard sat beside Nicholas's bed: the precious minutes with Richard there. At last he got up and said he ought to be going.

Outside Nicholas's room, Caroline closed the door and said: 'How d'you think he looks?'

'Oh, he's a strong lad. As long as the bones have been

properly set he'll soon be back on form.' Richard took out his watch.

'How will you get to Yarmouth?'

'There's a passenger-boat to Wisbech from the quay at noon. I'll take that and go on to Lynn and go by water from there, that should be quickest. Are you glad to be home, Caroline? Is it – I mean, is everything made up?'

She nodded. 'It was the right thing. I didn't realize there'd been such trouble while I was away. Father's been very low . . .'

'All that will change now,' Richard said gently. 'You can set your father on his feet again – I think he's one of those men who need occupation, isn't he? You can make things all right between him and Nicholas. You're strong, Caroline – no, you are, you've shown me that. They need you here.'

'Yes . . . And your ship needs you. Oh, I wish sometimes the world would just stop a little, just give us a space to catch our breath. But it just goes on . . .'

The maid had appeared at the other end of the passage with bucket and broom, as if to hurry them away. To her own horror, Caroline was crying. The tears wouldn't stop. 'Oh, damn, damn, I'm sorry, I didn't mean to do this . . .'

He looked at her with a strange, surprised expression. 'And I don't suppose you've got a handkerchief,' he said.

'No . . . I'm sorry, really – '

'Hush, it's all right,' he said. He took out his handkerchief, touched it gently to her face, then put it in her hand. 'There's one last thing I can do for you before I go.'

'Oh, Richard,' she said, quelling a sob, 'don't forget me.'

'There's no fear of that,' he said, pressing her hand. And with a confused moment of pause, and a quick bow, he was gone.

The sound of his rapid footsteps down the stairs, the door opening and closing, the vacancy where his figure had been, the tears drying on her cheeks, the echo of his last words, all fused in a single moment of vivid loss.

Caroline stood motionless by the banister, and Nancy the maid came near her and asked if she were all right.

'I – yes, Nancy, I'm all right . . .'

2

When Charles came back to Greek Street after seeing Caroline off, wishing he had had more time with his cousin, he found Edmund waiting for him at the door.

'There's two men here to see you,' Edmund said. 'They insisted on waiting. They – one of them seems to be a Bow Street Runner. I – I didn't know what to do, they would insist . . .'

Charles stared at his brother a moment, then patted his shoulder and mounted the stairs.

The Bow Street Runner was standing by the window in their parlour: the other man, a sandy-headed gentleman with an imposing display of white shirt-front, was sitting in the wing-chair.

'Can I be of assistance to you?' Charles said. The gentleman rose slowly. 'You are Mr Charles Hardwick?'

'I am.'

'My name is Peters. Private secretary to the Duke of Portland at the Home Office. Are you willing to answer a few questions, Mr Hardwick?'

Charles put down his hat and gloves and indicated the Bow Street Runner. 'And this gentleman?'

Mr Peters shrugged. 'A formality. We can send him away if you like.'

'No, no.' Charles sat down. 'I take it I am not compelled to answer any questions, whatever they may be about?'

'My dear sir, it's quite a simple matter. Concerning internal security at a time of national danger.' Mr Peters produced a paper from his breast pocket. 'This pamphlet printed by Jonas Spurling of St Paul's Churchyard bears the name C. Hardwick.'

'Yes. I'm its author.'

'I see. You have been an associate of Spurling's for some time?'

'I would hope to be called his friend – yes, yes, I have.' Charles glared at his questioner. 'You people have come down on Mr Spurling again, have you, is that it?'

'Spurling is to appear before the magistrates next week under the terms of the sedition acts,' the gentleman said. 'He's well known to us as an agitator and a disseminator of treasonable material. Now, as to your own association with him . . .'

And so, out the questions came. Charles's involvement with Spurling, with Burdett and the campaign over Cold Bath Fields, his informal contacts with radical activists, even his resigning from the Soke Volunteers: Mr Peters knew a great deal about him and wanted to know more. Charles, to his own surprise very cool and calm, answered all the questions. 'I've broken no law,' he said.

'I didn't say you had,' Mr Peters said, at last putting away Charles's pamphlet and his own notebook. 'Mr Hardwick, would you object to our examining any papers and documents you may have in these rooms?'

'Now wait a minute – you'd need a magistrate's order for that – '

'Certainly, certainly,' Mr Peters said peaceably. 'I merely asked if you would have any objection while I'm here. It doesn't matter.' He got up. 'Thank you for your time, Mr Hardwick. You do not anticipate changing your address in the near future?'

'Why should I?'

'Mr Hardwick, please. Just in case – anything crops up at Spurling's trial. One never knows. Good day to you.'

When they had gone, Edmund came timidly in. 'Are you all right, Charles?'

'Yes, of course,' Charles said. He held up his wrists with an effort at a smile. 'No handcuffs.'

But he was frightened, though he told himself that that was just what they wanted. They cast a web of threat and innuendo spun from the vague embracing powers of the Two Acts: one felt oneself caught, and panicked. That was why he had not had the presence of mind to ask from where, or from whom, most of the information came.

He was sleepless that night, and ended up oversleeping till half-past ten. Edmund had already gone to the Academy. Seedy and headachy, Charles lit a fire and made coffee, and saw the note on the mantelpiece.

From Lydia.

This was not easy to arrange. Much as I dislike acting like the heroine of a romance, I will ride out to Mother Red-Cap's on the Hampstead road this afternoon at two. Meet me there or not as you wish. Only do not think badly of me.

He had little time to wonder what this meant: he had to wash and shave, and he would have to hire a saddle-horse. He was in his bedroom, his face covered in lather, when he heard the voice of the maid from downstairs say 'Gentleman to see you Muster Hardwick.'

He went through in shirt-sleeves, drying his face, and found Sir Thomas Fairburn standing with his hands behind his back examining one of Edmund's watercolours

355

on the wall. He glanced round briefly. 'Ah. Your brother's work, I think?'

'It is.'

'A young man of some talent.'

Charles watched the elegant man as if he were a snake. 'As you see, Sir Thomas, I'm in a hurry, so – '

'I'll be brief then.' Sir Thomas turned sharply, straight-backed. 'You've disregarded my instructions, Hardwick. You've continued to pester my daughter. These letters, calls. I've warned you to keep away. Now this is my last warning. Unless you cease to have any communication with her immediately you must face the consequences.'

A monstrous suspicion reared up before Charles, and for a moment he could not find a voice. 'Can it . . .? I had a visit yesterday from a man from the Home Office . . . Is this your doing?'

Sir Thomas shrugged slightly. 'It is my duty to warn the government, of which I am a part, of those who seek to overthrow it. That I shall continue to do – unless you undertake to get away from my family.'

Charles laid his towel down on a chair and said slowly: 'You'll – you'll bring all that pressure to bear on me, simply because you disapprove of – '

'Listen, Hardwick. The person responsible for prosecutions under the sedition acts is the Treasury Solicitor. He is a very good friend of mine and would be more than happy to examine your case. I know plenty about you and the Jacobinical scum you associate with. I can have you before the Privy Council as easy as that.' Sir Thomas snapped his long white fingers. 'Am I understood, sir? You'll lie in prison and rot with your revolutionary cronies and it'll be no more than you deserve! Now, will you give me your answer!'

Charles lost his head. He lunged out and grabbed Sir Thomas by his ruffled shirt. Scent of pomade, light and tactful; Sir Thomas's eyes round with alarm; Charles's own fist raised. 'So, so, the ale-house agitator shows his true colours – this is what it comes down to!' Sir Thomas was babbling. 'Where is the friend of peace now, eh?'

Charles relaxed his grip, let go, moved blindly away. 'Get out, get out,' he said incoherently, scarcely able to look at the man.

Sir Thomas patted his shirt-front and put on his hat. There was triumph in his melodious voice as he said: 'Well, I think you've taken my meaning. I don't expect to see you again.'

Charles stared down at his own hands and did not see him go.

Mother Red-Cap's was an inn that stood outside the city where the Hampstead and Kentish Town roads met. Lydia, in velvet riding-habit, was standing by her horse holding its bridle outside the inn.

'I'd almost given you up,' she said, when Charles came cantering up. He had ridden like the wind and was out of breath.

'I'm sorry. Your father – I've just seen him.'

She gave him a quick glance, then swung easily into the saddle. 'Come. We can't talk here.'

She led him away at a brisk pace in the direction of Highgate Hill, turning at last down a lane between bare hedgerows and pulling up at a stile where a path led between trees. They tethered their horses and she walked quickly ahead of him down the path, swishing her riding-crop. 'You went to Curzon Street?' she said.

'No. He came to see me. Lydia, unless I keep away from you he's threatened to have me prosecuted. He's set the Government spies on me. Sedition. He can do it. He really means it.'

357

Lydia stopped. 'I knew something like this would happen,' she sighed. 'And what did you say?'

'Nothing. I nearly struck him.' She was keeping her face averted. 'I can't give in to his threats. I would be betraying everything – '

She turned sharply to him. 'You'd go to prison?'

'If need be. There's a principle – '

'Oh, damn your principles.' She walked on. 'I knew this would happen. Oh, Charles, you're a fool. Isn't this enough? Isn't this enough to convince you that it's no good?'

'No. No, it isn't. Don't you believe me when I say I love you? Don't you believe I won't give you up, no matter what he does?'

'You've got to,' she said dully.

'Lydia . . .' He tried to take her arm, was shaken off. 'I don't care what he does. I won't give in.'

Her face, pale and framed by her black straw riding-hat, was very solemn as she turned to him. 'What if I tell you to give in?'

A few dead leaves were shaken down from the trees in a sough of wind, and the word 'Why?' was shaken from him in the same way, dry, helpless.

'Do you think I like sneaking and conniving like this?' she burst out. 'Do you think I like my father mistrusting me? I've had enough of it. I always told you I was selfish, didn't I? Do you suppose I've enjoyed these past months, since you came along and caused all this trouble in my life? I had a contented life, a peaceful life, doing just what I wanted. You've spoilt all that, Charles. You've caused me nothing but trouble, there, that's selfish and all the rest of it and it's *true*. I just can't be bothered with it. Do you understand?'

His breath steamed in the air as he fought back waves of hurt. 'I don't know,' he said. 'I thought – that time at

Ranelagh – I began to believe you loved me. I *did* believe it.'

'Then you're wrong.' She winced and turned away. 'It's no good. I can't live like this, Charles.'

'I'll defy him! You can defy him –'

'*No*. You're living in a dream, Charles. It – it just can't be.'

'Have I got to convince you how much you mean to me?' he cried. 'Since I met you I've thought of nothing else. No one else. Thought of nothing but being with you, even dared to hope to marry you. You're everything, Lydia, everything I want; and if it's wrong, if it's – oh, not practical, then perhaps I know that. In my head. But not in my heart. I love you so desperately, Lydia, there's no help for it, nothing you do or say can change that. The thought of losing you – it's unbearable, it's . . . Only if I hear from your own lips that you don't feel anything for me –'

'Very well, then, I'll say it!' Her cheeks were stung with furious colour: she looked pointed and dangerous. 'I don't love you, Charles, not if it means all this suffering, all this bitterness, all this disruption of everything I hold dear. That's not what I want in life. You believe in romance. Well, I don't. It's foolish, it's destructive – Damn you, I want to enjoy my life!'

The pain was like a blow in the stomach. 'Well. And that you are plainly not doing at the moment,' he said.

'Oh, God, Charles, be practical.' She took hold of him by the shoulders. 'And when I say that I'm not being heartless for once. We mustn't see each other because my father means what he says, he means it – and, God help me, I suppose I must love you enough not to want to see you locked away in prison with your precious radicals. I don't want that, and though no doubt you are ready to be defiant now, sooner or later neither would you. I'm a cold creature, but I'm not so cold as to let you waste away in gaol for my sake . . . We're in a trap, Charles. Perhaps I should hate my father for it but I can't. The only way is to go away and forget.' Tears were running down her cheeks: she released him to brush them impatiently away. 'And it will be the best way, believe me. You've caused trouble in my life, but nothing compared to what I'd cause you. I'd rather you hate me now, then have you ruin your life in prison for love of me. Do you see, now, you wretched man? You must promise me you won't try to get in touch with me again. Promise me, promise me for the sake of this damned love you've decided to feel for me, God knows why.' She bit her lip. 'All I can say is, if there were any other way – but I don't believe in *ifs*. I can't marry you, Charles. If it's any consolation, I don't intend ever marrying – yes, because no other man would suit me after knowing you – but also because it's a fool's game. There, now it's said, and you must promise me . . .'

The sight of her in tears sharpened his pain till it was almost intolerable. 'You're asking me – to go away and never see you – '

'I'm *telling* you,' she sobbed out. 'It's the only way.'

'Lydia – this is all so – so *wrong*, that it should come to this . . .' A terrible vacancy confronted him as if all the innocence and hope of the world had been suddenly ripped away.

'Oh, wrong, whoever said right and wrong had anything to do with it,' Lydia said, with a heartbreaking echo of the old brittle carelessness. 'It's the world. I used to be quite at home in the world but I'm not any more . . .' She reached up and touched his face and then with a wrenching cry turned from him. 'God bless you, Charles,' she said, 'you'll thank me for this one day, truly,' and she ran to her horse and he stood numb and still and watched her ride away.

Eventually he stirred. Dead leaves crunched under his boots. He walked to his horse slowly and gingerly, like an old man. Was it perhaps true that your heart could break? His own felt as if it were being torn, pulled, stretched like putty. He patted the horse's neck, waiting for the strength to get in the saddle, while his mind roamed quickly over the terrain of the future and found no hope there.

3

Shortly before Christmas 1800, Russia, Sweden, Prussia and Denmark signed a treaty of alliance that revived the League of Armed Neutrality against Britain. The Baltic was closed to British ships, and with it the source both of timber and naval supplies and of imports of wheat. On Christmas Day the Austrians signed an armistice with the victorious French at Steyer, and Britain was alone. With 50,000 soldiers tied down in Ireland, Pitt made plans for the Union of the British and Irish Parliaments to try and solve the Irish problem once and for all, and set himself on course for a collision with a violently anti-Catholic King.

They were dark days, particularly for the head of a shipping house. But Caroline's return roused Luke from his depression. For the first time since Nicholas's accident he went to King's Lynn, and came back glowing and energetic. They would just have to concentrate on coastal trade, he said. The *Pride of Lynn* could make eight trips to Tyneside a year on his reckoning – they'd been taking things too slow. He even began to pick up the newspapers again.

As for Caroline, she was so concerned with healing the

damage at home that she had scarcely thought of her own situation – of the fact that there would be much interest in her reappearance in local society and not all of it benevolent.

The gossip had long died down, but not before certain conclusions had been drawn from Caroline's absence and from her father's ceasing to be agent for the prisoners-of-war. Clearly something very scandalous had gone on, and she had been sent away in disgrace: when Caroline began to go out again she saw speculation in people's glances and could see them itching to ask. Mrs Butterworth fished indefatigably: so, Miss Hardwick had been with relatives in London, she understood, was that correct? – dear me, such a long stay – someone said she was ill, and really they had been quite concerned – but she was not ill? – well, where did such rumours start . . . But Caroline, mentally heaping abuse on the woman, smiled sweetly and said yes ma'am and would give nothing away. If she was going to continue to live here again she must be strong. Richard had said she was strong.

So, she and her family felt their way back to firm ground together. But there could not be perfect ease until Luke had been up to see Nicholas. He still seemed to shun the guilty thought of his son lying injured, and would not face him.

Just before Christmas the doctor came, and with Caroline and her mother in attendance pronounced Nicholas much improved and removed the splint from his left leg. When Caroline came back to Nicholas's room after seeing the doctor out, she found her brother hobbling about with a crutch and whooping with delight.

'You're not supposed to be up yet!' she said.

'But I am, Caro!' he said, dancing around her. 'Huzza! God's life, I'm glad to be out of that bed . . .'

An idea came to her. She put her finger to her lips. 'Stay where you are a minute.'

She found her father in the study, avoiding the doctor. 'Father,' she said gravely, 'I really think you ought to come and see Nicholas. I – I know you haven't liked to . . . I understand, and so does he. But I really think you should.'

Luke looked grey-faced and helpless again. She took his arm. 'Come.'

At the doorway he paused, and looked at Nicholas in his nightshirt, smiling anxiously, balancing in the middle of the room. 'Well, father,' he said, 'dancing the hornpipe next week, eh?'

A muscle moved in Luke's cheek. His son came hobbling towards him. At the last he overbalanced, and Luke put out his arms and caught him.

Caroline quietly left them. Richard had said she could do it.

Richard. She thought of him constantly, imagining him walking the decks of his ship in the grey cold of the North Sea.

Christmas passed with no news of him, and she was beginning to fight with spectres of her own making when a letter came at last, on the first day of 1801. He was on board the *Desirée*, cruising in Yarmouth Roads, in conditions he tersely described as 'pretty uncomfortable', but they were all in good heart.

Her mother said: 'I suppose there's no knowing when he'll be back.'

'No.' Caroline said. 'Not really.'

'What your father said, Caro, about Richard being welcome here when he comes back to shore. He means it, you know. I hope Richard's not as stubborn as your father when it comes to matters of pride! It would be a pity if they couldn't be reconciled. Anyway, I hope he does come back.'

Caroline hoped so too. Even if that was all she had to hope for.

Book Three

CHAPTER 1

September 1801

1

> 'Since Freedom and Neptune have hitherto kept time,
> In each saying "this shall be my land";
> Should the army of England, or all they could bring land
> We'd show 'em some play for the island.
> We'll fight for our right to the island,
> We'll give them enough of the island,
> Invaders should just, bite at the dust,
> But not a bit more of the island!'

Frederick Amory was leading the singing, and Caroline, at the pianoforte, struggled in vain to make her accompaniment heard. But Frederick was more interested in volume than melody, and by the time he finished the song with a great whoop he had wandered off into a key known only to himself.

There was a lot of clapping and cheering and a few groans among the guests in the large drawing-room at Morholm, and then Frederick called to Caroline to 'give us another country-dance – a brisk one'. The party was for the fifteenth birthday of Frances Hardwick, George and Mary's youngest child: she was rather like Frederick Amory in her boisterous spirits and lack of self-consciousness, and the pair of them were soon prancing down the room, in which the furniture had been hastily pushed back, whilst the other guests clapped them on.

It was a young party. Caroline and Nicholas and their

parents had ridden over to Morholm from Peterborough with Lucy and Lawrence Squire; and besides Frederick and Louisa Amory there was a clutch of Frances's schoolfriends and the young Bellaers and Sedgmoors. Mary Hardwick was thoroughly enjoying it all, but George had not looked too disappointed when the steward had called him away from the party on business.

As for Caroline, she felt a certain ironic amusement at being, as it were, in the background of the occasion. People seemed to think that was where she would be happiest, since her re-emergence in local society. There were those, like the Butterworths, who scarcely covered their disapproval that Caroline Hardwick, who had disgraced herself with a French prisoner-of-war – and had probably disgraced herself *all the way* – should go about among decent folk. Most people, though, looked on her with prurient curiosity, or else they handled her with kid gloves: she might have had some peculiar disease.

Well, to those who mattered she was still the same Caroline.

At last, her aunt Mary came to relieve her at the pianoforte. She went to the sideboard for a glass of punch and was going to speak to Charles when she saw he was talking to Louisa Amory. She took a seat away from them: she wouldn't interrupt that.

She wondered if she was doing the right thing in encouraging Charles to see more of Louisa. That Louisa doted on him was clear; but her cousin's feelings she could only guess at.

He had returned to Morholm from London last Christmas, and he had not gone back, even when his father went up to Westminster. He seemed to have lost interest in his old preoccupations. His father and Edmund, who was still at the Royal Academy, had said they feared it was something to do with the girl he had known in London; but Charles would say nothing about it. He had stayed at Morholm and thrown himself into the work of the estate: he had been outside a lot this summer and looked brown and healthy. And yet not truly healthy. There was a gnawing discontent about him, and a reserve very unlike his old candour. He was not actually irritable, but there were wrinkles in his formerly smooth temper.

If he had been jilted by this girl, then Caroline supposed it wasn't really fair to thrust someone else at him as if that would 'cure' him. Of course she herself had emerged at last from disastrous infatuation; but into what?

She had not seen Richard since he had parted from her last December: he had been at sea ever since. Perhaps fate had devised this as a way of subduing her burgeoning feelings for him. She tried; but thoughts of him ran like an unbreakable thread through her every waking minute.

He had been with the North Sea fleet at the Battle of Copenhagen in the spring, and she had read his letters to the Bridge House and to Charles so often it was as real to her as if she had been there.

The fleet had sailed from Yarmouth on March 12th under Admiral Sir Hyde Parker with, as his second-in-command, Lord Nelson, a discredited and somewhat forgotten figure since his triumph at the Nile. The object of the action had been to break up the hostile League of Armed Neutrality by striking at Denmark. The voyage had been cold and stormy, in the teeth of bitter north-easterlies with sleet and snow: Richard said even the fenland weather was nothing to it. They had anchored on the 22nd off the Sound, between the Kattegat and the Baltic, with the wooded slopes and battlements of Kronenberg on one side and the rocky coast of Sweden on the other, and a frigate had been sent with an ultimatum to the Danish government at Copenhagen. After the rejection of the ultimatum there had been a period of waiting, and dispute among the captains about what to do. Nelson was for attacking immediately. 'I did not greatly fancy advancing on the great shore batteries of Copenhagen,' Richard wrote, 'but as we could hardly be more uncomfortable than where we were, with ice on the spars and the rigging, on our hair, even our eyelashes, I was for going on.' At last, on the 30th, there was a favourable breeze from the north-west, and the fifty-two-strong fleet made sail down the Sound. 'There was a great thundering of cannon from Kronenberg Castle sounding the alarm down the coast; and soon we were under fire from the batteries at Elsinore – yes, Hamlet's Elsinore, but the blazing was enough to put any ghosts to flight. But we stood over to the Swedish coast, and not a shot reached us; and we were able to look about us and see the beauty of this old kingdom we had come to fight. I believe few of us harboured any hatred for the Danes, and they were fewer as we came in sight of the stone spires of Copenhagen – the most handsome city I have ever seen. No wonder it was so well defended.'

Parker's squadron remained in the Sound, whilst Nelson led his squadron – including the *Desirée* – through the perilous channel of the Hoellander Deep. 'The reconnaissance was carried out by Nelson himself,' Richard wrote. 'I saw this slender man, who stands no higher than my chin, with his shock of white hair and empty coat-sleeve, go tirelessly back and forth in a boat among sheets of ice, in showers of sleet, marking out the buoys that would lead us through; and I began to understand the devotion he commands from his men.' The fleet anchored that night to the south of the city. 'Nelson and many of the captains dined and conferred on board the *Elephant*; and we knew that tomorrow we would fight. Ahead of us was the Danish line, and the great Trekroner battery, and I was aware that this would be a fight such as I had never experienced before.'

On the morning of April 2nd the squadron weighed and steered through the Channel towards the Danish lines. 'Disaster seemed to threaten immediately,' Richard wrote. 'Three ships of the line, the *Bellona*, the *Agamemnon* and the *Russell*, ran aground on the shoals. These were to engage the formidable Trekroner Battery, and so it fell to the frigates to take their place.

'The action began at ten and for four hours there was bitter and terrible fighting. At times the air was black as night with powder-smoke. Around noon it looked as if we might suffer a defeat. We on the *Desirée* were at the south of the enemy line, and ahead of us the *Isis* was in difficulty; several of her guns had burst and she was being almost overwhelmed by the heavy fire of the Danish ship *Prövestein*. Captain Inman, with quick decision, placed us across the bows of the *Prövestein* and we poured in a raking fire. She fought on until all her guns were dismounted, and there was grim slaughter on board. The Danish flagship *Dannebrög* was in flames and began to drift before the wind: she at last blew up with an explosion that I thought would leave me deaf for a week. The Danes began to surrender their ships, and Nelson sent a letter to the Danish Crown Prince under a flag of truce.'

As they learned later, the bloody Battle of Copenhagen, though fulfilling its object, had been in a way unnecessary. Shortly before it, a group of Russian noblemen had assassinated the insane Tsar Paul I, who had been the dominating spirit of the League of Armed Neutrality: the Danes had joined chiefly from fear of him. The fleet proceeded up the Baltic, but found the new Tsar Alexander I had reversed his father's policy, and in May the League was dissolved. At the end of July Richard wrote that the Baltic fleet was to be sent home: his ship went to reinforce the Channel squadron, for in the summer there was a renewed invasion scare.

But the invasion scare came to nothing more than a few popular songs like *The Snug Little Island*, bellowed out by Frederick Amory. There was war-weariness in the air – especially in the new government. Pitt, who had been Prime Minister as long as Caroline could remember, had resigned in February over the Irish Catholic question, and his successor, Addington – 'the Doctor' – was known to favour peace. The Continent was at peace: France under Bonaparte was as supreme on land as Britain was at sea. With the reopening of the Baltic, trade was thriving again. People openly wondered why they were fighting on.

So life at the Bridge House had become stable again – Nicholas recovered, the family reconciled – and Caroline had lived through Richard's letters and her imagination. They had all made one trip to London, in the spring, and had a headstone put up on little Anthony's grave; and she felt those terrible ghosts had been laid. Her mind should have been at rest; but it could not be. Not until she had seen Richard again.

. . . The dancing went on while Mary played, and eventually Charles, dodging Frederick Amory's elephantine gyrations, came over to where Caroline was sitting.

'You played very smartly,' he said. 'Have you been working at your music again?'

'Yes. I neglected it too long. Your poor carpet! Where does Frederick get his energy from?'

'An empty head,' said Charles. 'And youth, I suppose.'

'You speak as if you were an old man, cousin,' she said. 'Aren't you going to dance, and show him how it's done?'

'I'm sorry, Caro. Do you want to?'

'No, no. But I'm sure Louisa would like to.' That was hardly subtle. She wished she hadn't said it. Charles half-smiled, and did not look at her. 'Well – I'm not much of a dancer really,' he said.

'Do you hear anything from Edmund in London?'

'Oh, yes, he's prospering mightily. He has a commission for a portrait, a rich brewer who fancies himself in oils. Edmund chafes and complains it is not real painting, but the fee's not to be sneezed at.'

'You . . . have no thought of joining him there again?'

Charles shook his head. 'A waste of time, really. Playing at politics. I'm more use here.' There was a stubborn look about his face. She would have disliked it, had she not perceived that it was a cover, a dressing on a wound one shrank from looking at.

The party broke up at dusk, though the Hardwicks from the Bridge House were to stay the night. The Amorys were the last to leave: the family went out to the front of the house to see them off, and were treated to a last display of exuberance from Frederick who tried to ride his horse facing backwards whilst Louisa blushed and laughed on her pony beside him.

'Dear life, what a day,' Mary said, with her arm around her young daughter. 'Did you enjoy it, love?'

'It was *magnificent*,' said Frances, who liked emphasis. 'I wouldn't mind marrying Frederick if he weren't so fat. Where did papa go to?'

'Oh, I think he's still hiding at the gate-house,' Mary said smiling.

Across the stubble-fields beyond the village the sun was low in a limpid sky and the whole landscape was a mellow bronze. As they turned to go in Nicholas said: 'Hullo, who's that – a late guest?'

Caroline shielded her eyes with her hand. There was a figure in the distance, striding towards the house. The sunlight was behind it. Her mouth had gone dry.

'Looks like a man in uniform,' Nicholas said.

373

'It can't be . . .' Caroline breathed. There was a glint of gold braid.

'Is that Richard Lindsay back at last?' Mary said. 'Oh, I'm glad – we must give him some supper . . .'

If Caroline had been trusting to separation to cool and rationalize her emotions, she knew as Richard walked towards them that the hope had been in vain. She could scarcely get air into her lungs.

He looked lean and tanned from his Channel duty. In the heat of the sun he had untied and loosened his stock, and this glimpse of informality – Caroline knew how personally impeccable he was – gave her a peculiar, concentrated, longing pain.

It was both fortunate and frustrating that there were so many people there to greet him. For the moment there were only enquiries and explanations. 'Got to Peterborough this afternoon – no one at the Bridge House, servant said everyone was here – farmer's cart took me as far as Werrington . . .'

'Have you jumped ship?' Charles was saying. 'So unexpected – '

'We came into port to revictual, and suddenly we were granted two weeks' shore leave. I'm overdue anyway.' He turned from shaking Charles's hand, saw Caroline.

'Richard.'

'Miss Hardwick.' He shook her hand. 'I hope you're well.'

'Yes. Even without your care of me.'

He smiled faintly. 'You – you look well.'

Then Charles pressed him in to supper, and he was lost to her again in the crowd of people.

Later, after Richard had gone to Stamford to see his old aunt, Charles went to the large drawing-room with Jim

374

Benwick, the manservant, to help shift the party-scattered furniture back into place.

His uncle Luke, he noticed, had gone out of his way to be cordial to Richard this evening. There was a noticeable tension still between the two men, but things were better.

Charles glanced out of the window and saw Caroline walking alone in the garden. She had been quiet this evening. She looked lovely, though. Back to her full bloom – indeed, a maturer bloom – since her terrible experiences last year. His cousin had come through.

So can you, so can you, he told himself. High time this moping was at an end. Caro didn't mope. She fought.

Young. That's what I am, Charles thought. Not yet twenty-five. A ridiculous age to have this feeling of everything being over, of nothing being left. But then that was part of being young – each disappointment seemed a tragedy, the end of the world; and then you bounced back.

His thinking was full of platitudes today, none of them comforting. It was the profound disillusion that had afflicted him most sorely since Lydia had broken with him last Christmas. So much that had seemed important and worthy, so much that had seemed to glitter and shine had turned out to be so much paste and dross. His own naïveté pained him to think of. Everything had seemed clear and shapely, bathed in a pure light: it had been a shock to see at last the dusty half-shadows, the complex world of equivocations and hypocrisy and mixed motives in which everyone, including himself, moved.

He supposed Lydia had been right. Perhaps he himself had been wrong, charging about trying to save the world. Certainly he had achieved nothing – except perhaps getting Jonas Spurling another spell in prison.

The bitterness was so strong in him he could have been sick whenever he reflected that if he had been a safe

Church-and-King man proposing death to Boney he might have been with Lydia now.

But even that seemed doubtful. There had been a failure of courage on both sides. There was nothing to take out of the wretched affair, except this brooding and longing for what could not be and what was besides probably not worth longing for.

He bent to pick up the pieces of a plate that had been broken, thinking of Louisa Amory today, with her skin like milk and her submissive smile. He had promised her to go over to Leam House next week and sit for her; she got tired of drawing the same faces at home.

Everything was pushing them together, and he did not have the heart to pull away. And if he could not value Louisa's charming, accomplished womanhood, what could he value? Perhaps he had been naïve there too – thinking love could only manifest itself in the stormy magnetism of romance. Perhaps this mild mixture of respect and affection that he felt for Louisa was what people really meant when they talked about love. He wished he could tell. He wished he could be certain about things as he used to be.

2

Richard spent his leave in the fenland.

Luke was not half-hearted in his desire for reconciliation, and encouraged Richard to call at the Bridge House; and with the autumn weather set fair, Charles arranged outings in which Caroline usually found herself included.

They hired a small sail-boat and in the last misty gold of September they went down the Nene to Gunwade Ferry. As they slid between the reed-banks and the flat meadows, she looked up at Richard trimming the sails, tall and brown in his shirt-sleeves, his dark hair combed back and tied in a queue, the muscles of his back and thighs shifting slightly as he adjusted his balance; and she thought: some might say I hardly know him. Oh, during their time in London she felt she had gone some way to understanding him, but certainly there was a part of him that was mysterious to her. But wasn't that love too – the mystery of another presence? Antoine had been presented to her like an open book – except, as it turned out, he had his own hidden element, an element that was weakness and deception. Richard was more ambiguous. His quick temper, his unpredictability, his introspection – these were parts she had known before the warmth, the integrity, the singleness of mind and heart.

Not once in their meetings did he refer to that time in London. Perhaps it was delicacy on his part, to refrain from calling up a time of sickness and sorrow for her. Or perhaps he was gently relegating it to the past where it belonged, a unique and specific episode with no bearing on their relations in the world outside the sick-room. Whatever, he was reserved and correct. Indeed, often when he spoke to her he used what she thought of as his court-martial voice.

She fully intended betraying nothing of her feelings to him. But then, on Friday 2nd October, something happened that burst the tight bonds she had placed on herself.

It was market day morning, and she was walking in Peterborough with Charles and Richard, when a mail-coach, decked out with laurel and ribbons, came hurtling down Narrow Bridge Street with horns blowing and a man perilously perched on top ringing a bell and yelling. The horses were lathered with sweat. The coach came to a thunderous halt in the square, lurching and almost overturning on the cobbles, and the man on top fell over;

but he continued to shout, at the top of his voice: *Peace! It's peace!*

A crowd collected round the coach. Cheers went up; and others took up the cry: *Peace! Peace!* Great bundles of broadsheets were flung down from the coach into the square.

Caroline picked one up. It was an *Extraordinary Gazette*. It announced in bold type the conclusion of an armistice between the governments of Great Britain and France. The French army in Alexandria had capitulated. Hostilities between the two countries were to be suspended on land and sea prior to the negotiated Treaty of Peace.

People were dancing in the square. From the door of the Angel the landlord rolled out a barrel of ale. Someone began ringing the bells in St John's Church.

'It's real, isn't it?' Caroline said. 'Oh, Richard, it's peace! Now you'll be safe, you won't be in danger any more . . .' Hardly knowing what she was doing, she had seized his arm and held it tightly. 'I'm so happy – now I'll know you're safe . . .'

She recovered herself suddenly, withdrawing her hand, but not before she had seen the startled, transfixed look in Richard's blue eyes.

There were celebrations that night, and Caroline's father, with the prosperity of peace at last in view again, drank rather too much brandy. The next morning Rebecca dragged him out, protesting feebly, for an early ride to clear the cobwebs; and Caroline was alone when Richard called at the Bridge House.

He sat with her, murmured a few gruff commonplaces, then sprang up again as if to leave.

Instead he walked to the window and frowning out at

378

the river said: 'I set out for Portsmouth at noon, Miss Hardwick.'

'Oh?' she said, trying to keep her voice light.

'I must report to my ship as normal, though of course yesterday's news will affect all naval dispositions. The blockade will surely be lifted, and I will probably be told to return to shore. I wished to take leave of your – oh, damn it.' He began fumbling in his pocket. 'You must forgive me for what I'm about to say. But I have to say it. Yesterday, when you – well, perhaps I have misread matters . . .'

She waited, feeling sick.

He turned suddenly, unwrapping some cotton, and held towards her a necklace. 'This . . . this is from Copenhagen. It has been with me over miles of sea. I hope the salt air hasn't tarnished it. I – no doubt I'm starting from the wrong damn end asking if you will accept this, but I just don't know how otherwise to – to . . .'

Trembling, she took the necklace from his hand. It was of silver filigree with a single garnet.

'I thought of you when I saw it,' he said, pacing. 'I – God, I'm making a mess of this. I've cooked up reasons aplenty for not speaking out. In London we'd been close because of your illness, and I thought it would be – well, trading on my position to ask any more. Taking an unfair advantage. We'd become friends, and I didn't want to lose that, even that meant so much to me, I didn't dare press for fear of . . . I should have been grateful for what I had, but being with you, coming to know you, cherishing you, I knew it was more than friendship I sought . . . God knows, I even tried to convince myself that was all, when I was at sea, trying to pretend nothing was amiss while I had your face before me every moment of the day . . . And now, here, with your family welcoming me and thanking me for – well, whatever little I did for you, it seems like taking advantage again, but I can't help it.' He stopped, looked at her. 'I can't go away again without knowing, Caroline. I'm sorry if I've distressed you. I'm so used to ordering damned sailors about and I can't find the right words . . .' His face was disarmed, vulnerable, desperate. 'If there are any right words . . .'

Caroline laid the necklace down and pressed her hands to her face. She was numb, like a blind person who gains sight and reels half-afraid at the onslaught of vision. The painful gnawing of her own love was suddenly, frighteningly transformed by the knowledge of being loved in return. All the passionate feeling for Richard that she had striven to suppress was liberated and leapt forth to meet his; and for the moment she was paralysed.

'Strange, isn't it,' he said softly. 'That time at the Mere, I saw you, a grown woman, so beautiful – such life and wit, so fresh . . . I felt like a clod of earth beside you. Perhaps I even knew then that I loved you – or would love you, if you were not so far out of my reach; further than ever you seemed then, in spite of that lieutenant's coat I was sporting so proudly. And then when we met again, it was just we two; and I allowed myself to hope . . .' He looked with concern at the tears running down her cheeks. 'Caroline, I'm sorry . . .'

'Don't be,' she said, with a breaking sensation across her chest. She held her arms out towards him. 'Oh, Richard, dear Richard, don't be . . .'

She did not know how long she had stood there, crushed in his embrace.

'I'm dreaming,' he said, pressing his lips to her skin. 'I must be. Oh, Caroline, I didn't dare to hope . . .'

'So long not seeing you,' she said in a sobbing rapid way. 'Not knowing if I would *ever* see you. That time you

380

brought me home . . . I couldn't bear it when you went away. Drawing away from me . . .'

She pulled him down to the settle, caressing his hands and his face as if to reassure herself he was real.

'Let me look at you now,' he said. 'These past weeks I've been trying *not* to look at you: wouldn't allow myself to. Yes . . .' He touched her hair. 'That's the lovely face I saw before me, all the time I was at sea. That's the face I saw in London. Lovely in all that sorrow and squalor. The face I saw, beginning to smile again and laugh. Beginning to look to me and rely on me, that was the terrible thing; because then my feelings began to run away with me. I had to remind myself I was only a clumsy sort of nurse, that it was joy enough just to see you well and smiling again, that it was wrong and unfair of me to look for more . . .'

'Richard.' She kissed him, her tenderness tinged with a certain awe: it had not occurred to her that he too could be wary of love through fear of its rejection. 'After the way you found me in London, can you really – ?'

'Caroline, listen.' He took her hands in his and looked with great earnestness into her eyes. 'I love you and am your servant. Nothing can or could change that. What happened to you before doesn't matter to me, except insofar as you've suffered and I want to make it better.'

'And you have,' she said. 'And you will do – Oh, I hope I haven't hurt your shoulder,' she added, for she had hugged him to her so hard he gasped aloud.

'No, no.' He smiled. 'It's all healed since you nursed it.'

'The necklace . . .' She put it in his hands, then removed the ribbon-band from her neck and looked at him. His fingers, trembling very slightly, were warm on her neck as he put the necklace round it.

'It's beautiful,' she said. 'You've brought me back two

381

beautiful things,' and then his lips were on her neck where his fingers had touched. In a drowning dizziness she said: 'You've brought me back yourself, Richard . . . Oh, I've wanted you so much.'

'Before I go away again,' he said, 'I want to tell you – all the things I couldn't say before – how much I love you, everything.'

'There'll be time,' she said. 'Lots of time.'

'God, I'm a fool,' he said vehemently. 'Now I've got to get down to Portsmouth. Fact is I expected to be turned out of here in two shakes . . .'

'But you'll be back here soon, won't you?' she said.

She walked with him down to the Cross Keys, where he was to take the coach south. She was still dazed; and on Richard's face there was a stunned, uplifted look as if he had seen a vision. He had kept a mistrustful guard on his emotions so long that now he seemed like a man liberated from prison.

Light rain was beginning to fall. In the innyard he took her hands and drew her into the shelter of the archway and looked at her, wonderingly. 'Caroline, I've blundered in so far, and so fast, I hardly know what to say now . . . at least, I don't know how. You remember that time at Whittlesea Mere?'

She nodded. 'And you gave me a dressing-down for my bad seamanship.'

He smiled, but there was a frown on his brow. 'I – I believed you hated me,' he said. 'Or perhaps I even courted it.'

'You seemed to resent me,' she said soberly.

'Did I?' He caressed her fingers. 'Perhaps I resented what you were. So beautiful, so carefree. Everything that was beyond my reach. That's always been there in my feelings for you, that consciousness of where I stood. Turning me ever more tongue-tied and surly. Making me

382

bridle even as I admired you. You see, my love, that time at the Mere . . . you're probably aware I quarrelled with your father. Lost my temper. He accused me of disrespect for you. And that – that just seemed to crystallize all the bitterness growing inside me. It was as if I knew then I could never be worthy of you. Not in his eyes. Not in yours. And not in my own.'

'But father's so grateful for what you did – '

'I know. That's part of what I'm trying to say. I wanted to prove myself independent of him . . . And if I'm to ask you what I didn't expect to ask but, damn it, I must, then you must understand. You know I'm not rich. If this peace really is permanent then I shall want for occupation. And when I quarrelled with your father I swore I wouldn't come to him for help any more. A point of honour. And now it would seem as if I'm trading on his gratitude for bringing you back. If I were to ask you to think of marrying me . . .' He stopped.

Her heart thumped. She licked her lips, and studied his face, young now and unguarded, but clouded with the anxious questioning of his proud and self-critical nature. A man whose reserve was actually the product of an ardent nature, she saw. And its expression was for her alone.

'Oh, Richard,' she said. 'I'll do more than think about it. Oh, I'll do more than think about it, my darling.'

He gave a sort of laughing gasp, his face bright and radiantly hopeful. 'My God,' he said. 'Dear God, I've come out and said it. It's – You did say yes, didn't you? Say it again. You did, didn't you?'

'Yes,' she said laughing. 'Yes. Yes. Yes. Yes – *Richard*!' as he lifted her up and, to the stares of the people in the innyard, swung her round and round in his arms.

'I don't know when it will be – '

'Doesn't matter.'

383

'Nor where we'll live.'

'Doesn't matter.'

'Nor how we'll live.'

'Doesn't matter – Richard, I'm getting giddy!'

'Good,' he said, lowering her slowly. 'I'm giddy too. With happiness . . . But it does matter, Caroline. I must see your father when I come back. If he thinks I'm, well, fortune-hunting, relying on him – '

'No. Listen, love. There must be none of that. I do want to marry you – *you* – to be with you and make a life with you. And for that we'll have enough. D'you see? All the rest, all the past, just let it go. Dear Richard, we beat the fever, and nine months apart, and the Danish navy! – What have we to fear?'

There was a shout from an ostler. The coach was ready. She kissed his lips and cheeks urgently. 'I'll be here, waiting for you, Richard. Hurry back. And it will be all right. We're not mad, are we? We haven't gone mad?'

'Probably,' he said. 'But I don't care.' Abruptly he seized her hand and pressed it to his lips.

The coach took him away, waving to her. She stood in the square long after it had disappeared from sight. The numbness overtook her again: compounded not only of joy but also of a certain fear. She knew now – if there had ever really been any doubt – that her heart was his: that much was unanswerable. But now they must go forward together into an uncertain future.

CHAPTER 2

1

Caroline and Richard had two attitudes to their engagement to face, once the news went beyond her family.

On the one hand it would be a bad marriage: Luke Hardwick's only daughter to throw herself away on a poor naval lieutenant of no family. That, Caroline guessed, was the idea Richard was sorely conscious of. On the other hand, she had done well for herself, to get *anyone* to have her after she had made such a disgrace of herself. So, on the one hand he was the lucky one: he was marrying her for her money. On the other hand, she was lucky: she was being made an honest woman.

Caroline was able to imagine all these arguments going on in the drawing-rooms of local society. But, they had her parents' blessing.

When Richard reported to Portsmouth after the armistice he found his ship, *Desirée*, was to strike her flag at Spithead: the formal Treaty of Peace was still being tortuously negotiated in Paris, but already Addington's government was winding down the armed forces. Richard was placed on half-pay and told to await news from the Admiralty. So, he came back to the fenland in November to ask for Caroline's hand.

Perhaps, Caroline thought, her parents felt a certain relief, after her last disastrous involvement: Richard was at least a safer proposition. And her father, she could tell, was determined never to be heavy-handed with his children again. The couple were in love, and so it must be accepted. That was not to say that Luke hadn't formed a genuine gratitude and respect towards Richard, though there was still a fund of unspoken tension between the two men, only that he would keep any reservations to himself, as the wisest policy. His daughter and prospective son-in-law had both shown themselves pretty headstrong characters in the past.

An unconventional couple, an unconventional marriage. But Caroline had been through enough to disregard wagging tongues. And she had him with her at last. She cursed the protocol that required he stay at his aunt's house in Stamford, wasting their precious hours. As she remarked to him, if he stayed at the Bridge House it wasn't as if she was going to creep into his room every night. 'Oh, I don't know though,' she added.

They were walking down by the river, and his eyes kindled as he looked at her. 'You forget I've seen you very intimately. Not in a compromising way, but certainly in bed and in your nightdress and so on. Though of course at the time you were drenched in sweat and white as a sheet and skinny as a shotten herring.'

'Ugh,' she said. 'It sounds awful. How did you stand it?'

'You were still my Caroline,' he said feelingly. 'Though then I had no right to call you such. You were still beautiful to me, in everything you represented in my life.'

She stroked his arm. 'Well, at least you've seen me at my worst. At least I *hope* it was my worst. Still, I wish you could be here all the time. But that's the way of it. Safeguarding one's virtue . . .' She stopped and flushed. 'Not that I have any virtue,' she said soberly.

'No more have I,' he said. He gazed out across the green river. 'God knows I've been no libertine. Damn near virginal by seamen's standards. But I've had my own adventure in – in disappointment, in short. Oh, I know

386

it's supposed to be different – what's excusable in a man is not so in a woman. I don't know about that. All I know is when you love someone, it isn't in hope of finding an ethereal angel. You love them for what they are, right or wrong. I've learned that.'

'I think I've learned it too.'

He smiled at her. 'Which is not to say,' he said, 'that I wouldn't creep to your room also. So perhaps it's just as well.'

'Dear me,' she said, moving him on, feeling an agreeable featheriness inside. 'Such talk on a Monday morning. By the way, is your shoulder quite healed?'

'Yes.'

'Good,' she said, smiling and then laughing low and softly. 'I'm glad about that.'

As for the future – what everyday shape it would wear – she had meant it when she said it didn't matter. She wanted to be with him, that was all. Above all she must reassure him of that. He worried that he was poor, that the life he could offer her was insecure. The Battle of Copenhagen, which should have yielded good prize money, had yielded nothing: Sir Hyde Parker had had all the captured prizes burnt and sent to the bottom of the sea, leaving the men who had fought the battle, as Nelson disgustedly pointed out, with nothing. Richard's pay, without prizes, was less than £120 a year. Of course she would bring a marriage portion, but that was the one question which still raised Richard's proud hackles. She told him it was nothing unusual, that any woman whose parents had any money at all had some settled on her when she married. In society there were plenty of fine gentlemen who unashamedly went hunting for dowries, and it was accepted. He nodded, and agreed, but the old defensive look came down over his eyes again. It was the fact of taking money from her parents, she knew: it raised the spectre of dependence that was his *bête noire*.

So, she must reassure him. She had recovered her own self-esteem since the disasters of last year, but she saw it was a more complicated process with Richard. He said to her, later that day on the river: 'Every morning I wake up, and I have to think and – and make sure that all this isn't part of a long dream.'

'If I was there beside you when you woke,' she said, 'you'd know it isn't a dream.' She was deeply moved.

So, the sneers and insinuations with which their local society seemed pregnant must be disregarded. They must show their pride in their love. Mrs Butterworth was no doubt saying: my dear, I don't give that marriage five minutes. They would show them: they would make it work.

2

Standing down on half-pay was not the best way for a naval officer without means to begin married life. But in the meantime Richard was free to look for other work: there might be openings in the revenue service or the east coast packet-service. And they wanted desperately to be married.

That they were able to do so at all was because of Caroline's settlement. Besides his pay Richard had only two hundred pounds in Squire's Bank, saved from his prize money. From her father Caroline had a settlement of nine thousand pounds.

'It's *our* money,' she impressed on Richard. 'There's no patronage, no gift. It's my marriage settlement, and it would be the same whoever I married. And it's you I want to marry, my darling. Nobody else will do.'

She thought she managed to quell the restiveness of Richard's proud nature in this regard. But in the matter of a place to live they really were indebted to her father.

The fenland village of Elm was just outside Wisbech, and here a retired merchant of Luke's acquaintance was putting up his house for rent. He was going to live at Bath for his health: the tenancy would be a year and probably renewable if the waters agreed with him. In December, soon after Richard was decommissioned, he and Caroline and her parents went to see it.

Elm Cottage stood back from the road, half-hidden by apple trees. It was seventy years old and had a gracious look: mellow stone, hipped tiled roof, good sash windows on both storeys, and a scrolled canopy over the front door. Downstairs there was a comfortable back parlour with a moulded mantelpiece and wainscoting, and a dining-room opening out from the hall, and a stone-flagged kitchen and still-room. Upstairs there were five small bedrooms. Behind the house there was a stable and barn, and a walled garden with more apple-trees; and beyond that the property included twelve acres of land, ploughed but not sown. An elderly woman named Mrs Welney was looking after the house, and was willing to stay on as housekeeper to the tenants. The furnishings were rather heavy and old-fashioned, but that they would have to put up with. They might count on plate and silver coming their way as wedding gifts. Caroline would bring linen and drapery. As for Richard, the entire worldly goods with which he would promise to endow his bride would fit in one trunk.

From the back the house gave on to an almost uninter-rupted fen vista, mile after mile of rich black earth with a grid of straight dykes and causeway-roads; but the apple-trees would screen it at least partly from the east wind, and though it was a cold grey December day when they viewed it, Elm Cottage had a warm feel.

'Well, there's less space than you're used to, love,' Rebecca said, peering dubiously into the big beehive oven. 'Less light too. I suppose Wisbech is just in walking distance – '

'Dear mother, I could walk there and back with no trouble. And we may be able to afford a saddle-horse.'

'You like it, don't you?' Rebecca said smiling.

Caroline nodded. As soon as she had seen it she had warmed to it. Never mind the fusty panelling and the low teak beams in the bedrooms: she could imagine living here with Richard. She had never really considered herself a homebody, and she was surprised to find herself already planning little touches and rearrangements to improve the place. But then, since becoming engaged to Richard, she had realized that since his father died he had never had a home at all, only ships' cabins and drab port lodgings. It would all be new to him, and she wanted to make it special.

'I dare say it might be lonely for you here when Richard's away, if he goes to sea again,' Rebecca said.

'I'll be lonely wherever I am, if Richard's not there,' Caroline said soberly. 'He's made my life, mother. I thought it was all wrecked, ruined. But in truth it hadn't begun.'

Her father had proposed to pay their first year's rent. He steered Richard out into the garden to discuss it.

'I want you to think of it as a wedding-present, Richard,' Luke said. 'And perhaps it will make up for – well, some harsh words in the past. Unthinking words. Anyway, we've both learned a lot since then. And securing this place for you is in earnest of that.'

'Sir, I don't know what to say.' Richard licked his lips and gazed out over the clay field. 'This bit of land – I know nothing of farming, but I dare say it would yield something worthwhile, cattle-feed perhaps. I could ask at Morholm about that.'

'Then you've a fancy for the place?'

'Yes, indeed. It's not that . . .' He turned to Luke. 'I will look after Caroline, Mr Hardwick. I'll do everything in my power.'

'I'm sure you will, Richard. You've done it before, and we've not forgotten that. So we want you to think of this house as yours for the year, and not worry. Don't begin married life under any sort of cloud. There'll be plenty of openings for a man like you, I'm sure. If this peace is ever finally signed. They say Cornwallis is having a devil of a time thrashing it out with Boney.'

The two men went back into the house, and found Caroline and her mother in the parlour. There was a large window-seat overlooking the garden, and Caroline called to Richard from it. 'Oh, Richard, come and sit here. Think of this in the summer.'

He sat down beside her and took her hand. 'Draughty in the winter,' he said.

'No, I can't feel any draught – oh, you're teasing. You do like it, don't you?'

'It's more than I ever hoped for. Like you.'

So it was settled, with the wedding fixed for the new year, and over Christmas they were busy with making the house ready. Charles and Edmund drove a cart over to Elm loaded with spare bits and pieces from Morholm, as well as some geese and chickens from the home farm there. Susannah Downes sent a young mare from the stables at Great Baston, a generosity that made them uncomfortable.

1802 came in bitterly cold, but there was no snow on

the day of the wedding, at St John's Church in Peterborough. Charles was Richard's groomsman. Caroline was twenty-one, Richard a few weeks short of twenty-three.

Nearly all Caroline's relatives were there: the family from Morholm, her lawyer Uncle Peter Walsoken up from London, her Uncle and Aunt Milton from Helpston. Susannah and Stephen Downes had come over from Great Baston. There was Richard's old aunt from Stamford, and two of his fellow officers who had come all the way from Portsmouth, and the Amorys and the Squires and the Sedgmoors and the Bellaers and the Emmonsales, filling half the old church, to see the young couple leaving behind a turbulent and uncertain past for a future no more certain: Caroline in a high-necked silver satin gown with long sleeves and pleated bodice and a veil of old lace, Richard in his full-dress lieutenant's uniform with the gold braid and white lapels with silver anchor buttons and white breeches and stockings and cocked hat.

Caroline looked at Richard's lean profile as he knelt beside her and thought: now life is ours. It's not snatched from time and circumstance, it doesn't have to be chopped and curtailed like in that brief idyll in London, it doesn't have to be shared with the demands of other people and etiquette and the Navy and war. Surely sooner or later it will have to be, but for now he's mine and I'm his and I can make him know what he means to me. He's brought such happiness into my life where I thought there could never be any and I must make him know that and bring the same happiness to him. Because I know he loves me but he's still not sure, it's come so fast, he's lived all his life on a doubtful edge, it's written on his unquiet face and those grey-blue eyes that can look so wary and so warm, he's still not sure that everything will be all right. Once I thought him an arrogant man but now I know it's really that he doesn't value himself enough, that he's too hard on himself. Dear Richard. I love him so, it's through him that I've begun to learn what love is, and we must go on learning. Learning and loving.

They came out of the church into winter sunlight and showers of rice, and she saw across the street the Butterworths, who had not been invited but who had obviously allowed curiosity to get the better of them, all in moral black, like the bad fairy at the christening.

'Do you see them, love?' she whispered, and Richard said: 'I can't see anything but you.' They heard Charles cheering as they joined in an unrestrained kiss for the Butterworths' benefit.

The great wedding feasts of Luke Hardwick's youth belonged to a more rumbustious eighteenth-century age and were going out of fashion, but still he and Rebecca had laid on quantities of food and drink at the Bridge House, for the Hardwicks never celebrated halfheartedly.

Charles came to shake Richard's hand and kiss Caroline, and Frederick Amory followed him, giving Caroline a hearty buss like a horse hoping for sugar. 'By God, we could do with a few more junkets like this,' he said slapping Charles on the shoulder. 'We must get this fellow spliced next, eh?'

'Oh, what about you, Frederick?' said Caroline quickly.

'Gladly, if anyone'll have me!' he boomed.

Soon the post-chaise that was to take the newlyweds the eighteen miles to their new home was brought round from the livery stables, and the guests gathered outside the Bridge House to see them off.

Louisa Amory was next to Charles, waving as the coach rattled away, and she said: 'Doesn't your cousin look lovely? I'm so glad everything's worked out well for her – after – well . . .' She blushed painfully.

'Yes, so am I,' said Charles gently, knowing that Louisa

393

was one person who never meant anything maliciously. She looked glowing with the enjoyment of the day: she did not get many outings. He found himself taking a sort of quiet pleasure in her pleasure and wishing to add to it. 'Well, no need to break up the party,' he said, offering her his arm. 'Let's go and see if Frederick's eaten all the food. By the by, is your drawing of me finished yet?'

'Oh! yes – at least – it lacks some shading, but – well, that really needs to be done from the life, but it doesn't matter . . .'

'I'll be glad to sit for you again, if you can bear it.'

'Oh, would you? That's very kind – you must come over to Leam whenever you wish, father's always glad to see you . . .'

Charles went up the steps with Louisa, and saw her eyes brighten and the sight gave him a mixture of satisfaction and perplexity. He liked Louisa in a peculiarly protective way, and wanted her to be happy because she deserved it. That it was in his power to make her happy was a surprising and uneasy thought: like finding a way of making endless money that was shady but would never be found out.

Even Richard had spoken to him the other day about Louisa. Charles had put him off, awkwardly. But he reflected on what a change an observer might have discerned between him and Richard. Once it had been Richard who had been defensive and unapproachable. His love had unwound some of the tension of his temperament, liberated the deep springs of generosity and sympathy. With Charles the opposite was true. His feelings had once been free and open. Now he felt something small and tight and complex within him and he did not know how to unlock it or even whether he wished to.

* * *

394

The January sky was black when Caroline and Richard set out for Elm, and by the time they crossed the river at Guyhirn the rain was pelting down and drumming on the roof of the carriage.

She had changed into a round gown with a short-waisted spencer buttoned over it and a helmet hat. Her hands in her thin gloves were cold and Richard warmed them in his.

'We've left them all behind,' she said, 'still eating and drinking and proposing toasts. It feels nice, to know that they're thinking of us, but we can leave them behind and it doesn't matter, nothing matters but us. You and me.' She reached up and stroked his hair. The naval pigtail was gone and he had cut his thick dark hair shorter: it felt soft at the nape of his neck. 'D'you know, in London when I was ill, and you used to stay with me sitting in the chair all night – in the morning your hair was all ruffled, and I always wanted to smooth it down.'

They smiled at each other.

'How strange life can be,' he said. 'Folk who are bored, cynical, who see no mystery in it – how can they? To be alone – it's nothing, emptiness. To be with you – everything. Such a gulf between those simple things. D'you know, when we were making for Copenhagen, approaching the Sound, I came on deck one morning just in the fore-light of dawn, and everything was grey. The sky and the sea and the cliffs in the distance, all one grey, and I couldn't find any colour anywhere. Horrible. Like those folk who can't distinguish colours. But that's what you are in my life, Caroline. A world without you is like a world without colour.'

When at last they reached Elm the afternoon had gone dark and the rain was a torrent. Mrs Welney had placed lights in all the windows of Elm Cottage and clucked around them, fussing and welcoming, as they ran in laughing and shaking the rain off.

'There's a fine goose for your dinner, sir, ma'am,' said Mrs Welney, a woman with a long mournful face beneath a frivolous lace cap. 'Sent over by Mr Charles Hardwick from Morholm, with his compliments, with a half-anker of best port.'

A wood fire was burning in the dining-room, and the old brocade curtains were drawn against the filthy night.

'What a good fellow Charles is,' Richard said over dinner.

'I love him dearly . . . I think he's unhappy, Richard.'

'So do I. I tried to talk to him – don't know if I did right. About this girl who threw him over. I'd always thought of him as the type to bounce back.'

'I wish we could help him somehow.' They were silent, with a certain guilt, too happy to be able to genuinely contemplate unhappiness.

The goose was excellent. 'Well, this beats minced chicken in a tenement room,' Caroline said.

Richard smiled at her. 'Do you remember? But it seemed like a feast at the time to me.'

'And me. But now I must start learning the things you like and don't like. Minced chicken I know.'

'Oh, I'll eat anything,' Richard said. 'As long as it's not ship's biscuit. And what about you? What don't you like?'

'Well. There's parsnips. Fish that's all bones. Porter. Though *not* port, and I think we should have another glass. Getting up early. Mrs Butterworth. Writing letters, except to you. Mr Butterworth. Little stubby fingernails. Charity Butterworth . . .'

They laughed. Richard said: 'Dear God, how your eyes shine.'

Mrs Welney came in, her face a mask of despair. 'Oh, sir, I hardly know how to tell you. I've just been to lay a fire in your bedroom, and, well, the roof's leaking, I don't know how it is, and it's wetting the rug, and there was me wanting to give you such a comfortable welcome . . .'

'Damn,' said Richard, 'I thought I'd mended those slates just this week. Show me, Mrs Welney.'

In the room that was to be their bedroom there was a steady drip-drip of water into the pan that the housekeeper had placed on the rug.

'There's a ladder and tarpaulin in the barn,' Richard said. 'It won't take me a moment.'

'Richard!' Caroline said. 'You can't go up on the roof in this, you'll get soaked!'

'Oh, I've a boat-cloak. I'll not be a minute . . .'

She followed him downstairs again. 'But it's dark, it's dangerous!'

'There's a storm-lantern in the barn. I can weight the tarpaulin down with stones.'

She watched from the porch as Richard set the ladder against the roof and went briskly up as if he were walking up a flight of stairs. Fortunately there was no wind, but the rain was sizzling down, cascading from the gutters. With a cloth over her head she peered out and saw the lantern flickering on the roof, and then Richard was descending as swiftly and casually as he had gone up and splashing back to her.

'There!' he said triumphantly. 'I saw where the damage is. That'll be all right now.'

'Richard, you're drenched,' she said, pulling him into the porch.

He looked down at himself, a little shame-facedly like a boy caught out. 'Ah – well, I had to kneel in the gutters to hoist myself up, and – sorry. . .'

'You are a lamentable husband!' she said. 'Come in before you catch cold.'

She thanked Mrs Welney and told her to go to bed

when she was ready, and marched Richard up the stairs. 'We must get you dry.'

In their bedroom Richard pointed up at the beams. 'See, it's stopped,' and he looked at her apologetically. 'We – we didn't want water dripping all night,' he said, and seeing his expression she laughed and held him close. 'Oh, my lover, it will take a lot more than that to make me cross with you. Now, get by that fire – see what a shrewish wife you've got, ordering you about . . .'

She took off his coat and hung it up and then felt his waistcoat. 'You'd better take this off too,' she said, and when he had done so she saw his shirt was clinging to him in great wet patches. 'And this,' she said, and as she touched it she did not want to take her hand away, and his hand came and closed over hers. 'It's – it's soaking,' she said in an altered voice, and watched as he unwound his stock and pulled the shirt over his head. He stood there naked to the waist, lit and shadowed by the fire.

'I dare say your breeches are wet too,' she said, not really knowing what she was saying, her eyes fixed on his.

He shook his head gently. 'Your turn,' he said.

'Very well.' She put her hands up to the back of her neck, then abandoned it. 'This dress – hooks down the back,' she said indistinctly, and felt his fingers lightly on the skin of her neck and then his lips. He undid the hooks and his hands slipped round her waist, and she leaned back against him with a gasp and reached up to touch his face. As the dress slid rustling down his hands moved on her breasts and he kissed her bare shoulders. 'Oh, darling Richard, I've waited so long,' she said, turning to him and putting herself into his arms as if she were giving him herself to carry. 'I thought I'd die of waiting . . .'

The rain had stopped, and between the curtains a ray of moonlight penetrated and lay like a luminous ribbon across the foot of the bed. The candles had burnt down but the embers of the fire still glowed, and it was light enough for her to see Richard's face beside her and the soft beat of an eyelash as he looked at her.

'Warm enough?' he said, and his voice had a precise clarity in the silence, like the drop of a stone in a still pool.

'Mm.' She put her finger to the roughness of his chin. 'Worth the wait, love,' she said. 'It was worth the wait, wasn't it?'

He looked up at the beams and stretched up his hand. 'I'm trying to think of something poetic,' he said. 'And all I can think of is how beautiful you are and how much I love you.'

'That'll do,' she said, folding her nakedness softly and comfortably into his. The curtains stirred a little in a draught, enlarging the shaft of moonlight, and she saw the wooden chest beneath the window, Richard's shoes on the floor, the brass candle-sconces, the wash-stand, the statuette on the mantelshelf. 'It's a nice room,' she said. 'D'you know, I've scarcely looked at it till now.'

'I wonder why that is,' he said, and they laughed together, softly and hoarsely. Richard stretched with a sudden catlike relaxation, his arms above his head, and she rested her chin on his chest and looked up at him. 'Caroline!' he said, a sort of contented exclamation, as if his happiness was too much for silence and had to be given some expression.

'Hullo, Richard,' she said.

Beside his face, tanned from seagoing, she saw his arms and chest were paler: the half-light silvered the contours of the muscles. This man, she thought, with whom she had shared such intimacy, who was so guarded and now so unguarded, eyes dwelling on her with a disarmed tranquil look, as if just to see her were perfect pleasure;

who was so cherishing and so cherished; with the strong uprightness, born from a mixture of hardship and formality, of the naval man, and the young smile as he lay luxuriously uncurled watching her from lowered lashes: this man, so known and elusive, the tight fibres of whose being had opened to mesh with hers.

She had a sudden sensation of luck and fortune: seeing, in a kind of reverse presentiment, the two of them lying in this bed and beyond that the long trail of hostility and mishap and misunderstanding that had somehow, as by a winding path, brought them here. 'We're lucky, aren't we?' she said.

He lifted her hand and kissed the inside of her wrist. 'I'm lucky,' he said.

She settled herself against his chest and listened to the beating of his heart. 'I think we'll aways be lucky,' she said.

3

Richard had led such an active life that leisure came strangely to him: though there was plenty for him to do in fitting up and repairing Elm Cottage.

'I oughtn't to worry about it,' he said one morning. 'I'll just have to get used to being an idleton.'

'A what?'

'Idleton. Haven't you heard that? My father used to say it. Like simpleton.' He put on a look of mock affront at her laughter. 'I don't know. Lives all her life in the fens and she's never heard of idleton.'

With the help and advice of Charles from Morholm, as the bitter winter gave place to an early spring, they sowed the fields behind the house with peas and beans and turnip and onion. They took on a youth from the village for outdoor work and for harvesting when the time came. Charles promised them a couple of pigs from the next litter at Morholm, and Richard, with permission from their landlord in Bath, began work on a sty in the yard next to the barn.

'With a couple of heifers, perhaps,' Richard said optimistically, 'and brewing ale in the still-room, and the apples – why, we could be self-sufficient or near enough.'

One thing Caroline did miss was a musical instrument. Her old pianoforte was still at the Bridge House, and no one there played it; but she restrained herself from bringing up the idea of having it sent to Elm Cottage. It was exactly the sort of thing that would revive Richard's consciousness that he could not give her the sort of life she was used to. So far there had been none of the old chafing self-criticism. She did not want to risk spoiling their happiness together – a happiness like a deep clear stream. That meant so much more than being able to strum on the piano when she felt like it.

They soon came to know and like their neighbours in the village: mostly labouring people who worked in the rich black fields and had all the stoicism, canniness and dry humour of the fenland race. With only one horse, they walked a lot, from necessity and for pleasure. They walked west to the edge of Marshland Fen, where the smell of the sea was in the wind; south across Laddus Fen to the Old Nene River. Caroline had always been a town-dweller and Richard had spent much of his life at sea, and they found a special pleasure in observing the progress of spring after the thaw at the beginning of March.

They saw fenland flowers, hardily blooming in sheltered places: lady-smock and cowslip and primrose and cuckoo-pint and marsh-marigold amongst maidenhair fern, and violets under hawthorn hedges, and in the streams the young shoots of bulrushes. The fen droves were brilliant

401

in new mossy green with dramatic swathes of purple grasses. In the mornings great clouds of starlings went whirring from the reed shores to the newly-sown fields. Formations of wild geese appeared again in the sky, returning to the marshes and flood-meadows; crows clowned and congregated noisily in the sparse elms. By the dyke-sides they saw the moorhens beginning their nests, bustling importantly back and forth below the budding fringe of catkins; and in the hedgerows little boys hunting snail-shells. They walked by old field-paths and lanes, and ditchers and hedgers in leather gloves and leggings grew to recognize them. They walked back glowing to late dinners, and Caroline had never felt so healthy; and if she still could not get up early in the mornings, it was not because she was sleeping.

It would have been easy to have isolated themselves here from the doings of the wider world. But Charles quite often made the journey across the fen from Morholm to bring family news, and the busy port and market town of Wisbech was close by. It was at the end of March that a special issue of the *Stamford and Peterborough Courant* at last announced that the Treaty of Peace between Great Britain and France had been signed by Lord Cornwallis at Amiens, and a week later the whole country celebrated the official Proclamation of peace. The Prime Minister Mr Addington called the Treaty of Amiens 'a genuine reconciliation between the two first nations of the world'. A few dissenting voices spoke of 'the peace that passeth understanding', deploring the concessions made to France; but most people felt only release from the gloom and uncertainties of war. As far as Caroline was concerned, it meant that even if Richard was to go away again, it was not to face cannon and the marine snipers' bullets.

He had grown so quickly into her life, and she into his.

He had been thought difficult and reserved – by herself, once – but she who had penetrated that surface found him easy to live with. His deep loyalties and loves and antipathies, the single-mindedness that meant when he gave himself he gave entirely, found an echo in daily life in his absence of pettiness. Small things did not bother him, like small discomforts. She liked to see him standing out in the cold wind in his shirt-sleeves, thoughtfully watching as the floor of the new sty was laid or talking to the field-hand about the crops. Punctilious in dressing to go out and in hygiene – most men of his age scarcely took baths – there was yet no fuss about him. When she was grumpy with the onset of her menses, he did not take it personally and look hurt. If they were to fall out, it would be over something clear and fundamental. What she had always most disliked was niggling: she liked things open and straightforward and never let the sun go down on her wrath.

As for the past, that was gone and it cast no shadows across their life at Elm. Until one day at the end of April, when they went together into Wisbech.

She had finished her shopping, and they walked down to the North Brink to see the ships. Just below the bridge, way was being made between the merchant craft for a flotilla of barges. Caroline recognized the colours of the uniforms, bright yellow and red . . . the prisoners-of-war from Norman Cross, released and on their way to Lynn to be sent back to France and Holland.

Caroline watched in silence as the barges slid past. The sight of the prisoners, laughing and cheering with relief, made her burn with a sense of injustice directed at Antoine. In the happiness of her recent life the thought of him had been lost. But she remembered now that all this time he had had his own happiness, freed from

403

captivity while these men remained, reunited with his wife. An undeserved happiness.

Well, her own was such that she regretted nothing. She had found something more real and profound than Antoine could ever have offered. But still it was not fair. Whilst she and Richard had struggled to take hold of life in a turbulent world, everything had been smooth for Antoine Clairet. With a sudden, lucid, mature insight she perceived that it had always been, and always would be, like that for him. He would go through life smiling his sad smile and using people and feeling guilty and no one would ever tell him just what pain he had caused.

If there were any mechanism of retribution in the world, it ought to work on Antoine Clairet, if it were only to make him face the small unpleasant truth about himself.

At the beginning of May Richard went down to London to call at the Admiralty.

His applications to the East Coast Revenue Service had come to nothing. The service had been expanded during the war to cope with the depredations of coastal privateers and now it had a surplus of men rather than a shortage. The packet-service likewise had no vacancies.

'Wouldn't they summon you if they had a commission for you?' Caroline asked him.

'Well, in theory,' Richard said. 'But it can do no harm to go and make a nuisance of myself.'

Richard had made a garden-seat from the framework of an old sofa – he had an eccentric, untaught and very effective way with such things – and they were sitting here, enjoying the thin pure spring sunshine that was drying the dew on the grass.

'What openings will there be, nowadays?'

Richard frowned at his tea. 'It can't make sense to

dismantle the Navy completely, with a vigorous power still in control of most of Europe. But, old Billy Pitt dug us deep in debt to fight the war, so I suppose economies have to be made now. But there'll still be fighting ships. Convoys. Expeditions for map-making. Transports of convicts to Botany Bay – '

'Oh, no!' Caroline said.

'What's the matter?'

'Botany Bay – that's the other side of the world! You'd be away for years!'

'Well, not quite.' He reached out and took her hand. 'I'd not relish that, love. I'd not relish any time away from you. But I'm a sailor. It will come, sooner or later. Even if I only skipper a fen-lighter down to Northampton. Anyway, we must see what their lordships say. Perhaps they'll tell me to go away and buy an estate like Nelson.'

'Well, you've got your Lady Hamilton,' she said. 'And one you don't have to share with her husband.'

'A friend of mine from the *Olympia* saw her once. When he was at Sicily. A very pretty face but enormously fat, apparently. And Nelson's such a little wasted slip of a man.'

Caroline breathed in the soft air. The apple-trees were breaking into blossom: the winter aconites were over but in the borders stocks and forget-me-nots were coming into flower. 'This is estate enough for me,' she said.

'If only it were our own,' Richard said.

'Well, father thinks Mr Westmore would be willing to sell eventually. There's my money . . .'

Richard glanced at her. 'It's tempting,' he said. 'Too tempting. We've little enough to live on as it is. That's why – well, I want to be employed again. Bringing in money, with promotion in my sights.'

She studied his face, lightly stroking his hand. 'But you do like being here, don't you?'

'Of course. This is the place I want to call home. But – I'd feel I had more right to do so, feel more entitled to enjoy it, if I were doing something to earn it. Does that make sense?'

'I know how you feel, Richard. But it's you I married. My cousin Susannah married Stephen Downes and he could give her a great estate and carriages and all the rest of it, and I daresay that's the life she wanted. But that's not what I want. I knew all this when I married you.'

'Bless you, love. But you know I – I hate the thought of dependence. I want us to be beholden to no one. It's pride, I know, and perhaps that's a luxury like others we can't afford. It's just the way I'm made. Bear with me.'

'I will. As long as you remember I'd rather have a poor Richard with me than a wealthy Richard in Botany Bay.'

He was away in London two days. Caroline had not been alone for a long time, and she did not much like it. At such times she was liable to the odd chill of the spirit, born of the terrible time in London two years ago. She busied herself furiously with the garden and with baking, and was at the door to greet him when at last he came home.

He was dead tired from the long rattling coach journey and the walk from Wisbech. His eyes brightened when he saw her, but she could tell from his face and the set of his shoulders that the news was not good.

She mixed him a rum-and-water. 'Supper's ready if you want it,' she said.

'In a moment,' he said. He drank his rum quickly, bent to pull off his boots and gave it up, lay back in his chair. 'Whew, I wish one could travel down to London by water. I was never so shaken in a north-wester.'

She knelt to help him with his boots. 'How were their lordships?'

He smiled briefly. 'Unwelcoming. I did meet an old

406

friend at the Admiralty, on the same errand as me. The ante-rooms are fairly haunted with hopeful young officers.' He put his arm round her shoulders. 'Well, I suppose I should have expected it. They say they've no employment for me. St Vincent's disarming us at a prodigious rate. The Grand Fleet at Torbay's to be broken up. There are about a hundred ships of the line in commission now, and that's to be halved at least. Same story with the army. Oh, I'm not alone by any means. There'll be hundreds of men in my position. It's peace-time, after all. But I suppose I was hoping against hope that . . . Well. No carriage and four yet, love.'

'And I had my heart set on one too.' She looked at his lean introspective face, put a hand up to push his hair from his brow. 'Serious, Richard. You know how I feel. We've enough to get by. I remember what it was like to be cold and not have enough to eat, and that's something we know we don't have to fear. And I remember what it's like to be alone and without love. That was the most terrible thing of all. And you changed all that, just you. Whether you're an admiral or – or a landlubber.' She kissed him. 'Do seamen really say landlubber?'

He kissed her. 'Never,' he said, and the restive doubting lines of his face broke up in his young smile. It never ceased to touch her heart when that happened.

When he undressed for bed that night, however, she saw the way he looked at his lieutenant's uniform hanging in the closet. 'Better put this in mothballs,' he said lightly; and she perceived that his self-esteem had taken a knock today, that what other men might dismiss as the accidents of circumstance he took as his own failings.

A week after this, they received an invitation to a ball in celebration of the Peace at Thorpe Hall, a handsome, square, three-storeyed mansion standing among formal gardens just outside Peterborough. The Barnards of Thorpe Hall were of good family but not dismayingly so, and they could safely entertain the mixture of landowners, bankers, merchants and brewers who made up local society, without anyone standing on his dignity.

Richard and Caroline were to spend the night with her parents at the Bridge House, and they arrived in Peterborough in the late afternoon.

'Peace and plenty,' Luke said, tapping the front page of the *Courant*. 'Let's hope so. Fact remains that Boney's still left most of Europe closed to our goods. Still, trade with the north's thriving. Step into my study, Richard, will you? I want your advice.'

Richard looked blankly at the sketch of a ship that Luke handed him.

'There, what do you think of her? It's Nicholas's sketch. We went over to Yarmouth last week to see her. There's details written on the back. French prize, condemned for sale by auction. A privateer sloop, name of *Justine*. She was operating in the North Sea, and taken without damage. Hundred-foot. Built only a couple of years since, I reckon. What do you think of her?'

'I dare say she's a swift sailer,' Richard said. 'French privateers often are. You think to buy her, sir?'

'Already have done,'. said Luke with a pleased smile. He looked strong and vigorous again now, braced by activity as an invalid by salt air. 'Three thousand pound. She'll need refitting, of course, for what I plan for her. Tell me, d'you have any news from the Admiralty? Sit down, sit down, Richard.'

Richard told him.

'So, the government's winding the Navy right down, think you? Well, it seems a little hasty to me. We're a maritime nation after all. There'll be less demand for timber, that's a pity. But the Baltic's crying out for

English goods. Hamburg, Denmark. All my ships are at sea now. Lynn's full of sailors looking for work – I've got full crews again. This is the time to expand. What do you say?'

'Certainly, conditions are favourable. You needn't fear the press gang any more. And you won't have to wait for convoy now.'

'Of course, I can't offer pay like the East India Company, I'm sure you appreciate that,' Luke said. 'But I can offer the same as a Captain's rate in the Navy, in fact rather more, they're damned parsimonious at the Admiralty, I reckon. What do you say?'

'There'll be officers aplenty seeking employment,' said Richard. 'I should think you'd only have to say the word at Yarmouth or Lynn and – '

'My dear Richard, I'm not interested in other officers. It's you I want to command the *Justine*.'

'Me?'

'Well, who better? After your Copenhagen expedition you must know those waters. You've had two years' experience as a lieutenant in men-o'-war, that should fit you for the command of a merchant sloop. And I know your character. Have you had another offer, is that it? Tell me what it is and – '

'No, no, it isn't that.' Richard frowned at the sketch of the *Justine*. 'I – this is a very generous offer, sir – '

'Not a bit of it. I'm a man of business. I want a good man to command this vessel. You'd be ship-master for the House, too. Like your father was. That's my proposal. Forget the past. Why, it's a family business, and you're part of the family.'

Richard struggled, oppressed with the strong cross-currents of his nature, with recoiling pride and gratitude. A merchant captain's pay. Not to be sneezed at. There would be lots of young poor lieutenants who would jump at it. Caroline – he could support her. No longer reliant on her fortune.

'Now I realize that when you've been in the Navy, with great deeds a-doing, taking cargoes to Hamburg may seem a trifle mean,' said Luke.

'No, indeed, the merchant service is held in great respect in the fleet,' said Richard absently.

'You surely don't think you're not up to the job?' Luke said.

Richard smiled slightly. All the avenues against refusal seemed to be closing.

'I would hope to do you and the ship justice, Mr Hardwick,' he said at last. 'But will you give me a little time to think it over?'

'Surely, surely, my boy,' said Luke. 'She's not ready to sail yet. Talk it over with Caro. Of course it means you'll be away for periods of time, but nothing like as long as Navy cruises – and she expects that, marrying a seaman. Well, I'll go flig myself up for this jaunt tonight. Give me your answer when you're ready.'

Richard went back to the large parlour and found Caroline who had been unable to resist it, playing the pianoforte.

She finished playing and turned to him, pleased. 'There. I'm not *too* rusty,' she said. 'Applaud, husband.'

'Very good,' Richard said. '*Little Brown Jug*, wasn't it?'

'It was a sonata by Clementi,' she said, throwing a cushion at him. 'See how he torments me, mother? Anyway, what were you and father cooking up in the study?'

'Men's talk,' said Richard gruffly. They laughed together, but she saw that something was deeply troubling him.

* * *

There were perhaps a hundred guests at Thorpe Hall. The spring evening was mild, and lanterns had been hung in the gardens, so they could stroll along the gravel walks beneath the cypresses to the accompaniment of a string band playing on the balustraded terrace.

Richard had never met Sir Robert Barnard in his life, and was surprised when his host sought him out. Sir Robert, it transpired, was a keen admirer of all things maritime, and somewhat to his embarrassment Richard found himself treated as an oracle on everything from the effectiveness of blockade to the private life of Lord Nelson. His host told him of his collection of antique seafaring books and prints, and when Richard expressed a polite desire to see them Sir Robert was all enthusiasm. 'They're in the library, Mr Lindsay – I'll have candles and a fire lit in there directly – please, go and make free with anything that takes your fancy.'

Richard had become separated from Caroline, and it was a kind offer, so he found the library on the ground floor of the Hall and spent a while in there among the model galleons and brass compasses. He was turning over a copy of Falconer's *Universal Marine Dictionary*, when from the voices in the next room, opening by double doors on to this one, he caught his name mentioned and recognized the accents of Mrs Butterworth.

'. . . Well, apparently Mr Luke Hardwick has set them up in a house over at Wisbech. Really, I was surprised to see her at an assembly such as this, after all the scandal . . .'

'Oh, that was a long time ago,' said another voice.

'Maybe so,' said Mrs Butterworth. 'But it all seems a very strange business to me. Carrying on as if nothing happened. Why, this young sailor she's been married off to – '

'What is his family? Has he any?'

411

'Not a bit, my dear.' Mrs Butterworth again. 'I hear he's only the son of some employee of Mr Hardwick's. And glad to have her, I dare say, for the sake of her fortune. A squalid little arrangement.'

'Well, mama,' came the unmistakable mincing accents of Charity Butterworth, 'some expedient had to be found. When the goods are damaged, one's lucky to find any buyer!'

There were smothered giggles, and Mrs Butterworth said sepulchrally: 'Hush, child, you express yourself coarsely . . .'

Richard opened the door and confronted a ring of surprised female faces. A blush turned Charity Butterworth's sallow complexion an unpleasant shade of puce.

'Mr – Lieutenant Lindsay,' said Mrs Butterworth, taken by surprise. 'I – you, you are not at sea, I take it.'

'Well perceived, ma'am,' Richard said. 'At least your bad manners do not proceed entirely from stupidity.'

Mrs Butterworth's hooded eyelids came down. 'If you were a gentleman you would take that back.'

'If you were a lady I might consider it.'

The ball broke up late, and it was past two when Caroline and Richard at last closed the door of the guest bedroom at the Bridge House.

'Strange to be the guest in the house where I used to live,' Caroline said, sitting in the chair by the fire and lazily pulling off her stockings. They talked for a while in the drowsy, desultory way of pure companionship. Eventually Richard, trimming the candles, said: 'When your father called me into his study earlier, he had a proposition for me. I've been thinking it over all evening. He's invested in a new ship, a captured French prize, and he wants me to command it.'

'A new ship? A coaster?'

412

'No. For the Baltic markets. It's a substantial invest-ment.' Richard unwound his cravat. 'What do you think I should do?'

She stared at the fire, her mind wakeful now. 'The Baltic . . . It would mean your being away. But I like it better than Botany Bay.'

Richard sat down on the bed. 'The sea is all I'm fit for,' he said slowly. 'And in peacetime the merchant service is my best hope. And the pay I would get as captain of one of your father's ships would be twice what I get as a lieutenant in the Navy. We'd be substantially better off. Able to afford a second horse. Take young Ned on as indoor servant. And then if children should come, it would be very useful.'

She looked at him. 'But?'

He sighed. 'I'd almost made up my mind to accept, if you agreed. It's a tempting prospect. Oh, I could wring Charity Butterworth's wretched little neck.'

'Come on. Tell me.'

At last she wheedled it out of him. They sat together on the bed and cursed the Butterworths for a few minutes.

'Well,' Caroline said, taking his hand, 'I can't pretend I like being called damaged goods. But I don't care, really. Do you? We can't let them hurt us?'

'God forbid,' he said. 'Though I'd like to hurt them. But, you see, coming after your father's offer, it made me think . . . I wanted to prove I could look after you, love. Make a life together of our own, independent. It's a handsome offer, and I'm grateful, believe me, but it would be as if – well, as if your father were keeping us.'

'No, Richard. I know my father and I know he's very serious when it comes to business. He wants the best seamen for his ships. And you've proved that. There's no question of favour.'

'You think I should accept?'

413

'Well, as you say, the sea is what you're trained for. I can't see you being happy just cultivating the turnips at Elm. But it's for you to decide, love.'

'Working for your father, like my father did . . . It would add fuel to the Butterworths' ideas about us. Our marriage – an expedient.'

'What's more important?' she said soberly. 'What Mrs Butterworth thinks, or what I think?'

He glanced at her and then down at the floor. 'Now you've made me feel ashamed.'

'I don't mean to, love. All I'm saying is they can talk till their tongues drop off and they won't change anything. I married you because I love you. There's no question of expedient. I know that and if you don't, if I can't convince you, then . . . You must do what you think's best, Richard. Those little extra comforts, yes, I'd like them, and if we don't have them, then that's all right too. As long as I have you and your trust and as long as I know that you're not eternally chafing and gnawing away inside.'

He smiled ruefully. 'You certainly have the measure of me, love. Do I try you sorely?'

'Oh! not too much,' she said, stroking his face.

They went to bed at last, the question still unresolved but the air cleared. She was glad he had spoken. Such things could fester if left unsaid. He had a lifetime habit of brooding on things, she perceived, and he was only learning to break it with her.

Still, as she lay with her head on his shoulder, feeling his breathing slow and relax, she felt a regret at the complexities that were worming their way into the lovely straightforward life they had together. She had had more than her share of experience and was not innocent; but she was young and in love, and it is always a dismaying surprise when the unkind world exhibits its indifference to that fact, and contends that love is never enough.

CHAPTER 3

1

One morning at the end of June, Charles rode over from
Morholm to Leam House, as he did most days, to call on
the Amorys. It was generally, tacitly agreed that these
calls were specifically to see Louisa Amory; so he supposed it must be true. It was looked on as such an
obvious, desirable and suitable attachment that he hadn't
the heart to deny it.

Nor could he deny that he was shocked and deeply
touched to find Louisa that morning in tears. The volatile
family of which she was the quiet centre had exploded in
a row just before. It was Quarter Day, and in settling his
accounts old Mr Humphrey Amory had noticed that the
cost of keeping Frederick's hunters and dogs was threatening to outstrip the rents from an estate that was not
particularly large and was very particularly mortgaged.
Something in the sight of the unconcerned Frederick
sprawling booted and spurred in a chair eating a peach
had set off Mr Amory's hot temper. He had called him a
worthless hound, a haynish looby and a fat idleton and
said unless he spent a little less time in the hunting field
and a little more helping with the estate there would be
no horses in the stable for him to ride. Then Mrs Amory
had defended Frederick and Mr Amory had turned on
her, drawing attention to her finery and saying it was no
way for a married woman with two grown children to
dress, and then Frederick had said that was no way
to speak to his mother and Mr Amory had threatened to

horsewhip him, big as he was . . . It had all degenerated into a hurtful shouting match with Louisa trying to keep the peace and ending up most hurt of all.

'I can't bear quarrelling.' she said between her sobs, 'the things they were saying . . . oh, I'm sorry, Charles . . .' and in his pity and affection for her there seemed nothing more natural than to take her in his arms and hold her till she was quiet. And in a dry paralysed perplexity he felt how she held on to him and buried her face in his neck with such gratitude; and it was as if having expected a yawning chasm he found only a brook and he had merely to step across it.

That he did not love Louisa became clearer to him in that moment; but what became even clearer was the fact that the love he did feel was for a woman who could not be his, a poisoned, useless love that was nothing but a barrier to any kind of happiness. And if it was true that to give happiness to another person was in itself happiness, then he had that power, now, and it would be churlish not to use it, like hoarding vaults of corn in time of famine.

So he stroked her hair and kissed her cheek, and wiped her eyes with his handkerchief. 'Hush,' he said, 'everything will be all right.'

'Oh, Charles, I'm so glad you came,' she said, and kissed him back: trembling, blushing, but no longer crying.

He left Leam an hour later, with an engagement to go there for dinner tomorrow, if not exactly a formal engagement to Louisa. Tomorrow he would approach her father before dinner. Louisa said she would prepare the way for him. But there would be no problems. All her tears were gone and in her shy, modest way she was full of excitement.

No problems. Perhaps that was the trouble. Should it

all be this easy, this casual, this unimpassioned? Perhaps it was the best way. But something had made him say, just before he left, that before they made anything public there was something she should know and he must speak to her seriously alone. What he would say he was unsure: only felt the acute need to confess something, to convey that he brought to her a fond and respectful heart but not a whole one, that only if she was sure that what he could offer her was enough should they go ahead. And already he was half-afraid that the answer would still be yes.

At Morholm Frances came running out to the stable-yard.

'Charles! Father's here! Come home all unexpected. He brought me these ribbons from London. How do you think I look?'

'Like a maypole,' Charles said, getting a punch on the arm for his answer. 'Why's he come home?'

'Oh! I don't know, something about Parliament decomposing.'

Charles gave a shout of laughter. 'Dissolving,' he said. 'Parliament doesn't decompose, you idiot girl,' and he ran into the house with Frances threatening dire punishment after him.

They sat down to dinner early: George had broken his journey overnight and had had nothing since breakfast.

'I thought I could get here before a letter,' he said. 'I just upped and went as soon as I heard what was in the wind. Addington's dissolving Parliament and calling a general election. Looking to strengthen his position, I presume. You heard about the peace debate, Charles?'

'I heard the vote went in favour.'

'Two hundred and seventy-six to twenty-two. I was not one of the twenty-two. Debates went on for three nights. There are still a few who want to flourish the sword. But most people seem pretty well sick of war, and Addington's caught the mood. London reminds me of how it was before the war. The theatres and opera full again, a lot more drink taken, a lot less church attending and talking of sin. I must say I prefer it. So, what's the news here?'

Over dinner they told him: Charles, thinking of his own news, kept quiet. Tomorrow would be soon enough for that.

After dinner George smoked a pipe and began to look cheerful as he did when he came back to Morholm after a long absence, the lines smoothing out on his high brow. He proposed going over to the gatehouse to speak to John Newman, and said: 'Walk with me, will you, Charles?'

It was a beautiful June afternoon, and George paused by the hayfield to inhale the earthy scent. 'Looks well for cutting,' he said. 'God! Every time, I get used to the stinks of London and stop noticing them – and then I come back here and wonder how I ever endured them.'

'Have you seen the Earl of Exeter?'

'Not yet. He didn't come up this session but stayed at Burghley. I'll go over and see him tomorrow. That's why I wanted to speak to you, Charles. Well, partly.'

Charles waited. A lark sang somewhere up in the cloudless blue.

'You've not been up with me to London of late. I don't know whether you – well, you had your reasons, I'm sure. But I think, I presume, that a political career still interests you.'

'Well . . . In the abstract, shall we say.'

'And perhaps because it always seemed so abstract, so theoretical, you got rather disillusioned?'

Charles smiled.

'I shall be fifty this year,' George said, leaning his arms on the hayfield fence. 'Sometimes I feel it, sometimes not at all. I entered Parliament twenty years ago almost by accident. It seemed like a temporary expedient then. But somehow I got a taste for it. Even thought I could do some good there. I don't know about that, but anyway the point is I think I've done my share now and have no scruple about stepping down. What do you think about taking my place?'

Charles stared at the gently waving hay. 'Lord Burghley and the red republican in harness?' he said ironically.

'Well. There is that. But now we're at peace your views won't be – shouldn't be – quite so alarming. Personally I believe the Earl would be quite amenable to you taking my place as a Member for Stamford in his interest. So. That's my idea.'

Charles licked his lips. 'I – do you think to step down anyway? If I didn't do this?'

'I think so. I'd have to thrash that out with the Earl. I will say this. I'm glad of the peace. And I can see what Addington's trying to do. Strengthen the consensus around him, based on the blessings of peace. But it's not based on much else. There's the same old complacency and resistance to change. I think we need a few firebrands about now. So I suppose what I'm saying is I'd support you whole-heartedly, though I may not have given that impression in the past. I think we need some radicalism and I think you'd do well. Compliments from your father, whatever next?'

'I don't know what to say,' Charles said. 'It's been a while since I – since I've really thought about this.'

'I know,' George said. 'I'm not quite blind, Charles. You haven't wanted to speak of it but I know you've been unhappy. So, there's something else I should tell you. It's confidential, but I feel you'd like to know. It's about Sir Thomas Fairburn.'

At that moment Charles knew what the Methodists meant when they talked about the devil entering you: he

419

entered Charles for a second and whispered, *Perhaps he's dead*, before Charles could drive him away.

'The news is, he's been relieved of his sinecure post – Patent Inspector of Prosecutions for the Customs. In disgrace. Apparently, not content with the fat salary from the post, he'd been peculating the funds for several years. Oh, taking care to cover his tracks, and he's tried to throw the blame on a subordinate. The Government's saying nothing officially or unofficially. He continued to support them when Addington came in. But he's been dismissed, and that speaks for itself. My guess is that the Addington government, with a general election coming up, wish to present an appearance of probity and integrity. Sir Thomas Fairburn's public career is certainly finished. Well, more than that. He's pretty well ruined.'

George was looking out over the fields as he spoke, so he did not notice that his son had gone dead white. After a moment Charles cleared his throat and said: 'It can't . . . Not ruined. All that property – '

'The rotten borough in Cornwall? Mortgaged to the hilt. In itself it was worth little. The thing is, Sir Thomas had been borrowing for years on the security of that sinecure. Now there are no political places left for him to milk, and he's in deep trouble. That enormous mansion he's been building near Newmarket – '

'Stanningford.'

'That's it. Won't be finished now. He poured money into that like a drain. A stable of racehorses. Good arable land turned over to the stud-farm. Fairburn lived it high – and that means there's further to fall. God knows, I've been too deep in debt myself in the past ever to rejoice at this sort of thing. But given that moral stand he used to take – the guardian of the constitution and the laws of property and all the rest of it – there's a certain piquancy

420

in his being disgraced for corruption. It will be a shock to him. He was always so self-assured.'

Charles gripped the bar of the fence. He felt he must cry out to break the serene silence of the fields. A thousand whirling emotions pressed in on him and he could make sense of none of them. That morning, the gentle cooings with Louisa, seemed years ago. He gave his father a wild look. 'You're sure of this?' he said.

'It's common knowledge at Westminster,' said George, a little taken aback. 'I thought I should tell you, Charles. I never pressed you but I realize you were pretty thick with Sir Thomas's daughter and – well, it was when you stopped seeing her that this change came over you. I don't know if I've done the right thing.' As Charles did not answer he went on: 'There's another reason, which has to do with what I said earlier. I've heard of no public inquiry going forward into Fairburn's behaviour. It may be that the Government think his private ruin is enough and will keep quiet for past services rendered. But it could be brought up in the House. If you were in the House you could bring it up yourself.'

Charles looked at his father. He realized now that George had perceived much that he thought was hidden in his heart. He had never breathed a word of how Sir Thomas had threatened him with prosecution and prison without trial, how he had blighted all his hopes of happiness with Lydia, how all that bright part of his life had ended in disgust and disillusion the bitter taste of which had never left him. But his father was a man of sensitive insight. And now he was holding out to him a prospect of sweetest revenge combined with the fulfilment of a deep ambition. Even in the midst of his emotional anguish, Charles was seized with the consciousness of a new love and respect for his father.

But it was all much more complicated than revenge.

'Where is – Where are the Fairburns now, do you know?'

'At Stanningford, I presume. He made a hasty exit from town. The house in Curzon Street's shut up.'

There were pink smears in the sky. A beautiful day. A mad world.

George said: 'There's no need for me to see Lord Burghley tomorrow, of course. I can leave it a couple of days.' He patted his son's arm. 'Well, I'll go and see John.'

Left alone, Charles stayed leaning on the hayfield fence for a long time. The well-ordered estate stretching around him, prosperity, safety. Two miles away across the fields, Leam House. More safety.

And now *this*, whisking the soft carpet from under his feet. If it had come a little later, he would have been definitely engaged to Louisa, and the news should have been no concern to him.

But it did concern him. He could not go on with that half-hearted, decorous courtship with this news hanging over him. In his disillusion he had brought himself to distrust the impulses of the heart, but now there was no question of trust or distrust: he could only obey.

But first, he must see Louisa and tell her where he was going.

2

Charles reached Cambridge on the *Truth and Daylight* coach at two the next afternoon, and enquired immediately about local coaches to Newmarket. An ostler directed him to the White Lion on the other side of the town, and he got there just in time to snatch an outside place on the Bury *Elegant*.

From the top of the coach he had a sweeping view of Newmarket Heath, a brilliant green under the June sun. Several times he saw quadrangles of stables, and horses being exercised. He wondered if any of them were Sir Thomas Fairburn's. He wondered what Louisa Amory thought of him now.

Her quiet dignity had cut him up more than any tearful outrage could have done. There was no formal undertaking between them, she said. He had tried to explain that this was what he had wanted to speak to her about before, that he had had a previous attachment which had never, on his part, been truly severed, that he had to ascertain what had happened to her, that he had fully expected this to be dead and buried but now that it was not it exerted a claim on him that . . . He lost himself in windy exculpation, and broke himself against the small quiet rock of Louisa's dignity. She thanked him for being candid with her. She gave him a cold little hand in goodbye and he knew he had packed himself a burden of guilt that one day he would have to shoulder.

But for now all he could think of was Lydia and her father's disgrace. He had to see Lydia, but he asked himself whether he had also come to triumph over Sir Thomas. There were many questions he could not answer about his feelings, and there was a kind of blind imperative in his hope that this visit would answer them all.

They reached Newmarket in mid-afternoon. There would be no time to get back to Morholm tonight whatever happened, so he stowed his luggage and took a room at the Bushel Inn in Market Street. The town seemed full of men whose appearance spoke of an interest in horseflesh: short bow-legged men in top-boots, shrewd seedy sportsmen in raffish cravats, sleek gentlemen of Sir Thomas's own type. Stanningford, his enquiries revealed, was about two miles north of the town on the Ely road. To his astonishment he found himself unable to hire a saddle-horse in Newmarket, so he set out to walk.

He had not expected the house to be so ugly. Impressive, but ugly. It stood at the end of a short drive behind wrought iron-work gates, amongst yew topiaries. There was a castellated roof and many pointed chimneys and at the corner a hexagonal pepper-pot bay up which a creeper had been unsuccessfully trained to give an effect of venerable age. It was Gothic at its most gaudy; and on walking down the drive, which curved slightly, Charles saw that the wing at right-angles from the front was unfinished, with the roof only a skeleton and the windows unglazed. The effect was like a stage set seen from the side. But somehow appropriate. This place that he had never seen, but always identified in his mind with the power and fashion and assurance of the Fairburns, was built on sand.

The footman told him the family were not at home to visitors. 'But they are at home?' Charles said, seizing on some hesitancy in the man's manner, and was admitted.

'I really don't think Sir Thomas is fit to see visitors, but – '

'Fit but unwilling,' came a voice from the dark staircase. Sir Thomas was descending slowly. 'Hardwick, is it? Ah, the vultures, the vultures.'

'I came to enquire – '

'You came because you heard what has happened. A natural impulse, to gloat. Though of course, Hardwick, you're the one who believes man's impulses are all good.' Sir Thomas at last reached the bottom step, where light from the tall leaded windows was thrown on him. His appearance was painful to behold, perhaps because he had always been so impeccable. His hair was brushed lankly back as if he had just got up. He was in an old morning-gown and slippers. His eyes had the glassy look

424

of drink and his skin was grey. For the first time he looked his forty-five years, and more.

He gazed, dull and unsurprised, at Charles. 'Reed, is there some canary left?' he said. 'Bring a bottle into the drawing-room. Did you perhaps expect to see dust-sheets everywhere, Hardwick – and bailiffs making inventories? Ah, no. Not yet. There's still a certain stately leisure about these things. Come.'

'Is Miss Fairburn not here?' Charles said, following him.

'She has gone into Cambridge. In Mr Spencer Murrow's carriage. You remember Mr Murrow? His place is at Soham, not so far from here. He has placed his carriage at our disposal. Unfortunately we have had to retrench in the matter of carriage-horses. She'll not be long. You've come a long way for this entertainment, Mr Hardwick.'

Charles marked the *Mister*. He did not know what to say.

'Vultures, vultures. I do not include Mr Murrow in that appellation. As you may know he is of Evangelical persuasion, and calls my fall the will of God, like so many things. As for the will of society – that is against me too.' Sir Thomas poured two glasses of canary with an unsteady hand and sat down close to the embers of the fire, gathering his morning-gown around him, though it was warm and stuffy in the overfurnished room. 'People are treacherous, Mr Hardwick,' he went on. 'They are without loyalty. You will drink canary with me, but then you were never my friend. With my friends it is the opposite. I have been made a leper.' He poked the fire, his aristocratic face pinched and petulant. 'It has confirmed my view of human nature. Rotten within. You and your Jacobin fellows with your cant – man is good and institutions have made him bad, social improvement, equality . . . Man is *rotten* to the core. There is nothing to be

425

hoped for him. Everyone has judged me, condemned me. It isn't fair,' he added plaintively.

'Do you intend selling Stanningford?' Charles said.

'Who will pay for a half-finished house with money still owing to the builders?' Sir Thomas's wine was gone. Charles passed him the decanter. He saw there was no colour in the older man's delicate hands. 'It's all down to the lawyers. And they too will require their pound of flesh. I have no one to turn to. Men have done worse than me,' he said querulously, gesturing at the fire as if it were an audience. 'A few peccadilloes – who is free of those? Men have done far worse.'

'But not while pretending to be pillars of the establishment,' Charles said.

Sir Thomas glanced at him: the instinctive haughtiness came out in his face, but there was pathos too, as if he knew himself to be naked and defenceless. 'You don't understand,' he said, rubbing one hand restlessly up and down his knee, 'when a man – undertakes great projects, when he becomes a figure of consequence, his – his responsibilities, the claims on his resources, they seem to multiply. Look at Stanningford. It is a grand project, is it not? My life has not been conducted on a petty scale. But my fault is seen as mean and lowly. After Dr Johnson died men hurried to attack his reputation. Samuel Parr said "now the old lion is dead, every ass thinks he may kick at him." And so it goes. I am snubbed by men who should be beneath my notice. One is carried on, you see, one cannot maintain a place in the world as I have through – through a penny-pinching, grocerish carefulness. A man of consequence cannot make economies . . . I – I am the victim of my own success in the world. You understand, don't you, Mr Hardwick?' he said with a sort of proud, pathetic appeal.

Charles understood: he understood that Sir Thomas

was unwinding this tortuous thread of self-justification to him because he had scarcely seen anyone else to say it to. He had gained power by sycophancy and used it to inspire fear; neither produced staunch friends when the power was gone. He had been shunned.

And rightly, oh, so rightly. No one had more right to feel a triumphant, vindicated contempt at the sight of Sir Thomas now than Charles. The contempt was there; but it rubbed uncomfortably against something else that was like pity. And the two together created a realization in Charles – something that had never occurred to him: Sir Thomas was a weak man. He had only one side, like his great unfinished folly of a house, and no resources behind it, only an enduring vanity that was more pitiable than repulsive. His hostility to Charles seemed to be lost in the need to explain himself, to reconstruct the shattered façade, even for the sake of a young man whom he hated.

And Charles considered his own hate, and found it like a meal for which one has no appetite. This man had sought Charles's downfall and would have been happy to see him imprisoned without trial for opposing his will. I want to hate him, thought Charles, but I can't. I hate what he did to me, I hate what he did to me and Lydia, I hate his views, his conceit, his hypocrisy . . . But I can't hate this shell.

Sir Thomas held up his hand, his face suddenly alert. 'Carriage. That's Lydia. Lydia's back,' he said, and his expression was childishly, abjectly hopeful.

There were voices in the hall, and Sir Thomas called out: 'In here, my dear. We have a visitor.'

With sick excitement Charles turned to see Lydia at the door, and behind her Spencer Murrow, gaunt and starched and buttoned-up in black.

She was in a grey écharpe cloak and muslin bonnet. A muscle moved in her cheek when she saw Charles, but then she removed her gloves calmly and put out her hand. 'Mr Hardwick.'

'Mr Hardwick and I have been drinking canary together,' Sir Thomas said. 'Is there any more there, Mr Hardwick?'

Lydia went to her father and touched his shoulder. 'Dinner won't be long, father,' she said. 'Don't you think you should go and dress?'

'Dress?' He looked up at her with the same humble, obedient devotion. 'Yes, of course. Mr Hardwick will stay to dinner, I'm sure. And you, Mr Murrow?'

'Thank you, sir,' Spencer Murrow said, bowing gravely, 'but I must be getting back to Soham. I'll call again on the morrow if I may. Please remember that my carriage is yours to command, indeed anything that is within my power and that of my family.'

Lydia steered her father upstairs, and Charles saw Spencer Murrow to the front door.

'Mr Hardwick,' he said in a low, portentous tone, giving Charles his boneless handshake. 'It is Christian of you to call on the family in this time of trouble. Many former friends and acquaintances of Sir Thomas have withdrawn themselves. I, and my sister, leave judgement to the Almighty. If a man sins, it is the duty of his fellow mortals to direct his feet back to the rock of salvation.'

'How long has Sir Thomas been like this?' Charles said flatly.

'In this sadly discountenanced condition? Some weeks. He is as yet unable to grasp the spiritual comfort that awaits all who seek it.'

'He seems to be taking liquid comfort instead.'

Mr Murrow coughed and tweaked his long nose. 'H'm yes, well, I believe Miss Lydia seeks to – to moderate that. My sister and I call whenever we can and offer our services, as Sir Thomas seems little able to rouse himself on his own behalf. Miss Lydia is proving a tower of strength.' He put on his tall funereal hat. 'Who knows, Mr Hardwick, but that this fall may not be a blessing, an opportunity furnished by the Maker to lead one of His children from the paths of worldly vanity? Providence is inscrutable,' and with a little smile, as if to say that inscrutable as Providence might be to the commonalty, it favoured him with its confidence, Mr Murrow took his leave.

Lydia came down the stairs. 'Father's lying down,' she said. 'I persuaded him to.' She went into the drawing-room and picked up the empty decanter. 'Did he have it all?'

'Most of it.'

She nodded: stood there willowy tall, pale, proud, and unhappy.

'I had to come,' Charles said.

'To crow?'

'That's what your father said. That's – what I thought myself on the way here . . . My father told me the news just yesterday.'

'Well. Now you've seen us. This is how we are. It's all true, by the way. About father. I'm not about to deny it. I suppose it all goes to prove what you always thought of us, the way we lived. The come-uppance. You've been vindicated. I hope that's a satisfaction to you.' She rubbed a hand across her cheek. There were shadows under her eyes. No. If he had expected change in himself, he was wrong: his heart went out to her, his tangle of feelings resolved into the old, unchanged, passionate love at the sight of her, infused with a new protective tenderness.

'You're tired,' he said. 'Why don't you sit down?'

'Tired,' she said. 'Yes, I am tired.' She sat, rubbing her hand still against her cheek in distress. 'I've been to see father's solicitor in Cambridge. He won't do anything for

429

himself, he won't leave the house. We see no one but the Murrows.'

'What is the – how long – ?'

'Till we're declared bankrupt?' she said. 'Oh, it won't quite come to that, or so the lawyers tell me. Such property as is disposable is already being sold. Much depends on the attitude of the bank. We must hope for mercy. I suppose I should have expected something like this. Oh, not the fact that father had been stealing. That's what it comes down to, though they use fine words like peculating and embezzling. Stealing. That was a shock. But I should have known we couldn't go on living at the rate we did and not be in debt.' She sighed impatiently. 'But then that was just like me. The money kept coming. I lacked nothing. I took it for granted, yes, of course I could have new gowns, jewels, a new blood mare . . . I really think I believed that it – well, not grew on trees, but that it grew somewhere. But then father always protected me from that. I was the precious daughter for whom nothing was too good, who had only to be adorned and indulged and never be made unhappy. We have not been good for each other, my father and I. It's only right we should both suffer now.'

Charles sat at a distance from her, letting her talk on, perceiving that like her father she had had no outlet for her feelings since the collapse and now she could not stop.

'It's made him so helpless. He won't even face the truth. The stud was the first thing to go, it had to be, there was a ready buyer, it was only common sense. But he couldn't accept it. Not that, he said, can't we keep that? He thought the world was being malicious taking that from him. Wounded and outraged. He can't face the fact that *he's* responsible. Tradesmen demand payment of bills and he feels they have a personal grudge . . . Well. What do you think of Stanningford? More vulgar than

430

you expected?' Without waiting for an answer she went on: 'I always said it would never be finished. I'm not offering you much hospitality, am I, Charles? There's brandy in that cabinet if you want it.'

Charles got up. 'I think you should have some,' he said, pouring a glass. She took it but did not drink. She looked up at him. 'What has he been saying to you?'

'Oh . . . Nothing really.'

She gave him a straight, weary look.

'Well, self-justification. More for himself than for me, I think. He wasn't – '

'Hostile? No. Of all people, Charles, you are the only one who's visited him since it happened. Oh, except the Murrows, of course. They've taken our cause to heart. They're kind in their way, they've helped a lot.' She suddenly gulped down her brandy. 'Of course, if we do stay solvent that may not be the end of it. Father's relying on his friends in the Government – *former* friends – to keep things reasonably quiet. Hopefully they'll decide he's suffered enough. If there were a parliamentary inquiry, prosecution – it would finish him. He's my father,' she added, as if Charles had challenged her, 'I still love him. It would be better if I didn't, but there it is. You can't just stop loving someone like that.'

Charles nearly spoke then. But something made him wait.

'I've never had to do anything for myself before,' she said. 'Or for anyone else. Absurd, isn't it? I always thought myself very independent and confident and even, in my conceit, rather daring. And now I have to do all these things father's not up to doing, the lawyers, the bailiffs, the stewards . . . and I realize what a pampered protected little wretch I've been all these years! Just when our condition is about to be such that I certainly shan't be pampered any more. Give me some more of that brandy,

431

Charles. I can tipple now while the Murrows aren't watching . . . My father's a weak man, you see, and I never knew it.'

'And you're strong,' Charles said. 'And you never knew it.'

'Am I? I don't know. Someone has to be. Well, Charles – ' she made a brittle effort at a social tone, 'what have you been doing since I – since . . . what have you been . . .?'

Tears were collecting on her long eyelashes, beading but not falling. She looked down, miserable, helpless. 'Lydia,' he said, 'oh, Lydia,' and knelt down beside her and put his arms round her. As she held on to him a wave of pain and love broke itself into a brilliant unreal spray of joy as he felt at that moment that she was his.

'What have I been doing?' he said. 'Nothing. I can't do anything without you, Lydia.'

'Damn you,' she said gently, 'why can't you be fickle like other men?' She took his hand in both of hers and kissed it and then held it and looked at it with a kind of anguished regret. 'Why can't you find someone else, Charles . . .?'

'There isn't anyone else,' he said. 'How can there be? All I want is you.'

'Offspring of a disgraced bankrupt father,' she said, 'soused with brandy, with a runny nose – '

'Not an attractive prospect in theory,' he said. 'But everything I want in the world.'

'Charles, that last time in London – '

'It doesn't *matter*,' he said. 'Your father – none of it matters now. Poor Lydia. I can see what a strain you've been under. And how strong you've been. But now you won't have to – '

'Charles.' She released his hand, got up and went to the window. 'Don't say that. Strong . . . yes, if it were a matter of only being strong for myself, then . . . But it's not. You've seen father. He has no one but me. He relies on me completely.'

'Does he deserve you?'

She shrugged, looking out at the yew-planted grounds. 'I'm all he has. It's up to me to save him. I once told you I loved you too much to want to see you in prison for my sake. Well, I love my father and I don't want to see him in the debtor's prison. You've seen what he's like now. Any further down, and – I don't know what he might do.' She put her hand up to the heavy brocade curtain and he saw her fingers close tight around it as she said: 'I've hurt you often, Charles – strange, of all people in the world I least wish to hurt – but I'm going to do it now and this will be the last time. I'm going to marry Spencer Murrow.'

For a moment he thought it was a burst of her old wry flippancy. But she was not laughing.

'Spencer Murrow,' he breathed. It was grotesque . . . 'You don't love Spencer Murrow,' he said harshly: a statement, not a question.

'Oh, love. If it were only a question of love . . . Strong. I'm going to have to be strong for my father,' she said. 'So I'm going to marry Spencer Murrow.'

'Why? In God's name, *why*?'

'I'm a woman,' she said in a dead, muffled voice. 'I can't go and make my fortune in the City or at the Bar or – or Westminster. But that would take too long anyway. What I can do is make a rich marriage. By doing that I can save my father. Spencer Murrow has a large estate and an independent fortune of thirty thousand pounds.'

Charles stared at her, but she would not look at him. 'You're engaged to him?'

'No. He hasn't asked me yet, but he's hinted. It's in the wind. There's no question of love in such a situation. I can't make any excuses for my father, what he's done, but

I can't see him brought down. Please, Charles, say you understand. You'd make sacrifices for your parents, wouldn't you, if they were in distress?'

'*Sacrifices*.' A storm of anger welled up in him at this terrible calm slaughter of hope. 'Marrying a man you don't love – for – for – '

'For money. Just what I once said I'd do, isn't it, in my perverse way. But at least it's not for my own uses. Not for my own uses. Oh, Charles, please don't hate me.'

'He brought it on himself!' Charles cried.

She shook her head. 'If I could feel that for certain it would make things easier. But I haven't exactly lived an ascetic life, Charles.'

Charles stood frozen. His mind searched frantically for arguments whilst all the time it saw the ghastly death's-head of defeat. It saw defeat in the straight, slim, determined figure of Lydia at the window and the unnatural baldness of her words. The brittle frivolous immaturity was not there; but still she was part of her father's world. She could not escape from it. The wit and gaiety and warmth of her nature had been confirmed in a temple of materialism and now they would be sacrificed at the same altar.

Spencer Murrow . . . it was obscene.

'I've always been a selfish creature,' Lydia said. 'You know that. It won't hurt me to change my ways and be unselfish for once.'

'For life,' Charles said. 'For life. Have you thought of that?'

'I'm not doing this lightly, Charles,' she said in a breaking voice. 'Do you really think I haven't thought about it? Spencer's not an unkind man. Pompous perhaps. But there are worse faults. I've had twenty-two years of living just for myself. Now I must do something for someone else.'

If he had been in a way to be objective he would have admired her quiet determined courage. But he was not objective. He went to her and seized her arms and turned her to face him.

'I won't let you do it,' he cried. 'Oh, God, Lydia – all this time I've never stopped loving you. If I'd come here and found you were in love with someone else, if you'd thrown my love back in my face, I'd have been shattered, despairing; but at least it would have been *your* choice, your decision, your happiness. But *this* . . . Does your father know what he's doing? He'll blight two lives, yours and mine – and he lies upstairs with a belly-full of wine sleeping it off!'

'I know I've begged you to understand,' she said miserably, limp in his grasp, 'but I can't really expect you to.'

He released her. The consciousness of defeat struck him like a blow in the chest. But in his anguish one thing remained to him: like the snake, crushed beneath the heel, that turns to deliver a poisoned bite.

'What will you do if your father is prosecuted?' he said. A horrible calm was on him now. She looked at him without comprehension.

'You'll make this obscene sacrifice to save him from further pain,' he said perseveringly. 'But what if, in the new parliament, someone stands up in the House of Commons and demands a public inquiry into the infamous conduct of Sir Thomas Fairburn at the Customs Office?' His breath was coming in sharp jabs. 'What if that person was me?'

Her lips moved involuntarily as she began to understand. He saw her expression with a deathly satisfaction.

'He once threatened to have me ruined and thrown in prison,' Charles said. 'There would be a certain justice, would there not, if I were to mark my entrance in the House by doing the same for your father?'

Lydia lowered her eyes and turned from him. 'I – I couldn't blame you if you did, Charles,' she said indistinctly. 'But if anything could destroy the love I feel for you – and always have . . . that would be it.'

'Oh! yes, oh! yes,' he cried, stung, hopeless, his vindictive anger already turning to bitter ashes. He made a sweeping sardonic gesture. 'Oh! yes, your love for me. Much joy we've had of that. A great comfort that'll be when you're married to Spencer Murrow. What difference can that make to anything? It never has yet.'

'I don't blame you for feeling like this,' she said in a low voice. 'I don't know what else I can say.'

He stared at her graceful form. All her beauty, all the hope and joy and disappointment she represented seemed to be blasted on to his sight like a flash of unbearable light, leaving behind only seared blackness.

'Well, I wish Mr Murrow luck with you, Lydia,' he said, his voice spent and sickened. He picked up his hat. 'God knows he'll need it.'

'I'm sorry if it's placed you in a difficult position with Lord Burghley, father,' Charles said.

George went to open the large parlour window: the evening was very mild. 'Oh, not really,' he said. 'There was no definite undertaking. It's just that . . .' He shrugged. 'I must confess I thought you'd jump at the chance to be in Parliament. You used to be so keen – '

'Well, one changes, you know,' Charles said, looking without seeing at the close columns of print in the *Stamford and Peterborough Courant*. 'I dare say I'm a trifle young anyway.'

'Well, as I said, I think we need some young men.' George came and sat down again and frowned at his son. 'Is it the fact of being under the patronage of a peer? Plenty of reformers are, you know.'

'No, it isn't that,' Charles said. Frances was strumming at the spinet and producing jangling discords. 'For God's sake, Fanny, leave off that dreadful noise,' Charles said irritably.

'I'm allowed to play the spinet, ain't I, mother?' Frances cried.

'Yes, but not just now, love,' Mary said.

'It's not fair! It's not my fault if Charles comes barging home all in a bad temper!' Having scored a victory, Frances beat a retreat.

'Well, it's your decision,' George said. 'But opportunities like this don't come along very often. If you were to stand another time, you might have to look further afield, pay your own expenses – '

'I'm well aware of that,' Charles said.

A glance passed between George and Mary. They knew he had been to the Fairburns', but since he had got home that evening he had said nothing about his visit. George said, with an effort at casualness; 'Did something turn up at the Fairburns' to make you feel differently?'

'Why should it?'

'Well,' said George patiently, 'as I said, someone could make a fuss about this corruption of Sir Thomas's. The man should be answerable publicly, before the law, for what he's done. And if you – '

'I dare say he should, father,' said Charles, getting up. 'But I'm not interested in it. Let it lie.'

'Charles,' said Mary, making a gesture to George not to say any more, 'Frederick Amory came to see you earlier. He said he'd call again this evening.'

It occurred to Charles that Frederick had come to give him a thrashing for breaking what amounted to a promise to Louisa; but when Frederick turned up it was more in sorrowful commiseration than anything. He'd had his heart set on them getting spliced, he said, and now that Lou said it was all off he was bitterly disappointed.

'Can't you make it up, Charles?' he said awkwardly. 'You know, it's like learning to ride a horse – when you fall off it's best to climb straight back on again. I'm sure it can all be sorted out.'

'I'm sorry, Frederick,' Charles said. 'It just wouldn't be right.' He grimaced. 'Does she think very badly of me?'

"Tisn't that,' said Frederick. 'Nor me. I know these things are delicate-like. 'Course, there'll be folk who'll gossip . . .'

'True.' Charles patted Frederick's shoulder. 'Well, I think perhaps I'll take myself off for a while. That should help.'

'Go away? Where?'

'I don't know yet. But I've got to get away.'

3

Richard was to sail for Hamburg as commander of the *Justine* at the end of August.

With the guns removed and the whole newly painted in the Yarmouth yards she was a smart ship. There were thirty crew, with a second officer and a master and mate: they were competent and willing, with the camaraderie of the merchant service, a pleasant ambience after the harsh discipline and brutality of the Navy.

Yet, Caroline knew the decision to take the position had gone against the grain of his nature. She also knew that what had turned the balance was the consideration of money – his wish to offer her a better, more secure life. That by doing so he bound himself to her father, whom he had once sworn to be independent of, was the bitter paradox.

She would be lonely when he went, she knew. They had friends in the village, and her parents would send the carriage over to bring her to Peterborough whenever she wanted, and Charles would be a frequent visitor; but though she liked company it was not that she would miss, but Richard, her husband and lover. Still, there was no other way. She knew he was a man for whom inaction, after a while, became tedium. And she hoped that the mere fact of being at sea again, of finding himself useful, might soothe the constraint she knew him to be feeling at receiving what he saw as favours from her father. That was the one thing with the potential of a wedge to come between them and spoil a marriage that had so far been such a beautiful success.

Two weeks before he was due to sail, clouds filled the sky and there was heavy rain just as they were preparing to harvest their fields. The drainage failed at Elm, and their crops were spoiled.

Elm Cottage's small enclosure was dependent for drainage, like the manor fields it adjoined, on the cut to the Old Nene over towards Emneth. A small breach in the dyke, rendered hard and fissile by the hot summer, added to the sudden downpour, was enough to put their fields under water just at the crucial time.

It was a story that had been repeated time and time again all over the fenland, and had been the ruin of many farmers. For Richard and Caroline, with their few fields of roots and beans, it was not a disaster; but living straitly as they did with little room for manoeuvre, it was a blow. They had hoped the produce would keep them through the winter, with money for extras from the market sale of the surplus.

Charles and Edmund came over from Morholm to commiserate.

'Well, Charles,' Richard said, 'does it just go to show a sailor shouldn't go meddling with a farmer's business?'

'Bit early to say that,' Charles said. 'Floods happen. I don't know. This is very powerful land, more so than at Morholm. I wonder, when the dyke's repaired, if it might be worth trying wheat and oats next year. Never mind. We've plenty of silage at Morholm for your pigs.'

There was another reason for the brothers' visit. They were planning a trip to Paris, and asked Richard and Caroline if they would care to go with them. Edmund had sold portraits of a whole merchant family in London and wanted to use the money to go to Paris to see the art treasures of the Louvre, Napoleon's plunder from the galleries of conquered Italy. Charles was ready to go anywhere as long as it was away from home. They would be happy to bear the expenses of the trip, which should not be great. A great flood of English tourists was crossing the Channel that summer to see the new France of Napoleon Bonaparte that had risen from the confusion of the Revolution: there was a strong urge to travel after ten years of siege in the 'tight little island'.

Richard's sailing so soon put it out of the question, of course. Caroline was disappointed, for the idea greatly attracted her, but it couldn't be helped. She did not realize that Richard had perceived her disappointment, until that evening, when they went for a walk down to the river.

'There's no reason why you shouldn't go,' Richard said.

She looked at him in surprise. 'To France?'

'You would like to, wouldn't you?'

'Well, yes. But I'd rather go with you.'

'I'd rather you went with me. But it would be a pity to miss this opportunity. It'll be winter soon. And besides . . .' He took her hand and held it. 'When I'm at sea, I don't really have time to brood. Of course I'll miss you, but there's so much to do, I'm constantly occupied . . . and I don't like to think of you here, alone, not enjoying life.'

'But I do like it at Elm, Richard. I'm not discontented.'

'Bless you. I suppose what I'm trying to say is you've not had much of a life – in terms of happiness. Oh, perhaps as a girl, but then – you suffered a great deal. That time in London. Your child. You do think of that sometimes, don't you?'

'I – sometimes.'

'And the more you're left alone here, with nothing to occupy your mind, the more that will, well, come back to you.'

She squeezed his hand, touched by his perception. 'There's truth in what you say, love. But you've changed all that. You've brought me more than my share of happiness.'

'Have I?' He looked warmly, possessively at her. 'I hope so. But I hope I'm not one of these husbands who wants his wife to sit quietly at home waiting for him while he's at sea for months on end. I want you to have more, Caroline. And as for me, well, I've seen plenty of foreign parts, so it wouldn't be as if I was missing out. And I know you'd be safe with Charles and Edmund. By all accounts Paris is full of English people just now anyway. What do you say?'

She stopped and kissed him. 'I would like to go. And if you don't mind, then I will. But it's only because I can't be with you at the time that I'll even think of it. When you're home, that's where I want to be. With you. That's where my happiness is, Richard.'

'Very well then. But one condition. It's kind of your cousins to offer to pay the expenses, but I'd rather we paid a share.'

'Can we afford it?'

441

'Well, I'll have a bonus from this voyage. And Charles reckons ten days in France will cost little enough. I called on Squire's Bank when I went into Peterborough the other day and we're on an even keel.' They walked on. 'In fact, with these boom conditions we could do better. Mr Squire was telling me of several investments that he's made for smaller clients of late. Of course your money is in three per cents – '

'*Our* money.'

'Well. Our money is in three per cents, which are solid. But there are other things. East India stock. The new manufactures in the North. The peace has opened up investment.'

'Speculating? I don't know. Perhaps I have more of my uncle George's landowner-blood in me than I thought. I've always rather mistrusted that sort of speculation.'

'So have I. But there are such opportunities now, and instead of standing still like we are – '

'Richard. For richer for poorer, remember? I have everything I want. We're still young. Perhaps you should ask my father's advice before you go any further.'

'Perhaps,' he said after a moment. 'Still, it's worth bearing in mind. A little more money, and when you go to France you could bring back some of those shocking Parisian gowns we hear so much about.'

'So, your appetites are jaded already, sir?'

He glanced mischievously at her. 'What do you think?'

She passed her arm through his as they turned back for home. 'Paris!' she said. 'Strange. I shall be expecting to see guillotines everywhere. And *sans-culottes* with severed heads on pikes. I shall be able to tell Mrs Butterworth I was in the same city as Napoleon Bonaparte and lived to tell the tale!'

CHAPTER 4

1

Caroline, with her cousins Charles and Edmund, and Jim Benwick, a manservant from Morholm, set off for Dover at the end of August.

Richard was due to sail in two days' time. He was glad of the leeway this allowed him, to do something he had been thinking of for some time. With an advance on his pay, he ordered a Broadwood's pianoforte for Elm Cottage. It should be there in the parlour when Caroline returned from France, when he would still be at sea. She would like that.

It took another bite out of their income, of course. But the idea planted by the banker Mr Squire had taken root in his mind. Surely now was the time to speculate and take advantage of the buoyant markets? Caroline had wanted him to ask her father's advice, but privately, though not saying as much to her, he was resolved against that. No doubt Luke knew much more than he did about these matters; but he already controlled so much of Richard's life. Too much. For once, Richard was determined, he would act independently. Here was a way to be able to say to Caroline in a year, in six months, 'By the way, love, we can buy Elm Cottage.' And *he* would have done it. Not through borrowing, not through favours, not through ploughing her father's furrow.

She said she was content, and he believed her. But his own sense of security was always precarious, and he wanted her to have more.

Dover, which for years had been bristling with grim, fortified readiness for war, reflected the new attitude of England that summer of 1802. Life had been dour and embattled for a long time. Now the cartoons left off their bellicose images of John Bull squaring up to Boney: instead he was shown in cheerful reunion with his old friends beef and beer and butter. Pleasure was no longer a thing to be guilty about. The theatres and the parks and the spas were full again; families flocked to the new sea-resorts, Weymouth and Brighton and Southend, to try the beneficial effects of sea-bathing, in the shadow of the abandoned beacon-towers.

The Hardwicks made the journey to Dover on the London mail-coach, but there were several private carriages on the Dover road, gleaming yellow and red, with liveried coachmen and postilions, making for the same destination. The great Dover inns, the City of London and the York Hotel, were full of English travellers. In the supper-room of the City of London where they put up for the night there was a large and full-voiced party of fine gentlemen and ladies who were loudly complaining of the food, the coffee, the service, the beds . . . What would the Republican French think of them, Caroline wondered? The men with their starched collars and frills and their pinched faces expressing high-born *sang-froid*, the women powdered and hatted, fingering jewelled necklaces, upbraiding the servants in hard confident voices: they seemed the very type of arrogant, effete *aristos* the Revolution had done away with. Caroline said something of this to Charles, hoping to draw him out, for he had been quiet on the journey.

'As if they owned the whole country,' Charles said. 'Which, of course, they do.'

For his own part he was anxious to be off and across the Channel in the morning. Restless activity was the only thing that was bearable for him. He had, he supposed, a curiosity to see the egalitarian republic at last, but he was running away from rather than towards something. The horrible, complete loss of Lydia – the horrible *circumstances* of it – afflicted him like a painful debilitating disease. And it was aggravated by his own self-disgust. The prospect of aptest revenge had been held out to him, of going into Parliament and exposing Sir Thomas Fairburn, of delivering the death-blow to the detested man; but the relish he should have felt at that had turned to ashes in his mouth even as he had travelled home from Newmarket that dreadful day. There was no satisfaction in it. There was no satisfaction to be had from the whole business. In the end, his bemused father had decided, pressed by Lord Burghley, to stand for Stamford again, and had been duly elected.

If it were only Charles who had been hurt it would not have been so bad. But his behaviour towards Louisa Amory was a constant, burning shame to him. He should never have allowed himself to have become involved in the first place. That was a great wrong to her. She herself had loaded him with no reproaches, but the Misses Emmonsales at the Rectory had soon spread a story around the neighbourhood of Morholm that featured broken promises, trifling with affections, jilting, caddish behaviour – even that old Mr Humphrey Amory had taken a horsewhip to Charles. But they could not paint him any blacker than he saw himself. Weak, he had been weak, he knew, and it was a bitter knowledge.

Both Caroline and Edmund, however, were in high

spirits the next day, when they boarded the Calais packet-ship in brilliant August sunshine, with the coast of France a visible smear in the distance. The sailing was delayed by the aristocratic party, who were taking their own carriage and horses, and made a great fuss about the boarding; but when at last they set sail there was a fair wind, and by noon they were, in company with a great crowd of coasters, fishing-boats and merchant ships, facing the fortifications, the ramparts and drawbridges and watch-towers, of Calais, and a pilot-boat was guiding them into the friendly harbour of a nation which for a decade they had been taught was the bloodthirsty enemy of humanity.

They stowed their luggage at the Hôtel de Dessein, the chief inn of the port, and over a meal at the *table d'hôte* discussed the best way of proceeding to Paris. The *diligences*, the big unwieldy coaches that were the equivalent of England's stage-coaches, left for Paris at frequent intervals, but they had a poor reputation for speed and comfort. They decided instead to hire a post-chaise, which cost three *louis*, something over three pounds, and proceed at their leisure. They agreed also that at the inns on the way they would eat privately where possible: the custom of the *table d'hôte*, where all the guests sat down at the same table and competed for the general fare, meant that the most thrustful people got the most food – in their case that had been their aristocratic friends. It was just about the only thing that struck strangely so far. Calais was full of English people and most of the natives spoke English: as Caroline remarked, it didn't *feel* like France.

They set off for Paris in the morning in clear sunshine, leaving the bulk of their luggage to be sent on from Dessein's. The country of Artois through which they passed was flat and gentle, with occasional stretches of woodland, reminding Caroline of parts of Norfolk, though the carriage-road was much better. It was harvest, and they saw many people working in the fields: women especially, in lappet-caps and aprons, often with their legs and feet bare. The enclosures were small, and the villages through which they passed modest and self-contained; there was not the busy traffic and commerce of the English coach-roads. There were glimpses to be seen, through open cottage-doors and in market-places, of the material benefits brought by the Revolution to the peasantry: polished pewter and copper, neat clothes, abundant vegetables, smoking chimneys. They saw no mob-demolished châteaux, though they saw several new villas of the *bourgeois* standing back from the road. Once they caught sight of a gutted convent building and, when they put up at Arras for the night, a ruined church; but the landlord of the *Clef d'Or* Inn told them that it was being restored: Bonaparte had given the people back their religion and it had enhanced his popularity.

Eschewing the *table d'hôte*, they ate supper in their bedrooms, for French inns did not have the supper-rooms and curtained booths that made English inns so comfortable. But the meal was excellent: soup, sweetbread and green peas, two chickens, and veal cutlets, with biscuits, peaches and plums, liqueurs and a bottle of wine, all for 40 sous, less than two shillings. The earth-closet was a less pleasant surprise: the drone of the flies could be heard down the corridor. And Caroline was disconcerted by the spitting. One gentleman stood aside very civilly for her at the foot of the stairs, but at the same time let fly a gob of spittle that narrowly missed her skirts.

They continued at a leisurely pace the next day, stopping at Amiens to view the cathedral. It was a bustling town, with many cloth-workers, and merchants' houses, and here for the first time soldiers were much in evidence, cavalrymen clattering through the narrow streets in buskins and plumed shakos. Everywhere, in village and town, the travellers were met with friendliness. Despite the years of war there was no hostility: one man eagerly wanted to shake hands with *les anglais* – had they not made peace, so we could all go back to ease and prosperity?

On the splendid gravel roads they continued through Picardy, in a country of woodland, small meadows, fruit-trees and Lombardy poplars: as Charles remarked, no evidence of the kind of large-scale scientific farming seen in England. They put up for the night at Liancourt. It was beginning to feel most definitely a foreign country. They were amongst the first vineyards here: the woman who waited on them at the *Belle Image* Inn wore wooden sabots and a red camlet jacket; there was garlic and a rich strong coffee quite different from the stuff they drank in England. After supper Charles got hold of a newspaper, the *Moniteur*, and with Caroline's help read some of it; but he was disappointed. 'Bonaparte has taken the press in hand,' he said. 'Sadly he seems to be learning from the old Bourbons in the ways of authoritarian government.'

It had been a long, tiring day, but Caroline could not sleep. She supposed that in coming to France she should have expected to be reminded of Antoine Clairet, but somehow she had thought herself proof against the insistent memories that were pressing in on her more and more forcibly as they travelled towards Paris. Perhaps it was hearing French spoken all around her that did it. Whatever it was, the image of him came back to her more vividly than it ever had since he had left her at Yarmouth over two years ago.

There was certainly no nostalgia or longing attached to the image. Her feelings were sharp and mature and trenchant. She thought of how she had proposed running off to France with him and how he had calmly accepted it. She saw now how absurd the idea was of her coming to this strange country with him and just 'settling in'. If her youth was some excuse for the naïveté – though she wasn't sure about that – there was certainly no such justification for him. She saw now how he must have known all the time the impossibility of the plan, not just in the fact that he was already married, but in the whole atmosphere of feverish girlish optimism in which she had been carried along. It must have given him many a bemused smile in the privacy of his room in Little's Yard. And she thought again of the Norman Cross prisoners she had seen with Richard at Wisbech that spring, laughing and relieved, on their way to freedom after bearing their imprisonment with patience and fortitude: she thought of the warmth and hope infused by the unknown prisoner into the straw tower he had crafted – put away in the attic at Elm now – and how Antoine Clairet had managed to slide his way back to freedom, evading everything, evading responsibility, using, destroying, like a heedless child: back to the arms of his wife and the comfortable farm at Torcy. And at some point – perhaps at the moment before drifting into sleep – the idea came into her mind, just an idea, a speculation, of how sweet, how fitting it would be if she were to turn up at his house, confronting him with the fact that she had survived: him and his *wife* . . . to break in and destroy the security of his life as he had hers.

The approach to Paris was not, like the approach to London, a succession of villages and suburbs and brickyards and industries and swelling traffic: they seemed to go straight from country to city, and moreover there was not the great mantle of thick coal-smoke that often obscured London entirely. But once inside the city, past the grand new approach of the Norman Barrier with its huge pillars and a long avenue of elms, their progress was extremely slow, caught as their post-chaise was in a bewildering concourse of ponderous country waggons, laden asses, *diligences*, laundry-carts, one-horse cabriolets, and *fiacres*, the hackney-coaches of Paris, with their bony underfed horses fearsomely belaboured with the whip by the cursing drivers. They had the whole city to traverse to get to the Faubourg St Germain, where the Hôtel des Cordeliers had been recommended to them. It was dusk by the time they had settled into their set of rooms, on the third floor, shabbily furnished but airy; and they were so tired they ignored the strange noisy streets that beckoned them and went straight to bed.

They were awoken next morning by the cry of a water-seller with his cart in the street outside, and over the next few days, as they explored the capital of the *Grand Nation*, it became familiar to them, for it seemed fresh water was hard to come by in Paris. It was impossible not to be fascinated. Charles seemed to wake somewhat out of his impenetrable mood, and take his old interest in things political and social. Caroline was glad, for in the absence of Richard she wanted someone to share her enjoyment with. Edmund, with his long sleepy eyelashes and dreamer's face and phlegmatic temperament, was by nature undemonstrative and, besides, he spent most of the time in the Louvre. One visit there was enough for Caroline and Charles: the long galleries of paintings and sculpture, all the plundered riches of Italy crammed together, made an experience that was curiously oppressive. Edmund went even quieter, and in the evening Caroline saw him take out the sketchbook he had brought and gaze at it. At last he sighed and murmured: 'I shall have to start all over again.'

As much as they could they explored on foot, for the *fiacres*, negotiating the thick traffic, were nerve-jangling and expensive. Several times along the boulevards they spotted the unmistakable sight of English carriages: the French had never invaded England, but it seemed as if in peace the English had invaded France that summer. The hotels and restaurants were full of them. They had come either to be sceptical or dazzled by the new Paris, and probably most of them, like Caroline and Charles, felt a mixture of the two.

There was a lot of rebuilding going on: in some places there was a choked medieval squalor, in others the broad new streets had been laid out to great effect in the neo-classical style that was influencing everything. The city bore the scars of its recent history. Many of the great mansions of the nobility in the Faubourg St Honoré had been converted into ballrooms and baths and the ubiquitous restaurants – a type of establishment completely new to the English travellers, where one could eat at separate tables choosing from a bill of fare, and a very welcome one to Caroline and Charles. They were amused to find in the Rue de Richelieu a *Taverne anglaise*, which served, expensively as befitted foreign delicacies, roast beef with boiled vegetables.

There seemed to be a great vitality about the capital, as if the springs of energy released by the Revolution were still bubbling. People thronged the public gardens, the Luxembourg, the Tuileries, parading and promenading: the gardens were much more formal than English parks, with many fountains and much statuary. Martial statues and columns seemed to be everywhere. There were brilliant shops, gaudy with silk and ormolu and bronze and gilding and great mirrors and gold hangings. There were coffee-houses, rotisseurs, billiard-halls, dancing-rooms, and a frank enjoyment of gambling – there seemed to be a lottery-office in every street. And there were the theatres, many more than in London. On their second night Caroline and Charles went to the Comédie-Française and were ruefully forced to admit that the acting, the singing, the music, the scenery, the very building, which was circular like a temple, made the London theatres seem dreadfully feeble. But then even the streets seemed theatrical. In the Boulevard du Temple they saw tumblers and jugglers, and rope-dancers and egg-dancers who blindfolded cut nimble capers between patterns of gaily painted eggs; there were mountebanks crying up quack remedies and sellers of *tisane*, barley-water, with great kegs and jugs mounted on their shoulders.

They went to the Palais Royal to see the famous pillared arcades of shops, and found themselves caught up in the afternoon promenade of the *demi-mondaines*. Nothing was quite what it seemed: many of the gorgeous jeweller's and hairdresser's and draper's shops were genuine, but often one saw a shabby staircase at the side leading to cafés and gaming-rooms and other rooms, and Caroline innocently entered a 'milliner's' to find no hats and no pretence of hats. Supping later in a restaurant in the Palais Royal called *Les Trois Frères Provençaux* they met up with some fellow English travellers who were highly shocked at the immorality and vulgarity of it all. One scarcely saw a single well-bred face, they complained: all the money was new, and how it showed; and the fashions were positively indecent.

Certainly they were striking. The emulation of classical Greece and Rome was marked in the costume of the ladies. The muslin gowns were of the finest, slightest, most transparent material, with shoulders and arms bare, flesh-coloured stockings and sandals and a minimum of underclothing: the hair was cut short and full and anointed with oil. In the interval at the theatre the *citoyennes* stood in groups and formed elongated, waistless, diaphanous shapes as if on a classical frieze. The men wore cropped, natural hair, huge coloured neckcloths, elements of military uniform – hessians, hussar boots, cockaded hats – tight pantaloons, or, strangely enough, costume *à l'anglais* – the practical, basically egalitarian dress of the English country gentleman. Yes, Caroline and Charles agreed, perhaps there was vulgarity, but it had the breath of fresh air about it; and the most eager *habitués* of the upper rooms of the Palais Royal seemed to be the visiting Englishmen.

And the centre of this thrusting confident society was the court of the First Consul, the conqueror of Italy, the victor of Marengo, the little Corsican who had reinstated religion, brought back the *émigrés*, saved France from the debilitating corruption of the Directory and made himself the cynosure of all Europe. On their fourth day the Hardwicks made friends with two young married English couples from Kent, tourists like themselves, who had influential friends and had gained an entrance to one of the levées that had been continually held as part of the celebrations, still going on, for Napoleon Bonaparte's birthday several weeks ago. The two couples – confusingly, the Browns and the Brownings – regaled them with descriptions of the magnificence of the consular apartments in the Palace of the Tuileries, the silk and ivory and gold, contrasted with the modest bearing of the First Consul himself, who, defiantly un-aristocratic, shared the one bedroom with Madame Bonaparte. And it was they who helped them get the best places at the review of the troops in the Place du Carrousel, where, with a large group of gaping English travellers, they got a fair view of Bonaparte as he took the salute of his brilliantly uniformed guards. He rode at the head of a train of bemedalled generals and his own Mameluke orderlies dressed in exotically coloured Egyptian costume: ambassadors and legations of all Europe followed him in Court dress;

the sun glinted on polished brass and silver and the points of uplifted sabres, and the arena thundered with wild cheering. He was a small man but not a dwarf as the caricatures portrayed him, and he looked pale rather than swarthy, with a high brow and cropped hair. His own dress was plain, the uniform of the Chasseur Guards: a black cocked hat without lace and blue coat and white breeches. He looked determined and alert and every inch a soldier. For a few moments there passed before the eyes of Caroline, Charles and Edmund the mortal flesh, unadorned but by no means unimpressive, of a man whose name had already gathered to itself a misty screen of heroic legend; and then the procession was gone.

After that, they went to see the guillotine left as a monument in the Place de la Concorde, formerly the Place de la Revolution, but it was something of a disappointment. Caroline had ghoulishly imagined it towering into the sky but it was not large at all. They also went to the Opéra, and though this again was far superior to anything in England, it was here that both Caroline and Charles suddenly found themselves irritated with the constant presence of soldiery in Paris: they even kept order in the pit of the opera-house. Coming from England, where even in spite of the martial spirit of the last few years the army was mistrusted and kept out of sight, it was oppressive to be constantly surrounded by saluting, marching figures, creaking with leather and webbing, or else the frozen poses of military statues.

'The power, the order they like so much, is founded on the military,' Charles said. 'One knew it, of course, but all the same . . . it's disappointing that it should be so flagrant.'

The Browns and Brownings were preparing to leave Paris and go on a tour down to Orléans and back through Normandy towards Calais; and when they asked the

Hardwicks to go with them they were glad to accept. They had been a week in Paris: Edmund had absorbed as much of the Louvre as he could take without being overwhelmed, and Caroline and Charles felt that, in spite of what Parisians said, Paris was not all France.

Moreover, when they looked at the Browns' map and planned an itinerary, Caroline saw they would travel in the vicinity of Alençon. Slightly dry-mouthed, she suggested they should go there on the route: she had heard much about the famous Alençon lace-factory. Everyone agreed, and no one thought her suggestion strange – as why should they? The village of Torcy, of course, was not on the map. She even thought it quite possible that Antoine Clairet had invented the whole place, the farm, the ruined tower among the trees. Well, there could be no harm in travelling through Alençon anyway.

Orléans, which they came to after two days travelling from Paris through a flat, populous countryside of quarries and tilled fields and woods, had somehow an air of greater reality than the capital. It was large, perhaps the size of Norwich or Bristol, and there seemed to be more trade than parade: boats and barges crowded the quay on the Loire, bringing timber and wine and grain, and there was a heavy sweet smoke from the sugar refineries. Once again, however, there were the ubiquitous barracks.

'I don't know what to think,' Charles said in the post-chaise, when they set out again from Orléans. 'Military institutions must always be prejudicial to freedom. Yet the people seem to love Bonaparte. They're prosperous and France is a conquering nation. He's taken so much power to himself – I wonder if they realize quite how much. The Senate, the Legislative Assembly, the Tribune, it's all dependent on his will. So much is centralized: from him come the appointments of Prefects and city

455

mayors. And he's taken education in hand, which is a good thing, but from what I can gather that too is made military. A sort of Spartan ideal. Oh, I see the appeal. After the corruption of the Bourbons, what the country needed in the end was good government. But – '

'Too much government?' Caroline said.

Charles sighed. 'I'm sad that the press has been muzzled. Even more than in England, if that's possible. You know, for years, I and a few like me looked to France as the sun of freedom. Well, if not the sun, at least the place where men tried to put the ideals of liberty into practice, where the hope of a new world was kept alive. Now, I have a horrible feeling that Bonaparte's next move will be to get rid of his wife and marry some little German princess. Now that would be the end.'

They were travelling now in truly rural France, and people working in the fields stopped to stare at the Hardwicks' post-chaise and the Brown-Brownings' carriage. Through Perche and into the well-watered country of South Normandy the country became increasingly rich. The soil was a dark loam: there were lush green pastures, enclosed by red mud walls, with fat cattle, and plantations of fruit trees. This was the land to which Antoine Clairet had longed to return, at any price.

They reached Alençon in the evening, seeing in the red dusk a market town of handsome substantial stone houses and church towers, and put up at the *Lion d'Or* Inn in the Place Lamagdeleine. There was no avoiding the *table d'hôte* this time, but there were only a couple of wool merchants at the long deal table, and there was plenty of food to go round: eels, sole, ducks, roast mutton, salad, Camembert cheese, apple pie swimming in cream, and the local liqueur, Calvados, a powerful apple brandy. Fortified with Calvados, and making sure none of the others heard, Caroline casually asked one of the merchants if

456

there was a village called Torcy near here. To be sure, he said, only about a league to the north of the town, on the Sées road.

She was startled that it should be so close. And her whole being was suddenly shaken with the conviction that she should do it.

As she undressed for bed a voice told her that she was a happily married woman and the bitterness of the past was over. She should leave well alone. But natural human curiosity got the better of her, for it had a powerful ally in the vague sweet notion of revenge. Time had not created forgiveness in her heart. She had been wounded so deeply by Clairet that there had been a long period of numbness before the full force of resentment had risen to the surface. The sight of this fat peaceful country where he lived, contrasted with the memory of her painful lonely childbed in a grim lying-in hospital, had intensified it.

Probably he would not be there. Perhaps he had moved, or decided to go to sea again after all. But she would go and see.

She rose early the next morning, knowing that the others, after a hard day's travel, would not stir before nine. Jim Benwick, the Morholm manservant – he had taken France in his stride and picked up in a week enough French phrases to manage a comprehensible sort of argot – was up and talking to the maid in the dining-parlour.

'Jim, could you fancy a ride this morning?' Caroline said. 'I thought to go out to a village near here and enquire after a family we were introduced to. Could we hire a couple of ponies, d'you suppose?'

To ride out alone, she realized, would be seen as strange and risky. Jim Benwick had been remote from the Clairet business and would suspect nothing. He had no trouble in procuring the ponies, and presently they were riding out of the cobbled streets of Alençon, past weavers' cottages and packhorses and the two-wheeled carts of farmers coming in to market, into a tamed pastoral country of droning bees and earthy scents, with the dark mass of the Forest d'Ecouves on their left.

Caroline's heart missed a beat when the ruined tower of an old château came into sight above a small copse. The tower. It was as disconcerting as if the landscape of a dream should prove to be real.

'This the place, ma'am?' Benwick said.

'Yes . . . yes, I believe so.'

A modest handsome village of stone cottages, a few old timber-framed houses, a tavern, a stream and watermill. Torcy. She rode a little ahead of Benwick, her heart beating fast. She stopped a woman driving a few geese and asked for *la maison Clairet*. The woman pointed down the village street.

The house stood back from the road behind a thatched mud wall. It was somewhere between a large farmhouse and a manor, built of stone with a mansard roof and several chimneys. On one side was a row of pear trees, on the other a brick stable and yard and several outbuildings. Birds were singing. It was charming and peaceful. It was a peace she could shatter.

'Will you wait here, Jim?' she said, dismounting at the gates. 'I shouldn't be long.'

She walked down the path towards the front door, and as she did so a man emerged from the stables to her left, whistling and carrying an empty pail. He was dressed in waistcoat and shirt sleeves, rough breeches and boots. '*Bonjour, madame*,' he called out, coming towards her. '*Puis-je vous aider?*'

'Hello, Antoine,' she said.

Six feet away from her he stopped. The pail fell out of his hand and rolled away on the grass.

He had put on weight: he looked sleek and tanned. He looked like a prosperous gentleman-farmer. He looked as if he were going to faint.

'Caroline,' he stammered, staring at her as if she were a ghost. 'Caroline, oh, *mon Dieu, ce n'est pas possible* . . . what do you do here?'

'Why, I've come to see you, Antoine,' she said, and she was horribly, exultantly conscious of power, and of hate, and of the two swelling within her. 'I've come a long way. Aren't you going to ask me in?'

He stared and stared. He was white as death. She had never seen such pure and naked fear: she felt that if she were to take a step towards him he would fall down gibbering at her feet.

'Are you – alone?' he said at last, the words torn from his throat, and he looked wildly around.

'There's a servant at the gates with the horses,' she said. 'That's all. No, I haven't brought my father – or my husband. Though I'm sure he'd like to meet you.' She lifted her hand to untie the strings of her bonnet, and he flinched. 'You're looking well, Antoine. *Confortable. Bourgeois.*'

'You are – married?'

'Oh, yes, does that surprise you? And how is Madame Clairet – what was the name, Amélie?'

'She – is in the house . . . Caroline, you should not be here. Believe me, I am grateful, eternally grateful for what you did for me, but – '

'*Grateful.*' Her fingers tightened round her riding-crop. She could manage a good blow across the face from here, several probably, he did not look in a way to resist. 'Oh, well, that's all right then. Antoine Clairet is grateful, so my life hasn't been in vain. And what about the little Clairets, are there any yet? Or do you confine that sort of thing to your affairs with silly, trusting English girls?'

For a moment he obviously did not understand. Then his face crumpled. 'Oh, no, no, *Dieu*, it is not true, it cannot be – '

'Oh, don't trouble yourself about it, Antoine,' she said. 'But then you never do, do you? You like to keep truth and reality at a nice safe distance. Unfortunately I'm not at a nice safe distance any more. I'm here. I couldn't come on a tour in France without visiting you, could I? You and Madame Clairet.'

He gave a panicked glance back at the house, took a step towards her, trembling, sweating. 'Caroline, please, I beg of you, please go away. We – it was all a long time ago, a different world, a little madness, yes, a little madness of the wartime . . . Amélie is in the house, she must not, we must not – think what you like of me, but please, please go . . .'

'Why, you poor man, you're afraid of her!' said Caroline. 'How many lies have you told her, too? Is she like you? Or can she take a dose of good strong truth?'

'Caroline, no – please . . .'

His energy seemed to run out. He stood paralysed, hunched, his eyes desperately imploring, mutely abandoned to her will. And suddenly the ground-bass of contempt that underscored her feelings for him took up the whole theme. Contempt. This quivering jelly of a man, all complacence and then all fear, afraid of her, afraid of his wife . . . A man of straw. She could blow him away with one breath. And he was so pitiful as not to be worth it. The grandeur of revenge required a grand object. And she saw now that her life had moved beyond this impoverished soul: she had lifted the knife, but there was no need to strike it home. Coming here had accomplished a purpose rather different from the one she had anticipated. She had seen enough. She was free of him.

She turned to look at the house, the flowers in the

460

window-boxes, smoke curling from a chimney, barns and buttery, fields beyond the pear-trees. The Clairet estate. The fat of the land. No doubt all that rich Normandy cream had put that weight on him. Let him enjoy it, to the full capacity of his chilled, confined little heart. It must be terrible to be weak and not know it.

'Well,' she said. 'Benwick will be tired of waiting. We're staying in the district – perhaps I'll call again.'

She left him that to chew on, but she knew quite well, as she walked back to the gates, that she need not come again. She did not look back.

'No,' she said to Benwick as she remounted her pony, 'not the right family. Never mind.'

The party set out from Alençon that noon, after visiting the lace-factory, on the coach-road north to Rouen.

Caroline could say nothing to the others, of course, of where she had been that morning. But though she did not know it, perhaps Charles might have understood her feelings, after going in exultant hate and finding it all turned to pitying contempt: he too had seen the tower revealed as an illusion of one dimension only. But for him the experience had ended in bitterness, and Caroline felt liberated.

But, she could say nothing. And she felt with a curious conviction that she could not even say anything of it to Richard. This was something private to her. It touched Richard, insofar as her love for him was strengthened and deepened, and her appreciation of him as a man thrown into even brighter relief by the despicable spectacle of Antoine Clairet. Indeed, it was as if, after their whirlwind marriage and brief time together, she was struck for the first time by the full force of her love for Richard: she apprehended suddenly the sheer beautiful fact of him, rather as if she had suspected these recent months of her life, for all her happiness, might be a treacherous dream. A residue of bitterness from the Clairet affair had made her hold back a little: it had prevented her from ever being quite sure that what she had was real and lasting. Now that residue was gone, and she could bring to the marriage a whole heart.

But Clairet was one subject that could chill and wither the profoundest and most subtly intertwined roots of their mutual love: she supposed it could hardly be otherwise. She felt that Richard, so understanding, would not understand what she had done; the heat of honourable emotion would blast the cool surfaces of reason. Clairet must be left in the past. And for herself, she knew now that at last she had left him there and closed the gate.

They still had three days touring in France, and she liked the great city of Rouen, with its incomparable cathedral and narrow medieval streets and humming cotton-mills, better than anywhere they had visited; but they were all becoming surfeited with sightseeing and with statues and pediments proclaiming *Liberté*. And for Caroline, the abiding image of the trip was Antoine Clairet, quivering and feeble in shirt-sleeves in front of his snug smug house.

They made the journey back to Calais with the Brown-Brownings, and at Dessein's Inn, waiting for a fair wind for the Dover packet, they found the same stridently aristocratic party that they had made the crossing with. They were as loudly dissatisfied as ever; France, they had found, was a country of upstarts and parvenus, no breeding, the horses were wretched and the stables worse, they gave it a year and the whole system would collapse, they'd be begging for a Restoration.

'They may as well have stayed at home,' said Edmund, making a rare pronouncement of opinion. 'They've seen only what they wanted to see. Whatever else this France is going to do, it's not going to collapse.'

462

CHAPTER 5

1

The pianoforte was standing in the corner of the parlour when Caroline came home to Elm.

She had been wishing sadly that Richard could be there to greet her, and this wonderful gesture melted her entirely.

She was also a little worried. A pianoforte was an expensive article. She had already spent more than their accustomed housekeeping as her share of the expenses in France. Her pleasure in touching the pianoforte's white ivory keys was mingled with a little guilt. She had always sought to hide the fact that she missed an instrument. But then Richard was particularly good at quietly perceiving what you thought was entirely concealed in your heart.

'Oh, Richard,' she said, when he returned to Elm from his Baltic voyage at the end of October, 'you're that good to me.'

Her expression was so doleful as she said it that he laughed. 'You make it sound as if I were *bad* to you.'

'No, no. I do love it so but – well, when did you last buy a new coat or pipe or – or have anything for yourself?'

'I had something for myself on the 9th of January this year, when you became my wife,' he said. 'That will do for me for a long time yet.'

She embraced and kissed him. 'You smell different, somehow. Can it be the sea?'

Richard laughed. 'That's a nice way of putting it. Bathing facilities are rudimentary even on a smart ship

463

like the *Justine*.' He put his nose close to her cheek. '*You're* still as sweet as ever, though. God, I've missed you.' He burrowed his lips into her neck.

'Do you get nothing to eat on that ship, sir?'

'Nothing as good as you. So tell me. How did you like our old enemies across the water?'

'I'll tell you after you've had some supper. And you can tell me about the fleshpots of Hamburg.'

'Fleshpots! I've seen none of those in Hamburg. A very business-like town full of God-fearing burghers with round bellies. And stern *fraus* with weather-beaten complexions.'

While he ate supper she and Mrs Welney heated water for a bath and carried the tin tub and ewers up to the bedroom. Caroline helped Mrs Welney clear away and then went upstairs again and softly opened the bedroom door. In the bath Richard, with soap in his eyes, was blindly groping about for a towel. His naked back was shining in the orange afterglow of dusk.

She crept up, picking up the towel, and put her hand on his wet shoulder. 'Oh, Mester Lindsay,' she said in Mrs Welney's voice, 'scrub your ba-ack, shall I?'

He blinked through startled smarting eyes, seized the towel from her and wiped his face. 'Why did I get a tormentor for a wife?' he said, then made a grab and seized her hand. 'Room for two – coming in?'

'Richard – no, Richard, no, please!' She almost over-balanced as he tugged her but at the last managed to pull herself from his slippery grasp and danced away across the room. Richard flung a towel around his waist and went after her. When he finally caught her he toppled her down on to the bed. 'Richard, you're wet!' she said.

'So are you, now,' he said, kissing her and then beginning to tickle her in a place where he knew she was

464

very ticklish. 'No, Richard, love – no!' her voice rose as she tried to wriggle away.

He laughed. 'Shh. Mrs Welney will think I'm beating you.'

'Which you are. Brute.' She suddenly hugged and kissed him, her hands roaming over his back and shoulders and damp hair. She wanted him and it burned through her. His hands began to go slowly over her flanks and breasts. She sighed. She opened her eyes to look at him, naked above her, and then at the ormolu clock by the bed. 'Dear me,' she said primly. 'And only seven o'clock . . .'

'Not decent,' he said.

'Not decent at all,' she said, touching his nipples with her thumbs.

He reached over and opened the clock-face and turned the hands forward. 'There,' he said. 'Now it's night.'

Later, with the parlour windows open on the cool blue night, they sat together on the old oak settle. She told him of her experiences in France – omitting mention of her meeting with Antoine Clairet. She was more than ever convinced that she should say nothing of that to Richard. Marriage, she supposed, was meant to be a temple of absolute confidentiality. But Clairet was the grim past and Richard the bright future and she was resolved they would not touch.

Cold settled in early, with penetrating mist and fog. Fog on the fens was like nowhere else. On November evenings, when they closed the heavy curtains and added dried turf to the fire, Elm Cottage might have been a ship at sea. The great flat distances were grey, shifting, and enigmatic: the world seemed to lose all shape and coherence, resolving into something that was neither earth nor water.

The sunny mood of England's summer of peace began to chill too. In September Napoleon had annexed Piedmont to France and in October sent troops into Switzerland, to the disquiet of many in England. The lasting amicability between what Addington had named the two greatest nations of the world was showing signs of severe strain. There was contention over the terms of the Treaty of Amiens, both sides accusing the other of disregarding and manipulating them. The accession of Lord Castlereagh to the Cabinet was a sign of stiffening attitudes: his instructions to the new British Ambassador in Paris were to take a stand on the right of England to her say in the affairs of the Continent, a principle renounced at the Peace; and the British had refused to evacuate the garrison of Malta. A collision seemed more and more likely.

At the beginning of December Richard skippered one of Luke's small coasters, whose master was ill, up to Newcastle, and he was back in time for Christmas, which they spent, together with the family from the Bridge House, at Morholm.

George was back from the new Parliament to which, promising himself and Mary it would be the last time, he had been elected as Member for Stamford. Morholm, alone amongst its neighbours, still held old-fashioned Christmases, with evergreens, Yule-log, a feast and gifts for the local people, and a good deal of ale and punch and conviviality. Caroline loved it. She was surprised and disappointed that Charles was not there. He was travelling in Scotland with an old schoolfriend.

'Like me at that age,' George commented. 'Could never sit in the same place for five minutes at a time.'

All the same, George privately knew that his son's malaise was more deeply rooted. He did not know all the details of his disastrous involvement with Lydia and Sir Thomas Fairburn, but he had made some shrewd guesses

– and also about his guilt over what he saw as his irresponsible behaviour to Louisa Amory. The militarist nature of Napoleon's France, of which Charles had hoped so much, as he had admitted to George, had disillusioned him. Somehow a scar had been drawn across his spirit at an unfortunate age; an exceptionally open, generous nature had shrunk and drawn in on itself at the wound. Only time would tell if the breach was fundamental.

The snow began just after Christmas, and when 1803 dawned in the fens the fields were one expanse of dazzling white, broken only by blobs of dirty yellow where sheep searched patiently for grass on the droves. The dykes and flood-meadows were glazed with dark ice, and the air crackled with the sharp whizzing sounds of fen-skaters, faces frozen into exhilaration by the bitter scourging of the wind.

In Elm Cottage draughts whipped through the old windows, and Caroline longed to tear them out and replace them with new sashes. But they could make no such alterations to a rented property, and they had to do their best with thick curtains and banked fires. They lived simply. The nearby port of Wisbech provided its share of society and entertainment, but she was content with Richard. Alongside the intensity of physical love there was the quieter but no less mysteriously satisfying pleasure of affectionate companionship – so apparently commonplace, but only those who have never had it can think it so.

Then in February, during a spell of milder weather, Richard went to Yarmouth for two days with Luke, to inspect the damage to one of Luke's coasters which had run aground on a sandbar in the Roads. Caroline rode into Wisbech to shop: she had candles to buy, new stockings for Richard, sugar, a few other small purchases. She had some silver and a bank-note from Squire's Bank.

To her surprise the haberdasher would not take the note: when she pressed him he said he had not enough change.

It was strange, for Squire's of Peterborough was one of the oldest established banks in the region, and its notes were usually accepted for fifty miles around. She asked her father when he came back to Elm with Richard next evening.

'Oh, I dare say there may be some rumour-mongering, what with all this talk of war, and it's frightened the tradesmen,' Luke said. 'In '97, when Wainwright's collapsed, there was panic and folk wouldn't take bank-notes, but Squire's has always been steady as a rock. But look here, I don't fancy making the rest of the journey to Peterborough tonight, and the horses are tired. If you can find room for 'em in your stable, and room for me in a bed somewhere, why don't I stay the night and then you two can come with me in the carriage tomorrow and we'll go see Squire ourselves? There's sure to be a simple explanation.'

They were not the only ones trying to see Mr Squire at the house in Priestgate. Several farmer's gigs were waiting outside and blocking the narrow street, and little Lucy Squire showed them into the rear parlour and sat with them a few minutes before bursting into tears.

At last Mr Squire himself came to them, and as Luke Hardwick was an old friend and associate he did not attempt to mince matters.

Luke had been partly right. The apprehensions of war had sent a spasm of panic through the City markets, notably in India stock. Mr Squire, after a lifetime's prudence, had been buoyed up by the optimism of the summer peace and the opportunities for investment. Not only had he encouraged his customers to take up such investments, he had speculated on his own account, underwriting his speculations with bank stock. Now he was having to sell stock at a discount to meet his demands and rumour was doing the rest: his bank-notes were not accepted, Gurney's Bank would not handle them, depositors were withdrawing their money. Mr Squire, white-haired and red-faced and still looking the model of stout English probity, confessed that the bank might have to close its doors within a few days. Suddenly everyone was feeling the cold wind and he was not sure he could meet all his liabilities. He was most of all sorry that he had ever prevailed on Mr Lindsay to make those investments . . .

Richard had been very silent. Even as Mr Squire had begun speaking a suspicion had raised itself in Caroline's mind that the consequences were somehow graver for them than she thought.

So it was revealed, what neither Caroline nor her father knew. Guided by Mr Squire, Richard had made investments in the hope of a quick return, as had many in the hopeful glow of the peace. The funds, of course, had been diverted from the account on which they relied, including the fortune Caroline had brought to the marriage. That money, if it had been left in safe three per cents, would probably have been recoverable even in this crisis. As it was, not only Richard's carefully saved prize money but two thousand pounds of the settlement were irretrievably lost in the crash of the markets. Mr Squire shook his head and said over and again that he should have seen all the signs of a financial bubble. If the bank did have to close there was a good chance its affairs would be taken over by one with large capital reserves like Gurney's, and eventually they would get the remainder of Caroline's money back. He should have known, he said . . .

Caroline and Richard dined at the Bridge House. Rebecca, finding that her daughter, her son-in-law and her husband were all silent in different ways, tried to keep up a flow of hopeful talk.

'Mr Squire has influential friends, surely?' she said. 'There can't be a complete collapse . . .' And: 'I remember my father lost a lot of money in a banking crisis. That was during the American war. These things do happen. You can weather this storm, I'm sure . . .'

After dinner Luke had the carriage made ready to take Caroline and Richard back to Elm. He would canvass support among the mercantile community, he said; there was a lot of goodwill to Sydney Squire. They wouldn't see the bank go under without a struggle. He would keep them informed about developments. He had been very calm and thoughtful all day. But at the last moment he burst out to Richard, as if he could keep silent no longer: 'I suppose you weren't to know, Richard. But for heaven's sake, boy, if you'd this sort of thing in mind, why didn't you come to me for advice? You're a sailor, not a financier. I could have directed you to much safer . . . But there, it's done now.'

It was said without ill-temper. Only Caroline suspected how it affected Richard and only she guessed how he was feeling, how a blow had been struck at the most vulnerable part of his nature. The fact that they rode home in her father's carriage was unfortunately appropriate.

They were quiet on the way home. While Caroline sought for a way to convey to Richard that it was all right, that he must stop mentally heaping ashes on himself as she knew he was doing . . . while she thought this, the implications of what had happened began to sink in.

On the rational level she knew her mother was right. And she herself had constantly impressed on Richard that her marriage settlement was *their* money, after all. Such things happened. They were not destitute. Some money would be salvaged. They were young and must rub along . . .

But a deeper, emotional voice cried out in disappointment, especially as the carriage bounced into the village of Elm. She had so hoped that they could buy the house soon: now that would have to be put off, for who knew how long.

Richard handed her out of the carriage. There is a certain state of love, confusion and frustration where the warm touch of a lover's hand can set off a sort of mental gust: the consciousness of love throws the frustration into bolder relief and makes the world seem inimical. The gust blew up in her as she went into the house. This place, their security, their happiness, that was so valuable – he had *risked* it: not on the turn of a card, but on something that to her seemed equally unreliable. It was not the fact that he had not told her what he had done – it was the fact that he had not *known* her, not known that she was happy as they were. Did he not believe her when she assured him that she had what she wanted, that *he* was what she wanted?

Abruptly as it had come, the gust blew itself out. In the hall she took off her bonnet and reached out for him. He was suffering.

'My love,' she said. 'I don't know what you're thinking, but whatever it is, it's not as bad as that. There, I'm lucid as ever, I shall have to go into Parliament. What I mean to say is – well, you only did the same as Mr Squire, and he's been a banker for thirty years.'

Richard shook his head. He kissed her but his face was closed and grim: in such a mood the light clear blue eyes became almost transparent, seeing nothing around him, looking inward, critically and with distaste, at his own character. 'The difference is,' he said, 'that I was trying to prove something, and proved the opposite. And also we are in no position to gamble.'

They sat down to supper, and she noticed the way he

swallowed his food in lumps, unheeding. When this sort of introspection descended on Richard it was as if the physical world scarcely impinged on his consciousness at all.

'You do see why,' he said suddenly, 'I didn't go to your father? When I had the idea of investing for profit. You do see, don't you?'

'I know you don't like depending on my father. I see that. And really, love, it doesn't – '

'I'm not excusing myself in any other regard,' he said. 'Just wanted to make sure you realized that. For once I wouldn't be placing myself in your father's hands again, that was the idea. Acting for myself . . . Well, at least I know better now.'

'You're too hard on yourself, Richard. You know you are.'

'Am I? I go and throw money away on speculations I know nothing about, money brought to me by my wife whom I love more than anything in the world, but of course I don't tell her what I've done. The money is lost and so we will have to struggle along and that same wife will have to go without.' He flung down his knife. 'And I shouldn't be hard on myself? I should be horsewhipped,' he said with great disgust.

'I know why you did it,' she said. 'And all I can do is repeat, again and again, it doesn't matter to me. I didn't marry you to eat off silver platters. And I know you didn't tell me because – '

'I didn't tell you because I had this same childish idea of showing I could do things for myself. Look, mama, I did it all myself. At least that's how I rationalized it. I realize now I didn't tell you because you would have had the sense to stop me.' He looked at her with a sudden, unhappy fondness. 'And still you've said nothing about this house. Poor love. If you'd married anyone else this house might have been yours by now – '

'Stop it, Richard,' she said. 'Marry someone else? Who else would I marry? What would I be without you?'

'Some few thousand pounds richer,' he said shortly.

'Oh, God, don't talk like that,' she said. 'I can't bear it when you talk like that. I'm nothing without you, I don't give a damn about the money, two thousand, twenty thousand, what good is that to me without you . . .?' To her horror she began to cry. 'If I can't convince you of that I don't know what to do. It's when you won't trust me, won't believe in me, that I can't bear it, when all I want to do is be with you. And then you go and talk about me marrying someone else . . .' She had never had such an outburst before and the tears wouldn't stop coming.

Richard looked at her: he was one of those men on whose faces sorrow is scored like physical pain. 'You're wetting your apple pie,' he said gently.

'Oh, bugger to the apple pie,' she said, using one of his own naval expressions: and they laughed together, tensely, dangerously, a laughter of emotional exhaustion.

Later that night in bed, Richard said, staring at the rafters: 'The *Justine*'s not to sail again until the spring. No money coming in till then. Well, your father was right. A sailor not a financier. God, what a mess. I really thought that at last I'd . . . Oh, no matter.'

She sensed him lying awake and thinking for a long time. And she felt with a certain helplessness that whatever she said, Richard would torment himself with reproaches, his own and her own.

Superficially their life continued as normal over the next few weeks. But there was a cloud over the house and the old contentment was gone.

A constant avoiding of the subject of the money characterized their exchanges. Her fear of seeming to reproach him, his own pricking consciousness of what he had done, together created an empty gulf between them into which all sorts of misunderstanding might flow. They ate together, slept together, talked about the house and the fields and the livestock, and all the time the tension was racked up higher.

It could not, of course, be entirely ignored. A letter from Luke confirmed that Squire's Bank had closed its doors. Eaton, Cayley and Co. of Stamford were taking over its accounts and most of its liabilities, and it seemed the remainder of Caroline and Richard's money would be recovered when the transfer was complete. In the meantime there was the question of the renewal of the lease on Elm Cottage. Luke proposed to advance them the money for another year's rent.

Caroline might have predicted that Richard would not like this, but not the vehemence of his reaction.

'There must be some other way,' he said. It was a bitterly cold day with a north-east wind keening through the apple trees. He stood staring bleakly out of the parlour window.

'We'll get our money, eventually, that's the main thing,' she said.

'What's left of it.'

'All right, what's left of it.' His black looks, his bitter tongue, were trying her nerves. 'But there is no other way.'

He turned with an impatient gesture. 'And so we take another handout from your father. And we rely on him to provide my next employment.'

'It's a *loan*,' she said.

He gave a half-laugh. 'And so it goes on. I might as well wear your father's livery.'

She looked at him resentfully. 'Which do you love most,' she said, 'your pride or me?'

He was breathing hard. 'The two are inseparable,' he said. 'How can it be otherwise? Dear God, folk must be thinking they were right about this marriage all along. Married off to that sailor fellow, they'll have to support him of course, that's understood – '

'Don't ever say that again,' she said quietly. 'Don't ever.'

Something in her tone gave him pause. He glanced at her and turned back to the window. 'Well,' he said flatly, 'we've no choice, have we?'

'Whatever you say, I'm going to write to father and accept with thanks. Though the letter would look better coming from you.'

He went to the door. 'Your father's opinion of me now,' he said, 'is such that one letter can make no difference.'

She did not know what to do: she only knew she could not live like this. It had always been her principle not to let the sun go down on her wrath. This muted, explosive atmosphere was intolerable.

At the beginning of March, when Richard rode over to Morholm, the frost was still hard, and the black fields at Elm had yielded reluctantly to the plough. After the failure of their last crops he was seeking advice at Morholm: George was at Westminster, but he expected to find Charles there. To his surprise, he was not: Mary said that after his travels in Scotland with his old school-friend he had gone to stay with him in London.

'I have some news from my husband at Westminster that may interest you, Richard,' Mary said, taking a letter from her apron. 'George writes that a few days ago a Royal Message was read to Parliament reporting hostile preparations in the ports of France and Holland and calling for a state of readiness. Now Parliament has voted unanimously for an addition of ten thousand men to the Navy. George says all the talk at Westminster is of war against the French again. Have you ever been at Malta, which seems to be what all the argument is about?'

'No, ma'am. I've never been posted to the Mediterranean. Who knows, perhaps now it may come about.'

The news was food for thought. Richard was abstracted as he went over the home farm with the steward, John Newman, and only half-listened to his advice on ploughing and sowing. Before he left, Mary offered him some seed of radish to take back. In the stables, Jim Benwick tied the sack over his horse's saddle and remarked: 'Looks like it might be war again, sir. Reckon you'll be in it?'

'It could be, Jim.'

'Still, it may come to nothing. No telling which way the Frenchies'll jump.'

'Oh, of course, you went on the trip to France, didn't you? What did you think of it?'

'We-ell . . .' Benwick reflected. 'Paris was all very fine, as you'd expect. But it was all top show, I reckon. The countryside, now, was a different matter. There was a place we went to – Normandy. Town called Alençon. Mrs Lindsay, sir, she rode out one morning to this little village – calling on some family she knew. Now that country was so rich, with these good stone cottages – I thought to myself, we're supposed to hate the Frenchies and all the rest of it, but I could settle here and be happy. That's the real France, I reckon.'

'You went with Mrs Lindsay, you say?'

'Aye. Big house, handsome place, but it warn't the folk she was looking for, anyhow, so we went back. Beautiful, it was. But, that was summer, I daresay it's all cold and grey there too, now.'

476

It was cold and grey across the fens as Richard rode home, the wind tossing crows around a sky mottled with broken cloud.

Caroline had made her own decision that day: to prepare a large extravagant dinner of roast duck and veal, break open the last wine in the cellar, dress in her best, light a score of candles, and throw defiance in the face of the god of money. And, if Richard objected, to have it out with him, to break the ice if she couldn't thaw it.

When he came in he made no comment on the rich cooking smells or the candles. With a brief greeting he went upstairs to change.

Fifteen minutes later he had not come down, and she went up to find he had not even taken off his boots and was sitting in the wicker bedroom chair looking into the fire.

'Dinner won't be long,' she said. 'I hope you're hungry. We have two roast ducks.'

He nodded. 'Your aunt Mary has news from Westminster. It seems there may be war,' he said. He looked up. 'Duck? Where did that come from?'

'Gaffer Clare's poultry-yard,' she said.

He raised his eyebrows. 'I thought it might be a gift from your father.'

His cold stubborn tone set off something inside her. 'Oh, God, Richard, this just cannot go on. I've made a special dinner and I want us to eat it and be damned to the expense. And if we end up in debt then very well. I just can't live with this – this endless gloom, this silence, these self-reproaches! I know why you are like this and if there were anything I could say or do to help I would. I've *told* you I don't give a damn about the money. What I do give a damn about is being able to live and talk and laugh with my husband! Or even, if it comes to that, have a good downright row with him! But I can't live in this –

this *freezing* atmosphere all the time.' She stared impotently at his still figure. 'Are you listening to me?'

He stirred. His eyes looked absolutely grey and flat and colourless, his strong jaw rigidly set. 'Who do you know in France?' he said.

'What?'

'Who do you know in France? In the country. In a village. Near a place called Alençon.' He got up and leaned on the mantelshelf. 'Jim Benwick told me you went to see someone there alone. You didn't tell me about this.'

Caroline's heart thundered, and she instantly knew that either she should not have done it or she should have told him straight away when she had. To tell now . . . But her determination to clear the air was screwed to such a pitch that even this must be brought into its service.

'No,' she said. 'I went to the village of Torcy, where I knew Antoine Clairet lived. I wanted to see him. It was a thing I felt I had to do. I didn't tell you because I felt you wouldn't understand.'

Richard's tanned face had gone white. He gripped the mantelshelf. 'In that regard,' he said at last, 'you were wrong. I understand all too well.' He turned away from her. He said with a horrible calm in his voice: 'Thank you for your frankness, at last.'

'You do *not* understand,' she said vehemently. 'Have you forgotten what Clairet did to me? I certainly haven't. And that he never paid any price. And when we were in Normandy I decided that if I could find him I would confront him. Him and his *wife*. I had the power to destroy his life as he had mine. I went there in *hate*, to confront him with the fact that I had survived, to show his wife what her husband was really like. For revenge. That's why I went. And in the end I couldn't do it. Because what I felt for him was no longer even hate. It was contempt. I saw him for what he was. He was terrified when he saw me, terrified of his wife, and I went away knowing that I didn't care, that he wasn't even worth revenging myself. That was all. It was something I had to do.'

'Dear God, how it trips off your tongue.' He examined the candle-snuffers on the shelf. 'You hadn't forgotten what he had done to you. Clearly not. Clearly you weren't averse to a repeat of the operation.'

She seized his shoulder roughly and turned him about to face her. 'You're *detestable*,' she said, 'saying a thing like that! Do you really believe I could feel *anything* but hate for that man? How stupid do you think I am?'

'It seems to me that I've been the stupid one,' Richard said. He clenched his fists and threw his head back. 'Dear Christ, to think – you didn't *tell* me. Well, it shows what we've come to. No, I should have known. I thought it would come before this . . . My wife takes the opportunity to visit her old lover, but, oh well, his wife's still in the way, never mind, needn't say anything of this to old Richard, he's just grateful for what he's got. And now I'm supposed to meekly swallow this on top of everything else? Well, after all, she married that sailor fellow, matter of convenience really. Inevitable that this would come out in the end. A handsome house, Benwick said, rich land. It must have raised some very unflattering comparisons in your mind, my dear.'

'Yes,' she said, her heart swelling. 'A very handsome house. Rich land. All very desirable. But not to me. All I wanted was to come back *here*, to *you*, to this marriage that you seem determined to ruin . . .'

'Oh, this marriage? Well, it's already revealed its true colours, hasn't it? The Butterworths and all their kin were in the right of it. You needn't tax your ingenuity with these explanations, Caroline. It was a resort, an expedient, was it not? You felt a certain something for me, a certain grateful something, after all I was around when you were ill, and at the time it seemed a good idea. But now the discontent comes out, does it not? Poor Caroline. She throws herself into this living death with a sailor who can't keep two halfpence in his pocket without losing it and of course her mind goes back to her real love.'

'What do you want me to say?' she said, her soul too desolate for tears. 'Tell me, Richard, what do you want me to say? Time and again I tell you, it's you I want, not Clairet, not wealth, not anything else in life. Seeing Clairet made me realize that more deeply than ever. All I can do is tell you this and show you this, and if it's no good, if trust and belief and love are no good, what can I do?'

'Trust,' he said with disgust, as if the word were obscene. 'Let's not mention that. But a little honesty would not come amiss.' He moved away from her to the window. 'And that you've given me, though you perhaps didn't intend it. It was foolish of me, I dare say, to have ever let it happen. It was wrong of me, perhaps, to take advantage – to get you to marry me, when I knew that eventually you must regret it. But, I was so – it seemed like the most marvellous, wonderful thing, more than I ever dreamt of, and I even allowed myself to think, perhaps she does love me, perhaps it is real . . .' His voice trembled. 'Unfair to you, Caroline. I knew it must come. The day you would regret it.'

'If this is what marriage to you must be like,' she said indistinctly, her eyes misting over, 'then I do regret it.'

A muscle moved in Richard's cheek. Outside the dark wind raved and the trees shook. 'I'd better go check the outhouses,' he said. He opened the door. 'You're stuck with me, my dear,' he added tonelessly. 'I'm sorry for that.'

* * *

A hellish two days followed. There was a canyon between them across which she made futile gestures that were either unrecognized or unheeded.

She should have known. Their instincts had been right in casting a veil over the fact of Antoine Clairet and she should have left it like that. Lifting even a corner of the veil released a cloud of demons.

The man with whom she had shared such intimacy became a blank wall to her. Richard, in his hurt, his anger, his feeling of betrayal, locked his spirit up in its old defensive fastnesses. With great labour the foundations of trust had been built and now they were shattered. And knowing Richard's unyielding character Caroline feared they were shattered beyond repair.

She tried to reach out to him, but everything resolved into antagonistic silence. Protestations of love for him were no use: that was a coinage she had debased by the simple mistake of going to see Clairet, and it was worthless. The more so, in that the last prop had been pulled from beneath Richard's self-esteem, already tottering from the disaster of the lost investments.

And to have her love refused and discounted, sharpened her own resentment. He said their marriage was a failure, a convenience doomed from the start: his abrupt, complete acceptance of this hurt her; it was as if it was a relief to him. Richard's words about Clairet had been said in the heat of anger but she could not forget them. In her frustration she experienced moments of hate; for it is hard to be painted the villain of the piece. Oh, yes, of course, *her* love was insincere, sullied, but *his* of course had always been pure and he could retreat into this proud hurt holiness . . . she screamed this at him, trying to elicit some reaction. But he merely froze her away from him. And the worst thing was that the hate was not liberating, for it was twined in a strangling knot with her love for him – too strong to break but, it seemed, too weak to hold them together.

On the third day, a letter came to deliver them, in a perverse sense, from their anguish. It was a summons from the Admiralty: he was to report there immediately. With the mutterings of mobilization and war they both knew what that meant.

She helped him pack his trunk: he said, 'You don't have to do that,' but she ignored him. A carrier in the village was going down to Ely, from where he could get a coach to London.

Even as the carrier waited in the road outside, in the frosty morning, she could not believe this was happening, not this way. It couldn't be happening, it was a nightmare . . . In the hall he spoke to her about money. 'I dare say your father will let you know the position as regards Squire's Bank,' he said. He glanced at the pianoforte in the corner. 'You could sell that. Might fetch thirty pounds.'

She shook her head, unable to speak.

'Well.' He put on his hat. Back in his lieutenant's uniform he looked stiff and remote. 'I'll arrange to have my pay paid into the bank when I can. I'll write you with details of my new commission. It may – '

'Richard, we can't part like this,' she burst out. 'We *can't* . . . it's so wrong . . .'

He glanced away from her, drawing in a deep shaking breath. 'It's . . . there's no time now, we – I don't know, war may not come, I may not be away long. We'll have to decide then . . . what we're going to do.'

He opened the door. Agony tightened across her heart and she said: 'Richard, will you kiss me?'

He hesitated. 'If you wish,' he said.

She broke down at that. She turned away from him and ran into the parlour, sobbing hysterically; and she did not see him go.

A little while later Mrs Welney came into the parlour and put a motherly arm round her shaking shoulders. 'There, there,' she said, 'don't take on so, dear. It's natural.' The master had gone to sea and the mistress was crying; it was natural. Mrs Welney did not know how unnatural it was; did not know that it was the end of everything.

The spring was slow, the earth sluggish after its winter coma. Caroline threw herself into the work of the farm at Elm: with just the one outdoor servant there was plenty to do, and she craved exhausted oblivion. To know that your love, your marriage, your happiness were disintegrating was pain enough; to be left in this suspended state, with no way of settling it one way or the other, no knowing what Richard was thinking, was the torture of the damned. So, she worked herself mercilessly and dropped into bed at night aching, lonely, and revolving in her mind a hundred scenarios of her and Richard's future and trying to find a thread of hope in one of them.

His new commission was as second lieutenant on the frigate *Serapis*, Captain Meade, crew two hundred and eighty, at Torbay with the re-forming Western Squadron. They were waiting on events. That was the substance of her husband's letter.

Waiting on events. Everyone thought there would be war. The Norman Cross prisoner-of-war camp, which had been put up for sale, was prepared for use again. While the news continued to come in of the decorous wranglings of Lord Whitworth and Bonaparte's brother Joseph to come to some accord over Malta, there were other more forthright indications of mood. Bonaparte ordered the permanent military occupation of Holland and Switzerland. Invasion craft were said to be assembling in the Channel Ports. In the City the Funds went haywire.

It was in the second week of May that Caroline received another note from Richard. Admiral Cornwallis had hoisted his flag at Torbay and the fleet was to sail directly to resume the blockade of Brest. With the same post came a special issue of the *Stamford and Peterborough Courant*. It had been announced in Parliament that the ambassadors of Britain and France were being recalled. The 'enduring peace' was over.

Not surprising to Caroline. Her own peace was over. It too had been brief and lovely: perhaps it too had been an illusion.

2

George Hardwick returned from the House of Commons to his lodgings in Buckingham Street, tired and aching and glad of the mild spring night air after the fug of the chamber. The renewal of war, and the news that one of Bonaparte's first acts had been to intern all British civilians in France, had set the place buzzing like smoke in a bee-hive. All sorts of little cabals had formed. Pitt had returned to the House for the first time in months amid rumours that he would lead a new ministry, but he looked ill and seemed to have lost friends. Fox was implacable in opposition and the Grenville faction without broad support. It looked as if the Addington government, uninspiring and unpopular, would have to make war as it had made the peace.

When he saw lights in his rooms he cursed – not more intriguers. He just wanted supper and bed. His landlady wore a curious expression. 'It's a young lady, sir. She would wait, wouldn't take no denying . . .'

'I don't know any young ladies,' George said crossly, going into his sitting-room and finding Lydia Fairburn.

He recognized her immediately, though she was much thinner and considerably less well-dressed than he remembered her. She sprang to her feet and stood looking tall as a sunflower, holding her bonnet by its strings, gazing at him with frank, apprehensive green eyes.

'Miss Fairburn. How d'you do? This is a surprise.'

'You must forgive me, Mr Hardwick. I assure you I'm not in the habit of – loitering about the chambers of statesmen. But I wished to see you very urgently . . .'

'We're only statesmen when we're dead,' said George with a brief smile. 'I'm just going to have supper, Miss Fairburn. Basic fare, but I'd be pleased if you'll join me.' He had no reason to like this young woman, given her effect on his son; but then, he did not know the whole story, and he had old-fashioned manners.

Lydia shook her head rapidly. George saw she was very agitated. 'I came here,' she began, 'I – it was the only address I knew . . . I had hopes of finding Charles, or if not, that you might tell me where I could find him. I wouldn't blame you if you refused,' she said hurriedly, 'not at all. I don't know how much Charles has told you about me – whatever it is I'm afraid it can't be more unpleasant than the truth. But I have to see him if it's only for him to tell me to go to the devil, and I didn't know – if he was in London, or at Morholm . . .' She spoke rapidly, staccato, her eyes lowered and her fingers jerking the bonnet-strings into fearful knots. 'You see, Mr Hardwick, you must know what happened to my father – his disgrace – and it was he who stood between me and Charles – well, it wasn't, it was *me*, I see now – anyhow, I became engaged to a man who had wealth enough to rescue my father; and Charles I dare say thinks I'm married to him – and I'm not – I know Charles was right and – it would be the best thing if you were to tell me that Charles is happily married to a charming woman

485

who is worthy of him – and if he is, then serve me right but I have to *know*, you see – I've left my father and I've *woken up* – this must sound most peculiar, Mr Hardwick, I'm sorry – but I have to know . . .'

George suddenly perceived that the girl, for all her rattling energy, was near to collapse. He put his hand under her arm and propelled her into a chair and poured her a glass of brandy. 'This must be worse than listening to speeches in Parliament,' she said, subsiding miserably. 'But you were the only person – '

'You did quite rightly,' George said. 'Miss Fairburn, Charles is not married. Nor is he here – '

'Then he's at Morholm? Oh, will you allow me to go and see him? I promise not to make him unhappy again, only let me – '

'Miss Fairburn. I'm afraid my son is not at Morholm. He is currently at Chatham, with the 30th Cambridgeshire Regiment of Foot. He obtained a commission in the army last month.'

3

It had not been difficult for Charles to gain a commission as an ensign in the army, once the decision was taken. The expanding army wanted officers. If you were keen to join an élite regiment – the cavalry or Guards – you might have to buy a commission, but otherwise all that was needed was an ability to read and write and a letter of recommendation from someone with the rank of Major or above. Caroline's mother Rebecca had a brother, Paul Walsoken, who had recently been promoted Major in the Royal Fusiliers. The letter – *I beg leave to recommend Mr Charles Joseph Hardwick as a gentleman fully qualified to*

hold an ensigncy in his Majesty's 30th Regiment of Foot –
had been all that was required.

The more difficult part was explaining his reasons to his
parents. The idea had been in his mind for some time and
had taken root after his trip to France and the threat of
renewed war. His basic convictions in favour of reform
and liberty were unchanged, but like many radical young
men, he had been disappointed by the imperial pomp
beginning to surround Napoleon. The changes he wanted
in England wore a different shape, and if it came to
invasion, as seemed likely, he wanted to help repel it. But
why the Regular Army, his mother had asked – there
were the Volunteers, or the Militia, a perfectly genuine
service . . . Charles shook his head. The home services
were admirable in intent, but they were basically ineffectual. He had made up his mind that for once he would
not compromise: do something whole-heartedly. He was
sick of himself, of his own moping discontent and self-
loathing. A complete change, a plunge into a life of
action, seemed to offer salvation: a testing and scourging
of self. Sighing around Morholm was not going to help
him recover so he might as well go where he could do
some practical good.

And so with the rumours of great invasion fleets across
the Channel flying about he had reported to his regiment
at Chatham. Chatham garrison was the chief of a whole
string of barracks and encampments hastily reassembling
to meet the threat of invasion that spring. Chatham Lines
and the Forts guarding the great naval dockyard were
being reinforced. Semaphore towers were erected along
the Medway to London. When Charles arrived all seemed
chaos. Long trains of ordnance and baggage waggons
crowded the coach-roads out of London. As a consequence of the government's panic to get as many armed
men as possible to the threatened coasts, incoherent

bodies of Volunteers and newly-embodied militia regiments straggled here and there with no plans for their reception. Chatham itself seemed less a town than one large excrescence of war, with seedy streets clattering with dragoons, with sailors and dockyard-workers mingling and fighting in fishy taverns, with smoke swirling from armourers' and blacksmiths' shops, with the thunder of battery-testing and a discordance of trumpets calling to foot-parade. And everywhere figures in shakos and white breeches and black gaiters and red coats with a bewildering variety of regimental facings. Charles felt conspicuous for a moment until he recalled that he was dressed in exactly the same way.

He had had only very basic training with the Soke Volunteers; but his training with the 30th Regiment of Foot was less rigorous than he had expected. His long-limbed frame had always been quick and athletic. He had first got on a pony when he was three, and did not find the daily riding-school difficult. There were exercises with the fire-lock and bayonet. As well as taking instructions in company drilling, he and the other young officers were required at first to drill along with the men: this was less congenial, but he even found a kind of mindless relaxation in it. There was plenty of time for eating and drinking with his fellow subalterns in the mess. It was a simple, undemanding companionship: one was automatically friends. And for further instruction there was the *Regimental Companion*, which included helpful warnings about bringing prostitutes into the barracks. They need not have troubled about that. Affairs of the heart or otherwise were things he kept at a touchy, watchful distance.

George had never believed in interfering in the private lives of his children. So when he came to Chatham with

Lydia Fairburn, the day after she had turned up at his lodgings, he wondered if he were doing the right thing. To tell her where Charles was might not be interfering: what he was doing now most definitely was.

But, the girl was all for travelling on the coach to Chatham alone, and he would not permit that. Moreover, she had impressed George in spite of himself. There was intelligence there, and a forthrightness that he liked; and as she told him her story he perceived that the flippancy went alongside a clear-eyed honesty about herself and others. His judgement might be at fault but he would risk it: she deserved a chance to see Charles. He would arrange it and leave them to it.

So, that afternoon they put up at the Bull Hotel in Chatham, and George booked a private dining-room and sent a message to Charles's barracks, saying that Ensign Hardwick's father was in town and would like him to join him for dinner.

The spring afternoon was chilly and a maid had lit a fire in the small room. Lydia stood by it warming her hands. She looked composed, George thought, but he guessed that that was an effort of will. She had always struck him as a wilful young woman, but now he would call it purposeful. Absently he admired the slanting green eyes and white complexion. The sparkle had been dulled but a maturity added to the beauty. Even from the brief account she had given him of her story he surmised that suffering had played its part.

'I'll leave you alone when Charles comes,' George said. 'There is a coach back to London at six, remember.'

Charles came to the Bull willingly: afternoon parade was over and there was only the prospect of a meal in the mess and dice with his fellow-juniors to beguile the evening. The landlord showed him through to the private room. He went in, ducking his head under the low beams.

'Charles. Glad to see you. You're looking fit.'

His hand was grasped. 'Father. This is a delightful surprise – ' He saw the tall young woman standing by the fireplace, and stopped dead.

George had slipped past him to the door. 'Well,' he said, 'the House is forever debating the state of our defences: I'll go take a turn about the town and arm myself with a few facts.'

Charles turned to call his father back, but he was gone.

'Hullo, Charles,' Lydia said.

Charles took a deep breath. 'This must be a joke,' he said carefully. 'But I'm afraid it's one I don't appreciate.'

He turned to the door, in a black wave of fury and misery. Was she determined to shatter what little peace of mind he had regained? But just then the landlord and a maid came in with covered plates and bottles and with great ceremony began to lay the table for dinner; and in a ridiculous, constrained silence he stood there helplessly, holding his hat, unable to look at Lydia, unable to move.

When at last they were alone Lydia came forward to the table. 'It isn't a joke, Charles,' she said. 'I'm so very sorry to – to spring this on you. I had to see you and it was the only way . . . I went to your father in London and he insisted on accompanying me – '

'You've left your husband at home?' Charles said. 'Not the best recipe for married contentment. But then that was never part of your – '

'I have no husband,' Lydia said. 'I'm not married.'

He glanced suspiciously, resentfully at her. 'But what about – ?'

'I'm not married, not to Spencer Murrow or anyone else. Oh, Charles, will you sit down and let me explain?'

'I've wasted a great deal of time listening to your various *explanations*,' Charles said. 'I really don't think – '

490

'*Please*, Charles,' she said. 'Just give me a few minutes – just hear me out and then . . . Just hear me out. I am quite serious.'

Charles looked at his tall cockaded hat and at last laid it down on a chair; but he did not sit. 'Very well,' he said. 'But I really can't see what there is to say.'

She gazed at him soberly. Her hands gripped the back of a chair. 'As I said, I haven't married Spencer Murrow. Nor am I going to.'

'Well, so you've toyed with another man and then cried off. Nothing unusual about that, surely? Who else are you baiting your hook for? Some bigger fish than Spencer Murrow? Some . . .' Suddenly he could not go on. The blasts of bitterness came and went, leaving him scorched and arid, and miserably conscious of being back in the toils of complex feeling from which he had never truly escaped.

'I know why you feel this way,' she said, 'believe me, I expect nothing else. But I had to see you because you were *right*. I couldn't marry Spencer Murrow. Yes, I became engaged to him and I fully meant to go through with it. But I couldn't because I knew you were right. I didn't love him, and it was *wrong*, like you said; and I knew that it was you I loved – '

'Oh, God in heaven,' Charles burst out. He strode to the fireplace. 'Spare me, Lydia. Spare me that, for God's sake. Say what you have to say, but don't insult me with *that*.'

'I can't help it,' she said. 'Because it's true. That time you came to Stanningford – when in spite of everything you came to me – I was such a fool, for what I could have had then, just by . . . But all right. The point is in the end I knew it would be wrong to marry Spencer Murrow. I broke off the engagement. I was sorry to hurt him, but it would have been worse if I had married him . . . But of

491

course, father was already making preparations. Spencer had pledged to rescue my father's fortunes. Father was cheerfully making ready to start anew once his daughter married this man of huge wealth. He could go on living as he had always done. Stanningford would be finished and . . .' She swallowed painfully. 'So I had to tell him it wasn't to be. It's odd when your own father becomes – like a stranger to you. When suddenly it's as if you see him from a distance . . . Well, perhaps I should have expected the reaction, but I didn't. Somehow – even knowing him as I did – somehow I had this comforting picture of him saying well, child, then we must sink together, we must reconcile ourselves . . . But it was the *violence*, the hatred. I'd betrayed him, he said. I was a wicked daughter, I had betrayed the memory of my mother. That was the chief thing. My mother, the paragon. *She* would not have done it. *She* knew the meaning of love, of duty, of sacrifice, she would never have been so mean, so cruel . . . It went on and on.' Lydia drew in a sharp breath. 'It isn't easy to look at your own father and suddenly know you despise him. To look at him and just see selfishness, this terrible abject selfishness all the way through. And to see that I had come close, so close, to being exactly like him. Anyhow, I knew then that it was all over. He tried all sorts of things, tears, appeals, threats. Even when he struck me it didn't matter because my mind was already made up. Once you've seen your own father as I saw him, there's no going back – '

'He did what?' Charles was staring at her. 'He struck you?'

'But it couldn't make any difference then. I've deserved that blow a thousand times over, Charles: from you among other people. But this time, when it came at last, I knew I did not deserve it. And there was father still convinced that things could go on as they always had. No.

492

It was over and I would have to be alone. He still wouldn't believe that I could leave him. In stubbornness at least we're still alike . . . Anyhow, Stanningford's sold up now – everything's been sold up. The debts were finally met with a little over. Of course, he said, I'd not get a penny of what was left; I was never to come to him, I was an unnatural, ungrateful child, a disgrace to my mother; and he still didn't realize that I didn't *care*. It was too late.' Her voice had become low and calm now, almost impersonal. 'He's living with poor Aunt Clarissa now. Trying her sorely and raging at the world that conspired against him.'

'Aunt Clarissa . . . But what about you?'

'I've been living in London. With a family named Paige. He's a stockbroker in the City. I very much dislike children, as you know, but the little Paiges aren't too repulsive and they even listen to what I teach them occasionally.' She gave a sad smile. 'Yes, Charles, I'm working as a governess. I'm not entirely brainless, you know, and I have the appropriate French and drawing and I suppose the gentility. I think they found quite a *cachet* in having a Fairburn teaching their children. If only they knew how little I valued that name. They're quite kind to me – they gave me this leave to come and see you, though I said I was visiting a sick relative.'

'A governess . . . How long . . .?'

'About six months. Don't look like that, Charles, it won't kill me! As I said, what little money was left father refused me, but I didn't want it. It was when I realized that he wanted to sell his daughter into a loveless marriage for the sake of his damn horses and silk waistcoats that I realized there was something very wrong about the way we had been living. It would do me a power of good to work for my bread. And I think it has. It's given me the courage to come and tell you, because I owed it to you. I owe much more, but at the very least this . . .'

Charles, frowning, came to the table and poured himself a glass of wine; then, recollecting himself, poured another glass and handed it to her, not touching her fingers. 'What will your father do?' he said, going back to the fireplace.

She shrugged. 'Aunt Clarissa worships him, and looks after him. The money that was left might last out, if he lived *very* frugally. God knows, I've begun to see how little people can contrive to live on. It doesn't matter. I've no part in his life now. It's the best way.'

Hardly knowing what he did, Charles came back to the table and lifted the covers. 'We – we may as well eat this,' he said absently.

He sat, and after a moment Lydia did the same.

'So you went to see my father,' he said dully, looking at the chicken on his plate. 'And found I'd joined the army. Did that – surprise you?'

'Yes.' Her long fingers traced the stem of her wineglass. 'Do you – do you like it?'

'Oh, I . . .' He rubbed his forehead. He couldn't think: reeling under this new knowledge he felt a numbness like that of extreme fatigue. 'It's not so bad. There's a brutality of discipline that I can't like . . . I still can't believe it really. I'm startled when I look in a glass and see this uniform.'

'I don't wonder.' Lydia smiled nervously. 'But you look very fine. And to think I once made fun of you – some tradesman's son, wasn't it? What a horrible little creature I was. But then you've always been – the Paiges have a son about nineteen who dresses the dandy and is universally thought an Adonis, but he couldn't hold a candle – I've always thought you the most beautiful man I – '

'Lydia, don't,' Charles said harshly. He flung down his

494

fork and got up from the table, unable to bear it, unable to look at her.

'I'm sorry,' she said in a small voice. 'Oh, Charles, I lied . . . I mean I *did* come to tell you this, because I felt it was right, but also because I had to see you – because I love you and while there was some small grain of hope . . . Oh, I had no *right* to expect anything, I know that – no right to expect you would even think of me after what I've done – and I thought, perhaps he's married, perhaps he's blissfully happy and in love and serve me right, but I had to see you, to – to know . . . I'm sorry. Believe me, I didn't mean to say this.'

'No, I'm not married. I nearly was, though.' He fell silent.

'. . . I'll go,' Lydia said.

He shook his head, motioning her to sit down. 'No, stay,' he said, 'stay until father gets back, I . . . Please excuse me just a minute.'

He went out. He had to get out, to be alone with his bewilderment.

He went out into the cobbled courtyard of the inn. An open gate led to a kitchen garden and he stood there, leaning against the gatepost. Clouds were knitting together in the sky and the light was fading over the rooftops of the town. He caught the sound of a drum from the garrison and further off a bell rung on a ship in the docks.

He wrestled with the strange pain of being offered love and being unable to receive it. Unable, or unwilling? He didn't know. All he knew was a twisted confusion and a fear that his capacity for love had gone: that disillusionment and bitterness had cut something away.

He remembered a time when love had given him no rest, lifting him in a fine-drawn exhilaration that made every moment seem charged with brilliant meaning; he remembered how the loss of love had so hurt and reduced him that he could barely tolerate himself. He had abandoned all thought of it and plunged into a new life. Now that the love he had sought so passionately was offered to him, he looked into himself and saw emptiness, and did not know if he had any love to offer in return.

Oh, life was a wry business. A cynic would find great relish in this situation. But Charles was not a cynic: he was the opposite. Perhaps, he thought, that was his trouble.

And Lydia. He had been moved, deeply moved by her narration, moved by the sight of her, moved by her proud, humble determination. If some might have said, in the past, that she was scarcely worthy of love, then they could not say so now. She had acted with courage and honesty. All the qualities that he had seen in her, amongst the worldliness and frivolity, had come to the fore. Worthy of love . . .

A face loomed close to his in the dusk, peered suspiciously. 'Oh! beg your pardon, sir.' It was the innkeeper, carrying a pail. 'Couldn't see you right for a moment . . . Everything all right?'

'Yes,' Charles said. 'Breath of air.'

'Coming on to rain, sir,' the innkeeper said, passing by him.

'Going in presently,' Charles said. He had not noticed the rain.

What the innkeeper said about not seeing him struck a chord in Charles. He felt the same suspicious doubt towards himself: saw himself with the same lack of recognition. The image was blurred and distorted.

He thought of what Lydia said about her father: the shock of seeing her own father for what he was, selfish, mercenary, cold. He thought of his own father and the deeper love and respect that he had begun to feel for him after their old disagreements. He began to see how Lydia had suffered in facing the truth about Sir Thomas. And yet, it had liberated her. Was the truth about himself something he too did not want to face – the embittered, mistrustful figure hiding in the regimental uniform?

'Charles.'

Lydia's voice spoke hesitantly behind him. He turned to see her with a cloak around her shoulders. He registered for the first time the fact that the cloak, and the plain woollen gown beneath, were rather shabby.

'I wondered where you'd gone . . . it's starting to rain . . . Charles, there's a London coach leaving soon. I'm – '

'D'you know why I joined the army, Lydia?' he said, looking out over the garden. 'Oh, certainly because of the danger of invasion, and the England I want to see is not one dominated by Bonaparte . . . but why I'm here, really, how I came to this pass?' He ran a hand over his damp hair. 'You know, I've been thinking all this time of you married to Spencer Murrow. I tried never to think of it and of course I never stopped. It isn't easy to – to take in . . .'

'I know I've made you unhappy, Charles,' she said. 'I don't expect you to forgive me and I know I never shall forgive myself.'

'We're right on the edge here,' Charles said. 'The edge of England. And somewhere over there, the French invasion fleet, so they say . . . The front line. I suppose I've run away as far as I can. Can't go further.'

'Will they come?' she said after a moment. 'The French?'

'No telling.' He turned to look at her. Her face was a pale oval above the cloak. 'Yes, you've made me unhappy, Lydia. But . . . but I don't suppose I've exactly made your life a season of joy.'

'Oh, Charles, you're wrong there. What do you suppose gave me the strength to leave my father and be alone and work for my living? It was the thought of you. The thought that even if I'd lost it now, I once had the love of that man . . . I lost it because I threw it away. Oh, I used to say that we belonged to different worlds and all the rest of it, but that's true of all lovers. And the truth was I wouldn't leave that world – I had everything all arranged to my satisfaction, and I could keep all the deeper things at a nice comfortable distance. And the deepest of all was you. But my father's disapproval was at hand, a nice excuse, and I believe at heart I must have really connived at his separating us. It took all the responsibility away from me. So I could go on being a child. Not even that. I was only half-human. And in the end I had to be rudely shaken out of that world, and thank God I was . . . it nearly destroyed me . . . Dear Charles, you're soaking . . .'

'So I am.' He had not noticed it; through Lydia's words had dawned a vision of how he had nearly destroyed himself: not through love but the fear of love. In his fear he had drawn back into a shell, dry and sterile: he had embraced pain and refused to let it go.

'Charles . . . it would be wrong of me to say I could make you happy – after all I've done to you. All I can say is I'd try, I'd spend my last breath to make you happy, because you're everything to me . . . Oh, please, tell me yes or no, send me away if you like but just say – '

'Oh, God, don't go,' he said, and a great suppuration of feeling burst the tangled knots within him. 'God, don't go away, Lydia,' he said, and he found her hands in the folds of her cloak and clutched them, 'my darling Lydia, don't leave me . . .'

'Never,' she said. 'I never will.' She threw her arms

498

around his neck and pressed her face against his. 'My love, can you forgive me . . .?'

'Nothing to forgive,' he said. Drained and released, drenched with rain, dizzy and alive, he held her. 'Nothing to forgive, my lover, nothing . . .'

She enclosed him in the folds of her cloak, hugging him against her, shielding him from the rain that pattered harder on the cobbles and formed pools glistening yellow in the light from the inn windows. Only the sudden thunder and rattle of a coach swinging through the arch into the yard roused them from their embrace.

'That'll be the London coach,' Lydia said.

'To hell with it. You're not going on that.'

'No. No, I'm not. Oh, Charles, don't stop holding me.'

He shook his head. 'I've got you caught, Lydia. Safe caught. Love, I can't believe I'm saying this – what I mean is, I can't offer you much now, I'd always dreamed of taking you back to Morholm, but I can hardly walk out of the army now, at least until . . . Well, it's an uncertain life, and – '

She silenced him with a kiss. Rain was beading on her eyelashes as she smiled at him. 'It's an uncertain world,' she said. 'Bonaparte may come next week. The sky may fall next week. But whatever happens, we've got our own certainty, haven't we? I know I have.'

'You'll be a soldier's wife, and live in lodgings in Rochester and – and twiddle your thumbs while he goes to parade, and be patronized by the Colonel's wife?'

'Try and stop me. Oh, just try and stop me.'

'We'll do it tomorrow. I'll get a licence and father can give you away – '

'Charles, your poor father! He's still wandering around the town in this rain!'

'Serve him right for playing matchmaker, God bless him.'

499

'I'm glad he did.'

They turned to go back into the inn. The rain was still heavy but to the east the clouds were dispersing to reveal the lights of the fort at the dockyard, warm and hazy in the moist darkening air. With Lydia's hand in his, Charles lifted his head and fancied he could smell the sea in the distance, hear the laughter in the barracks and the stamping of horses and the fiddling and singing in the dockyard taverns: life crowded vividly in on him as if he had just gained his senses anew, and with it came the future – just as complex and uncertain, but now to be embraced without fear.

The London coach was ready to go, and the coachman, seeing them, called out: 'Anyone for the London stage?' But the soldier and his lady only laughed at him and went into the inn together.

CHAPTER 6

1

The spring of 1803 ripened into a summer of exceptional fineness: the sort of summer folk said they remembered from their youth. And yet it was like no season anyone had ever known. There was an unreality, a fearful suspense curiously heightened by the calm sunshine and the fields of waving corn.

There were posters everywhere. Even the little church at Elm had patriotic addresses pasted to the door, together with blood-curdling accounts of what would happen when Bonaparte's army rampaged its way through the English countryside. In the public prints simian Frenchmen were shown impaling babies amidst the ruins of London, or, more hopefully but no less gruesomely, John Bull flourished Bonaparte's surprised head on a pike. There were sham playbills: 'In Rehearsal, *Theatre Royal of the United Kingdoms*. Some dark, foggy night, will be *attempted*, by a strolling company of French Vagrants, an old Pantomimic Farce, called *Harlequin's Invasion*, or the *Disappointed Banditti*.' Rousing songs were bellowed in theatres and by ballad-singers in the streets: from the inevitable *Britons, Strike Home* to *United and Hearty, Have at Bonapartee*.

Everyone who could afford one was in uniform. At Elm, farmers and farm workers drilled on the green in the evenings, and gentlemen held county meetings to discuss vague plans of driving all the cattle and sheep before the invading French. Volunteers guarded the great piles of

501

furze and turf, stretching across the fens to King's Lynn, that were to form the bonfire-beacons warning of invasion. Rumours of spies proliferated. Naughty children were told that Boney would eat them. Broadsheets showed huge flotillas crossing the Channel – great floating rafts the size of towns, complete with fortified castle: one pamphlet assured its readers that the French would come in balloons. In the meantime the small Regular Army, including the newly married Ensign Charles Hardwick of the 30th Cambridgeshires, was massed at Kent with preparations to fall back to the fortified positions at Chatham when the enemy landed.

Not, of course, that the enemy would come. The Navy would see to that – notwithstanding the fact that the service had been drastically wound down during the peace and was short of supplies. The sight of a sailor caused cheers. At Elm Caroline found herself bathed in reflected glory as if she had been married to Nelson himself. Neighbours continually asked for news of Richard. They were disappointed when she said all she knew was that he was with Rear-Admiral Collingwood's squadron in the blockade off Brest.

It was true. The one note she had had from him told her that, and that he had arranged to have his pay forwarded, and no more. Presumably he thought she did not care to know any more. Presumably he did not care.

The terrible scenes of their parting became as familiar to Caroline as a play an actor has played for fifty years. She rehearsed them obsessively in her mind, trying to find some gloss of comfort, trying to interpolate or change passages so that they would yield a more hopeful interpretation. There must have been something she could have said or done, some key that would lead them back to understanding. But the more she brooded the more it seemed the crisis was inevitable. She could trace its roots back to the moment she decided to visit Torcy and see Clairet, or to when Richard had taken employment in her father's service, or to when they had decided to marry with no money, and always the roots seemed to go deeper and she lost them. So, people said how proud she must be of her husband, and she smiled and nodded and all the time thought: I don't have a husband, I don't have a marriage, it's all poisoned and withered by suspicion and mistrust and *I can't do anything about it*, I have to just wait and wait and not know whether he loves or hates me, whether he's indifferent and has simply given up. I don't know how *I* feel for him when he's brought down the barriers like this, slammed the door of his soul in my face.

And still she had to go about as normal. The fields were ripe for harvest and young Ned was continually coming to ask her questions about the farm: sometimes her cousin Edmund rode over from Morholm, but mostly she was alone and the business of running Elm Cottage and its glebe was down to her. It was like being a widow, but she supposed even a widow had the comfort of memories, and hers were ambiguous, yielding as much pain as pleasure.

The society of her parents was something she avoided as much as possible. Her mother's subtle penetration would soon discern that something was wrong, and as for her father, with the Continent closed to his ships he was full of enquiries after Richard and the progress of the blockade.

It was the silence from Richard that was unbearable. Always he had found time for letters – long, loving letters in which she could hear the accents of his quiet baritone as clearly as if he were in the room with her. There would be no difficulty in mail reaching England from the Fleet at Brest: there was constant exchange between the block-ading squadrons and Torbay and Portsmouth, ships re-victualling and refitting and carrying communications to and from the Admiralty. She woke every morning in hope of a letter, even if it were cold and impersonal – even, yes, if it were a bitter outpouring of resentment, she could bear that. One day in June when she came down to breakfast Mrs Welney said: 'Nice fat letter come for you, mistress,' and her heart bounded. But when she seized the letter she saw it was from Charles, at Chatham. It was a long, happy, affectionate letter telling her in detail about his marriage to Lydia Fairburn and how married life agreed with him and that he couldn't wait for Caroline to meet her . . .

She wept then. And in tearful fury she went up to the attic and dug out the straw picture of the tower and tore it out of its frame and threw it on the fire. She stood there watching the golden marquetry blacken and disintegrate in the flames. It was the nearest she could get to erasing the fact of Antoine Clairet's existence in her past. She stood there and tried to feel better but she knew no symbolic act could draw the poison. Not even aiming a pistol at Clairet could do that. Mistrust, misunderstand-ing, division – those monsters fed on themselves and fattened.

The nights were warm and close as the summer deep-ened. In the July night Caroline undressed listlessly and opened the window and looked out, as one habitually did, to see if the bonfires were lit. It was said that Bonaparte had made an inspection of his invasion barges and troops at Boulogne: at Chatham, Charles said, all leave was cancelled and officers forbidden to leave their posts for more than two hours. Invasion. Caroline did not share the fears of many of her compatriots. If it came, it came. There were much more fearful things in life.

She lay down in her shift. This was when the loneliness became like a physical ache. And just before she slept, as always, her soul seemed to leap out and protest: *Why don't I hear from him? Oh, Richard, it's cruel . . . So long now . . . Richard, can't you hear me? Why doesn't he write me? Cruel . . .*

In July, Ned began cutting the hayfield, and one morning in brilliant sun she took him out a stone jug of ale and a plate of rabbit pie and stayed there talking to him for a while. The heat shimmered over the fields and when she saw the carrier who brought the mail walking up to the house he almost seemed to be floating in the sultry air.

She ran; she met him before he reached the door. Another fat letter.

'Reckon this weather's too good to last, missus,' the carrier said with a fenman's pessimism.

She did not answer. The writing was not Richard's. Some part of her mind dully recognized it. Stupefied with heat and disappointment she walked into the house.

The hall was dark and cool. She opened the letter: there was some printed matter enclosed in it. The sweat went suddenly cold on her body: it seemed to freeze on her skin.

The letter was from her Uncle George, in London.

'. . . I saw this in the *Naval Gazette*: I don't know whether you get the Gazettes at Elm. I presume this is the same Lieutenant Lindsay – you will no doubt have heard more about it by now, but I thought I would send the report anyway . . . I expect to return to Morholm shortly and I am most anxious to hear how Richard is, though I have no doubt you will give me a favourable report . . .'

Barely comprehending, she stared at the cutting from the *Naval Gazette*.

Captain James Meade, His Majesty's frigate Serapis *(24)* . . . *May 20th . . . On signs of assemblage of troop transports on the north shore of the mouth of the Iroise, the* Serapis *was detached from the blockading squadron under Rear-Admiral Collingwood . . . The raid achieved its aim in causing extensive damage by shot to a number of barges there under construction . . . On retiring the* Serapis *was deflected to a north-easterly course by the approach of the enemy ship* Puissant, *80 guns, and sustained a raking fire from the shore batteries at Point St Mathieu: however the* Puissant *retired on the prompt appearance of His Majesty's ship* Minotaur, *Captain Coney, then at the head of the squadron in the Roads . . . Wounded in the action, and commended to their Lordships' attention for courage under fire, Second Lieutenant R. Lindsay, Able Seaman Ball, also Sergeant of Marines J. Matheson . . .*

Mrs Welney heard Caroline's cry from the kitchen.

She steered the mistress with difficulty into the parlour and made her sit down. At first she could get no sense out of her, and at last took the letter from her hands.

'Oh, bless you, ma'am – wounded, it says, no more than that, why, sailors are always taking all manner of knocks – '

'But don't you see,' Caroline cried, 'the 20th of May! Two months, more! And this is the first I've heard . . . don't you see? Two months ago and not a word – he would *write* me, or have someone let me know. Look – it says the *Serapis* was taken into Portsmouth for repairs. And I've heard *nothing* – he'd let me know, I know he would, if – oh God – '

'Now stop it, ma'am,' said Mrs Welney, seizing Caroline's wrists. 'You mustn't even think it. I know there must be some reason behind it, I'm sure of it, and not the one you're thinking. You mustn't think it, you mustn't!'

'He'd let me know, just let me know he was all right, I know he would . . . All this time . . .'

Her struggles at last subsided and she slumped back,

staring at the crumpled letter, the innocent little pieces of paper that were charged with all the diabolical evil in the world. Mrs Welney patted her hand. 'Now sit there, and I'll go brew a strong dish of tea with a morsel of brandy. And then you can go see your father, he'll know what to do.'

'No . . .' Caroline sat up. 'He's up at Boston this week – and besides, there's nothing he . . . I must go to London. The Admiralty. Uncle George is at Westminster, he's at the centre of things, he'll help me.' Feverish energy seized her. 'The Cambridge coach leaves Wisbech at one. I can sleep at Cambridge and be in London tomorrow. Help me pack a bag, Mrs Welney . . .'

'Go alone, ma'am? Are you sure? Why not have Ned go with you – ?'

'I am alone without Richard,' Caroline said. At the foot of the stairs anguish immobilized her a moment. Alone. Richard . . . The unthinkable possibility loomed before her, its foul breath was on her face, it gestured with ghastly hands to the future in its train, her future, empty, bereft. She broke free and ran up the stairs. *Keep going.*

'Oh, ma'am, wouldn't it be better to wait?' Mrs Welney said. 'Wait for news – write a letter to the Admiralty, or – ?'

'I can't wait,' she cried, dragging a carpet-bag from the closet. Waiting was death. Oh, God, no. *Keep going.*

2

She got to London the following afternoon.

The wheels of the Cambridge coach had beaten out a rhythm in her head that would not leave her. *Two months ago . . . he would have written . . . Two months ago . . .*

He'd at least let me know, he'd at least let me know, he'd at least let me know he's alive . . . If he's alive, if he's alive . . .

She flung open doors in her mind, looking for an avenue that was bearable. It was all over, and he hadn't even cared to let her know, it didn't matter because he felt she didn't love him, he didn't love her – no, that one was not bearable. He was dead – he was dead, and he had died feeling betrayed, died with the memory of failing her, the memory of that last, terrible parting from her in bitterness and division. *If this is what being married to you is like, then I do regret it.* That parting without even a kiss. No, no, that was most unbearable of all. Slam the doors, slam them all shut, think nothing, only act, keep going. The other passengers in the coach thought her mad. She babbled, blew away thought with a ceaseless gale of chatter, on the weather and the roads and the harvest, the villages and towns through which they passed, recited their names and wondered where they came from, Haverhill, now what did that mean? Keep going.

They put up at the White Bear in Piccadilly. It was a short walk to George Hardwick's lodgings in Buckingham Street. Stink of undrained streets, smoke of sea-coal and tanneries across the river, confusion of carriages and drays. Coloured transparencies in print-shop windows: *Bob Rousem's Epistle to Bonaparte!* In Buckingham Street, a knife-grinder with his cart, a gossiping maid. Caroline ran up the stairs, and met her uncle coming down.

With him was a fat, red-faced man whom he introduced as Mr Sheridan.

'I'm sorry, Uncle – please let me speak with you . . .'

There was no mistaking Caroline's agitation. George took her arm. 'I'll see you at the Cocoa Tree,' he said in farewell to Sheridan, and he guided her into his parlour and poured her a measure of brandy.

'This is a surprise . . . You've come alone?' George said.

Caroline nodded, swallowing the brandy, without water, feeling it burn.

'I'll be getting a bad reputation with my landlady. Not so long ago Charles's young wife descended on me, and now – ' He stopped, seeing the urgency in Caroline's face. 'You got my letter, Caroline?'

'It was the first I knew of it, I've heard nothing from him – uncle, I must find out – '

He held up a hand. 'I've just written you again this morning. I enquired at the Admiralty myself after Richard – I know the under-secretary there – and you've heard nothing? – typical Admiralty muddle . . .'

Caroline closed her eyes.

'He's at Portsmouth, in the Haslar Naval Hospital. Wounded – that's all I know.'

She resisted the waves of faintness. 'He hasn't written me – nothing – I thought . . .'

'I see. Well, no doubt Captain Meade – it's strange, I must say. You came straight away? Your parents – ?'

'No. I've told no one. I came straight to you, I thought – oh, Uncle, are you sure? He's alive?'

'He's wounded, at the hospital. I'm afraid I know no details . . . Caroline, you look exhausted. Have you eaten?'

Caroline shook her head. 'I must go to him, Uncle. I must. You do see, don't you?'

'Of course.'

'Portsmouth – there are coaches – '

'It's too late in the day now. The best way will be to go post. I'll go with you. You must sleep here and we can hire a carriage in the morning and be there quickly.'

'Oh, but I can't wait, I . . .' The frantic fire of energy seemed to go out suddenly, its fuel spent. Her legs were like paper. She sank into a chair.

Her uncle patted her hand. His face was furrowed with kind concern. 'You're dog-tired,' he said gently. 'You need rest.'

She put a hand to her brow, her whole body sapped and weak. Bright lights danced before her eyes. 'I thought . . . I just couldn't stop thinking that he . . . Oh, he never wrote me . . .'

Portsmouth. It was as familiar to Richard as his home and he had often described it to her, but she had never been there.

She travelled with her uncle in a swift post-chaise through a country of downs and villages, in hot sunshine. The carriage wheels beat out no rhythm this time: she was quiescent, her mind cleared and swept, ready for whatever it had to receive. Last night had been the time for speculation. The horrific images had tormented her for hours, wormed their way into her dreams when at last she slept. Now there was only truth to face.

Through an arched gateway and into Portsmouth High Street; elegant old houses, coffee-shops, curtained bow-windows. A teeming place. Sailors, tanned, pigtailed, in glazed hats and loose trousers, braided officers, soldiers from the garrison, market-women bearing huge wicker baskets, fishermen, Negroes, Jews in beards and gaberdines. Seagulls screeched and quarrelled over leavings of fish. The harbour glittered like a mirror between the haphazard roofs and chimneys.

They put up at the Fountain Hotel. Caroline remembered that this was where, Richard had told her, the naval lieutenants stayed when in Portsmouth – midshipmen at the Blue Posts, senior officers at the George. He had made her laugh, telling her the story of when he was first made lieutenant and had marched proudly into the Fountain dining-room and hit his head on the low beams.

'The Haslar is across the harbour, at Gosport,' George said. 'You've eaten nothing. D'you want to have a meal first?'

She shook her head. He did not press her. They drank a mug of ale and her uncle took her arm and they went out.

All was vitality, the harsh vitality of war. Talking nervously, George pointed things out: the swarming dockyard with its rigging-loft and rope-walks and tarring houses and saw pits and mast-ponds where the great timbers were seasoned, the tower of Fort James over on Rat Island and beyond the wharves and smoking brewhouses of the victualling-yards. In the harbour for refitting were two big men-o'-war around which buzzed, courtier-like, smaller craft, cutters and barge transports. A new-built sloop was being towed in from the Hamble to be fitted out by the dockyard craftsmen.

They came through the crazy, stinking, congested streets of the Point, amongst beer-shops and brandy shops and heaped baskets of oysters: an atmosphere of brothel and fishing-village combined. At the Point Steps they boarded one of the many wherries and rowing-boats, like hackney-coaches, that ferried people across the racing waters of the harbour mouth. Mudlarks scrambled for coins thrown by passengers.

Crossing the harbour mouth they could see several men-o'war at anchor off Spithead, massive ships as big as mansions, each caught in a spider-web of intricate rigging. A magnificent sight, sun glinting on the water, a beautiful day. The beauty of the world went on, thought Caroline, the beauty and the ugliness, indifferent as the tides. One floated, powerless.

The Haslar Naval Hospital was a large imposing building, fifty years old, built by the Haslar Creek. Her uncle was saying: '. . . has a fine reputation. Lind was surgeon here – the curer of scurvy.' She was not listening. She was thinking of the Lying-In Hospital in London where she had had her baby. Oh, this was better – she could tell as soon as they entered the lobby: immaculately scrubbed floorboards, light windows, fir-wood burning in a brazier to keep off infection. But it was no place to get well, to wish for life. No place for her husband, her lover.

A porter fetched the house surgeon, Mr Lanyon. He was an elderly, stiff man, in naval surgeon's uniform, which absurdly gave Caroline confidence.

'Captain Meade was here just the other day enquiring after Lieutenant Lindsay, in some concern that his relations should be informed,' Mr Lanyon said. 'Lieutenant Lindsay has scarcely been lucid since he was brought here, ma'am. Certainly unable to communicate with you.'

'What are his wounds?' Caroline said, detaching herself from her uncle's arm.

'You must prepare yourself for some change in your husband, ma'am. No, he has lost the use of no limbs nor senses. In the action in which the *Serapis* was raked with fire he received a blast of splintered shot and wood along his left side from the ear to just below the knee, causing extensive lacerations to skin and flesh. One piece was deeply embedded below the shoulder, taking in shreds of his shirt, and I had to dig for it. This has not so far proved infectious, but the dressings are changed regularly for signs of putrefaction.' The dry voice croaked on. *I shall never forget this voice.* 'I'm afraid, ma'am, Lieutenant Lindsay was already suffering traumatic fever when he was brought here. It was of unusual duration and a remittance was only followed by the condition under

512

which he now labours. Your husband has served in the Indies, ma'am?'

'Yes.' She found a voice, though it was not her own. 'Some years ago.'

'I would surmise he contracted malarial fever there. A recurrence in later life is not uncommon. He is very low with it, ma'am. I will not hide the truth from you. He is dangerously weakened and has passed the point at which I normally expect men to show signs of recovery.'

Caroline stared, faintly mesmerized, at the row of silver buttons on the surgeon's coat. An age seemed to pass, during which she drew a deep breath, a long age that left her previous life a dim, primeval memory. Now was all. 'Let me see him,' she said.

They passed through a long ward where several men lay in beds laid parallel to the walls, and others sat up and talked and played dice. One had a stump for an arm. More fir-wood was burning, and in the centre of the room were long trestles and barrels of water. Mr Lanyon called to an assistant-surgeon to follow him. They came to a passage at right-angles. Mr Lanyon indicated a door with a grating. 'We have begun isolating fever cases,' he said. 'Though I am considering moving Lieutenant Lindsay to the ward.'

There was nothing in the room but a low cot-bed and a table on which stood a jug and basin, an hour-glass, a spoon and a glass jar of leeches. Light filtered through a high grated window. The figure on the bed was still. Caroline went forward.

Richard had pushed back the blanket and was lolling up on the bolster. His right side was to her. The first thing she noticed was he was unshaven. He was always scrupulous about shaving. The growth of beard was intensely black. His skin was white, or grey – like no colour living

513

skin ever had. His hair was matted with sweat. One hand was feebly clenching and unclenching.

She bent over him. His eyes were open but they did not see her. They were shallow and unreflecting like a doll's. He was thin, so terribly thin and gaunt: the bigness of his bones showed through the nightshirt. He smelt of stale sweat. His breathing was thick and impatient, like that of a man struggling to untie something in desperate haste.

She touched his hand. Such tender, intelligent hands. That was unchanged. 'Hello, Richard,' she said.

'I fear he will not recognize you, ma'am,' said Mr Lanyon.

Caroline nodded. Then she went round to the other side of the bed. There was a long puckered scar reaching from his left ear to the neck of his nightshirt. She bent and pulled back the blanket and began to open the nightshirt. Mr Lanyon put a restraining hand on her arm but she shrugged him off. 'He's my husband,' she muttered.

She looked at the body she loved. It was white and wasted. The contusions went on, down his hip and thigh. They were mostly healing but just below the shoulder was a thick bloody dressing where the surgeon had dug for the splinter. Richard moaned and stirred a little but did not move to cover himself up. Gently she did it for him.

Mr Lanyon was saying something to his assistant about the dressing. Her Uncle George was standing in the doorway, looking grave and old. Richard was moving his lips but making no sound. And Caroline was thinking of something Antoine Clairet had said: perhaps the only true thing he had ever said. *Men rush to battle . . . but it is women who are the courageous ones*. She hoped it was true. Now was the time to test it. Test her courage and strength. The worst was over. There was only one thing

514

more to fear, and that thing she was going to fight, fight with all her resources of life and love.

'How is he nursed?' she said abruptly.

Mr Lanyon raised his eyebrows. 'The assistant-surgeons are in charge of nursing. Women from the town are employed, boat-women and others.'

'Boat-women?'

Mr Lanyon coughed. 'Nursing is an indelicate trade, ma'am. We do our best to ensure . . . Of course, some of the men have their wives come here to nurse them.'

'That is what I wish to do,' Caroline said.

'Ma'am, I appreciate your concern, but – '

'If the men have their wives to help, why not the officers? There can be nothing indelicate. I am Lieutenant Lindsay's wife.' She looked round the bare room. 'Would it be possible to place a truckle-bed, a chair even in here, so I might rest a little at night?'

'You think to nurse at night also?' Mr Lanyon frowned and glanced at George. 'Ma'am, if you wish it, I cannot prevent you, though I assure you your husband receives the best of care . . . But I will be plain, ma'am. Your husband is dangerously low. The remission usually found in these fevers is yet to come and I do not know how long he can bear up under it, given his condition. He suffers delirium and is sometimes violent. He is – not clean. It will be a noisome task.'

She did not answer. She was thinking of herself lying in the room in Jackson's Rents, and Richard looking after her. Had she been 'clean' then? Did they really, truly, expect her to sniff her handkerchief and retire to a hotel in the town and send a servant to enquire each morning whether her husband was alive or dead?

She looked at her uncle. George nodded. 'I'll send your bag over from the Fountain,' he said. 'I'll stay there tonight and write your mother and father.'

Caroline gazed at the wreck of her husband on the narrow bed. She took off her bonnet and pelisse. 'Tell me what to do, Mr Lanyon.'

The night was surprisingly quiet in the hospital. War having been not long resumed, and no major engagements fought, it was not full. One or two of the men called out for water or moaned in their sleep: from outside, the odd drunken shouts of dockers, the ringing of a bell on board a ship. Most of the noise was made by Richard.

His frame was wasted, and yet there seemed to be pockets of frenzied strength there somewhere. In the intervals of genuine sleep he lay as if comatose, limbs sprawled, totally still. But in his delirium a weird energy took hold of him. He writhed and twisted. He babbled, in a bewildering variety of tones, now fearful, now conversational; now in a contented peaceful way, now with a throaty urgency that was like a horrible parody of sexual passion. He struggled to get out of bed and she had to hold him down, pushing his shoulders, trying not to touch the part where the wound was still not healed, feeling the muscles bunched and taut as if they would snap. Other times he would lie quiet, looking around him, and she would steal to his side and speak his name, convinced he was growing lucid; but his eyes would flick unseeing over her, continuing their restless exploration of the high ceiling beams.

She wanted food in him, whatever it took. Milk and gruel and broth were the only things it was possible to feed him, and often, raving, he rejected them. The assistant-surgeon and the day-nurses tended to give up when he grew too strenuous. Caroline would not. She fought with him, spooning the stuff down his throat, pinning him back with her weight. She even held him by the hair. Nourishment, he could not fight the fever without it.

On the second day, Captain Meade of the *Serapis* came to see her. He explained that he had been unable – as she could see – to elicit her name and address from Richard and had finally written to the Admiralty for the relevant records, with inevitable delay. He told her how courageous her husband had been in the action off Brest and said he would make a fine commander. She was grateful but listened absently. Courage, courage, that was what he needed *now*. She did not know if she had enough for both of them.

Her Uncle George stayed in Portsmouth for two days, periodically descending on her to make her come away for a break and a meal at the Fountain. He had reserved her a room there, but she spent the nights in Richard's room. On the third day her mother and father arrived, having come at once on receiving George's letter.

She was glad to see them and embraced them warmly. They were shocked and moved at the sight of Richard: Luke, who had not led a sheltered life, went white to the lips. But she shook her head impatiently when they spoke of hiring good nurses to look after him, getting a doctor from London. She felt, but could not explain, that *she* only could help him. They took rooms at the Fountain and came each day. But they seemed to sense their powerlessness.

All but a few of the twenty-four hours of the day she spent with Richard. She was there when the dressings were changed and when Mr Lanyon came to check the wounds. They were healing well and only the gash beneath the shoulder still bled. Every time Mr Lanyon sniffed the bandages for infection she went rigid with fear. But the flesh, he said, seemed sound. He took the leeches away: the patient was not strong enough to bear a bleeding.

'The scarring on the face, hip and thigh should be quite superficial,' he said, 'that on the shoulder perhaps more pronounced. That is to say, of course, if – '

'If he lives,' said Caroline.

Mr Lanyon pulled down his brows and coughed. He still did not quite know what to make of her.

Scarring, she thought, what was this talk about scarring? It was the fever that was taking him away from her, pulling him down, sapping his denuded strength as he struggled with it, as the whirlpool saps the strength of the flailing swimmer.

On the third day Able Seaman Ball, who had also been wounded on the *Serapis*, came to see Richard. He had his arm in a sling. He told her what a peppering the lieutenant had taken that day. 'Coh! Such blood! He didn't half bear up, though,' he said. 'Reckon he'll get his command soon, ma'am, for sure.'

'If he lives,' Caroline said again.

'Lives?' said Able Seaman Ball. 'Oh, I 'spect he will, ma'am. Don't reckon he's the sort to die meself.'

This visit roused her. The young sailor did not seem in the least disconcerted at the sight of Richard. Her strength revived.

But not long after Ball had gone Richard broke into one of his delirious, broken, cross-grained laughs. It was a more terrible sound than screams of agony.

Each day she managed to wash him. She knew instinctively that if there were any gleams of consciousness in his mind, they would register distress at being so dirty and sweaty. He had always been clean. Lying in bed at Elm she liked to be aware of the fresh smell of his body beside her. But no matter how she washed, how she wiped his

518

forehead and chest, the sweat still poured. It only stopped for the shivering.

She hated the shivering. Often it came on at night. It racked him. His hands juddered like those of a palsied old man. She tried to hold him, to caress and soothe and warm him; she laid warm bricks at his feet, but nothing was any good. And then his eyes would flick open and he would stare up at her with an expression of anguish and she could only stroke his hair and whisper his name and fight her own fatigue because she knew if she fell asleep he would die.

But on the fourth night, when at last his shivers subsided, he was lucid for a little while. He looked at her with his eyes screwed up in the candlelight. 'Caroline,' he said. He dozed and then woke again and reached out to touch her hand – feelingly, not with the blind grasping of his delirium. 'Caroline,' he said again.

'Yes, Richard. Yes, my darling, I'm here. I'm here with you.'

He gasped and twisted, his breath rattling. 'Love,' he said. Soon he was delirious and unseeing again. But she knew then that whatever part of his mind was able to surface above the fever, knew she was there. He knew she was there.

But throughout the next day he was rambling badly. Even her tireless exertions would not make him take food. Her parents came to the hospital, but this time she would not leave him. She took a little hasty dinner with Mr Lanyon in his parlour upstairs. 'Mrs Lindsay,' he said, 'I speak *in loco parentis*. I am full of admiration for you, but you are overtaxing yourself.' He examined his wine and seemed to choose his words. 'My dear madam – there is only so much you can do. You cannot defeat nature.'

But he didn't understand. Once Richard had dragged her back to life, or so it seemed to her. Could she not do the same? She *had* to be there. Where else? Richard was her love. Perhaps Mr Lanyon didn't understand that – Perhaps that was not fair. Probably he had a deeply cherished wife. And in this situation *he* would know too. But perhaps she herself had never truly understood love till now.

She ached in every limb: her body, traitor, told her to go to the hotel where her parents were and get a wash and a change of clothes and a good sleep in a proper bed. Her mind burned on. She went back to Richard.

It was close that night. The assistant-surgeon who brought candles climbed up and opened the high window but no breeze of salt air came through. Caroline's light muslin gown still clung to her. The heat oppressed Richard. He threw off the blanket and tossed about, muttering. She pressed damp cloths to his head but the very water in the stone basin was tepid.

She slept, sitting on the truckle-bed leaning against the wall. She hadn't meant to. She woke with a start. The candle had gone out but streams of milky moonlight were in the room.

Richard was gabbling. 'Too close, too close . . . Clear that gangway, damn you! Falling short, sir . . . No, in range, in range – Look to yourselves!'

He sat bolt upright, gesturing with sweeping arms. She went to him, tried to settle him back, but the feverish strength was on him. 'Richard,' she said, 'it's all right, darling, I'm here, it's – it's a dream, it's not real.' His skin was burning.

'Get that man below! Able Seaman Ball, sir . . . Captain's compliments to Mr Bowyer, and begs . . . Pump sufficient . . .' He gave a convulsive writhe. '*Minotaur*, sir . . .'

She fumbled with tinder and flint and lit a candle. Richard's face was chalky. They had managed to shave

520

him the other day but the stubble was thick again. 'Darling,' she said. 'Come back to me. It's me, Caroline.'

Richard snorted and gestured as if brushing flies from his face. 'Caroline . . .'

'*Yes*, my love.' Her heart leapt.

'Caroline, I'm sorry. I shouldn't have made you come on this voyage – it's no place for – I shouldn't have done it . . .'

He began talking to her – not talking to her in this room, now, but as if she were not there. 'My fault, my darling . . . not much of a berth, is it? Oh, I was wrong to do this to you, Caroline, but I loved you, do you see, I loved you so much, I couldn't bear to be parted from you, so I made you come with me . . . She's a swift ship, my love, she won't be taken, they won't take us . . .' He was seized with a shudder, a groan, the two things dreadfully commingled – and cried: 'Oh, you can't forgive me, you can't . . . My fault . . .'

He raved on, sinking into sudden peace and as suddenly lurching up and thrashing about in panic. He was lost in the labyrinths of a recurring waking nightmare that seemed to revolve around the action in which he had been wounded. But she was there too – he had involved her in it somehow and he cursed himself and begged her to forgive him. In the ghastly light of candle and moon, with uncouth shadows springing up the walls, she held his tossing body down and lived in the nightmare of his pain. And though she beat off sleep her own nightmares defied her pricking eyes and pranced about the room. Antoine Clairet was there, and he was grossly fat, and he was on a horse reviewing the troops in the Place du Carrousel in Paris; and then with a bound he was at Dover leading the invasion, and his first object was Elm Cottage, to burn it to the ground, and her father was there, he was skimming across the fens in one of his coasters towards the advancing army, but a cannon-shot blew him away, and then her cousin Charles was there, in his red coat, with a company of soldiers, and he called 'Fire' but the army rode over them, and she ran and Richard was there, with a ship on Whittlesea Mere, and they sailed away on it but then there was a boom and a puff of smoke from the shore and they were hit . . . And so her waking nightmare meshed with Richard's and seemed to become one and the same. And then he cried out and with supernatural strength burst from her embrace and staggered out of bed.

He was walking, weaving across the room. 'Look to yourselves . . .' he said in a low, slow voice, *'look to yourselves!'* he screamed. 'Take that man below, gently, damn you – Oh God Jesus, this one's for me, get out of the *way* – '

She ran to him, seized him, sobbing 'Richard, Richard, wake up, it's not real . . .'

He stared as if into the distance and quivered and then shouted 'There! Look out!' and flung her roughly aside. She fell, and the side of her head struck the table.

She lay dazed for a minute. She struggled to sit up and found that Richard was on his knees beside her. 'Caroline,' he said. He touched her hands and then, with infinite gentleness, her face. 'Caroline, are you – ? Caroline, love, I – where . . .'

He was shivering. She got to her feet and put her arm round his shoulders. 'Come, love. Get into bed. Get into bed, my darling.'

Meekly, helplessly, he sank into bed. She covered him up and, it seemed immediately, he was unconscious.

She applied a cold cloth to the bruise on her own forehead and splashed her face. Then she sat on the edge of Richard's bed and listened to his laboured breathing.

It was the darkest, stillest hour of the night, when there

seemed no hope of morning and no relief for her husband but the relief of death. But she would not allow him that relief: she did not even know if it was cruel of her, only that she was determined he would not leave her. To keep herself awake she began to talk, on and on in a low chant like an echo of his delirium. She strung out her despair and love on a long fragile thread of talk, while the candle guttered and Richard's chest rose and fell.

'. . . it's all war out there, Richard, soldiers and sailors, and cannon, and hammering in the docks, and beacons on the hills, and I know we can do nothing about it, and I'm not afraid of it, but I want peace, I want *our* peace, the peace we had together, loving, learning . . . All the things we had, Richard, the small things too, the sun coming up over the fens, over the mist, the taste of new-baked bread, a warm fire in the cold evening, and walking by the river where the moorhens nest – all the things to be *shared*, the things that are so different when you share them with someone you love. All our love, Richard, do you remember? – and we're going to have it again. Don't you know it's the one true thing in the world, and we can't let war and nations and fighting and money destroy it – they can't destroy it, it's too strong, it must be too strong. I've tried to be strong for both of us, darling, because I need you . . . apart from you I'm not *whole*. I love you, darling Richard, and *you must know that* . . . I know you felt I'd betrayed our love and, if I have, then I'll never forgive myself . . .'

She roused herself at last to trim the candle and found the moonlight had been extinguished by a sicklier version of itself, a pale, bleached dawn. She stood by the window a moment, lifting her face for a breath of air, and then went back to the bed. Richard lay very flat and still. In the scourging lye of dawn he looked ashen, the hollows of his eyes deep pits. He looked as if he had been washed up there, by a surging force too strong to resist, and left stranded and broken. Her heart jolted as if she had been punched in the chest and she put a hand to his head. It was dry and cold. He suddenly looked to her as if he were sinking, fading, melting down into the bed.

'Richard! Richard!' She shook him. 'Oh, God, don't leave me, Richard . . .'

Richard sighed and opened his eyes and peered up at her, frowning and puckered, as if she exuded a dazzling light. 'Don't shout, love,' he said weakly. 'My head's thumping like a press.'

She stared at him, barely daring to hope, looking for the glitter of delirium in his eyes. 'Darling . . . do you know me?'

His lips moved in a vestigial smile. 'Caroline . . . love.'

His throat was dry. She brought him water and he drank deeply, rapturously.

'Oh, God,' he said, laying his head back, 'that's wonderful. So thirsty . . . is it morning?'

'Yes, love.'

'What day?'

'Oh, Tuesday, no Wednesday, oh, I don't know. Richard, are you – ?'

'Dear God, I've had quite a dose, haven't I?' he said.

She nodded. 'Do you remember?'

'I – some parts. I remember being here – and these damn wounds being fresh and hurting like the devil . . .' He touched his left shoulder gingerly, seemed reassured by what he found. 'I knew when it was coming on me, I knew the signs, kept trying to fight it off; but then there's a blank, with just the odd bit here and there . . . How long have you been here?'

She shook her head. 'Nearly a week.'

'Have you . . .?' He turned his head to look at the truckle-bed by the wall. 'All the time?'

She nodded.

He found her hand and held it, taking deep relaxed breaths, as if the mere air were something ecstatically pure and sweet. 'I remember thinking, does Caroline know – does she . . .?'

'Does Caroline care?' She squeezed his hand and bent and kissed his face. 'Oh, darling, I've been so afraid – you've been so ill.'

He lifted his hand to her face, saw the bruise. 'Did I do that?'

'You were raving. You couldn't help it.'

He propped himself up on one elbow. 'Poor love,' he said. 'It must have been awful for you.'

'For *me*?' She laughed, in a breaking relief close to tears. 'Oh, Richard. Oh, darling.'

He sat up, feeling experimentally down his left side. 'Well, they certainly feel better . . . God, I must have lost thirty pounds in weight.'

'Are you hungry?'

'I feel as if I could even eat ship's biscuit.'

'Good.' She stroked his arm. 'I want some flesh on these bones, love. Embraceable flesh. Flesh against mine . . .'

He took her hand and looked down at it. 'Caroline, perhaps you think it's not the time, but I must say it, I – God, the nightmares are coming back to me now . . .' His voice trembled a little. 'I didn't want to live, Caroline – God forgive me, when I left you I didn't want to live . . .'

'Hush,' she said. 'It's all right now. You are going to live. I'm here with you. I love you, Richard. That's all I can say.'

He shook his head. 'But you see – I'd – I felt I'd *failed* you –'

'I've told you, love, all that doesn't matter.'

'Oh, but not just the money and the rest . . . No – it

525

was – the things I said. Oh the things I said to you, Caroline, before I left. Unforgivable. About Clairet. Unforgivable – throwing your love back in your face. I knew immediately that I'd failed you, that I'd gone too far and I had destroyed everything – it was *me* who'd betrayed our marriage . . .' He shifted restlessly, pushed back his damp hair. 'Always, constantly demanding – demanding love and when it was given, *doubting* it. And I knew this time, those things I said, I had gone too far. I said to myself as I left – you've broken it, ruined it. You can't expect anything now, my lad. This most wonderful gift I'd been given – your love – and I'd destroyed it like a pettish boy . . .' He suddenly put his arms around her and held her. 'Sorry about this, my darling,' he gasped, 'I'm not exactly a fragrant Adonis just now but I must hold you . . .'

'Oh, Richard, nothing's broken, nothing's ruined.' She kissed his lips. 'No more doubting, love, never any more . . .'

His eyes looked into hers. 'Dear life,' he said, 'you look beautiful.'

She smiled. 'I've not bathed for days,' she said, 'my hair hasn't seen a comb, I've lain down in this old frock, I haven't slept since the night before last – but if you say so then I must be, my darling . . . No more doubting.'

3

The humid weather broke at the beginning of August. A thunderstorm cleared the way for days of bright sun and a stiff breeze across the sea. The morning Richard left the Haslar Naval Hospital the wind was rippling the flags on Fort Blockhouse and setting the waves dancing at the harbour mouth.

Caroline came from the Fountain with her parents to meet him; but at the ferry steps on the Portsmouth side of the harbour Luke and Rebecca said they would watch the ships and wait there. They would travel back to the fens together, but this was an occasion for Caroline alone.

Richard had an extended leave. Captain Meade had come to the hospital the other day to see him, and told him it was very likely his promotion would be gazetted before the winter; but he was not fit for service yet. He had eaten like a horse after the fever had broken but he still lacked some weight and strength. His wounds were knitting well, and the scar on his face had sealed to a white line, but he was still stiff along his left side. 'I shall leave it to you, ma'am,' Captain Meade had said to Caroline, 'to effect a full recovery.'

'She's already done that,' Richard said with a smile.

She was dressed in her best white and silver poplin for this great morning, with a black straw hat with red ribbons; and when she came into the lobby of the hospital, Richard was there in his full dress lieutenant's uniform with the white cuffs and lapels, tall and erect, still a little pale, but with a warm light in his eyes as she walked towards him.

They shook hands with Mr Lanyon and the assistant-surgeon, and the porter said he had sent Lieutenant Lindsay's trunk to the Fountain; and Caroline took Richard's arm and they went out into the brilliant sunshine.

'There's a ship going out,' Caroline said.

Richard shaded his eyes with his hand. 'The *Challenger*,' he said. 'Just refitted. Going to join the blockade.'

'Let's go and see.'

They walked down to the quay below the hospital. The *Challenger*, a big second-rater, was leaving the harbour mouth guided by a pilot-boat. Her gun-ports were newly-painted and brass glinted on her fore-deck. People on the opposite shore were cheering and waving their hats, and from Fort Blockhouse came the boom of a salute as the great ship passed.

'I think I can understand why sailors go to sea,' Caroline said.

He smiled. 'Can you?' The wind ruffled his hair as he turned back to look at the vast white sails beginning to fill. 'Well, there's always a part of me that responds to a sight like that. But for now . . .' He smiled again.

'It will come,' she said. 'I know that. Like you say, the sea's part of you. But not yet. And I suppose some day the war will end, but not yet. All we can do is hold on to the present moment. Enjoy it. *Live* it.'

'You know, when I was in the hospital – at the worst time – when the fever let go of me and I dropped asleep . . . each time it seemed like an ending. All over. But there are no real endings, are there? If I've learned anything, it's that we always go on learning. Even in love. Most of all in love.' He raised her hand and kissed it. 'And I want to go on learning.'

'We'll learn together.'

'And just at this present moment,' he said, gaily taking her arm and springing her up the quay steps, 'I am in the sun with my lovely wife, and the envy of all eyes.'

There was new colour in his cheeks, she saw, and a boyish grin softened the strong bones of his face. 'Dear Richard,' she said. 'Dear love.' She felt weightless and airy like the fluttering pennants, the gulls balancing on the wind, the white foam in the wake of the ship.

'Oh! smell that air,' Richard said. 'It's as if I never breathed the fresh air before.'

'And the sea.' She pointed, to where the foamy wake of the departing ship was breaking into glistening spray speckled with sunlight. 'Look. The light on the sea. I don't think I've ever seen anything so beautiful.'